Passionate
Novels of

The Minister's Wife

"With great power and true understanding of deep emotions, fears, longings, and love, Delia Parr delivers another unique story that etches itself into your heart."
—*Romantic Times*

"Parr's latest is brimming with forbidden temptation, old scandals, dark secrets, darker betrayals, and the power of faith."
—*Publishers Weekly*

"THE MINISTER'S WIFE may be the 'breakout' novel that establishes Parr's reputation.... [It] reaches a new level of emotional suspense and dramatic complexity ... Parr's writing is fresh and original."
—*Milwaukee Journal Sentinel*

"[Parr's] characters are delightful ... Parr's book is one in which the reader can search for hidden meanings of life in the various situations she presents, or reading the novel can be taken strictly as a recreational pastime. Either way, the reader wins."
—*Raton* (NM) *Range*

The Ivory Duchess

"A heartwarming romance ... an emotional love story of hidden pasts, assumed identities, and unexpected love."
—*CompuServe Romance Reviews*

more ...

"Delia Parr has done a wonderful job in balancing an emotional love story with humor . . . highly recommended."

—*Under the Covers Book Reviews*

"Ms. Parr is one bright star to watch!"

—*Romance Forever*

By Fate's Design

"Delia Parr vividly depicts everyday Shaker life, and BY FATE'S DESIGN showcases both triumph and anguish for the human heart and soul. Ms. Parr's star is definitely on the rise."

—*Romance Forever*

"Delia Parr has given us an intriguing historical, laced with delightful characters, passionate romance, and a heartwarming tale of love, growth, and trust—an incredibly beautiful love story."

—*Rendezvous*

"An excellent tale."

—*Bell, Book and Candle*

"BY FATE'S DESIGN is an exciting Americana romance that brings alive the Shakers, an interesting part of our heritage. The lead characters are both superb, and the support cast adds the right amount of spice to make Delia Parr's par excellence novel well worth reading."

—*Affaire de Coeur*

The Fire in Autumn

"Empathy and passion mix superbly in this poignant, unusual romance written by the shining new star, Delia Parr."

—*Romantic Times*

"A powerful read, packed with conflict sure to set your pulse pounding . . . an intense emotional experience and a humbling journey into true love."

—*Pen 'n Mouse On-line Newsletter*

"A moving tale of a man faced with a choice between love and security, written with warmth and tenderness!"

—Anne Cleary

Evergreen

"A uniquely fresh book with engagingly honest characters who will steal their way into your heart . . . A one-sit read . . . I loved it!"

—Patricia Potter

"A poignant, beautiful love story, brilliantly crafted . . . A triumphant romance that fills the heart and soul with joy."

—*Romantic Times*

"Incredibly poignant . . . Not to be missed."

—*Heartland Critiques*

St. Martin's Paperbacks Titles
by Delia Parr

EVERGREEN
THE FIRE IN AUTUMN
BY FATE'S DESIGN
THE IVORY DUCHESS
THE MINISTER'S WIFE
SUNRISE

SUNRISE

Delia Parr

St. Martin's Paperbacks

SUNRISE

Copyright © 1999 by Mary Lechleidner.

All rights reserved. No part of this book may be used or reproduced in any manner whatsoever without written permission except in the case of brief quotations embodied in critical articles or reviews. For information address St. Martin's Press, 175 Fifth Avenue, New York, N.Y. 10010.

ISBN: 0-312-97091-9

Printed in the United States of America

St. Martin's Paperbacks edition/September 1999

St. Martin's Paperbacks are published by St. Martin's Press, 175 Fifth Avenue, New York, N.Y. 10010.

10 9 8 7 6 5 4 3 2 1

Dedicated to

Vicki Hinze

a talented author, treasured friend, and precious woman who blesses my world with her presence.

Acknowledgments

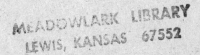 I am indebted to several generous people who helped me to understand the nineteenth-century legal system in Lancaster County, Pennsylvania. Evelyn E. Sullivan, Executive Director of the Lancaster Bar Association, directed me to Cindy Garman, Esquire, who graciously guided me with advice. James L. Stokes, Research Assistant at the Lancaster County Historical Society, directed me to actual nineteenth-century murder pamphlets as well as county historical resources which allowed me to accurately describe the courtroom in the old Lancaster County Courthouse. I am truly indebted to them all for their help, but any errors in interpretation remain mine alone.

Delia Parr

Prologue

How had sorrow and bitter disillusionment so quickly consumed the joy that had filled her very soul on her wedding day?

Heartsore and wearied from long days of work followed by sleepless nights, Jane stared out the window in her chamber above the general store. As dawn broke, she scanned the single street below, but the landscape only reflected her own desolation.

A sigh, emanating from the depths of her spirit, escaped from her lips. A harsh, frigid winter, made bearable only by the ageless promise of spring, had long ago eclipsed the sultry days of summer. Too forlorn to believe her married life would mirror the seasons of nature and love would blossom one day in her hapless marriage, she prayed she would somehow find contentment, if not happiness.

As blustery winds outside bowed barren trees into submission, sadness gusted in her heart and disappointment scattered the dreams that her whirlwind marriage had resurrected from beyond the shadows of her spinsterhood. Just like the misunderstandings that created countless obstacles along the path to marital happiness, banks of snow lined the deserted roadway. Only six months ago, the entire village had gathered there for the annual Fourth of July parade and celebrated, as well, her surprising marriage to Hiram Foster.

Choking back salty tears that blurred her vision and burned her throat, she turned away from the window, closed her eyes, and crossed her arms at her waist. As she leaned back against the wall for support, she fought the tight grip of despair that clutched at her spirit and struggled to reclaim a fragment of the joy that had swelled the moment Hiram had proposed to her.

You're a good, honest, and extremely capable woman, one I scarcely deserve. I would be honored if you would be my wife.

The very words he had used to win her hand echoed in her mind. Her heart trembled anew, and she caught her bottom lip to stifle a sob as vivid memories flashed in front of her mind's eye. With the noonday sun sparkling in his burnished gold hair and his pale blue eyes smoldering with open affection, he had been irresistible as he proposed on bended knee. Right on the planked sidewalk in front of the general store he had inherited from his father only months before. With half the village and her entire family watching them!

Her pulse began to race, just as it had in that magical moment, yet beyond his startling good looks and romantic smile, she remembered most the honesty in his proposal. Instead of pledging his undying love and pretending she was too beautiful to resist, he had spoken from his heart, admitting he wanted to make her his wife because he valued her for her skills and the depth of her character, just as she had dreamed would one day happen, if she waited long enough for the right man to come along.

Swayed by words that caressed her soul and convinced her that his transformation from a wandering wastrel into a responsible businessman was real, she had bid a grateful farewell to her days as Jane Glennings, a spinster clerk who had devoted herself to her younger brother, Sam, after their parents' deaths. She had joyfully welcomed her new role as Mrs. Hiram Foster—wife and beloved helpmate—as a dream come true.

As the prodigal son and the village spinster, she had known they made an odd match, but she had counted on one very strong common bond to unite them: Sunrise, a sleepy little hamlet on the banks of the Susquehanna River where each of them had extended families and deep roots that stretched well into the last century.

Her dream, as well as her joy, had been short-lived.

Now, only six months into their marriage, she realized she had sorely misjudged the man whose name she now carried, as well as the depth of the bonds that united them. Left with a wounded heart and broken dreams, she had a troubled marriage she did not know how to heal.

Not alone.

Not unless Hiram opened his heart to her, and she had the courage for fight for her dream: that he would one day treasure her as his wife.

She had little hope she could reconcile their differences easily, and she could scarcely begin today. He was leaving in a few hours for yet another business trip, but she could ill afford to ignore the ever-widening gap between them to wait until he returned.

She had to make some attempt to talk to him about their problems before he left. Before it was too late. Before their marriage disintegrated beyond the point of salvation, and before heartrending sorrow mired in self-pity stole the last ounce of her courage.

Determined to take the first step today, she wiped the tears from her face and straightened her work apron before walking over to her dresser where she began to brush her hair. Instinctively, she kept her gaze averted from the mirror, a simple act that stirred memories so painful her heart shuddered and her hands shook so hard she had to tighten her grip on the brush. Her cheeks warmed with shame at how many times her husband avoided looking at her directly.

Heartache, born long ago in her childhood, wrapped like a painful vise around her chest. An ungainly child, she had grown up to be an exceptionally plain woman.

When fresh tears welled and threatened to overflow, she counted mentally as she brushed her hair in long, hard strokes, but she could no more erase the memory of the pitying glances or scornful looks from men than she could transform her appearance.

She had believed her father when he had held her on his knee and told her she was his beautiful little girl, but schoolmates' taunts and a total lack of suitors had repeatedly sliced through his well-intentioned lie, leaving deep scars that Hiram's disaffection had opened within weeks of their marriage. Her chest constricted with unbearable pain. Unable to draw more than shallow breaths of air, she set the brush aside with trembling hands.

Without physical beauty to attract a man's interest, she had molded her character with strength and an uncommon appreciation for always telling the truth, no matter how painful it might be. Yet deep in the recesses of her heart, in a very secret place she hid from the world, still lived the dream that someday, one special man would find her beautiful—in face and form as well as character. Her pulse began to race as if chasing, once again, that impossible dream.

She bowed her head and sighed heavily. After her heartbeat returned to normal, she chose a dark brown ribbon to tie her hair back. When she heard the door to Hiram's adjoining chamber open and close, her hands froze in place. When his footsteps echoed down the hall, her pulse quickened.

Was he leaving early? Without even saying goodbye?

Desperate to speak with him before he left, she dropped her hair ribbon without tying it into place and rushed from her room into the hallway. Her husband was straight ahead, making his way to the parlor with his travel bag in his hand.

"Hiram?" She rushed forward past his bedchamber door, her heart pounding in a dull thud that echoed her

disappointment. She would have no time to talk to him
if he left now.

He turned around and glowered, his features harsh,
even in the pale dawn light. "What is it now?"

She braced to a halt in front of him. Her hair askew,
she smoothed it away from her face with trembling fingers. Her chest rose and fell quickly as she took quick
gulps of air. "Weren't you even going to say good-bye?"

"Good-bye," he growled, then turned and walked
into the parlor.

She swayed on her feet, and her cheeks stung as if
he had slapped her.

He opened the door and stepped onto the staircase
landing that led to the outside entrance at the rear of
the general store. She stumbled after him and reached
him before he had descended more than halfway down
the steps. "Please don't leave angry," she pleaded.

He sighed heavily, dropped his travel bag onto the
step, and turned around. They were practically face-to-
face, but she barely recognized him. Disgust and im-
patience distorted his handsome features when he
looked into her eyes, and she took a step back from
him.

"Stop chasing after me. Just go back to your room
and finish dressing your hair."

She recoiled from his bitter words. She had never
seen him look at her with such contempt. Until now.
She dropped her gaze, ashamed of herself for running
after him and giving him another chance to embarrass
her. "I only wanted to say good-bye," she whispered.
"I-I wish you could stay. I don't understand why you
have to leave again. You just got back—"

"I travel a lot. I thought you would have gotten accustomed to that by now."

Her gaze snapped up to meet pale blue eyes filled
with disdain.

"I have to meet with the suppliers. Your job is easy:
Take care of the customers and keep the books. Those
are the only two things you do well. It's been a perfect

arrangement, and I don't know why you insist on spoiling it."

Shame, deep and bitter, nearly arrested her cowering heart. Pride prevented her from swaying on her feet, but it was sheer force of will that kept her gaze steady and the words she wanted to lash at him unspoken.

His eyes widened with mock surprise. "What's this? No whiny protest? No clinging? No sappy requests that I write more often?" He snorted.

She caught her lower lip with her teeth and held her silence, refusing to give him another excuse to indict her.

His grin bordered on nasty. "Good. You've been a little slow to learn, but I didn't think you were totally stupid. And just to keep you quiet, I think I will write . . . if I think of it. Now hurry, or you'll be late opening the store," he ordered, grabbed his travel bag, and left her standing there listening to the echo of his whistling as he descended the rest of the staircase and disappeared from view.

Numb to the very depths of her soul, she sat down on the top step and buried her face in her hands. Deep sobs tore from her throat as she bid a final farewell to the dream she had embraced the day he had proposed to her and to any hope that they might easily reconcile.

Her disappointment and sorrow ran deep, but her greatest burden was knowing beyond any doubt he had exploited her qualities for his own selfish purposes when he had married her. He had no desire for a loving wife and devoted helpmate to share his life in Sunrise. He wanted a servant to run the general store so he could return to his wastrel ways and spend most of the store's profits on extensive business trips east where he satisfied his lust for fine clothes, excitement, and city entertainments.

She had the rest of her life to regret marrying Hiram, but she would keep her pain stored away from view in the hollow depths of her heart where her dreams now lay tattered in shreds that she feared were too ragged ever to be made whole again.

Chapter 1

Jane's hand trembled as she tilted the heavy watch that hung from a silver chain around her neck to check the hour. It was nearly six o'clock. With no time now to tidy her room, she had precious little inclination to ponder, again, why or how her marriage had withered away into nothing more than an illusion. She had responsibilities to meet to the villagers and area farmers who depended on the general store.

She left her chamber and gently closed the door behind her. Her heart pounding, she tiptoed down the hall, but when she reached Hiram's room, the door was ajar. She peered inside and realized he had already left for an overnight stay in Lancaster to meet with his lawyer in preparation for his next long trip.

Hesitating but a moment, she crossed the room and walked through an invisible cloud scented with his cologne, stepped over bed linens that trailed to the floor, and closed the door to the walnut wardrobe on her way to the window. Her fingers brushed against the tied-back drapes, but she paused to take a deep breath of tingling dawn air before she slid the window closed. She turned and walked back through the room he had left in the same total disarray as their marriage, apparently without much of a backward glance for either.

Once she was out of the room, she closed the door behind her and walked down the hall, moved through the parlor, and descended the stairway that led to a small foyer that adjoined the rear storeroom. Just inside the back door, someone had left three crates of eggs for barter, and she stooped to retrieve a handwritten note before continuing.

Daylight streamed through the curtainless windows in the storeroom, but she walked past each window without looking outside. When she reached the opposite end of the narrow room, she unlatched the wide doors that led to the loading platform. Working quickly and efficiently, she continued her morning routine and entered the general store through a second doorway, this one directly opposite the loading platform. She passed barrels of salted fish and flour and shelves bulging with sundry dry goods.

Shivering, she shoveled a good amount of coal into the warming stove in the center of the room and noted the pungent aroma of stale tobacco. She had cleaned out the boxes of sawdust placed next to the four chairs that circled the stove just last night, and she made a mental note to scrub the dark stains on the well-worn wooden floor—stains left by villagers who gathered here every day to share the latest bit of gossip, issue commentaries on the weather, call for the post, or fill empty hours with companionship and a wad of chewing tobacco or, occasionally, a pipe.

Outside, footsteps approached slowly and deliberately on the planked sidewalk that ran the width of the storefront and announced the hour. She had no need to check her watch. Aunt Nester was as punctual as she was reliable whenever Hiram was away. It was now six o'clock and time to open the store. Jane hurried to the door and greeted her self-appointed assistant with a smile as the sound of the door's warning bell echoed overhead.

Her mother's sister, now several years a widow, never broke her stride. Reed thin, with her face weathered by years as a farmer's wife, Aunt Nester still did not have a single gray hair on her head. With a wink, she strode past Jane, draped her black shawl around the back of her usual chair, and moved a box of sawdust several inches further away.

After a quick nod of satisfaction, she plopped into her seat where she had a clear view of the front door. She glanced around the store while balancing a small woven basket on her lap. "How long do you expect him to be gone this time?"

"Just overnight. He'll be back late tomorrow," Jane replied as she removed the dustcover from her desk in the front left corner of the store. "He's not leaving for Baltimore until next week, but then he'll be gone for seven or eight weeks. He's planning on meeting again with his lawyer before he's off to make the rounds of new suppliers." She folded the cover and placed it into the bottom drawer, wishing she could put her disappointments and concerns away as easily.

She ran her fingers over the new ledger book she had painstakingly prepared for use while Hiram was in Baltimore. She prayed he would remember to stop back in Lancaster on his way home to reclaim the old ledger books from the lawyer there. He was using them to collect on old debts owed by folks who had moved away and to sell off some of the promissory notes Hiram's father had acquired through the years.

"He's away far too often and too long, in my opinion. Turns out he never really wanted to settle down like his father," Aunt Nester commented. As far as she was concerned, Hiram had no name. He was simply "he" . . . until he acted more responsibly and earned the right to have a given name again. Jane was not sure she quite understood Aunt Nester's logic, but she knew better than to try.

"The crullers are still warm. Sit and eat with me before folks get here and interrupt our breakfast."

Jane frowned. "You don't have to come help me every time he goes away."

Aunt Nester laughed. "Never did like doin' a thing 'cause I had to, and now I'm old enough and ornery enough to do just what suits me. And helpin' you suits me."

Grateful for her aunt's company, Jane pulled a chair alongside her aunt, spread the offered napkin on her lap, and gratefully accepted a sugared cruller. She nibbled at the edge of the fried dough, mindful that Aunt Nester probably needed to be here at the store as much as Jane needed someone she could trust to help her. "Does it ever bother you . . . I mean, you've given up most of your home for nearly two years now."

Aunt Nester chewed thoughtfully. "Abram did his duty and provided for me as best he could, bless his soul, I have my two rooms and use of the kitchen as long as I live. I expect Felicity will be happy to see me outta the house for a spell, though." She shook her head. "Thomas is entitled to his birthright, and with four youngsters, he needs the old homestead more than I do."

She put her cruller down, and licked the sugar from her fingers. "It's a natural cycle women's lives follow, but don't you fret for me. I've lived nearly three score and raised a fine family. As for the years I have left . . ."

"Wouldn't you rather stay with Aunt Lily in Philadelphia?"

"And leave Sunrise? Never! This is my home. I was born here, and I'll die here, just like your folks. Besides," she added in a softer tone, "I wouldn't know how to survive in the city, and I don't have the funds to match Lily's. I won't be on the receiving end of her charity, even if she is my own sister."

She looked up at Jane and smiled. "*We're* family, too, and family looks out for one another. Always." Her eyes misted, and she turned away abruptly to set the basket onto the floor. "So . . . we'll follow the same routine as last time, I assume. I'll keep watch for the customers when you have to work in the back settlin' up with the farmers. Come noontime, I'll take myself upstairs and start fixin' somethin' for our dinner while you tend to the store. Unless you'd prefer I stay here and mind the store."

Her gray eyes twinkled. "What'll it be? You can keep me outta your ledgers or your kitchen, but not both."

Jane laughed out loud. "You're more than welcome to my kitchen."

"That's what I figured. Most of your customers would probably agree with you, too. Sometimes I think you're too honest for our own good. Makes it awful hard to be your replacement." Aunt Nester reached into her apron pocket and pulled out her pouch of chewing tobacco as a wagon approached. "Go on. Get busy in the back. Rael Meyers mentioned he'd be here early with milk and butter. That's probably him now. Sure wish Sam was stoppin' by to haul for you today. Now that he's got his own business and hauls for Jonas Peterson at the mill, too, I don't get to see him very often at all."

She shook her head. "Neither does that wife of his. Polly must get awful lonesome, even though he's not gone as much as your husband. I still don't understand why she wouldn't agree to let you teach her how to keep Sam's books. She'd be company for you, too."

Jane swallowed hard. "Polly is much more interested in spending money, not learning how it's made," she said honestly, but truth be told, she had a much more personal reason for not wanting Polly here often. Having her in the store on a regular basis would be like dangling a piece of frosted cake in front of Hiram and expecting him to satisfy his taste for sweets with a day-old crust of bread.

The woman Sam had married a year and a half ago was young and utterly feminine. With her pale blond hair decorated with fancy ornaments and piled high in the latest fashion or hanging down her back, she wore gowns with more lace and ruffles than half the women in the village combined. She caught the attention of every man she passed while Jane was as plain as a common sparrow.

In looks, most women fell somewhere in between these two extremes. When Jane and Polly were in the same room, Jane was not sure whether it was Polly's beauty that made Jane appear so unusually plain or she was so plain Polly appeared to be more beautiful.

Sam positively adored his stunning wife, and given the state of Jane's marriage, she had troubles enough without having Polly here as a constant reminder of how devoted Hiram should have been. He had not even come to her bed for nearly three years now, and she assumed if he had any carnal appetites at all, he sated them when he traveled.

In all fairness, she had no proof he had ever been unfaithful to her—only her finely tuned instincts about the man she had married and the gnawing suspicion that he found her less tolerable with each passing month they remained married.

Jane folded the napkin around her unfinished cruller and placed it in the basket. "Sam's away till tomorrow. I'm sure you'll see him then," she murmured before making her way to her desk. She picked up the ledger book and walked back to the storeroom, chiding herself for being mean-spirited and jealous of her own sister-in-law.

After being cooped up in the store all day, Jane found the prospect of spending another evening alone intolerable. With her supper cleared away, she walked the two miles to Aunt Nester's home and delivered one of the peach pies Mrs. Singletary had bartered for eggs and milk. Using the shortcut she and Sam had always used as children to reach the homestead he now shared with his wife, Jane traipsed along the footpath through the woods to visit Polly and bring her a pie—a visit she hoped would help assuage her guilt for the unkind thoughts she had had about Polly earlier that day.

With Sam out of town and her own family living miles away in Columbia, Polly was bound to be lonely, too, just as Aunt Nester had suggested. Since both their husbands traveled frequently, Jane made a mental note to extend herself more often to Sam's wife, if only for his sake.

The weather was still warm, and she slowed her pace to enjoy the waning autumn display of natural color before winter arrived, stripped the forest nearly bare, and painted the landscape white with snow. She followed the footpath, reached the main road linking Sunrise with the turnpike several miles to the east, and walked along the edge of the cindered roadbed for half a mile before her former home came into view.

She sighted the footpath that detoured around the house to end at the outbuildings hidden from view from the road. Filled with nostalgia for happier days, she opted for the footpath instead of the wider entry drive that led to the front of the house. Memories of the years she had spent raising Sam after their parents had been killed in a freak lightning storm filled her mind and brought a smile to her troubled heart.

She had only been nineteen; Sam was four years younger, and those first few months as orphans had been difficult as Jane assumed yet another role as disciplinarian. She chuckled softly as she walked, careful to keep the pie she carried from tipping. Sam had slipped out during the night one too many times before she had finally figured out how he had managed to get back inside without her seeing or hearing him approach.

Until she had remembered the footpath.

Sam never quite forgave her for scaring him half to death the night she surprised him by being there behind the barn when he finally made his way home just before dawn. He had never used the footpath again, either.

By the time she reached the barn and crossed the yard to the back door of the house, she had second thoughts about her decision to use the footpath. Since Polly was not expecting her, Jane hoped she would not frighten the girl by suddenly appearing on her doorstep without any advance warning.

Balancing the pie with one hand, she knocked on the back door which immediately swung open a few inches. She waited, rapped again a little harder this time, but Polly did not come to the door. Jane peered into the kitchen, saw it was deserted, and knocked again.

Still no response, although when Jane cocked her ear, she heard the low, distant murmur of voices coming from another room. Assuming Polly had company, Jane hesitated. She did not want to intrude, and she relished explaining her impromptu visit to the other guests even less, considering she still wore her work gown and apron.

Feeling foolish, out-of-place, and awkward, she turned to go back home and stared down at the pie. She could certainly make faster time if she did not have to carry the pie back with her, but she could not very well leave it on the porch. Critters would devour it before Polly even knew it was there.

Jane would simply have to put the pie in a safe place and leave a note for Polly to explain why she had not announced her presence. She let out a deep sigh, turned around, and slipped quietly inside the door. She was only halfway across the room when the voices she had heard earlier became louder and more distinct.

She froze in place and stared straight ahead. The door to the dining room was only open a crack. Just enough to let her hear the voices more clearly.

Her hands gripped the edge of the pie tin even harder. Her heart started to pound. Fingers of cold shock snaked around her spine and sent shivers through her body.

She heard Polly laugh.

Hiram's voice rumbled low and seductively. "What a delightful feast you are, my love. How I've hungered to taste your sweetness again."

Bile burned the back of her throat, and tears blurred her vision as she stumbled forward a few steps, her gaze locked on those meager few inches of space. Her mind rejected the limited view she now got of her husband and her sister-in-law as impossible.

She braced to a halt, paralyzed by unspeakable shock when she saw Polly's voluptuous body spread across the dining room table and Hiram, naked as well, standing as he suckled her breasts.

Horror. Outrage. Disgust. Each vied for control of Jane's emotions, but lodged in a painful lump in her throat that prevented any sound from escaping when she cried out. Battling nausea that threatened to announce her presence, she backed away, one shaky step at a time. Startled and disoriented when her back pressed against the outside door, she turned and raced outside as her mind screamed the horrible truth.

Lovers. Hiram and Polly were lovers!

Her slippered feet flew across the yard and along the barn. When she reached the footpath and entered the woods, she flung the pie to the ground. Dropping to her knees, she braced her hands on the cold earth and slammed her eyes shut. She retched violently and repeatedly until her stomach emptied, but she could not purge the vision of her husband and her sister-in-law, naked together, any more than she could silence the echo of their lovemaking.

She sat back on her haunches, wiped her face with the handkerchief she kept in her apron, and crisscrossed her arms at her waist. Rocking back and forth, she sobbed. "Hiram, my God, Hiram! What have you done to me? What have you done to Sam?"

She cried until she was hoarse and there were no tears left. Dazed, she could barely stand, let alone take a few steps, yet she chided herself for not having the courage to confront both Polly and Hiram back at the house, either moments ago or now.

Darkness had long chased away the twilight when she finally had the strength to struggle her way home, but with every step she took, she vowed to confront her husband. Her protective instincts for Sam surged, and she knew she had to find a way to force Hiram to end his affair with Polly so Sam would never have to learn the bitterness of his wife's betrayal.

She would never forgive Hiram for what he had done to her—or to Sam. And in the silence broken only by the sound of her own stumbling footsteps, she heard the gentle tolling of an inner bell that sounded the death knell for any hopes she might have had for redeeming her marriage.

One week later, Jane waited for Hiram in the parlor after supper, finally ready to confront him about his affair before he left for Baltimore in the morning. Sitting stiffly on the settee, she twisted the ring on her finger and tried to calm her pounding heart.

When she heard him come out of his chamber and enter the parlor, she looked up, shocked to see he was formally dressed and carried his travel bag. "You weren't supposed to leave until morning."

"My plans changed," he snapped without breaking his stride.

"But you promised you would have time to talk to me tonight," she insisted.

He paused, raked his gaze over her, and shuddered as if a chill raced through his entire body. "If you weren't so abysmally homely, I might have considered the prospect as bearable," he murmured as he dropped his gaze. When he checked his gold pocket watch, he scowled. "I'm late. Whatever it is that's made you so miserable this past week will have to wait," he announced and headed toward the door.

Angered by his words, she bolted to her feet and raced unsteadily to the door before he reached it.

"Get out of my way," he ordered.

She squared her shoulders in a display of bravado that belied her fears. "You can't leave. Not yet."

He impaled her with a gaze of stunning rage. "Don't ever tell me what to do."

"At least give me some idea of where you're going after you leave Baltimore," she pleaded, hoping she could stall him long enough so he would be forced to stay the night and she would have the opportunity to confront him about what she had seen on her fateful visit to Polly.

"I'll be back when I'm good and ready. In the meantime, don't question me. Ever," he snarled and shoved her aside to open the door.

Caught off guard, she tripped and grabbed the arm of the settee to keep from falling to the floor as he stormed past her and left without saying another word.

Fear kept her from chasing after him, and she quickly bolted the door closed to keep him from coming back inside. His chortle in response echoed in the stairwell. She turned, pressed her back against the door, and shoved her hand to her mouth to stifle her cries of frustration and outrage.

Tears streamed down her cheeks, but she made no attempt to wipe them away. She had missed several opportunities to confront her husband, a mistake she had hoped to remedy tonight, but she had failed.

Confronting Polly, instead, would serve no purpose but ill. She would only deny the affair, and Hiram would not be here to accept his share of the blame. Images of Polly and Hiram together, intense and painful, fired in rapid succession in her mind's eye. Jane blinked hard, forcing the images to the back of her mind and replacing them with thoughts of Sam.

A splinter of guilt for keeping the truth from him pierced her very soul, but she consoled herself knowing Polly would be faithful while Hiram was away. When he returned, Jane would demand the affair be declared permanently ended, or she would threaten to tell Sam— a threat she hoped she would not have to carry out.

Only then would she be faced with a moral dilemma too difficult to consider now. She would either break her brother's heart with the truth, or endure a lifetime with the truth hidden deep in her soul to spare him the heartache and disappointment she knew only too well.

Chapter 2

Desperate situations called for desperate measures.

Jane worked through the night at her desk in the general store and greeted another cold February dawn exhausted, but satisfied she had no choice but to swallow her pride and write to Aunt Lily asking for help. Hoping she had explained her circumstances well enough in her letter, she doused the lamp, stood up, and stretched her cramped muscles.

She carried the letter with her as she walked over to the warming stove and added more coal. After she moved a chair closer to the stove, she turned it so she could reread her letter in the natural light pouring through the storefront windows before sealing it in time for the arrival of the mail wagon.

4 February 1832

Dear Aunt Lily,

It is with a heavy heart that I write to you now to ask for help and pray you will intercede on my behalf as well as on that of the family and friends you left behind in Sunrise.

Hiram has not yet returned or written again since October. Although he has often extended his trips beyond his initial expectations, he has never been gone so long that he put the general store in jeopardy, which I must sadly admit he has done this time.

I wait for the mail wagon each week, half afraid I will be notified he has been taken desperately ill, or worse. I pray my fears are

*unfounded, but I have overheard others voice the
same worry.*

*Several weeks ago, Rev. Reilly claimed to have
seen Hiram approaching the rear of the store late
the previous night. He seemed quite disturbed
when I told him Hiram had not returned, but
eventually admitted he must have made a mistake.
To everyone's relief, he finally went to Lancaster
to be fitted with a pair of spectacles he's needed
for years.*

She paused, laid the letter on her lap, and rubbed her
weary eyes. Her head pounded with worry about
Hiram's reaction when he finally returned and learned
she had turned to her aunt for help, but she was prepared to defend her action as one that could have been
avoided if he had met his responsibilities to her and the
rest of the village.

While she had honestly described her concern about
his welfare to her aunt, she considered it far more likely
that he had simply extended his trip. It was also possible he had abandoned her. She refused to admit, even
to herself, which of those eventualities she preferred.
She was too emotionally spent, too physically exhausted
to waste what precious energy she had left on herself.

Never once, however, had she found herself missing
him as a wife should miss her husband. The opposite
of love, she had discovered, was not hate, but a complete vacuum of affection that frightened her in its in-
tensity. Before she could get mired in a bout of self-pity,
she turned back to her letter:

*Aunt Nester has moved in with me, a compro-
mise we reached only last month, but I still worry
that she has been working too hard here at the
store each day. Our stock has dwindled terribly
low, yet suppliers refuse to accept anything in
trade or extend credit to anyone but Hiram himself. Soon I will be forced to close the store unless*

I find a way to operate it in his absence.

   I traveled to Lancaster several weeks ago to see Hiram's lawyer, but he was not helpful. Neither were the other three lawyers I visited, and I had the troubling notion they were far more worried I was meddling in my husband's business than concerned about the villagers who depend so much on the general store.

With a deep sigh, she closed her eyes briefly and tried to block out the humiliating memory of her journey to Lancaster. Efrem Harris, Hiram's lawyer, had been rude; the others, simply condescending, and she had returned to Sunrise frustrated and angry—both at the lawyers and at her irresponsible husband who had left her and the villagers in such a vulnerable position.

When she heard the sound of an approaching wagon, she looked up, recognized the mail wagon, and quickly finished reading the rest of her letter:

   If you could use your influence to recommend a lawyer in Philadelphia who would be willing to come to Sunrise to offer a legal solution, I would be forever indebted to you and to him. I have few funds with which to pay him, but I would be willing to sign a promissory note—one I can repay when the store is operating at full capacity again.

   I confess that I have probably waited too long to ask for your help, but since you mentioned in your last letter you would be leaving for France to visit Philippe's family, I felt I had to write now, for it shall be far too late by the end of summer when you expect to return to do much good.

Affectionately,
Jane

Whether satisfied or not with her appeal, Jane had no time to rework the letter as the driver of the mail wagon, Edmund Farrow, came to a halt just outside the general **store.** She rushed back to her desk, sealed the letter, and met him at the front door with her letter and the rest of the postings the villagers had left with her during the week. With a quickly said prayer that he would have news from Hiram, she greeted him with a weary smile and handed him her stack of letters. "Getting colder, isn't it? Would you like to come inside and warm up a bit?"

He shook his head, and the red curls peeking out from beneath his woolen cap rustled. "Got to keep to the schedule. Nothing for you this week," he said as he handed her back a small stack of mail for other villagers and stuffed her postings into the canvas bag he carried. "I don't suppose Hiram's back yet, is he?"

Her heart sank, along with her hopes. "Not yet. Soon I pray," she murmured.

"See you next Saturday," he offered before climbing back aboard his wagon.

She nodded and closed the door. Weary steps carried her back upstairs so she could change and get ready to open the store and spend yet another day filled with worry about her future.

Jane's feet were nearly frozen, her mood was sour, and it was only ten o'clock in the morning. Still furious that two of Hiram's nephews, Jack and Willy Coombs, had invited her to their home only to threaten again to wrest control of the general store away from her, Jane let the March winds literally blow her down the main roadway. The gusts were bone-chilling, but did little to cool her temper. She trudged up the steps to the general store and hastily knocked the muddied snow from her slippers and wished she had thought to wear boots.

When she looked through the window, she saw a stranger sitting at her desk studying her ledger book and account receipts and realized the Coombses had done more than make an idle threat. They had deliberately lured her out of the store so their lawyer could peruse her books!

Since she had had no reply from Aunt Lily and had little hope of retaining a lawyer on her own, she had only her own outrage—and her wits—to protect herself. "How dare you!" she shouted as she charged inside, rushed to her desk, and yanked the ledger book out of his hands. "You have no right to examine my books, regardless of what Jack and Willy told you. Get out. And take your scheming, swindling plot with you!"

With her chest heaving, she drew quick, shallow breaths of air, fought the tears welling in her eyes that threatened to spill down her cheeks, and glared at the city-dressed man who gazed up at her with a startled, but angry expression on his face.

His frock coat and vest draped around the back of his chair, and the white linen shirt he wore stretched across his chest as he tensed. Broad of shoulder, he was solidly built, although he lacked the heavy muscles that marked most rural men. Dark, wavy hair framed classical features made extraordinary by large, deep-set hazel eyes. It was not their color or shape that was striking, but rather an unusual blend of sharp intelligence and deep commitment that made his features more compelling than handsome.

And dangerous, she noted with alarm, as his gaze hardened. Appalled he would be angry with her, she scowled back at him.

"You're misinformed. Mrs. Foster, I presume?"

Still clutching her ledger book, she was too outraged to do more than nod. She swallowed hard and glanced quickly across the room before she locked her gaze with his again. "Where's Aunt Nester? What ruse did you use to convince her to leave?"

"Ruse? Swindle?" He spat the words at her and seemed to be battling an anger that matched her own. "You either have a vivid imagination or you're so overworked you're overreacting. Your aunt is upstairs making coffee and preparing some refreshment and suggested I use my time to good advantage while waiting for her. If you'd allow me to introduce myself—"

"Don't bother." She huffed. "You're leaving. Now. Or I'll summon the constable and have him throw you out."

"You don't understand—"

"I'm perfectly aware of your intentions," she snapped, fearing he would simply abscond with her records if she left to get Noah Washburn. She knew she had no chance of grabbing hold of all the account books and correspondence that littered the desk.

Since she was standing and he was seated, at least she had the illusion of greater power, but she had no doubt when he did stand up, he would tower over her. She had no choice but to bluff him out of the store. "I don't know how you sweet-talked Aunt Nester into letting you examine my records, but whatever permission she granted to you is now rescinded. I want you out of my store."

He let out a deep sigh and closed the journal he had obviously used to take notes. When he spoke again, his words were no longer bitter, but controlled. "No, you don't. If you'll let me explain—"

"Save your explanation for someone feebleminded enough to listen."

He shook his head and reached around the chair to withdraw a paper from his frock coat pocket. He put the paper on her desk and tapped the document with one finger. "Read this first. If you still want me to leave, I will."

Having reached a standoff of wills, Jane stared at the single piece of folded paper. It looked more like a letter than a legal document, at least to her untrained eye, but she could not pick it up and read it without setting aside her ledger book.

Anxious to make him honor his word and leave, she walked over to the warming stove and set the ledger book on the chair Aunt Nester usually occupied before removing her gloves, bonnet, and cape and placing them atop the book.

When she returned to her desk, she picked up the

letter, but did not unseal it. "Once I read this, you'll have to leave, but your journal stays here since any notes you made concern my business and belong to me. I expect you to leave Sunrise today as well," she added as an afterthought.

"Agreed."

Surprise flickered in the depths of his eyes, and she had the impression he had somehow lured her into a trap. She kept her gaze on him as her trembling fingers broke the wax seal and opened the letter. She recognized the sprawling handwriting immediately, and a warm flush spread from her neck to her cheeks as she quickly read the short note:

> 5 March 1832
>
> *Dearest Jane:*
>
> *Forgive me for the delay in responding to your letter, but I was away until only last week and leave for France in the morning. Daniel Colton is my friend as well as my lawyer. His fees are already covered since he is on retainer and handles my legal and business interests. I entrust you into his care without reservation until Hiram returns.*
>
> *With greatest affection,*
> *Aunt Lily*

Jane gulped, refolded the letter, and closed her eyes. She could not will herself to disappear any more than she could take back the past few minutes and relive them, but she now understood why he had been so angry when she had accused him of plotting against her. When she opened her eyes, Daniel Colton was smiling at her, which only made her quickly planned apology seem more trite than it already was. "I'm . . . I'm truly s-sorry, Mr. Colton," she stammered. "I thought . . . I thought you were—"

"Please call me Daniel. Your aunt told me about the Coombses. Your mistake is quite understandable," he said softly.

"But not unforgivable, I hope. I apologize. I was rude and snappish."

He grinned. "Quite so, Mrs. Foster."

"My name is Jane."

"Jane. Given your circumstances and your concerns, you were quite within your rights to be so hostile."

She cringed and found it hard to accept her actions as justified. Hoping to turn the topic of conversation away from her poor behavior, she glanced at the volume of notes he had made in his journal and toyed nervously with the ring on her finger.

She argued with herself for feeling defensive and offered him an opportunity to address the concerns he apparently had about her business dealings. "You seem to have found some problems in my books."

"Areas of concern," he corrected. Without referring to his notes, he sorted through the copies of her correspondence and held one up for her to see. "Did you write a similar version of this letter to all your suppliers?"

She leaned to the side and immediately recognized the letter she had written to the Waring Company in Baltimore. "Nearly so. I felt it was only fair to keep them informed."

His eyes widened with a look of disbelief so close to being incredulous she felt the hackles raise on her neck.

"So you *told* them outright your husband was away indefinitely and you were operating the store alone?"

She squared her shoulders. "Of course."

"The suppliers wouldn't have known that. You could have forged your husband's signature and operated the store, forestalling any interruption of trade for yourself and the rest of the village."

"That's unethical!" she gushed and stared at him. Had he really rolled his eyes?

"But pragmatic, given your husband's extended absence and history of frequent travel. As long as you met your obligations, no one would have thought to question you. Frankly, if you had forged his signature, you could have avoided this whole bad situation."

She stared at him and returned his look of disbelief with one of her own, all the while wondering why Aunt Lily trusted this man as her lawyer. "The thought never occurred to me, and I find your suggestion an insult. Regardless of whether or not anyone would have discovered the forgery, I would have known it was wrong. I do business the only way I know how: with integrity."

"That's a refreshing notion," he grumbled, "but terribly naive. I do, however, apologize if you took my remarks as an attack on your character, but the basic fact remains that if you had forged his signature, you wouldn't be needing my services now. Sometimes, in the interest of justice, the law must be circumvented."

She pulled her head back and stared at him. "Justice is always done when laws are obeyed. To be honest, I wonder just what kind of lawyer would advise his client to knowingly break the law. Whose definition of justice should we use? Yours or the Constitution's?"

Silence. Thick, awkward silence.

Daniel flinched, clenched his hands into fists, and glared up at his client. The only thing that kept him from exploding was the fact that she had no idea how her attack on his view of justice and the law mirrored the criticisms his fellow members of the bar, not to mention judges, more often than not, leveled against him.

Jane Foster was a slight woman with long brown hair that hung, country style, in a mass over one shoulder and trailed nearly to her waist. Set in chiseled features, her dark jeweled eyes accented high cheekbones and lips too full for the size of her face. Unusually plain, and dressed in a dark brown gown topped by a canvas apron, she might have presented the image of a fragile fawn if she did not have such a sharp tongue.

She was not physically beautiful or even mildly attractive, but she did have a depth of character few women possessed. He might have considered her idealism and optimism enviable, but he knew otherwise from bitter personal experience. And she would, too, unless he could convince her to stretch the law, not break it, when justice demanded quick remedies.

"I'm sworn to uphold the law and the Constitution," he countered in response to her charges against him. "Unfortunately, there are times when the legal system moves too slowly or cannot address particular circumstances. I don't condone breaking the law indiscriminately, but there are times when—"

"When you decide the law is wrong?" She lifted her brows.

"When justice demands something the law countermands," he argued. "Your husband's account in the Lancaster bank is a perfect example. Under the law, you can't touch the money he deposits there, but in reality, you helped him to earn that money and need it to run the store." He paused and cocked his head. "Have I said anything to offend your idealistic sensibilities yet?"

"N-no," she admitted.

"But you wouldn't even consider withdrawing some of those funds to use for the store, would you?"

"Certainly not!"

"Then you agree with the law forbidding you access."

"I didn't say that."

He grinned. "No, but by complying with the law, you admit to its legitimacy. I'm not proposing you should have had someone withdraw the funds for you any more than I argued earlier you should have forged your husband's signature. I'm only suggesting—"

"Please don't. We'll just have to agree to disagree. For the moment," she said quickly, as if unwilling to engage him in a debate. "Is there anything else you found in the record books that you want explained?"

"Only one thing," he remarked, relieved to leave their philosophical differences aside. For the moment. "There are dozens of entries that indicate you continued to accept items for barter long after you knew suppliers would not accept them. Granting credit for goods received and then absorbing the loss was hardly wise, if not poor business practice."

Her backbone stiffened, her shoulders squared, and her chin tilted up defiantly. "Balancing entries in my account books is not as important as the villagers who depend on me. Where you see dates and names and numbers in the books, I see people. Real people who face untold challenges every day just to survive. By the time most of these seasonal goods were returned or refused by the suppliers, it was too late to give them back so the villagers could market them elsewhere."

Her words poured out in a rush, and her cheeks flamed a darker shade of pink. "They shouldn't have to suffer because my husband has been irresponsible. My books may not agree, and my business practices may not have been wise from the perspective of profit, but they were necessary. If you can't see beyond a set of business records and agree, then you might as well go back to Philadelphia right now and save us both time and wasted effort. I know you came here as a favor to Aunt Lily, but if I have to, I'll find another lawyer on my own."

He caught his breath and nearly held it. She had just threatened to dismiss him! Lord, the woman had gumption. Standing there alone, with only her convictions as a shield, she was stoic, forceful, and fiercely loyal to her customers as well as her own sense of righteousness.

He was about to tell her that her disregard for standard business practices was no different than his approach to the law and that they both valued justice above all else when two customers entered the shop. Jane immediately turned away from him, and the smile she wore to greet the two women was brittle.

"I'll be on my way now," he announced in a voice loud enough for the women to hear. He stood and redonned his vest and frock coat as the two women walked toward them.

Jane hid her disappointment beneath a smile and made quick work of introducing Libby Holtzman and

Penelope Washburn to Daniel. "He's Aunt Lily's lawyer, and he's come to help me find a way to keep the
store operating," Jane offered, although she was not
certain she wanted his help if he intended to give her
advice that would require breaking or stretching the
law.

Libby, the taller of the two women, spoke up first.
"I hope we're not interrupting."

"Not at all. I've finished for now," Daniel assured
her. He immediately excused himself to get a room at
the tavern and unpack, but agreed to meet with Jane
again later that afternoon. Both women watched him
leave with mild expressions of disappointment Jane did
not find surprising. Libby and Penelope enjoyed the un-
official position of village guardian—a title they had
shared for as long as Jane could remember.

What gossip or news one woman did not uncover,
the other one did, and they justified their nosiness on
the basis of their inflated views of their husbands' positions in the community. Ben Holtzman served as the
mayor and local justice of the peace while Noah Washburn was the constable. Their two wives would squash
a rumor before it started or stir up a stew of trouble
that would win a blue ribbon at a county fair.

Apparently, Daniel's arrival here had not gone unnoticed and warranted a rare joint effort, and Jane
could ill afford to offend either woman. "Can I help
you with something?"

Libby removed her bonnet and sat down near the
warming stove. "I was hoping to talk to Nester."

"She's upstairs making coffee."

"I'll wait."

Taking a different tack, Penelope pointed to a supply
of disinfectants and poisons Jane kept on a top shelf for
safety's sake. "I need a bit of corrosive sublimate. Red
ants. Such a nuisance."

"Already? It's only the middle of March." Jane went
behind the counter, pulled out a stepping stool, and
nudged it closer to the shelves.

"I'm not one to be caught unprepared," Penelope countered. "With your stock dwindling low, I thought I'd better get what I'll need now." Barely five feet tall, she leaned over the counter where her ample bosom spread out like a hug pillow. "I hope now that Mr. Colton is here you'll be able to get some new stock."

"So do I," Jane admitted, although she was not quite certain she and Daniel would be able to work together without clashing. Still shaking from her encounter with him, she climbed onto the stepping stool, reached up, and moved several jars and bottles aside to retrieve a canister to carry back down with her.

She moved so quickly, she momentarily lost her balance. Before she regained it, her hand knocked against the last bottle of concentrated tobacco juice, which fell off the shelf and smashed at the same time she put one slippered foot to the floor.

The highly toxic amber liquid, used to control garden pests, puddled the floor, saturated her right foot, and splattered the hems of her gown and petticoat with dark stains she would never get out. Only her work apron survived untouched.

"Oh dear, are you all right?"

Visibly shaking, Jane stemmed the panic racing up her spine. "I'll be fine," she insisted. She laid the canister of corrosive sublimate on the countertop, picked up her skirts and shook splinters of glass off the top of her foot. She pulled a handkerchief from her apron pocket to soak up the liquid before hurrying toward the staircase in the foyer at the back of the store. "I'll only be a moment," she called over her shoulder.

She had no idea how long it took for a person's skin to absorb the poison or how much of it would be fatal, but she was not about to waste a single minute. She had to get the poison off as quickly as she could.

She raced through the foyer and up the stairs, heading straight for the kitchen where she intended to pump water over her foot for a solid hour, even if that meant she had to sit on the sink to do it.

Despite her fears, a nervous giggle bubbled straight from her throat to her lips. She had given Libby and Penelope, the gourmet gossip cooks, quite a juicy tale to savor, perhaps long enough to let their recipe for lawyer stew simmer just a little longer before it boiled over and spoiled dinner for both of them.

As for Mr. Daniel Colton, she had the time now to think very carefully about meeting with him later this afternoon. By then, she would have to decide whether she wanted to bother listening to his advice or simply send him back to Philadelphia.

Chapter 3

Daniel had no intention of spending the next few hours in a dismal room at the tavern until he could meet with Jane again. He untethered his horse from the post outside the general store, mounted, and surveyed the hamlet of Sunrise nestled against the mountainside on a bluff overlooking the Susquehanna River and frowned.

The village itself covered no more than two city squares in length, although his ride from Columbia, which had begun at dawn, had taken him past scores of small homesteads and several mills in the rolling valley hills beyond the village. As far as he could tell from his vantage point, there were no intersecting streets separating the businesses and homes along the single roadway that led through the village proper.

Sunrise was exactly as Lily Dionne had described it. For a man born and bred in the city, he felt as if he had ridden back in time. No courthouse. No bank. No telegraph, newspaper, or stage office, either.

Not exactly the Promised Land when it came to practicing law, but certainly suitable for a haven he could sorely use after the past few trying, hectic months. His stay in Sunrise was bound to be short-lived, assuming he could convince Jane to make her rigid principles a bit more pliant, but he rather hoped to extend his visit into the country holiday he deserved after winning an acquittal in a hard-fought murder trial that only reinforced his reputation as a scrapping, practical lawyer committed more to justice than the legal system itself.

He spurred his mount forward into a slow walk and

headed toward the roadway he had sighted earlier that twisted to the right and fell in a sharp incline to the raft landing along the banks of the river. Dismayed to find his thoughts still focused on his last client, Debra Modean, instead of Jane Foster, he blamed his mental preoccupation with Debra on the murder pamphlets of her trial. These brochures continued to incite controversy and scandal, dying a long and tortured death.

He urged his mount to follow the curve that led down and away from the main road. He leaned far back in his saddle to keep his seat, yet ease the burden on his horse. Unfortunately, there was little he could do to erase his memories of the murder pamphlets filled with lascivious sketches and titillating tidbits from Debra's sensational trial.

When he reached the raft landing—used only during the spring trading season, which had yet to arrive—he tethered his horse and paused. For the second time today, he had the eerie feeling he was being watched. He looked around and listened, but saw and heard nothing beyond quite ordinary forest sounds. Dismissing the idea of someone following him as a touch of paranoia, yet another holdover from his last trial, he walked along the banks of the river until he found an outcropping of rock that contained a ledge where he could sit protected from the wind.

He climbed up, leaned back, and gazed at the gray ribbon of river flowing only a few feet away. Waves slapped at the banks of the swift-moving Susquehanna, which he suspected would be filling soon from a multitude of creeks and streams that would be overflowing with melted snow come spring.

In contrast to the cool, tranquil surroundings, his blood still boiled with anger at how Mercury Pine, so-called journalist and frustrated artist, had distorted the facts of Debra's trial. Despite her acquittal, the one-eyed snake had written and illustrated not one, but two scandalous murder pamphlets about her.

The masses of people starved for licentious details of

the case had wolfed down the first pamphlet the day after the prosecution had rested its circumstantial case, earning a fortune for Pine's publishers and adding yet another jewel in the crown Pine wore as the King of Sludge.

Daniel had cried foul to the judges until his throat had turned raw, but the trial had resumed, and he had guided it to a stunning verdict: not guilty. Not to be outdone by the unexpected acquittal, Pine's second pamphlet was even more successful than the first. Like voracious vultures, the public had devoured the first printing in less than twenty-four hours.

Tasting bile in the back of his mouth, Daniel wondered what poor accused soul would be Pine's next victim and what lawyer would be forced to contend with him. At least it would not be Daniel, and with that soul-satisfying thought, he tried to put Debra's trial behind him and focus on Jane, but his mind refused to do more than compromise and compared the two women instead.

Debra was a dazzling young beauty who had been accused of murdering her husband. Kindly speaking, she was a bit slow-witted, which had required Daniel to exercise extreme patience and overlook her petulance, vanity, and demanding nature to focus on her innocence. She was not, however, concerned with the methods he needed to use to secure her acquittal and quite willingly let him conduct his pretrial investigation and the trial itself without interference.

He could not have met a more direct opposite than Jane Foster. She was as plain a woman as he had ever met, and he wondered how she might look without the lines of exhaustion that creased her forehead and the corners of her eyes. Still, she had an inner goodness that added a soft luster to her features which he found uncommonly appealing.

To his consternation, she was also a woman whose rare character, commitment to honesty, and faith in justice highlighted how far he had had to stray to make sure justice prevailed when the legal system failed to protect the innocent.

He picked up a handful of pebbles and threw them into the river, watching them sink as he thought about the methods he had used for the past decade to succeed. "With just cause," he murmured, disgruntled at how lawyers manipulated the law every day and bilked or swindled unsuspecting clients in the name of the law and how often justice deserted people unjustly accused of a crime.

He picked up a heavy rock, attempted to skim it across the surface of the water, but failed. He had only been ten years old when his father died, but it was the memory of how the lawyer hired by his father's business partner had cheated his widowed mother out of her rightful due that had forever altered Daniel's view of justice and charted the path of his life's ambition.

Immediately dismissing a career in business, he had studied the law and modeled his tactics after the lawyer who had swindled his family. Cheated by death, he had not been able to wreak vengeance against the man who had stolen his mother's livelihood and Daniel's inheritance, but he had dedicated himself to preventing other legal vultures from exploiting unsuspecting clients.

Disgusted that Jane had already formed a low opinion of him, he refused to continue to justify his methods. She was obviously far too naive to understand that justice was not blind any more than it was fair because the laws designed to insure justice were as imperfect as the men who designed them.

He muttered under his breath, knowing full well she would change her mind when she realized she had little hope of saving her business without taking a few shortcuts through the law. Unless she held to her beliefs and dismissed him for good, a scenario he would find hard to explain to Lily Dionne.

Far more disturbing, he had already begun to question himself and his reputation as a champion of justice. Had he become so jaded these past ten years that he actually preferred working in legal shadows just within the boundaries of ethical behavior? Or did Jane's idealism and faith in justice shine just a tad too brightly for any pragmatic man to emulate?

He jumped off the ledge, walked back to his horse, and mounted up to take a good long ride instead of spending the rest of his time waiting to meet again with Jane mired in doubts about himself.

Debra had never made him question himself or his ethics, yet another difference between the two women that brought to mind a ditty his father used to sing to his mother as he waltzed her around the parlor after a disagreement. Loving memories of his parents and their undying devotion to one another brought the slow, romantic melody from his heart to his lips and eased his troubled mind.

He sang softly as he rode, his voice echoing in the wooded stillness: "Oh, beware of the jewel shining brightly. She will blind you from the start. Choose instead the jewel shining softly. She will capture you with her heart. Oh-h-h, my wife is the jewel that dazzled my heart . . ."

Fully recovered from her accident, Jane walked into the storeroom several hours later and climbed the stool to reach up to the top shelf. Her fingertips brushed the edge of the small box she wanted, but she could not quite get hold of it. She stretched up on tiptoes and dragged it forward until she retrieved it, unleashing a cloud of dust that set off a sneezing spell.

Undeterred, she slid back the box cover and removed one of four black velvet pouches. She did not stop to look inside. By feel alone, she knew she had found what she wanted and put the pouch into her apron pocket. She secured the box and slid it back onto the shelf, being careful to keep it closer to the edge this time.

When Daniel returned this afternoon, she hoped this symbolic gift would be a not-so-subtle reminder that she wanted his legal help, but only if he agreed to follow the legal course she set—one that would not conflict with her values.

If she were honest with herself, she would admit she almost needed to take one of these for herself. As strongly as she felt about finding a solution to her dire circumstances well within the law, she found Daniel to be attractive enough to be distracting. She liked the way his tailored shirt molded to his chest and wondered how it would feel to run her fingers through the waves in his dark hair.

"Now that's sinful," she exclaimed as her cheeks warmed. She had not thought about any man, other than her husband, *that* way, and her feelings for him had never been so strong. Thoroughly ashamed of herself, she was about to step down from the stool when she heard footsteps in the foyer.

Heavy footsteps.

A man's tread that sent shivers down her spine as she mentally reviewed the possibilities of who it might be. Daniel was more likely to wait formally in the store proper and send Aunt Nester to get Jane, especially after their confrontation earlier. Sam had stopped in just as she had opened the store on his way to Peterson's mill before leaving for Columbia.

By frenzied process of elimination, that left only one man who would be approaching the storeroom, and she panicked at seeing Hiram. Not now. Not today. She did not want to have to explain why Daniel had come to Sunrise.

The door creaked open beside her. His shadow fell into the room as he stayed out of her range of vision while he held on to the doorknob.

Her eyes widened with fear. The top corner of the door was a mere inch from her face! Instant reflex. She shrank back against the wall behind the door and gained a fingerful more space. She was afraid to breathe. She was even more afraid that if she called out to him, she would startle him and he would automatically flinch, sending the door smashing right into her face. Once he stepped into the storeroom and away from the door, she could safely make her presence known.

Her mind screamed disaster, and she held her breath while counting time by the hammering of her heart. Long heartbeats later, he simply stepped back and shut the door instead of entering the room. She heaved a heavy sigh of relief and waited for her body to stop trembling and her heart to slow to a more normal cadence before she stepped down from the stool.

When she heard his footsteps starting up the staircase, she smoothed her skirts and freshened her hair before opening the door and entering the foyer. With one quick glance up the staircase, she felt her heart lodge in her throat.

"Noah?" Gooseflesh crept up her legs and covered her body, and a sense of foreboding pooled like lead in the pit of her stomach as she stared at the constable.

He turned around and came right back down the steps. "Jane? I thought you were in the storeroom. I checked there, but—"

She started to shake. "I-I was behind the door. I was afraid to say anything for fear I'd startle you and the door would hit me." The sorrow in his eyes was palpable. "What's wrong? Is something wrong?"

"There's been an . . ." He held his hat in his hands and turned it round and round in front of him while he cleared his throat to start over. "There's been an . . . accident of sorts up by Peterson's mill."

Sam. He'd gone to the mill earlier. Her mind and heart latched onto her brother's name and would not let go. With her hand to her mouth, she backed away from him before he could say words she instinctively knew she did not want to hear.

Hushed voices. Soft sobbing. The sounds of grief grew louder as Jane backed through the foyer into the general store. She recognized the sounds, but she was too focused on escaping Noah to think beyond them.

Arms gently wrapped around her shoulders. Startled, she bolted free and found herself looking into Aunt Nester's tear-stained face.

"Jane. Poor, dear Jane," her aunt whispered as other women gathered in small huddles in front of the store, watching with identical expressions of sympathy on their faces.

Jane felt the blood drain from her body, one drop at a time. She grew cold and felt brittle, as though she might snap into tiny pieces if anyone touched her. Her mind worked in slow motion. Her vision blurred. Sounds echoed. Her heart thudded as if preparing for one final beat. She was unable to think beyond trying to understand what was happening to her body as each of her senses began to shut down, helping her to reject or deny that something horrible had happened to her brother.

Noah took her arm. "You should sit down. Let me take you upstairs where you can be more comfortable. Maybe Ben should be here, too," he added, typically flustered and overwhelmed. "He's still over at Dr. Birchfield's. Let me get him for you."

A rush of life force carried prickling warm tingles to her numb limbs, cleared her vision, and sent her pulse racing. Questions exploded through her mind that demanded answers. Here. And now.

She struggled to organize her thoughts. An accident. He had said something about an accident at the mill. Near the mill. The mill! She pulled from his grasp. "Sam! What's happened to Sam? Where is he? Take me to him. Wait. I'll get my cloak. And some bandages. No, the doctor will have those. Is Dr. Birchfield with—"

"Sam's fine. He's on his way here now." Noah dropped his gaze for a moment before he spoke again. "It's Hiram. They found him an hour ago. I'm sorry, Jane. He's dead."

Relief that Sam was all right delayed her reaction. "Dead? Hiram's dead? Hiram?" Her words echoed back at her like she had yelled them into a canyon. She swayed on her feet, but denial came swiftly. "Hiram had an accident at the mill? He couldn't have. He can't be dead. He's . . . he's not even here. He's—"

"I'm afraid it's true, dear," Aunt Nester crooned. Jane stepped back when her aunt tried to hold her again. "Sam is on his way here now. Please. Let me take you upstairs."

"No." Jane said the word out loud that ricocheted in her mind and crashed into others. *No. He's not dead. No. He's away. He can't be dead. Not Hiram. Not here. Not at the mill. The mill? He's in Baltimore or Philadelphia or somewhere else, but he's not here in Sunrise, and he certainly is not dead.*

"No," she repeated, stiffening her body and bracing her feet hard against the wooden floor. She kept her gaze lowered.

"Jane? I'm sorry. I'm so sorry, Jane."

A man's familiar voice whispered low just behind her. She looked up as she turned around and rushed into her brother's arms. "Sam," she cried. He crushed her in his embrace. "Tell them, Sam. Tell them it isn't true. It can't be true. It must be someone else."

"Everything will be all right," he whispered, stroking the back of her head when she pressed her face into his shoulder. "Just hold on and let me handle everything. Hiram's gone to his final rest, Jane, but we're all here to help you."

"He's . . . he's gone?" she murmured, trusting her brother without hesitation. Sam would not lie to her. If he said Hiram was dead, then it must be true. As the possibility began to take hold in her mind, she sighed and struggled against feeling cheated from ever knowing if her marriage could have been saved.

The truth tugged on her heartstrings and forced her to admit her marriage had ended the very moment she had seen Hiram with Polly. His death had only spared her a lifetime of unending heartache, and she wondered if she would be able to keep that in mind as she spent the rest of her days as a widow, just like Aunt Lily and

Aunt Nester. She would no longer have to fantasize about losing any chance she might have had to save a marriage that had only caused her pain.

She clung to her brother for support as images of her life with Hiram stacked one upon the other, like logs in a hearth. Kindled by betrayal and disappointment, relief flared into flames that licked and burned each hurtful memory until guilt, as heavy as iron, snuffed out the raging fire and left only the smoldering embers of her discontent.

She extinguished the embers with salty tears. Duty and responsibility, twin plates of armor, raced to shield her from emotions that ran wild. The question of how and why Hiram had died just as he had arrived back home needed to be answered. Immediately, before she tended to the tasks required of her now as his widow.

She took a deep breath, reserving the complicated grieving process she would face for later. She dried her tears with her hands and eased from her brother's embrace, only to find herself face-to-face with his wife.

Hiram's secret lover stood between Jane and the constable, the man who had the answers she needed.

Bright red stripes streaked Polly's dark blue eyes. Tendrils of blond curls damp with tears framed her pale cheeks, and her grief-stricken state added a haunting vulnerability to her beauty.

"How terribly shocked you must be," Polly whimpered as she dabbed at her tears with a lacy white handkerchief.

She stared at her sister-in-law, appalled by the woman's gall. She dared to offer condolences to the widow of the man she had taken as a lover?

Jane forced herself to remain calm and wondered how it might feel to lose a lover, yet not have the right to grieve that loss openly. It was easier for Polly, perhaps, because everyone in the village, save for Jane, would dismiss Polly's grief as a perfectly normal expression of sorrow for the death of a member of the family or sadness for her newly widowed sister-in-law.

For her part, she was momentarily able to set aside her disdain for Polly for a very selfish reason. With Hiram's passing, there could be no question now the affair was over for good. The threat to her brother's marriage had ended in a very sad, but final, way.

She had been spared her bitter confrontation with Hiram, but her dilemma about being honest with Sam or hiding the truth still festered in her soul. Troubled as well by the very difficult tasks in the immediate days ahead, she sighed. Hiram's death had only added a new dimension to the dilemma aching to be resolved these past six months.

Now that he was gone forever, he could not be made to admit to the affair and telling Sam now would force him to choose between believing his wife, who would no doubt deny the affair, and his sister. She could not do that to Sam.

Heart-weary, soul-sick, and overwhelmed by the uncertain future she faced, she made the only choice she could and vowed to take the knowledge of her husband's affair and their troubled marriage to her grave.

It took a huge effort, but she did not cringe when Polly kissed her cheek; instead, she set the past aside to focus on finding out what had happened to her husband. She took one look at Noah's face and turned to her brother. "Take me to see Ben," she murmured, her voice quiet, but firm.

He frowned. "Let me wait with you upstairs. Daniel is at Dr. Birchfield's with Ben and will be along as soon as the doctor can tell us more."

"Daniel? What's he—"

Her brother smiled sadly. "He's your lawyer, and he was incredibly helpful when I met him at Dr. Birchfield's. Don't rush over there now. Let Daniel do his job."

"You should listen to Sam," Noah insisted.

She tilted up her chin and met her brother's gaze with determination fusing her backbone into steel. "Will you take me, or must I go alone?"

Chapter 4

Jane dipped her head so the rim of her bonnet would block her face from the wind and used one gloved hand to hold her cloak closed. Sam held her other hand as they walked together down the roadway with Noah following behind. Straight ahead, a crowd of men stood gathered round an open-backed wagon she assumed someone had used to bring her husband's body back to the stone-and-brick residence that also served as Dr. Birchfield's office.

She saw the worn shingles on the small clapboard church further up the roadway where tomorrow her husband would be buried in the adjoining cemetery. Her breath clouded in front of her as she walked deliberately. Only her dignity kept her from running ahead and demanding answers to her questions about how Hiram had died, and she focused, temporarily, on what she faced after she had been told the circumstances of his death.

She was no stranger to the rituals surrounding death. She had buried her parents together when she had been only nineteen, and she knew from painful experience exactly what loomed in the hours and days to come. Her footsteps crunched on the frozen cinders in the roadbed, and she knew that unless she detached herself emotionally, she would not be able to carry out her final duties to her late husband.

Until then, she could not let her grief, however tainted it might be, prevent her from finding out the truth about the circumstances of Hiram's death and meeting her responsibilities to him.

As his widow, she was entitled to know. Later, she would wash and dress his body and receive mourning calls. Tomorrow morning, she would lead the mourners at the graveside service and watch her husband's coffin placed into the aboveground crypt next to his parents, completing the one homecoming she had never anticipated.

Only then would she allow herself time to find her way through a maze of conflicting emotions and properly grieve. Only then would she struggle to understand the answers to questions she was close to asking. How did Hiram die? Why was he up by the mill? When did this happen and why?

The men's voices hushed to whispers as she and Sam passed the wagon, and she nodded to acknowledge the men who had left businesses and farms untended to come here as word spread about Hiram's death. Sam gripped her hand harder and guided her around the wagon to the slate walkway that led to a door framed in a low A-shaped stone entryway that protruded from the rest of the red brick home.

Without knocking, Sam opened the door and stepped aside to let her and the constable precede him. Once inside, she took a deep breath of air laced with the smell of antiseptics as warm air stung her cheeks. With her heart pounding against her will, she grabbed for Sam's hand again.

Only a few feet away, the mayor was talking to Daniel in the wide hall separating the two parlors on either side that had been converted into an examining room to her left and a waiting area on the opposite side.

The minute Ben spied her, he fell silent and turned his surprised gaze immediately to the constable.

Noah cleared his throat. "She insisted she wanted to talk with you, Ben. I didn't get a chance to explain," he said meekly.

Ben frowned. "I'm sorry for your loss, Jane," he murmured to her. "You really shouldn't have come."

Daniel looked directly at her brother. "Sam, why

don't you take her back home? I promise to come to the store as soon as we know more. There's still a lot—"

"I came for answers before I take Hiram home," she said firmly. She refused to be intimidated either by the officials who were here or her lawyer. Daniel's role had changed dramatically in the space of only a few hours, and she was surprised he was willing to represent her interests here. Their differing views about ethical legalities notwithstanding, she doubted Daniel would be interested in such an ordinary legal problem and assumed he would simply return to Philadelphia.

She had often wondered what she would do if Hiram returned after she had engaged a lawyer, but never once considered her husband would arrive home in a coffin. Although her earlier meeting with Daniel had been for naught, there seemed to be little reason to continue their professional relationship now, unless he expected to help her wade through the legalities of settling Hiram's estate because of his friendship with Aunt Lily.

Voices from the waiting room drifted into the hallway. She ignored them and stared straight into Ben's eyes. He might be twenty years her senior, but she was not going to back down to someone she had known all her life. "I came for answers before I take Hiram home," she repeated.

He set his shoulders back, and his shirt stretched across his potbelly. "Not here. Noah was supposed to talk to you at home while the doctor finishes up."

She shook her head. "No, now. I want answers now. Then I want to see him and take him home with me." Ben flinched. Had her voice been that stern? She let out a slow breath. "Please, Ben."

Indecision filled his eyes, but only for a moment. He turned his head toward the others. "Noah, clear out those folks in the waiting room. Tell Jonas to take them all down to my house and don't dare let them stop at the tavern. Tell Libby to make them all something to eat, and you make sure they stay put till I get home. Understood?"

She gripped Sam's hand so hard her knuckles hurt as confusion rained away every thought she had in her head. What on earth was going on? Before she could pose that question, four men she recognized as mill workers followed Jonas Peterson, shuffling past her. They walked out the door, never meeting her questioning gaze. Neither did Jonas.

Noah did not reappear, but she saw him standing stiffly by the front window the moment Ben ushered her, along with Sam and Daniel, into the waiting room. A healthy fire gave the room a suffocating warmth, but she did not remove her bonnet or cloak. She refused Ben's invitation and Daniel's encouragement to sit down, and instead stood next to her brother in the middle of the room with her back to the fire and her gaze on the office door just across the hall.

She knew Ben would give her the details surrounding Hiram's "accident of sorts" now, but her legs were shaking and she had to lock her knees, praying she would be strong enough to hear the grisly news without swooning and proving the men right.

Ben seemed to be wearing a perpetual frown. "If you won't sit down, at least let me take your cloak and bonnet."

She answered him with a stern look and silence.

Daniel drew a long breath. "He's not the enemy, Jane. He's only trying to do his job. Actually, it's Noah's job as constable, but he seems to be a bit . . . overwhelmed. You're entitled to some answers, but you can't see Hiram yet and you can't take him home because the doctor is preparing the body—"

"That's my responsibility. I'm the one who should wash and dress my own husband, not Dr. Birchfield," she protested, upset Daniel had sidetracked her primary purpose for coming here.

Ben finally spoke up. "You can't do anything until there's been an autopsy."

Shocked nearly senseless, she caught her breath. "An autopsy?" Chills raced up her spine and back down again. "Noah said there'd been an accident. I need to know what happened. Why . . . why an autopsy?"

"I'm afraid things are rather more complicated than you were led to believe." He shot yet another harsh glance at Noah, but softened his gaze when he met hers again. "Peterson sent his men to clear out the gullies along the stream feeding the mill before the snow melts higher up the mountain soon and widens the stream. They found Hiram several hours ago. Peterson sent for me and Noah, and we had the body brought here to have the doctor—"

"But why?" she protested, cutting off his words before he could say "autopsy" again. The image the word created was so desecrating and frightening . . . and the procedure was totally unnecessary. She could not think of a single death in the village where an autopsy had been suggested, let alone ordered. Ever. Why now? "This has to be a mistake. Whatever happened to Hiram that you or the doctor can't tell what caused his death? Surely his injuries—"

"We couldn't find much. His body was frozen solid. The doctor had to thaw the body first. Even then, he still couldn't find injuries severe enough to have caused death."

The image of Hiram laying stunned or badly wounded for hours in the bitter cold only to freeze to death overwhelmed her. She swayed on her feet, and Sam moved closer to her. "Please sit with me," he said.

She shook her head, trying to keep the gruesome image from coming back and struggling to maintain control of her thoughts. "Tell them no autopsy," she insisted, knowing Hiram would abhor the very idea of someone marring his handsome looks with hideous incisions. "I have no idea why Hiram would have been up by the mill, or . . . or how he died," she offered, "but surely the doctor will be able to find something to explain all this. Noah said there'd been an accident. Did Hiram fall and hit his head or . . . ?"

Daniel shot a harsh glance at both Noah and Ben who recovered first. "Noah didn't make himself clear. We don't know yet what happened, but Hiram's death was not an accident. They found him buried under a mound of rocks, where he's been maybe as long as a few months. The coroner from Lancaster is with Dr. Birchfield right now trying to help us find out how and why Hiram died. While we're waiting for the results and the sheriff to arrive, all we know for sure is that Hiram was murdered."

Horror exploded, setting off bright yellow sparks right in front of her eyes. A wave of nausea weakened her before darkness swelled and engulfed her. She fell forward in the suddenly darkened room and heard Daniel's voice echoing far, far away.

"Jane? Grab her, Sam! Blast it, Noah, I told you I wanted you to keep her home and tell her there!"

Once Dr. Birchfield roused Jane from her swoon, Sam escorted his sister home, leaving Daniel at the doctor's office to await the results of the autopsy. He sat in the waiting room, his gaze glued to the door across the hall where on the other side, both Dr. Birchfield and the county coroner had resumed the autopsy.

Daniel had been just as surprised as everyone else when he learned Hiram Foster's body had been brought to the village, but professionally, he was more than ready to defend Jane, if necessary. For the past few years, he had been lead counsel for the accused in several infamous murder trials, the most recent, of course, being the beauteous Debra Modean.

Based on his experiences, he knew random acts of murder were actually quite rare. The spouse or lover of a murder victim was always the first suspect, followed closely by family members and friends which would place Jane at the forefront of the investigation that had just begun. He had not talked to her yet, but he was certain she had no idea how precarious her position was at the moment.

He was equally convinced she was innocent of any wrongdoing, despite the fact he had known her for such a short time. If anything, she might be guilty of trusting too much or waiting too long to seek a legal remedy to her problems, but murder?

"Not a chance," he murmured. He knew full well every man and woman was capable of murder, given the right provocation. Given their explosive meeting earlier today when she had used bluster and sheer courage against him instead of flailing at him or raking his face with her nails, he could not image Jane being provoked into physical violence, except perhaps in self-defense. Even then, she was too slight a woman to stand much of a chance against a man of any size, and from all reports, Hiram Foster was a tall, strapping man.

He took a deep breath and shook his head. Instead of enjoying a quiet country holiday, he found himself mired right back in a possible murder trial. On a more positive note, with the investigation still in the earliest of stages, he was hopeful she would quickly be eliminated as a suspect.

He sat back in the upholstered chair, expecting the autopsy to be finished soon. In the meantime, he hoped the sheriff from Lancaster would arrive, if only to learn as much as possible before Jane was questioned.

And when she was, Daniel had every intention of standing by her side and using any and all means to protect her interests.

Chapter 5

Freshly gowned and restored now after fainting at Dr. Birchfield's, Jane sat in her parlor with Daniel, Lancaster County Sheriff David Fleming, and Noah Washburn. Sam and Polly stood close by, but Jane had insisted Aunt Nester go home, if only to give her a respite from the scandalous commotion in the village center.

She found the prospect of answering the sheriff's questions easier with Daniel here, but she wished Sam had taken his wife home. Especially under these circumstances, Polly was like a brier on the stem of a beautiful rose, tolerable only at a distance, but Sam had adamantly refused Jane's request to leave once the sheriff arrived. Daniel tried to persuade Sam to leave as well, but relented, allowing them to stay as moral support for Jane on the condition that they remain silent during the questioning.

Oil lamps softened the shadows of late twilight poking through the drapes, but did little to chase the dark, troubling thoughts that lay heavy on her mind and heart. Despite her outward calm, she drifted on choppy waves of disbelief and horror in a sea rocked by the still-mysterious circumstances surrounding her husband's death.

A huge swell of grief was building inside her, growing stronger hour by hour. She could feel it in the pit of her stomach, rolling and crashing with furious strength. Holding it back behind a dam of dignity made her nauseous.

It was only a matter of time before the dam broke

and she was swept away, losing all control of her emotions. By sheer strength of will, she refused to let that happen before the questions that had been screaming in her mind ever since being revived from her fainting spell were answered. Who had murdered Hiram? Why? How?

She continued to twist the ring on her finger, which had now begun to swell. So far, she had managed to respond calmly to all of the sheriff's questions, recounting Hiram's vague plans for his business trip, the one letter she had received, and her attempts to keep the general store operating.

She also explained Daniel's arrival in Sunrise to help her, although he had not yet taken any action on her behalf. She had not, however, hinted at the troubles she and Hiram had shared within their marriage, especially with Sam and Polly here, not to mention Noah and Daniel.

Truthfully, Hiram had been entirely pleased with how their marriage had evolved. She had been the unhappy partner, and she had no intention of ever revealing her pain, especially in front of the woman who had contributed to the troubles in her marriage.

Now it was her turn to get answers to her questions. "I can't believe Hiram was *murdered*," she murmured, steepling her hands on her lap to avoid toying with her ring. "Are you sure?"

"We're still waiting on the coroner, but there doesn't appear to be much doubt." Sheriff Fleming wrested control of the investigation from local authorities, who handled only minor infringements of the law, and answered quickly. Overly tall and thickly built, he had an all-consuming presence. Too large for any of the chairs, he occupied the settee while Jane sat across from him in a chair next to Daniel and Noah.

The sheriff turned his gaze to Noah. "Are you sure they're going to send for us when Dr. Schultz is finished with the postmortem?"

"Said they would. I'm sure they will. They won't let

you down," Noah insisted in a rambling way. He sat on the edge of his seat and looked like he was ready to escape at the first opportunity.

Fleming chuckled. "Relax, Noah. No harm's been done." He looked back at Jane and apparently detected her confusion. "Dr. Schultz is the county coroner. He's a bit of a stickler for procedure—"

"That's only the half of it," Noah countered. "The man's got sandpaper for a temper. We did what we thought was best at the time. It's not like we ever had a murder in Sunrise before." He blushed. "Sorry, Jane. Didn't mean to be so . . . so blunt."

"Don't worry about Dr. Schultz," Fleming offered.

More confused than ever, Jane turned to Daniel. "I'm not sure I understand what's going on."

His eyes clouded with apology. "I'm sorry. The coroner conducts an inquest for all suspicious deaths and calls a jury of local men to the scene while he examines the body in their presence. They may testify later at the trial, assuming the murderer is caught and indicted."

The sheriff nodded in agreement with Daniel's explanation. "Unfortunately, Noah and Ben had your husband's body removed back to the village, and Dr. Schultz . . . well, he was a tad upset. He's had to improvise a bit, but the mayor has smoothed everything over. He got enough men for a jury, including the men who had found your husband, and took them to Dr. Birchfield's before they all went back to the scene where your husband had been found. Dr. Schultz will have enough information to submit later to the court once he finishes the postmortem examination and has the jury view what he finds. After that, he should release the body for burial."

"The . . . the jury will have to see Hiram's body after . . . Is that necessary?" Eyes wide, she felt her heart begin to pound. When Daniel nodded, she let out a sigh.

Hiram was probably watching from the other world, absolutely horrified to see his body mutilated by an autopsy, then displayed for a jury of men who had been his neighbors and friends. She could not imagine a greater humiliation for a man who prided himself on his attractive physical appearance, and she wondered if he had gone on to another place where inner goodness was far more important than physical beauty.

"We'll be able to share more with all of you tomorrow," the sheriff suggested and looked at Daniel before going through the notes he had made. "For now, I'd just like to review a few things. Earlier you said you haven't seen your husband since he left last September . . . September twenty-ninth. Is that right?"

She nodded.

"And he only wrote to you once in October?"

Another quick nod.

He flipped through a few more pages and frowned. "And you have no idea where he went, specifically, in Baltimore or Philadelphia?"

Daniel scowled, clearly growing impatient with the sheriff's attempt to shake her earlier comments. "Mrs. Foster already told you—"

"No, it's all right," she insisted and took a deep breath, reminding herself to be careful to phrase her answer honestly, but without implying she did not care where he had gone. "Hiram never planned a rigid itinerary or kept to a schedule. He traveled for . . . for pleasure as much as for business."

The sheriff cocked his head, raised one brow, and posed a question he had not asked earlier. "You never went with him?"

"Someone had to stay and keep the store."

"Did your husband usually carry large sums of money as he traveled?"

She swallowed her pride. "I don't know."

"What about other traveling companions? Did he take anyone else with him when he left or make a habit of bringing anyone back with him? Someone who might have then had the motive or opportunity to rob and kill him?"

"No. No one," she murmured. "He traveled alone."

As far as she knew, that was the truth, but it would not shock her later to learn he had female companionship during his travels from one city to another. In any event, he would hardly have brought a mistress back to Sunrise.

He already had Polly here, and from what Jane had observed between her husband and sister-in-law, the only way Polly would have killed him was by loving him to death. She was also half Hiram's size, and Jane could not imagine Polly overpowering him by any means.

Jane felt her cheeks grow warm, and she took a sip of water from the glass on the table next to her chair to cool her resentment. By rights, Polly's devotion belonged to Sam, and Jane could only pray this sordid ending to the affair would bring Polly to her senses.

The sheriff started to tap his pencil on his notes, and the sound brought Jane back from her mental wandering. "Is there anyone here in Sunrise who might have had some bad business dealings with your husband? Someone deeply in debt to the store, or someone who didn't like him?"

"No, Hiram was well-liked, and I . . . I kept all the books. He didn't really pay close attention to specific accounts. Not with . . . with anyone local." She furrowed her brow. "He did plan to stop in Lancaster to see his lawyer and drop off the other ledger books and some old promissory notes left from when his father owned the general store. I don't know much about that. You should talk with his lawyer, Mr. Harris."

The sheriff jotted down additional notes as she spoke. "Is that Efrem Harris?"

"Yes, but even if there was someone who was upset with Hiram, why would he kill him? And how would that . . . that person know Hiram was on his way home when I didn't even know?"

The sheriff scratched his head. "He could have written to someone, told them when he was coming."

She frowned. "Not here in Sunrise. I handle the post. I would have known."

He shrugged his shoulders. "Then maybe it wasn't someone from here. Maybe he met someone in Lancaster or Philadelphia or wherever who followed him home and waited until they were somewhere no one else would see them and—"

"Follow him all the way to Sunrise? That doesn't make any sense."

"Neither does this line of questioning," Daniel argued. "Since Mrs. Foster wasn't with her husband, she had no firsthand knowledge of what may or may not have occurred. While I want my client to be fully cooperative, I won't have her badgered by unnecessary questions. If you have nothing further relevant to what she may or may not have witnessed here in Sunrise, this interview is concluded."

The sheriff bristled. "Not quite," he stated, but hesitated as though struggling to find the words to phrase his next question. "I mean no offense, Mrs. Foster, but your husband was apparently . . . er, well, the ladies found him appealing. To your knowledge, was there any kind of misunderstanding that might have led to a confrontation between your husband and another woman's husband?"

The blood drained from her face, and she began to tremble. Her heart skipped a beat then pounded furiously to deny the traitorous thoughts jumbling together in her mind. Sam would not, could not have killed Hiram. Not Sam. Not her brother. He did not even know about the affair.

Guilt for even forming the thought that Sam had had anything to do with Hiram's death left her trembling even harder, and she was surprised Polly had not swooned. She gulped back a new wave of nausea and covered her mouth with her hand while taking deep, slow breaths of air.

"You don't have to answer that question," Daniel spat as he glowered at the sheriff.

"Now look what you've done," Sam barked, breaking his silence. He rushed to her side and rested his hands on the back of her chair. "We're all decent people here in Sunrise. We're not much of a place, compared to other towns or cities, but we're neighbors and friends. Hell, we're all related to half the other folks in the village."

He paused to glare at the sheriff. "Maybe Hiram wasn't the most reliable man God ever made. He had his faults about him, just like everyone else. Some folks might argue he put too much work on this woman here, but my sister never complained. She was a dutiful wife to him, and he was a good provider, a solid neighbor, and a loyal friend. I can tell you right now he'd never betray his wife or any of his friends or neighbors by stealing the affections from another man's wife. Never."

Sam's earnest defense of Hiram shoved new splinters of guilt into her soul, but the sheriff's response chilled her to the bone.

"Sunrise isn't Paradise, either. I've been sheriff long enough to know the most likely suspects are those known to the victim. If your sister didn't kill her husband, one of Foster's friends or neighbors probably did. And I won't stop investigating until I know the truth and see the murderer brought to justice."

Stunned, Jane could scarcely breathe, terrified the sheriff would discover the affair and point to Sam as a suspect, one who would have a very strong motive for killing Hiram.

The sheriff put his notes away and stood up, towering over both Jane and Sam, and Daniel quickly stood as well. Sheriff Fleming's dark eyes glistened with compassion laced with determination. "I'm sorry, Mrs. Foster. I didn't mean to upset you. As painful as it might be for you, I won't give up asking hard questions until I find your husband's murderer." He checked his pocket watch. "If the doctor isn't finished yet, he should be soon. I should probably get over there. Noah? Mr. Colton? Will you be coming with me or staying here?"

Noah leaped to his feet. "I'll go with you."

Daniel nodded to Sam. "Don't leave her here alone. I'll be back," he murmured and left with the other two men.

Jane held tight to the arms of her chair as the dam holding back her emotions began to crumble. Tears welled, and Sam put his hand on her shoulder. "We'll stay with you until Aunt Nester gets back."

"No. Go on home. I'm fine. I'm . . . I'm just feeling a bit exhausted," she insisted, looking at Polly who was still standing by the door. Her face was pale, her eyes were wide with fright. Apparently, she recognized the danger Sam would be in as the sheriff continued his investigation. Jane had no compassion for her, but she did need to be alone. "Take Polly home," she urged her brother.

He took one look at his wife and quickly relented.

The door had barely closed behind them when the dam broke. Pent-up emotions escaped in deep sobs that left Jane gulping for air as she rushed from the parlor to her room. She passed by Hiram's bedchamber, a room filled with bittersweet memories that only added more pain and regret to the salty tears that drowned her face.

She flew into her darkened chamber and crumbled atop her bed. Shaking uncontrollably, her body was beyond her control. Heaving sobs left her breathless, and the effort to stem the tremors in her limbs was futile. She muffled the groans that echoed in the room by pressing her face against her pillow.

No longer willing to be denied, fear and grief swept over her hard and fast, surprising her and confusing her as well. The sheriff's vow echoed in her mind, over and over, sending fear for Sam straight to her heart. She was certain Polly would never admit to the affair, not to the sheriff or to her husband. If Jane could also keep silent about what she had seen, the sheriff would be stymied and forced to look elsewhere for a suspect.

With her fears settled, at least temporarily, she tried

to understand why she would grieve so deeply for a man she did not love. She had long ago lost any affection for her husband, yet she was reacting to his death as though they had had a perfect marriage. She toyed with the wedding ring on her finger, a symbol now that was totally useless.

As her sobs waned to whimpers, all the years she had spent with Hiram unfolded, as though her mind had retaken control and flashed images for her to see, one by one, so she would understand her grief: his romantic, whirlwind proposal. The early happy weeks. Their quick estrangement. Her profound disappointment. His ultimate betrayal.

As the joy and hope that had begun her marriage died slowly again in her mind, she realized she was not a hypocrite for weeping and feeling sorrow at Hiram's passing. She truly did grieve, but not for losing a beloved husband. With his death, that stubborn, tiny ray of hope buried deep in her heart that they would somehow reconcile and discover some affection for one another died too.

And with her broken heart, she grieved for the dream of what might have been.

Soothed by her insight, she dried her tears. Her eyelids grew heavy, and her breathing shallow. Try as she might, she could not resist sleep and welcomed the deep darkness that descended as a welcome relief to reality—if only for a few hours.

Frustrated by the coroner's refusal to divulge the results of the autopsy until morning, Daniel had at least secured a private meeting for them all scheduled for eleven o'clock at Jane's home. When he went to inform Jane, he found the store locked and the upstairs windows darkened. Rather than disturb her, he walked back to his room at the tavern without being stopped by curious villagers.

Hoping his luck would hold till he got to his room,

he managed to get halfway up the stairs before someone called after him.

"Mr. Colton?"

So much for good luck. He turned and saw Jane's cousin, Louis, at the bottom of the stairs.

"Thought that was you," he whispered. The tavern owner looked from side to side before continuing. "Man came in about an hour ago. Said he was your friend and claimed you two separated earlier today on the road when his horse pulled up lame. He wanted to wait for you in your room, but I put him in the common room. Hope that's not gonna cause a problem."

Daniel immediately stiffened. Apparently, he had been right to be suspicious earlier and knew now someone had followed him from Columbia and had been watching him here in Sunrise. "Actually, it's fine. I didn't travel with anyone today. What's this supposed friend of mine look like?" he gritted, trying not to leap to any conclusions about the man's identity.

Louis narrowed his gaze. "City fella. Kinda shifty, but maybe I'm just leery of strangers after all that's happened today. Or maybe it's that eye patch he wears. Do you know him?"

"Unfortunately, I do," he admitted, "but he's not a friend."

Louis snorted. "Thought not."

"I'll handle him in the morning. Thanks," Daniel offered and started back up the steps. He clenched his teeth together so hard his jaw ached.

Damn!

He paused at the top of the stairs to let his anger shift from seething to controlled before continuing down the hall. He stopped in front of the door to the common sleeping room, took a deep breath, and summoned every ounce of self-control he possessed to keep from breaking down the door and strangling the one-eyed snake who had slithered into Sunrise and dared to call himself Daniel's friend.

Unless he handled this situation very carefully, however, Jane could very well end up the poor soul who would be this man's victim, and Daniel would once again be the unlucky lawyer who had to contend with him.

At least he had the time tonight to think of how to get rid of the man. He proceeded further down the hall to his private room and unlocked the door.

"Colton!"

Time had run out.

So had his luck.

His heart pounding, he turned around with a weary, but hard-fought smile on his face and hoped the dim light would hide whatever disdain he had not been able to swallow. Dismissing the impulse to bow mockingly before the King of Sludge, Daniel walked a few steps back down the hall before acknowledging the man. "Mercury Pine," he gritted, tasting bile just saying the man's name.

When Pine chuckled, the eye patch he wore to cover his disfigurement crinkled a bit. "You've looked better, Colton. You really should try to rest more. Had a busy day, haven't you? From dawn to well past dusk. Not a good omen—for either you or Mrs. Foster, although the late Mr. Foster might protest."

Daniel let his smile droop into a frown. Obviously, Pine had been snooping and eavesdropping outside the general store when he and Jane first met. Daniel could not afford to antagonize the journalist by taking offense, but refused to be baited into discussing the matter of Hiram Foster's death or its implications for Jane. "Actually, I came to Sunrise hoping to take a bit of a holiday. The good clean air and country fare here can restore a man, especially after a long trial. It's not a country estate in England, but Sunrise will do," he countered, trying to shift the conversation to Pine's most recent victim, Debra, who had fled to England to escape the notoriety Pine had created.

Pine lifted his free brow. "I'm certain your 'holiday' will have to be postponed considering the serious nature of the new widow Foster's difficulties." He shook his head slowly from side to side. "Confidentially, Colton, after enjoying a 'jewel shining brightly,' how hard is it to be 'dazzled' by one 'shining softly'? As a lawyer, that is."

Anger, swift and hot, sent his pulse pounding again. His hands clenched into fists, and he fought hard to keep his features frozen in place. That Pine had heard Daniel singing when he had been down by the river and then openly perverted the love song with lewd innuendo was more than sacrilege. It was a personal affront he would never forgive. If he had had a rock within easy reach, he would have lured Pine to slither underneath and squashed the breath out of him. "Mrs. Foster is an old friend," he managed.

"Who amazingly arranged for her lawyer to arrive on the very day her husband's body was found?" Pine chortled. "I can't believe that was a coincidence any-more than I can accept the illustrious Daniel Colton is her friend rather than her lawyer. There isn't a better lawyer in two hundred miles when it comes to setting a murderer free."

He put the tip of his finger to his forehead in a mock gesture and narrowed his one eye. "Or should I say murderess when I write about this case?"

Despite his best efforts, Daniel flinched. He had no choice now but to be more direct and meet the jour-nalist's assumptions head-to-head since he intended to make Jane his next target. "Maybe you need a rest more than I do, Pine. You're jumping to wild conclusions. There's no trial pending here. There hasn't even been a full investigation, let alone an indictment. Good Lord, the man hasn't even been buried yet."

"But there has been an inquest," Pine remarked ca-sually, "and from what I've been told by a juryman, it's only a matter of time before the grand jury indicts your client. This case may not have the same . . . shall we say 'attractiveness' as your last one, but the public is end-lessly fascinated with murder, particularly when a wife does away with her husband. Take your last case—"

"Good night, Pine." He turned and walked back to his room before red-hot fury melted the last of his control.

"Colton!" Pine called after him, refusing to be ignored or dismissed. "You won't have a beautiful woman to sway the jury this time or her wealth to buy them off." He snorted, and the sound echoed in the hall. "The public may not be overly enthused by a little mouse of a storekeeper, but I'm certain they'll find her late husband a more dashing victim than the late Simon Modean."

Daniel gripped the door handle so tightly his knuckles whitened. "There's not going to be a trial," he snapped, although he would have given half his wealth to know what Pine had learned about the results of the autopsy.

"You wouldn't be here if you didn't expect to defend Mrs. Foster against murder charges. That's what you do best. Granted, it may take some time for the investigation to mount up more than suspicion or circumstantial evidence, especially since the village seems to be rallying around the grieving widow, but once the coroner's findings are released, that will change. I'll be here to document the entire event, and this time, the hangman won't be cheated."

With his patience burnt to a crisp, Daniel glanced over his shoulder and glared at the damnable man. "It's going to be very satisfying to watch you waste your time while someone else is reporting on a real murder case."

"Oh, this one will be real. Trust me. I can sniff out a good murder trial practically before the victim draws his last breath. Talk to me tomorrow after the coroner's findings are announced. We might even be able to work out something to make your work here more profitable since the widow doesn't appear to have the access to funds like Debra did. I'd even consider—"

"Consider yourself a fool," Daniel spat. He unlocked

his door and stepped into the darkened room, but he did not manage to get the door closed before Pine dangled one last piece of bait that Daniel tried, but failed, to ignore.

"See you at the church. Ten o'clock."

He froze, but refused to go back into the hall. Rage was boiling so close to the surface, his skin felt like it had caught on fire. Why the church? Less than an hour ago, the sheriff and coroner had both agreed to a private meeting.

As if he could read Daniel's mind, Pine snickered. "Small village. Lots of interest and fears to be put to rest. They do things differently here than in the city," he taunted.

Daniel let out an expletive, slammed his door shut, and stood alone in the dark. He listened to the sound of Pine's footsteps as he retreated, his words reverberating in Daniel's mind and heart. Rationally, he knew Pine was full of bluff, resorting to taunts hoping to make Daniel lose his temper and reveal confidential information.

Professionally, Daniel had had years of experience that had taught him to manage his temper and keep control of his thoughts and actions to protect his clients—an ability Pine failed to credit to Daniel.

It was his heart that concerned him.

He closed his eyes. His pulse was normal now, but his heart had already started to swell with affection for Jane, a surprising and totally unacceptable development as far as he was concerned. He cared about Jane as any man would care about a woman who was very quickly and unexpectedly sneaking her way into his heart—a dangerous omen he could not afford to tolerate.

If he was going to stay levelheaded and guide her through the maze of an investigation that could place her in serious jeopardy, he could not give in to his feelings for her, no matter how sympathetic he might be, although his feelings for her were much more complicated.

For any lawyer, getting emotionally involved with a client was taboo. He had never done it before, never even been tempted, and he did not have the luxury of spending any time now to figure out why or how this had happened.

With Pine temporarily rebuffed, the most pressing issue facing Daniel now was how to get Pine out of town permanently, and he would get no sleep tonight until he had formulated a plan to accomplish that goal.

Chapter 6

Had everyone's world turned inside out, or just Jane's?

Instead of the church being a place where believers heard the Word promising eternal life, today villagers would hear only secular words describing death. Two doctors, one a virtual stranger, stood near the pulpit while the minister sat next to Jane in the first pew, and villagers who had not put a foot inside the church for months filled every row and lined the aisles, murmuring gossip instead of prayers.

With her face hidden by a dark veil and her trembling hands hidden in the folds of her cloak, she fingered her wedding ring and tried to remember everything Daniel had told her just an hour ago.

Her greatest concern rested on the city journalist who had followed her lawyer to Sunrise. Daniel had promised to see that the man left before he caused any more trouble, but she had seen a man wearing an eye patch enter just ahead of them which meant Daniel had not been able to keep his word.

Fortunately, Aunt Nester did not know about the disreputable newspaperman. She would be likely to confront him herself, even more so now that he was here in the church. Jane did not worry that the journalist would harass her here, not with Daniel sitting to her left and her brother to her right. Although she was grateful to have her brother's support, he had been giving Polly most of his attention. He had his arm around her so she could rest her head on his shoulder, and he had tilted his head to shield her face from view.

Sweet, devious Polly. Was there another woman in the universe who could look as stunning in mourning clothes? Probably not, Jane decided, and chided herself for being mean-spirited in church, of all places.

Sheriff Fleming raised his arm and signaled for quiet. When loud murmurs dropped to barely a whisper, he started by introducing himself and the coroner since most villagers had not met them yesterday.

"As a courtesy," he began, "I'm going to have Dr. Schultz present the findings of the coroner's jury. While it is too early in the investigation of the death of Hiram Foster for me to comment fully, let me begin by emphasizing that we will need your help to solve this terrible crime."

He paused and gazed around the room. "Gossip and innuendo serve no purpose but ill. I hope anyone who has information for me will step forward later today. Although I'll be leaving tomorrow to return to Lancaster, that doesn't mean I've abandoned the investigation. I will be returning to Sunrise, but in the interim, you can always contact me through Noah Washburn or Ben Holtzman, who will forward any developments here to me."

He turned and nodded to the two doctors. Dr. Birchfield stepped forward first. "As most of you know, it has been my sad, but necessary duty to assist Dr. Schultz with a postmortem examination. He is eminently far more qualified than I am to render an opinion in this case. We will not entertain any questions since those are best left handled by the grand jury if and when the inquest is directed to the court."

Facing the moment she had dreaded most, Jane held her breath. Everything was proceeding exactly as Daniel had said it would. When Sam reached over and took her hand, she let her breath out slowly and smiled. She held on tight and tried to still the hammering of her heart as Dr. Schultz moved forward to join Dr. Birchfield.

Slightly older than their local doctor, the coroner appeared to be in his late forties, although his gray hair and old-fashioned mustache made him look somewhat older. He took out a paper from inside his frock coat and held it up. "I have the jury's verdict right here and will keep possession of it until directed to provide it to the court. Today, I'll only give you a brief summary of my written report."

He stopped, cleared his throat, and produced a set of notes from his pocket. "When discovered, the body of Hiram Foster was buried under ice-glazed rocks and stones in a mound we have determined to be man-made. As the body was frozen, it was moved to the doctor's office where it was allowed to thaw after the clothing was removed and held for my review. Personal effects included only a metal ring with three keys and a badly torn playbill from a theater in Indiana. We found no travel bag."

Before Jane could register more than a glimmer of hope that robbery was the motive for killing her husband, the doctor resumed his report. "In company with Dr. Birchfield, I made the postmortem examination. From its general appearance, the body is presumed to have been dead a few days. I would be willing to suggest, however, that given the frozen state of the corpse when found and the particularly cold winter and isolated hiding spot, it is not only possible, but equally likely Mr. Foster had been dead and his body hidden for as long as two months."

Gasps filled the air, echoing Jane's surprise. Hiram could have been dead for two months? Her pulse began to pound, and she was glad her veil covered her face. She trembled when she saw Daniel's strained expression, but when she saw the bespectacled minister shift stiffly in his seat, chills raced up her spine. Two months ago, in January, was when he had claimed he had seen Hiram near the general store. Was it possible her husband actually had come back to Sunrise in January? Had he gone to see Polly as she had once suspected?

Had someone stopped or waylaid him? Or had the minister been wrong all along?

Jane had so many questions, she could not think straight enough to focus on any single one before another one popped into her head.

"Superficially," the doctor intoned in a louder voice to get the room quiet again, "there were a number of bruises on the body. None of these injuries caused death and occurred shortly before death or immediately thereafter."

Sam squeezed Jane's hand, offering moral support, and she held on hard to brace herself to hear the rest.

"We noted a slightly yellow staining on several areas of the body with no foul odor, only the faint residue of cologne. We then dissected the body and discovered no internal damage whatsoever. As coroner, I've conducted over eighty dissections, but recall two cases with similar evidence as to the cause of death."

He put away his notes, and when he again addressed the gathering, his voice rang clear. "Death was caused by asphyxiation due to poison absorbed by the decedent's skin, specifically nicotine, which is commonly sold as concentrated tobacco juice. Death would have occurred up to four or five hours after application of the poison. It was most likely mixed with the victim's cologne and used by the unsuspecting victim who suffered his end near Peterson's mill where the murderer then attempted to conceal the crime."

Hushed whispers erupted into loud conversation, but Jane only heard the doctor's last words echo and crash together in her own mind. Grappling with the irony of her accident in the general store and her husband's fatal reaction to the same poison, she gripped her brother's hand hard, intuitively eliminating robbery as a motive.

Poisoned. As long as two months ago.

Poison. Rubbed on his body, hidden in his cologne.

Poison. The perfect way for a woman of any size to overpower a man of Hiram's stature and strength.

There was only one woman Jane knew who was

close enough to Hiram to have access to his cologne, and the horror of that reality unleashed a swell of nausea almost as strong as when she had caught Polly and Hiram together and feared she would be physically ill.

Sweet, devious Polly. She had been welcomed by all the villagers into their hearts and homes over a year ago when Sam had brought her back from Columbia as his bride. She had dazzled them all with her blond beauty and captured their devotion with her sweet disposition and sunny smile. Then she had betrayed her husband and murdered her lover for reasons Jane might never know.

Unless she was wrong.

Unless there was another woman in Sunrise Hiram had taken to his bed and had spurned in favor of Polly. Someone Jane had not discovered having an affair with her husband. Someone who had taken deadly revenge.

She was horrified by yet another thought. If the poison took hours to kill her husband, that could implicate a woman from as far away as Lancaster or Marietta or Columbia or any of the other towns and villages within a range of four or five hours' travel time.

The possibilities were only as limited as the number of women in nearby towns and villages, for in her mind, a man willing to risk committing adultery so close to home would be even more likely to indulge himself elsewhere.

Even her assumption that Hiram had been murdered by a rejected lover could be challenged easily. What if the woman in question was also married, and her spouse had discovered the affair? What if he had decided to end the affair with murder?

As her initial assumptions began to crumble, she started to tremble again. Unless she was absolutely positive Polly had killed Hiram, she could do and say nothing. She had no choice but to tuck her suspicions away with the collection of life's disappointments she kept locked in the depths of her soul and pray she was wrong about Polly.

Strong twines of shame created by the circumstances of Hiram's death wrapped around her heart and soul, but she carefully, and willfully, tore them away. Any shame belonged to Hiram for betraying her and to the man or woman who had murdered him. Not Jane. She had kept her vows.

For a fleeting moment, she even considered the possibility that she might be accused of murdering her husband, but immediately dismissed the thought as absurd. Even if the sheriff posed the question, she had nothing to fear.

She was innocent.

There was not a single thread of evidence that could surface even circumstantially to cast her under serious suspicion because it did not exist. Even if it had, none of the villagers would give the evidence any credence. Jane had lived a good, moral life before and after her marriage, without ever voicing a complaint about her husband. She had nothing to fear for herself.

Only for Sam and his adulterous wife.

Daniel's apology and his warning about the journalist Mercury Pine rang an alarm bell in her mind that sent her pulse racing again. She had been surprised when Daniel had told her about his last trial and the shocking way the journalist had added to the scandal by penning murder pamphlets, the likes of which she had only seen once and promptly burned. It was not Daniel's fault Pine had followed him here, but with the notoriety surrounding his last few trials, Pine would not believe Daniel remained here only to help her with handling the legal matters concerning Hiram's estate.

If Pine stayed and uncovered evidence of her husband's adultery with Polly, the scandal would spread like wildfire along the eastern seaboard in one of his outrageous pamphlets, even if she had not been the one to poison Hiram—a scandal that could destroy Sam's marriage, Jane's loving relationship with her brother, and even the village itself.

She had to get rid of Mercury Pine, and the only way

she could think to do that was to make sure Daniel left before the investigation moved forward so the journalist would follow him. She would not be able to talk to him right now, but he would be present when the sheriff met with her after the public meeting. As soon as the sheriff left, she would dismiss Daniel and send him back to Philadelphia and pray Pine would follow him there.

As Daniel escorted Jane from the church, he looked back over his shoulder and saw Louis and several other villagers corner Pine and usher him out the opposite door without incident, although he was disappointed they had not sent Pine packing before the meeting. He only hoped their plan would work and Pine would leave Sunrise now, never to return.

As he walked her back to her home over the general store, Daniel was more concerned than ever about Jane and the impact of the jury's verdict on the cause of Foster's death. Poison was typically the weapon of choice for women rather than men, which was a limited factor pointing to her as the perpetrator of her husband's death. Poison was also the obvious choice for cowards who did not have the mental courage to use a more typical weapon or for someone who lacked the physical strength to commit murder.

Physically, Jane could not overpower a man, but she was morally strong and had a reputation in the village for being hardworking and honest. From firsthand experience, he knew she confronted issues directly rather than avoid them, which also undermined any thought she would resort to poison if she had had problems within her marriage.

Based on what he had heard at the meeting in the church, it was now clear Foster had at least attempted to come back to Sunrise. What was not certain was whether he had reached the village, gone home to his wife, and then died as he was leaving again or if he had died en route to home and had never arrived at all. Finding out which scenario had actually happened would be critical in defending Jane later, should that become necessary.

Just as important, there were other clues that pointed to robbery as a possible motive for the murder. The missing travel bag was one, and he needed to talk to Jane to find out if there were any other personal effects missing from her late husband's person. If so, then the focus of the investigation might point to a traveling companion Hiram might have met along the way from Lancaster to Sunrise as a suspect, which added credence to the question the sheriff had posed to Jane only yesterday.

Again, Daniel had many more questions than he had answers, and it was clear he could not get all of them here in Sunrise. The lure of Sunrise as an idyllic escape back in time was now more of a liability than ever. He needed everything at his disposal to help her—a telegraph, a courthouse, even a stage line, just to list a few. Riding back and forth from Sunrise to Lancaster, a large city where he would have the important tools he would need if called upon to defend her, wasted time and effort.

When they finally reached the general store, he guided her inside and chanced a look at the woman walking beside him. She made her way through the foyer and up the back steps to her living quarters with her head held high and her body straight, even though he was certain she was quaking inside from the shocking details the coroner had revealed.

Because of the dark veil she wore, Daniel could not see her face, but he could picture her lips pinched into a determined line and her chin tilted up just a tad. She created quite a different image compared to his last client who had been a weeping, hysterical woman whose personal flaws had cracked wide open under the strain of the trial.

Jane's character and will were stronger. She might not crack under the strain of the murder investigation, but she would suffer tremendously if eventually charged with her husband's murder.

Daniel simply could not let that happen.

His first task, however, would be to take a look at Foster's will and file for probate to guarantee her economic future. After that, they would have to talk about the murder, and he would continue to monitor the sheriff's investigation to protect Jane's interests.

If she were eventually charged, he would have to assemble a staff of associates to help prepare her defense, but it was premature to do so now. After their heated discussion earlier that morning before her husband's body had been found, Daniel had no doubt she would be a difficult, if not impossible, client to defend. Although her belief in justice and commitment to high ethical standards was admirably sincere, he also knew she would be far less idealistic if the time ever came when he had to defend her against charges that could take her life instead of her livelihood.

While he waited for events to unfold that would demand action on Jane's behalf, he had other tasks to complete for Lily Dionne. Although she had never anticipated her niece would be tragically widowed or suspected of murder, Lily had given him several directives, any one of which he was free to follow or disregard as circumstances warranted.

It was time to implement one of the directives so he had a bit more freedom than he enjoyed at the tavern where his every move could be monitored. As soon as he had taken care of Foster's will, he would implement that directive, although he was quick to realize Lily had not prepared either herself or her lawyer for one very disturbing factor that added to an already incomprehensible development.

He had found Jane Foster to be exactly the kind of woman who could dazzle his heart, a most dangerous place for her to be if she became the center of a murder investigation.

Chapter 7

Still shaken by the inquest findings an hour later, Jane carried the neatly folded set of Hiram's garments into the crowded parlor. Sam joined her and put his arm around her shoulders as she handed them to Dr. Birchfield.

"With the dissection, it's better this way," the doctor murmured. "You've been through enough. I'll do my best. Have Sam bring you by later to see Hiram."

She nodded, grateful to have her brother beside her without his wife. "I'll have to speak to Reverend Reilly about the burial."

Sam hugged her closer. "He's in the kitchen with Polly, Aunt Nester, and the others. He suggested tomorrow morning at nine, unless you want it to be later. Thomas offered to keep the store open in the morning, if you think that's necessary since it was closed today, but most everyone will be at the cemetery."

She closed her eyes briefly. After witnessing the packed church today, she could easily envision a crush of graveside mourners and shuddered just thinking how that city journalist might describe it. "I'd rather have a more private burial. Couldn't we have it done quietly later today?"

"If that's what you want, I can have Hiram ready," the doctor offered. His gaze glistened with compassion. "Today has been hard enough. Maybe you should rest a bit before facing your final good-bye."

She had said good-bye to Hiram with her heart a long time ago, and memories of their last parting moment when he had shoved her aside when she had tried to keep him from leaving brought tears to her eyes.

"The doctor's right. You should rest and build up your strength a bit," Sam urged.

"I'd rather today," she insisted. "Please ask Reverend Reilly if he can conduct the service at the grave."

"Jane, I really think—"

"Don't bother trying to change her mind," Sam cautioned. "She's a stubborn one. Family trait," he teased, giving her a gentle smile. "I'll arrange it with the minister. What time should I tell him?"

"Just before sunset. That way everyone can get home before it's fully dark."

With a shrug of resignation, Dr. Birchfield smiled. "Then I'd better leave now. Give me an hour or so, then stop by anytime you feel you're ready to see him. I'm going to take some of these folks with me so you can get a little rest. Unless you need to speak to the sheriff or Dr. Schultz again."

She chewed on her lower lip. Both men had been solicitous, yet reserved when they had come to speak privately to her for a few moments after the meeting in church. But there was one thing that still concerned her. "Could you just remind Sheriff Fleming about Hiram's pocket watch? And . . . and maybe you could check through Hiram's clothing one more time. The watch belonged to his father. I . . . I should send it to his brother if he can locate it."

"I can and I will. Sam, see that she gets some rest. Doctor's orders."

She put her arm around her brother's waist. "You won't have an argument from me."

He chuckled. "Good, especially since I tend to lose arguments to my big sister."

She might have been older than Sam, but she certainly was not bigger. His choice of words made her smile. They had been nearly the same size when their parents died, and she had watched him grow from a skinny boy to a strapping man who topped six feet by several inches.

With their father's sandy brown hair and dark brown eyes, and their mother's generous smile, Sam kept her memories of her parents alive with his physical presence alone. A guilty conscience nudged her soul, but she embraced the pain, vowing again to protect him from the heartache of Polly's betrayal. Telling Sam about the affair now served no purpose, other than to relieve her own guilt, a small burden her love for him would willingly carry.

As soon as Dr. Birchfield and the Lancaster officials left, Thomas and Felicity went home, too, followed by the minister who had agreed to a sunset burial. Sam closed the door for the last time and eyed her with a determined look. "First you need something to eat. Then you rest."

She grinned at him. "You're enjoying bossing me around, aren't you?"

"Every little chance I get." He ushered her to the settee and called Daniel from the kitchen for reinforcements. "Can you keep an eye on my sister? She's likely to slip downstairs and work in the store while I get her something to eat."

Daniel smiled back as he crossed the room to join them. "She does have a well-deserved reputation for working hard, doesn't she?"

"Too hard."

"Family trait," she interjected. Sam's days hauling freight had kept him away too often, and she wished he could stay closer to home for more than the obvious concern she had for his marriage. "Whatever happened to trust?" she prompted, feeling a little silly about having a sentry to guard her.

"Oh, I trust you," Sam replied as he made his way to the kitchen. "Just enough to know you'll have a real good reason for going down to the store."

She sighed and looked at Daniel sheepishly. "He's right. I probably would have gone to undo the past week of havoc Aunt Nester's created in my ledger book."

He smiled and took a seat across from her. "I wouldn't let her hear you say that."

"I already did," she admitted. "Most people don't argue with her anymore. They know I'll adjust their accounts later. First she complains I'm too generous. I argue back, and she finally uses her poor skills with figures as an excuse. We do this all the time."

When he sobered, his gaze still remained soft, and she felt like she was the most important woman in the world as far as he was concerned. "You're very fortunate to have such a close, supportive family," he said.

"I know. I thank God for them every day, especially . . . especially now." Finding it difficult to imagine how she would have managed without them while Hiram had been gone off and on for the past five years, especially during his last business trip, and now during this awful time, she shifted her thoughts to the man who sat in front of her. "Do you have family?"

He shook his head. "My parents passed on a long time ago. As an only child, I guess I'm always a bit fascinated by close-knit families, even envious at times. I think I'd like one of my own someday, though."

"But not now?"

He grinned. "I'll need a wife first. At least that's how it's properly done."

Her cheeks flushed warm, and she dropped her gaze. Although he had escorted her home from the meeting in church, she had not spoken with him privately. With others still present, their conversation had to be on a personal, rather than professional level, but she was embarrassed nonetheless. "I thought you might already be married."

He chuckled. "The Colton men tend to marry late. My father was forty-one, and his father was thirty-nine. My great-grandfather was over fifty. I'm only thirty-five so I have lots of years left to keep up tradition."

Before she could respond, Sam and Polly came into the parlor together, one carrying a platter of food and the other a cup of something that smelled like coffee laced with brandy of some kind. She wrinkled her nose and frowned at her brother, who was balancing the cup and saucer. "Did Aunt Nester think I wouldn't notice? I can't drink that now. I'll sleep for a month."

"Or at least a few hours, which is precisely her point."

She waved him away. "Just plain coffee."

He shrugged his shoulders and returned to the kitchen while Polly handed over a platter with enough food to feed a family of six. "I brought you a little of everything," she murmured as she handed Jane the plate.

Along with a waft of tempting aromas that stimulated her appetite, Jane detected the subtle fragrance Hiram had brought home for Polly from one of his trips. Jane's bottle of perfume lay untouched in her dresser. "Thank you," she managed, but Polly had already turned her attention to Daniel. With a sudden loss of appetite, Jane only nibbled on a wedge of warm cornbread and observed her sister-in-law in side-glances as she sat down on the settee next to Jane, engaging Daniel in conversation.

"Tell me all about Philadelphia. It must be grand living in the city," she gushed. Opened wide, her dark blue eyes sparkled like smoldering sapphires set in softly sculpted ivory features. Her pale blond ringlets curled over each shoulder and down the front of her black silk mourning dress like sunshine draped over the twin dark moons of her breasts.

At twenty, she had a way of looking at a man that was half innocent and half temptress, an alluring combination that fascinated every man she met. Obviously, Hiram had found Polly irresistible, and Jane had to admit Polly was more than beautiful. She was exquisite, although Jane also knew her sister-in-law had a flaw no one else had detected.

While Daniel entertained Polly with descriptions of some of the sights in the former national capital, Jane studied him closely as well as she continued to sample a bit from the platter. While he gave Polly his undivided attention, Jane also recognized a subtle hint of detachment in his eyes, as if he were studying and evaluating Polly without her even knowing it.

When Sam joined them with a fresh cup of coffee for Jane, an awkward silence ended the conversation as she exchanged her plate for the steaming beverage. "You barely touched this," he complained as he frowned at her.

Polly nodded. "You have to eat more. You're already wasted away. You'll need your strength back . . . for later." Shifting from sweet gaiety to sorrow in less than a heartbeat, she sniffled and dabbed at her nose with a delicately embroidered handkerchief.

"I'm sorry," she whispered in a shaking voice. "I can't seem to stop thinking about . . . about everything for longer than a few minutes. I don't know how you can be so strong, especially after the coroner's report. It's all too terribly shocking. If . . . if anything like this ever happened to Sam . . ." Tears choked the rest of her words, and she covered her face with her hands.

Jane stiffened and gripped the edge of her saucer to keep it from shaking. Polly was the last person on earth Jane expected to mention anything about Hiram's death to her directly, and she was loath to share her feelings with a woman who had been her husband's lover.

Fortunately, Sam intervened. He set Jane's plate aside and helped his wife to her feet to enfold her in his arms. "We all need to be stronger for just a little while longer," he murmured while casting Jane an apologetic glance. "Now, now. Nothing is going to take me away from you. Not for a very, very long time."

"Perhaps I should go," Daniel suggested as he stood up. "We can talk more tomorrow and get some legal questions about the estate settled."

"No, I'd really rather talk now," Jane protested. If she was going to get rid of the journalist, she had to inform Daniel she no longer needed his services. She did not want to embarrass him by telling him in front of anyone, but she could not afford to lose time and wait until tomorrow. If she spoke to him now, he could even leave for Philadelphia before the burial and arrive there before dark, taking his dangerous shadow with him.

"Sam, why don't you take Polly home for a while?" she suggested as she set her coffee aside.

With his wife gently weeping against his shoulder, he shook his head. "I have to round up the pallbearers, and I wanted to escort you to Dr. Birchfield's later. It would be easier if she could rest here. I'm sorry. We're not making this any easier for you, are we?"

Jane swallowed hard. "Why don't you take Polly to my room so she can rest while you're gone."

He cocked his head. "Are you sure? The doctor wanted you to rest, too."

"I will. I promise, but I need a little time to talk to Daniel. Aunt Nester is still here, and I'll be finished by the time she's got the kitchen tidied. She'll let me rest in her room."

"We'll keep this brief," Daniel added. From the firm look on his face, she could tell he had no intention of remaining very long, which would also serve her well. She was not capable of holding her own in a lengthy debate with him after all that had happened today.

Sam reluctantly agreed and led Polly down the hallway to Jane's bedchamber. A sudden thought sent Jane following quickly in their footsteps. She went straight to the wardrobe, found the apron she had worn yesterday, and retrieved the pouch containing the symbolic gift she had selected for Daniel.

After all he had done, she could not dismiss him without offering him some payment of her own for the hours he had unexpectedly spent on her behalf. Regardless of her original intentions for choosing this particular gift, it was the only thing of value she could think to offer him. She left the room as Sam guided his wife to the bed, closed the door behind her, and returned to the parlor to find Aunt Nester clearing away Jane's barely touched plate and beverage.

"I told Polly you wouldn't eat much," her aunt grumbled. "Look at this waste. You'd think the girl would have half a brain. Sometimes I worry for Sam."

"He adores her," Jane admonished, hoping to end her aunt's commentary. Daniel seemed more than mildly interested in what she had to say, judging by the look on his face.

"He'd better. He'll be working day and night and every hour in between to keep her. She's a sweet thing, and Lord knows she loves our Sam, but she's not one to buckle down when times are troubled."

"She's young."

Aunt Nester snorted. "At her age, you'd been raisin' Sam for over a year and workin' in the store to support the two of you. Polly needs a good stiff backbone like yours."

In spite of her best efforts, Jane's backbone did stiffen. "She's Sam's wife and she's family now," she reminded, scarcely believing she was defending Polly, of all people.

" 'Course she is. That's why I'm nice to her," Aunt Nester quipped.

By this time, Daniel had a definite twinkle in his eye, and Jane sighed. "Are you still convinced you want a close-knit family?"

"Only if I can borrow your Aunt Nester from time to time."

Her aunt sniffed at him. "You chargin' for your time today? If so, get on with it, or I'll have to write Lily and tell her you're overchargin' her."

He laughed. "Lily and I worked all that out before I came here."

"Good thing. Now I've got a few dishes to do up, and when I get done, I expect you to be gone so I can convince Jane to get some rest."

Jane gasped. "Aunt Nester!"

"Don't you argue with me, young lady. Sit down and say what you have to say in ten minutes, which is when I'll be back." Her aunt left in a huff that prevented either Jane or Daniel from arguing even if they chose to.

"Ten minutes is more than enough for today," he said quietly as he took his seat again.

"More than enough," she agreed. She sat down, too, but plunged ahead to wrest control of their conversation. "Thank you for everything you've done. I just wanted you to have this as a token of my appreciation for all your help." She handed him the black velvet pouch. "Maybe you'll find this useful the next time you have to travel to see a client."

His dark hazel eyes narrowed. "Lily has taken care of my fee. You didn't have to—"

"It's a gift. Open it," she urged, surprised by how much she wanted the gift to please him.

He untied the black ribbon holding the pouch closed and her gift slid upside down into the palm of his hand. When he turned the silver case over, he smiled. "A compass."

"So you won't ever lose your way," she explained, grateful he had no idea what she had originally intended the compass to represent. She had meant it to remind him that he needed to set a legal course for his clients that stayed strictly within the boundaries set by laws he seemed only too willing to circumvent or ignore. "It isn't much . . ."

"It's magnificent," he murmured. As he studied the heavily decorated case, his eyes glistened with emotion. "Thank you."

"You're welcome." She drew a deep breath and gathered all the courage she possessed. "I do value the help you've given me and hope you won't be offended, but since Sam's here to help me with . . . with everything else, I won't be needing a lawyer any longer."

Disbelief etched every feature on his face. "You're dismissing me? Now?"

She tilted up her chin. "Yes, I am."

"You're making a mistake. You need a lawyer now more than you did before."

She kept her gaze steady. "I was hoping you could leave this afternoon."

"Well, I'm not leaving. Not this afternoon or any-time soon. Unless you've been dissatisfied with my serv-ices and want me to refer you to another lawyer. That I can do."

"Not at all. I-I just don't need a lawyer anymore."

He leaned toward her. "Yes, you do. You're too bright to make me believe you're actually serious about dismissing me because you don't need a lawyer. Tell me the real reason you want me to leave."

Never one to back down easily from the truth, she handed it to him succinctly. "Mercury Pine. If you go back to Philadelphia now, he'll follow you. If you stay, he will, too, and if he's half the rabble-rouser you say he is, he'll do nothing but cause trouble here. The peo-ple in Sunrise are good, decent people, but he'll portray the village as Sodom and Gomorrah. I can't and I won't let that happen, all because of how Hiram died."

He frowned. "You're right about Pine, and it's en-tirely my fault he's here. I've admitted it, and I've apol-ogized. I also tried to reassure you I would see he left town. Obviously, I failed to do that quickly enough, but I can't leave now and let you face an investigation that could get very, very nasty while you attempt to have your late husband's estate settled. Not without legal guidance."

"Sam's here."

"He's not your lawyer."

"Neither are you. Not any longer."

"You're wrong again," he said firmly and stood up. "Ten minutes are just about up. We'll deal with this further tomorrow."

Exasperated, she felt her pulse skip into double time. "I thought I made myself clear. I don't need you here any longer. I dismissed you."

"You can't do that."

"Why can't I?" she argued, wishing he would just give in like Sam always did.

"Technically, you're not my client. Since Lily is paying my fee, she's my client. Until she dismisses me when she returns, which won't be for a good while yet, I'm staying put and watching out for your legal interests."

"But I paid you, too."

He grinned and held up her gift before putting it into his pocket. "The compass was a gift, not compensation for services rendered. Rather than waste time arguing or debating the difference, you'd be better advised to talk to your cousin, Louis."

"Louis?" she cried, thoroughly befuddled and caught somewhere between chagrin and relief. "What's Louis got to do with all this?"

Daniel walked over to the door, opened it, and paused before stepping out onto the staircase landing. "He's part of your family," he chided, "and 'family watches out for one another.' I hope I'm quoting you correctly. Talk to him. No . . . on second thought, sit still. I'll tell him you want to see him."

He closed the door behind him, leaving her sitting there with her mouth open and her mind crammed with questions. She leaned against the back of the settee and closed her eyes to escape into darkness where she might try to piece herself back together. She slowed her breathing and relaxed her body, searching for peace and calm.

She had once thought that death inspired only deep, dark grief and somber reflections, but after learning of Hiram's death, she had gone numb. Like a kaleidoscope, she felt hollow inside. Each of her emotions had turned into tiny, multicolored pieces of glass that constantly shifted into new positions with each new experience or encounter, twisting her emotions until one dominated the others.

Sorrow, joy, shame, pride, confusion, calm, exasperation, humor, or gratitude. She could never be sure which emotion would dominate the moment, but she recognized the uncertainty as familiar, even though her parents had died so long ago.

With a deep sigh, she let herself drift into a short nap while she waited for cousin Louis to arrive. Instead of worrying, she listened to the beating of her heart and thought about how disconcerting it would be to have Daniel stay here. She scarcely took notice as her brother slipped past her and out the door.

Chapter 8

By five o'clock, everyone was ready for the burial service. Jane looked at herself in the mirror on the wall next to the door in the parlor. She fidgeted with the veil that distorted her vision and decided to keep it off her face for now. Wondering why Louis had not come to see her as Daniel had promised, she flinched when a knock ruptured the heavy silence that had descended on the household. She took several side steps and opened the door before anyone else had a chance to offer.

Louis was only one of two men on the staircase landing, and Daniel stood several steps below. Her cousin greeted her with an apologetic smile. "Sorry we took so long. George wanted to come with me. He has something he wants to say first."

She nodded, her mind awash with questions, although she recognized George Gunther as one of the mill workers who frequented the general store. He was also one of the men who had discovered Hiram's body, and she remembered seeing him at Dr. Birchfield's yesterday. She glanced back into the parlor where Sam, Polly, and Aunt Nester all had curious looks on their faces. "It's Louis. I'll only be a moment," she explained, and quickly stepped out onto the landing and closed the door behind her.

Barely twenty, the young mill worker was as pale as a sugarloaf, but his cheeks were bright red. "I came to give you this," he murmured and awkwardly slipped several coins into her hand. "I shouldn't have talked to that newspaperman, and I'm . . . I'm real sorry for what

I done." He dropped his gaze and slumped his shoulders.

The coins were warm, as though he had been gripping them in his hand for a good while. "You were the juryman who gave Mr. Pine the information about the jury's verdict, weren't you?" she guessed.

He nodded and slowly raised a sorrowful gaze to meet hers. "I didn't think it'd do much harm. The coroner was gonna have the village meeting the next day . . . and . . . and I've been saving so long to bring my wife here from back home. I just couldn't let the chance pass. It's almost all I needed . . . I didn't know how he'd stir up trouble for you, not till I talked to Mr. Colton and Mr. Glennings here. You always treated me right at the store, Mrs. Foster. I asked them to come with me so they could see I meant what I told them about apologizing and returning the money."

Her heart swelled with compassion, and the coins grew heavy in her hand as she recalled how he had spoken so passionately to her about the wife he had left behind. He had come here and built a small homestead for them, working at the mill to earn the funds to send for her. "Matilda, isn't it?"

His eyes widened.

"Matilda. Your wife's name is Matilda, isn't it?"

"Yes, ma'am. Matilda Luanne Gunther. She's staying with her folks in New York for now." His gaze softened with love as he said her name, then clouded with shame. "She wouldn't be so proud of me right now if she knew what I done."

Jane returned the coins to him and wrapped her hand around his fist to keep it closed. "Use this to bring Matilda here to be with you. You shouldn't be apart," she whispered.

"I can't," he argued as he tried to pull away. "That's Judas money."

"No," she insisted. "You didn't tell Mr. Pine anything he wouldn't have learned the next morning."

He was too strong for her, and he managed to get

the coins back into her hands. "It wouldn't be right, and Matilda wouldn't come here if she knew how I got the money. I'll just keep working hard and earn it honorably," he protested with his shoulders squared and his expression proud.

"Then I'll give the money to the minister to use," she responded, unwilling to risk offending the young man. She could, however, offer to help him to reunite with his wife. "I don't suppose you have much free time, what with working at the mill and trying to build your cabin for you and your wife."

He smiled broadly. "The cabin's almost finished and just needs a few more touches on the inside."

She cocked her head. "Then you might have some free time on Sunday when the mill is closed. I need someone to help out a bit on Sunday morning before church to move stock and give the store a good scrubbing. I can't pay in coin, but I could pay in goods so you could save more of your wages. If you're interested," she added to avoid pricking his pride.

Eyes wide with disbelief, he gulped hard. "I'd work real hard," he promised. "Real hard."

She nodded. "Then I'll see you Sunday at six. Don't bother with breakfast. Aunt Nester will make you eat again anyway."

"Yes, ma'am. Thank you, ma'am," he gushed as he backed away and fumbled his way past Daniel to escape down the steps.

She closed her eyes briefly as she slipped the coins into her cloak pocket and prayed the love shining in George's eyes for his wife would never fade. When she opened her eyes, Louis was shaking his head and smiling. "Uncle Paul would be real proud of you. I know I am."

She smiled. Her cousin had always loved her father and had watched over her and Sam, helping them out after they were alone and times were lean. "You're family," she teased. "You're prejudiced."

"Protective, too," he admonished. "Daniel here told

me about Pine, although I had my own qualms about the weasel after he tried to get into Daniel's room under false pretenses." He put his arm around her and hugged her close to his stocky frame to whisper into her ear. "Pine's gone, and I doubt he'll be coming back anytime soon."

She chuckled in spite of herself when he finally released her. "Tell me you didn't tar and feather him and ride him out of town on a rail."

"Worse," he said with a serious look on his face. "I told Libby and Penelope what he was up to."

She covered her mouth with her hand. "You didn't!"

"Sure enough I did. A small town is an amazing thing to most city folks. Some just don't get smart and make sure they don't overstep their welcome. Don't get lodging or food at the tavern or a place to stable a horse. Don't even get directions from a farmer way outside the village if they're escorted out of town blindfolded and left a few miles from the road to find their way back to the city."

"No," she gasped. "How could you do that? Everyone wouldn't know to help."

He grinned and scratched his balding hairline. "We might not have a newspaper or a telegraph like they do in the city, but we've got Libby and Penelope and a whole bunch of womenfolk who can spread the word even faster."

His smile faded, and the twinkle in his eyes turned to a serious gleam. "Folks here are upset, but they're not going to let an outsider come in and stir up more scandal than we already have to contend with so he can make a profit and make us a laughingstock of village fools. I'm not saying there won't be gossip or rumors that divide folks' opinions about what happened to Hiram, but we'll deal with that here in Sunrise by ourselves. Now go on. Get yourself ready to do what you have to do. Daniel and I will wait at Dr. Birchfield's till it's time."

She gulped back tears and hugged him. "Thank you, Louis."

He squeezed her hand. "Just taking care of family," he managed before his voice broke.

She held on to him and wished she could talk to Daniel privately. She braced herself as she stood back from her cousin and hoped Daniel would accept her apology and agree to remain as her lawyer. She looked at him directly. "I'm sorry. I should have trusted you to keep your word. I-I suppose I just panicked."

"The important thing," he said softly, "is that Pine is gone now, and you won't have to worry about having your privacy exploited any longer."

She sniffed back a tear. "Does that mean you still want to be my lawyer and help me with Hiram's estate?"

He looked at her askance. "You mean since you tried to dismiss me? Happens all the time. I'm used to it."

She could not let herself off the hook that easily. "Well, I'm not. It won't happen again."

This time he grinned. "Yes, it will. The next time I'll just ignore you like I did earlier today."

"There won't be a next time," she promised, although she was certain they would clash wills if there were unexpected stumbling blocks that complicated settling Hiram's estate. When she heard footsteps approaching, she gave Louis a peck on his cheek. "I have to hurry. I'll see you in a little while."

She slipped back into the parlor just as Aunt Nester reached the door. "It's time to go. I'll explain later," she offered and turned to the mirror to adjust her veil into place. With one final glance at herself, she swallowed the fear suddenly gripping her throat and led her family out the door to complete the last of her duties as Hiram's widow.

With her closest relatives solemnly gathered in the waiting room, Jane stood with Sam at the entrance to the examining room at Dr. Birchfield's. He gripped her elbow and opened the door for her. Her heart pounding in her ears, she entered the room, turned, and looked up at him. "I'd like some time alone first. Please. Go back with Polly. I'll be fine."

He cradled her cheek with his hand. "Are you sure?"

She nodded and gulped back tears that threatened to overflow.

"I'll be right across the hall . . . if you need me."

She closed the door and dropped her gaze before facing the dimly lit room that held as many memories as medical instruments or medicinal smells. The day Sam fell and broke his arm. The day she fell and needed stitches in her knee. A sadder day when her baby sister came here highly fevered and never returned home.

This day, this very moment, would be ever so much harder, and she lifted her veil and turned to see the open coffin resting atop the examination table. Her gaze never wavered as step after tentative step took her to her husband's side. The moment she saw his face, she gasped, surprised to see how natural he appeared. The dim light, she realized, cast shadows that softened the bruises on his face and concealed the yellowish tint the coroner had described.

Hiram was still nearly as handsome as he had been in life. Choking back tears, her throat tightened as she laid trembling fingers atop his cold hands, which were folded together and lay at his waist. She looked at him, taking huge gulps of air, unable to do more than let the memories come and fade away with each deep breath she took until she had completely and silently emptied her heart.

She stroked his hand, wondering if she would ever know how he had spent his last hours or who had murdered him. But right now, in their final moments together, none of that mattered. This was the man who had swept her off her feet and had first introduced her to the joys and the sorrows of womanhood. He was also the man who had exploited her and rejected her emotionally long before he had betrayed her physically, a man who had broken her heart and shattered her dreams.

Now that he had gone on to whatever his reward might be, she remained, once more, alone. No longer a spinster or an abandoned wife, she had become a widow.

"I've come to say one last good-bye," she managed in a strained whisper. "I know you always hated good-byes. I . . . I just wish we could have been happy together."

She removed her glove and slipped off her wedding ring to place it beneath his hands before she whispered aloud the inscription he had had engraved on her ring five years ago. "From Sunrise to forever. HF–JG." She bowed her head and let the tears of regret flow freely. "Forever ended before it ever had a chance to begin," she murmured, as her emotions went numb and her body became heavy and lethargic.

She dried her tears with her hands, put her glove on again, and dropped her veil back into place before she walked across the room to open the door so her family could view Hiram for one last time.

The next half hour became nothing more than a blur. Hushed weeping, murmured condolences, and in some cases, stoic faces. A flurry of activity as the pallbearers assembled. The short walk to the cemetery. The minister's kind words of comfort.

Seemingly within moments, she was standing at the head of the granite crypt with the minister as the pallbearers slid the heavy cover back into place. Glancing up, she saw the crest of the sun hanging above the mountaintop across the river, drawing closed the curtain of light, formally ending her days as a married woman and Hiram's days on earth.

The investigation into his death, however, had just begun, and as surely as the sun would return tomorrow, so, too, would the questions and the suppositions. With each passing day, she would have to remain on her guard to keep anyone and everyone from discovering the secret about her husband and Polly, which Jane was burying today with him.

She listened closely as the minister ended the service for Hiram with words of caution from the gospel that her own thoughts might have inspired. " 'Do not judge, and you shall not be judged; do not condemn, and you shall not be condemned. Forgive, and you shall be forgiven.' "

Could she follow the minister's advice? She was not sure, but as her life as a widow unfolded, she was certain she would face many in the village who would judge and condemn Hiram once the details surrounding his death were discovered.

She only prayed they would not judge and condemn her as well.

Chapter 9

There was trouble in the Promised Land and exiling Mercury Pine created only an illusion of village solidarity. Now that their common enemy had been banished, Daniel hoped they would not choose Jane as another.

At least that's what he observed the day after Hiram Foster's private burial. Last night the tavern had buzzed with debate about the shocking announcement made by the sheriff and coroner. While many villagers saw Jane as a woman shamefully wronged by her husband, he was not sure if they truly felt that way, or if they had been intimidated by her cousin, Louis, from speaking against her.

As he made his way to the general store to see her about getting her husband's estate settled and discuss her position as a likely suspect in her husband's murder, he passed a number of villagers gathered in small groups, talking. Some merely acknowledged him with a nod while continuing to talk; others stopped talking until he passed, which suggested he had been right to question the support for Jane he had heard last night.

Overnight, the weather had shifted back to bright sunshine and warmer temperatures just above freezing, which made his short walk more pleasant, but he almost credited the scandal and heated debate, rather than a return to seasonal weather, for chasing away the bitter cold.

As he approached the general store, he was surprised to find it open for business. Aunt Nester greeted him from her usual seat as soon as he entered the store and started talking before the overhead bell stopped tinkling. "Don't ask me why we're open," she cautioned as she fumbled to open her tobacco pouch. "Wasn't my idea. She's in the back storeroom. Has been since six. Spent half the night writin' letters and the other half sortin' through papers and makin' lists for herself so she could get Sam on the road with a shipment by eight."

She finally got the pouch open and put a pinch inside one of her cheeks. "Maybe you can use those expensive lawyer skills of yours to convince her to take a few days to mourn that scoundrel husband of hers, even though he left a mess behind. Expect you'll be stayin' for a spell now."

He let her barb pass and saw through her bluster to the worry that deepened the creases in her forehead and troubled her gaze. "Lily wanted me to stay until I was certain Jane's difficulties were resolved. That may be longer than any of us anticipated, but I'm in no hurry to leave."

She eyed him suspiciously. "No big trials waitin' is what you mean. Jane told me about that newspaperman, Pine, and your last client's trial. You should have been more careful not to carry your troubles right to Jane's doorstep. She's got plenty of her own. Wasn't enough he left her alone to carry his burdens here while he traipsed about. Now he's gone and left her the shame he should have suffered," she grumbled.

"You're right," he admitted. "Hopefully we can both be here to help her until the sheriff can find out who killed her husband. In the meantime, I'll do what I can to help get her husband's estate settled."

She snorted. "You're lookin' at it. A half-empty store, probably a pile of debts, and a name scorched with scandal that folks here will talk about long after she's gone."

He had guessed as much and did not argue with Nester. He also knew Jane well enough by now to expect she would work day and night to pay off her husband's remaining debts and have the store fully operating before too long. "Do you want to tell her I'm here?"

"No sense wastin' my steps. She'll want to see you anyway. Go on back. She's avoidin' grief and workin' out her heartache on an empty stomach. Get her to go upstairs before she faints. And don't be surprised when you see Polly. She's probably mopin' about instead of cleanin'. Sam left her here to help Jane, but that girl's about as useful as a plug of chewin' tobacco without a spittoon."

When she added another bit of tobacco to her mouth, he decided not to comment. He had already formed his own opinion of Polly, which Nester only reaffirmed. As stunning and eye-catching as she might be, Jane's sister-in-law was neither as simple nor as guileless as she appeared to be. A true "jewel shining brightly," she was exactly the kind of woman his father had warned him to avoid, but she had her husband so infatuated, he was oblivious to her superficial vanity and selfish nature.

When he got to the storeroom, he found the door open. He stood in the doorway and saw Jane on tiptoe atop a stool at the far end, which had emptied considerably since he had last seen it. With her arms stretched over her head, she had her hands braced against a large box, which was balanced precariously on the edge of a shelf. He had an indecent view of her slim ankles, and the outline of her breasts underneath her tightly pulled apron he found hard to ignore.

She turned her head and smiled weakly. "I thought I heard footsteps."

He was surprised she had not heard his heart pounding as well. Rushing forward, he got behind her to reach up and hold the box steady. Before she removed her hands, he noticed she was no longer wearing her wedding ring. "Are you trying to take this down from the shelf or replace it?" he asked as his chest pressed against her shoulders and his chin brushed against her hair.

"Down," she gushed as she dropped back to the soles of her feet. She stepped down from the stool and moved it away so he could get closer to the shelf and pull down the box more easily.

He would have, if the box had not weighed over thirty pounds. Or maybe he was too preoccupied trying to get his mind to control his body's reaction to being so close to her. Using both hands, he barely managed to set the box onto the floor without dropping it. "How did you expect to get this down by yourself?"

"I didn't realize it was too heavy until I had it halfway off the shelf. I was trying to push it back, but I just wasn't tall enough to get a good grip. I'm glad you came by." She dropped to her knees and tugged at the lid. "Let's see what's inside," she suggested. Her eyes lit with excitement that did not chase away the exhaustion set in every one of her features.

"Don't you know?" he asked as he sat down on the stool.

"It's not marked. Sam spied it earlier when he took down a box in front of it. There!" She gave a final pull, lifted the lid away, and set it aside. She cleared away the dried moss used as a packing material and frowned as soon as she uncovered the top row of some kind of implement made of polished green marble. Oddly shaped, it was approximately a foot long and less than two inches wide and resembled a shriveled cucumber with a carved handle at one end.

Her shoulders slumped, and the corners of her lips shaped a frown. "The dibbles."

"Dibbles?" He reached down and picked one up by the narrower end and discovered markings along the length of the tool. "What's a dibble?"

"Just another costly mistake," she murmured. Her face grew solemn, and her gaze became distant. "Hiram had a flair for those."

He cocked his head. She had not said a word against her husband before now. It was clear her defenses were down, and Daniel was loath to take advantage of her exhausted state to explore her private feelings for her late husband. "What's it used for?" he asked, trying to draw her thoughts outward.

She blinked several times. "Oh, it's a garden tool. Here. Hold it this way." She turned the dibble around and wrapped his fingers around the handle end before she thrust it once downward toward the floor. "You jab it into the earth just like that and then wriggle it around to make a hole for planting seeds or flower bulbs. The markings here tell you how deep the hole is."

"Sounds handy enough," he commented, wondering how long it would take before she realized she was still holding his hand.

Only a heartbeat.

She dropped her hand away, took the dibble, and packed it away again. "Most folks here use a notched stick," she offered. "They couldn't afford a marble dibble even if they wanted to have one. Which they don't. Hiram never grasped the difference between luxury and necessity people in a small farming village live with every day."

"You couldn't ship them back?" he asked, hoping to offer some suggestion to soften the disappointment in her eyes and the defeat in her voice.

She shook her head. "No. At least that was the bargain he had made. He . . . he did that often to buy the goods cheaper to make a greater profit. These have been on the shelf so long I completely forgot about them." She lowered her gaze and blushed. "Just like the compass and a few other items. I-I hope you're not offended, but I'd rather you knew . . . in case someone here saw you with it. They'd remember the compass. I had four that sat in the glass display case for over a year. I finally just packed them away while Hiram was on another trip."

His heart swelled, and he had the sudden urge to pull her into his arms and hold her until there was no hint of sorrow left in her heart or her face. "I consider the compass a very special gift because it came from you. As for these . . ." He chuckled, trying to lighten the mood. "You could always give them away to your customers, unless you'd rather just have me put them back on the shelf."

"Give them away?" She met his gaze, and her eyes shimmered with the possibility. "I could, couldn't I?"

He shrugged his shoulders. "It's just a thought."

"And the other things, too, except for the compasses, of course. I could set up a display in the glass counter case. It's standing empty. And . . . and I'd make room for more storage at the same time. People could pick whatever they liked each time they made a purchase. That's a wonderful idea. Thank you!"

He wished he had a pocketful of ideas just to keep her smiling and shoved aside his worry she did not have the right to give anything away until Hiram's estate was settled. "You're welcome. Now where are these other items? I can stack the boxes in the store for you so you can fill the case whenever you decide you're ready."

"You don't have to do that. I can wait for Sam, or maybe George can help me on Sunday."

He rolled up his shirtsleeves. "Show me what you want moved. Then we'll take a break so you can get something to eat and make your aunt happy. We have to talk about filing probate for Hiram's estate, anyway, so I'll talk while you eat. Fair?"

She smiled again. "Fair."

For the next half hour, he carried boxes from the storeroom into the general store and lined them up in a row behind the glass case so she could unpack them later by herself. He had never seen such an odd assortment of goods: marble garden dibbles, pewter inkstands, ivory-handled scissors, and silver candle snuffers.

What had Hiram been thinking when he ordered these? Daniel mentally calculated their collective worth at over two hundred dollars—a sum he found to be as outrageous as the fool who had bought them.

Daniel stood next to Jane while Nester watched from the store side of the case with a disapproving look on her face. He scanned the boxes again and shook his head. "On second thought, maybe this isn't such a good idea. There are merchants in the bigger cities who might be interested in buying this whole lot. They wouldn't pay full value, of course, but you could recoup some of your loss."

Jane thought for a moment and sent her aunt a warning glance that kept her silent. "No second thoughts or wishful thinking. The past is spent, and all I want to do now is think about my future. I'd rather get rid of them now and give them to people who might enjoy them than store them and try to bargain with merchants who may or may not end up taking them."

"You have to think wisely about your future," her aunt warned. "If this lawyer fella thinks you can sell them—"

"At a fraction of the cost Hiram paid?" she argued. "I'd rather give them away."

Surprisingly, he felt a tug from his conscience. "Let's give that thought serious consideration upstairs. We need to talk about the legal steps you have to take first."

Jane brushed her hands on her apron. "All right. Aunt Nester, I think I'll ask Polly to come down here with you so I can talk with Daniel privately. Maybe she can wash the glass and wipe down the shelves in the case."

Grinning, her aunt moaned out loud. "This oughta be a sweet sight to behold. I'll make sure she doesn't hurt herself."

Daniel chuckled. "She's not going to move the case, just wash it."

"In that frilly little lace confection she's wearing? Give her an apron, Jane, and make sure you tell her I said she had to wear it."

Jane scowled affectionately. "She likes her pretty dresses, and she won't complain about wearing the apron to protect her gown."

"Oh, so you've got an apron all trimmed up in lace for her to wear?"

"No, but—"

"Expectin' her to wear a piece of canvas is like askin' a queen to the ball in her petticoats. Just tell the girl I'm waitin' here in case she has a problem. Go on, now," she urged as she tapped her foot.

Apparently, Jane chose not to continue the argument, and he followed her upstairs. With one step into the parlor and one glance at Polly, he added a new layer to his respect for Nester and peeled one away from the younger woman.

Polly was seated on a chair in front of the settee with her midnight blue gown carefully arranged to display the intricately woven flounces of lace that formed the skirt. Dressed more suitably for an afternoon tea or an evening soiree than for a day spent helping Jane at the general store or in her living quarters, Polly was the picture of genteel elegance and feminine perfection.

His attention, however, centered on the settee, which she had apparently draped with an assortment of fancy ladies' handkerchiefs.

"Oh, hello, Mr. Colton. Jane!" she gushed. "I had no idea you had such lovely things. You're always so prim and practical-minded. I hope you don't mind. I just couldn't resist taking one last peek at them."

Jane paled, and he saw her backbone stiffen. "You were in my bureau?" Her words were softly spoken, as if she could scarcely find the breath to utter them.

"Aunt Nester asked me to help you clean so I started in your room. See?" She pointed to a pile of bedclothes that littered the floor in front of an open door at the end of the hallway. "I put on fresh sheets and pillow slips after I dusted. Then I thought . . . well, with all that's happened I wouldn't be surprised if your drawers needed to be tidied, too. That's when I found the handkerchiefs. They hadn't been ironed, so I did that for you in the kitchen and then laid them here as I finished. Did Hiram bring them back for you from his trips?"

She gazed at Jane so innocently, Daniel wondered if the word privacy held any meaning for her at all. He glanced at Jane and saw her chin tilt up just far enough to give him fair warning she was not going to be swayed by Polly's lame excuse for violating Jane's privacy or to be distracted by her question.

Her lips formed a smile cooled by her steady gaze. "I appreciate your help, but I would prefer to straighten my own drawers in the future." She let out a deep sigh when Polly's smile crumbled and her bottom lip began to quiver. "Cousin Gabby made most of those for me," she added in an obvious attempt to soothe Polly's feelings. "The rest belonged to my mother. I don't use them every day. I save them for special occasions."

Polly dropped her gaze. "They were just so pretty. I didn't mean any harm."

"I know you didn't," Jane murmured. "Mr. Colton and I need to talk privately. Would you mind going downstairs? I have some things to display in the glass case, but it needs to be washed."

Her sister-in-law nodded, but the pout on her face belied her willingness to tend to the task. When she rose and leaned forward to pick up the handkerchiefs, Jane stopped her. "I'll put those away. Why don't you get a pail of vinegar water ready while I get you an apron to wear?"

"There's one hanging in your wardrobe," Polly remarked as she walked toward the kitchen, "unless you have something else a little—"

"I'm afraid that one will have to do," Jane quipped.

Daniel watched silently from his place near the door and waited there while the two women left the room and returned moments later. He took the pail of water from Polly and carried it downstairs while she stayed behind to don her apron. As he returned, they met one another on the staircase, and he had to turn sideways to let her pass.

Clearly unhappy with her apron, she had already untied the string holding the bib portion in place. "I'm glad I won't ever have to be a shopkeeper," she whispered with a quick glance back up the steps. "I don't know why she seems to enjoy it," she complained as she tugged the apron bib lower to reveal her bodice which tightly outlined her ample breasts.

He hid his amusement as well as his disapproval. "She's fortunate to have a way to earn her living now. Most widows don't."

The young woman shuddered. "If Sam's business grows as quickly as he thinks it will, I won't have to worry about that. Sam will be able to provide for me . . ." She paused to wipe away a tear. "I'm sorry. I never thought about being a widow at a young age, but seeing Jane have to struggle alone now . . ."

"Jane's a strong woman. She'll survive," he said reassuringly, even though he was certain Polly was more concerned about herself than anyone else.

She nodded and proceeded down the staircase, leaving her annoying perfumed scent behind her. When he rejoined Jane, she had cleared away her handkerchiefs and sat waiting for him on the settee. "I'm sorry. I didn't mean to keep you busy doing chores for me all this time."

"That's why I'm here," he countered. "To work on your behalf."

"But not doing menial labor. You wanted to talk to me about filing something for the estate?"

He sat down and smiled. "I just need to have you check through your late husband's papers to find his will, if you haven't done so already. Since there are no children involved, I'm hoping he left everything to you so it's a fairly simple procedure to have everything put into your name."

When she furrowed her brow, his heart skipped a beat. Any businessman with half a brain who traveled as extensively as her late husband had would have prepared a will to protect his wife and any issue they might have had. From what Daniel had learned about Hiram Foster so far, he had been an indulgent man who lived entirely for his own pleasures. It would not surprise Daniel if the man had been as irresponsible with his wife's future as he had been callous to her needs throughout the latter years of their marriage.

The fact that Foster's General Store had passed through succeeding generations for over a hundred years to remain in the same family, according to Lily, did little to stem the growing alarm that raced through his veins with every beat of his heart. He sat forward in his chair and kept his voice as steady as he could. "He did have a will, didn't he?"

He held his breath waiting for her to give him an answer. Exhaling slowly the moment he saw the flicker of fear in her eyes, he watched determination harden their color to dark brown marble.

"I couldn't find his will, but that doesn't mean I can't operate the store. Everyone knows we worked together, and I kept the store running when he was away, which was more often than not. I kept the books for his father several years before Hiram ever came home, and there's no reason . . ." She paused, apparently realizing she had been rambling, and dropped her gaze. "That doesn't matter, does it?"

"It might," he offered, stretching the truth only far enough to give her a little bit of hope.

She sighed and looked at him with defeat glistening in her eyes. "But probably not."

"No. Not if he died intestate, but we don't know that for sure. He could have drawn up a will and left it with his attorney in Lancaster. I think Lily mentioned you had been to see him several months ago."

"He wasn't very helpful."

"He doesn't have a choice this time," he responded. "There's no reason to be concerned until we've spoken to him. Odds are in your favor that if your husband didn't think about drafting a will, his attorney probably did." As he expected, she was not content to let the matter drop without exploring each and every possibility.

"And what if he didn't?"

He kept his voice steady to keep her from over-reacting. "Under the law, you could claim one third of the estate as your dower rights. The rest would go to his next of kin. Someone mentioned he had a brother."

Her face paled. She nodded stiffly, but did not dissolve into hysteria like Debra would have done. "Aaron. He's a riverboat pilot on the Mississippi. He lives in New Orleans with his family. I still have to write and tell him about Hiram, but I wanted to wait to see if the sheriff recovers the pocket watch Hiram was wearing when he left. It belonged to their father. I just hope the investigation doesn't take too long."

With the conversation veering in another direction, he wanted to seize the opportunity to discuss her status as a possible suspect in her husband's murder.

The sound of footsteps on the stairs, however, left him little time and only reminded him how hard it was to talk for longer than a few minutes at a time without being interrupted. The four-hour ride each way to Lancaster would guarantee both the time and the privacy they needed to discuss some very delicate issues, and he steered the conversation back to the matter of the will. "We'll both have to go to Lancaster to file for probate anyway, so we'll make an appointment with Harris first."

Wide-eyed, she pulled her head back and squared her shoulders. "I can't leave Sunrise. Not now."

"You don't have a choice," he argued, yanking the truth so far this time he expected it to break. He could only hope it would not boomerang. "We could leave immediately and be back here before sunset tomorrow. I'm sure your aunt would be able to keep watch over the store. If not, simply close it for a few days. People will understand."

She stiffened. "I can't go. I have too much to do here. Sam's already taken one shipment and—"

"And he shouldn't have done that. You don't have the right to ship or sell or give away anything until there's been a full accounting done for the estate," he

argued, finding it oddly to his advantage to insist upon
following the letter of the law when he had so often
ignored it. "We'll need to review all the ledgers again,
not just the one you've used since your husband left in
September—"

"Mr. Harris has those. Hiram delivered them when
he left in September to have the lawyer collect on some
bad debts and other promissory notes," she stated.

"Yet another reason you need to see him. In person,"
he urged. As the door opened, he wondered how much
of the money that Foster might have collected from his
lawyer remained in the bank account.

"Person? What person?" Aunt Nester asked as she
entered the parlor.

Jane cast him a warning look before answering. "Mr.
Harris. Hiram's lawyer. He probably has a copy of the
will, that's all."

Daniel jumped in quickly to get Aunt Nester to aid
his cause. "Jane and I will have to go to Lancaster."

The older woman looked at Jane's stricken expression and frowned. "So what's makin' you look like you
swallowed worms?"

"She doesn't want to go," he offered before Jane
could respond.

"I didn't say that," she grumbled. "I said I couldn't
go. There's too much to do here."

Her aunt sniffed her disappointment. "Close up the
store. It'll be waitin' here for you when you get back.
Besides, I need a day or two to rest, even if you don't."

Jane's cheeks turned a rosy shade of dark pink, and
Daniel could have kissed Nester all to pieces for adding
guilt to the list of reasons he had already given to Jane.

"I'm sorry. I should have thought of that. I suppose . . ."

"No supposin' about it. While you go pack a few
things, I'll take care of Polly before I close up downstairs. The careless girl cut her finger on one of the
shelves. Just a nick, but she's actin' like she'll bleed to

death without a bandage. I'll leave a note for Sam so he knows she went home."

She turned to Daniel and grinned. "Looks like you're goin' to Lancaster after all. See that you treat my niece good and proper and since Lily's payin' for this trip, get a couple of rooms at the Golden Swan. Best hotel in the city, or so they tell me. You can drop me and Polly off at home on your way."

He smiled back and deliberately avoided Jane's gaze. "My pleasure."

"Why do I get the feeling you two have conspired against me?" Jane mumbled.

"Because we're both on your side," he responded, praying she would keep that in mind when she found out he could have easily resolved the question of the will and the missing ledger books while she remained in Sunrise.

Chapter 10

With four people crammed together in the buckboard, Jane had little room to breathe, let alone sit comfortably and safely. With one hand gripping the front edge of the wooden seat and the other on the side, she held on tightly for fear of pitching sideways and landing facedown on the cindered roadway below.

Not that she could create any more of a spectacle than they already had. Half of the people who lived in the village center openly gaped as the wagon pulled away from the general store.

Sitting next to her, Polly cradled her bandaged finger in her hands, and if her skirts had not taken up twice the space she actually needed for her size, Jane would not have minded being so crowded. She only hoped she could keep her balance long enough to see Aunt Nester and Polly delivered home.

As they rounded the sharp curve just beyond the livery, Polly shoved hard into Jane's shoulder and nearly pushed her off the seat entirely.

"Oh, I'm sorry," she gushed sweetly.

Jane bit back a hasty retort and regained her composure as the roadway straightened, grateful there was at least another mile before they would round another curve near the home Aunt Nester shared with her son and his family. "I'm fine," she gritted, but in fact, she was not fine at all. Not while she was sitting close enough to Polly to feel her take every breath and to hear the little whimper she made each time the wagon hit a bump in the road.

She closed her eyes, seeing and hearing images of

Polly and Hiram together that disgusted her, and she tried to stare at the roadbed as it passed beneath the wagon to chase them away.

"There it is. Just like I told you. Slow down a bit," her aunt ordered.

It was too soon to have reached the fork in the road that led to Aunt Nester's home, and as the wagon slowed, Jane looked up to see the outline of the small stone cottage built into the mountainside less than a mile away from the general store.

Surrounded by overgrowth, the cottage was nearly obscured, but she could make out the line of the roof and smiled in recognition.

"That's where I was born," Aunt Nester said proudly to Daniel. "Lily and Charlotte, too. That's Jane's mother. Shame to see it sittin' empty again. The last folks who lived there, that'd be the Mcintyres, they moved on a couple of years back. Folks claim some city people bought it for a summer estate, but nobody's shown up."

"Actually, that's about to change," Daniel replied as he drew the wagon to a halt at the entrance to a narrow dirt lane that led to the cottage.

Unable to move to face him, Jane turned her head, but she could not see much beyond the wide brim on Polly's bonnet. She did catch a glimpse of her aunt's face to observe a fleeting expression, but it did not mirror her own surprise.

"Lily bought it, didn't she?" her aunt asked softly.

"About a year ago. It was right before Philippe died, and she became too distraught to do much about it. Now that she's back to being herself again, she's asked me to have it refurbished while I'm here so she can use the house when she visits, which she tells me will be more often now that she's alone."

While pleased that Daniel confirmed her aunt's suspicion, Jane was more moved by the surprising hint of envy she had seen on her aunt's expression and detected in her voice. She wondered what it must feel like for her aunt to have been left with only a few rooms in which to remain for the rest of her life while her sister, Aunt Lily, had her own home in Philadelphia, a chateau in France, and now another home here in Sunrise, along with more funds than she could spend in two lifetimes.

After finding it hard to ask Aunt Lily for legal help, Jane could easily sympathize with Aunt Nester's feelings, particularly with her own fate so questionable. She doubted if Hiram's brother would want to return to Sunrise to run the general store. If he did, the living quarters would scarcely accommodate his family or leave more than room for a cot for Jane in the storeroom.

Since she could not afford to buy out his interests, they might be forced to sell the general store, in which case she literally would be put out into the street. The mere thought of moving back to her family's homestead with Sam and Polly made her nauseous. She took a few gulps of air to ease her distress, although there was nothing she could do to ease the ache in her soul.

She would live in an unheated cave filled with hibernating bears before sharing a home with Polly.

If worst came to worst, she would simply have to ask Aunt Lily for a room in the little cottage and assume the role of housekeeper for her aunt, a prospect that also gave her a new understanding of Aunt Nester's refusal to accept charity from anyone, even her own sister.

Anger at Hiram gnawed at her spirit for making her question if she would be dependent on charity for survival, a very distinct possibility if he had died without a will. Even if he had not, she would scarcely earn a decent livelihood with one third of the store's profits, but she quickly suppressed her anger and held it at bay, at least until she knew about the will for sure.

She was so deep in her own thoughts she nearly tumbled off her seat again when the wagon started rolling forward and wished she had paid attention to the rest of Daniel's explanation about Lily's plans for the house.

She could see the road curved just up ahead and prepared herself, but this time Polly managed to do little more than shift slightly and press against Jane. Once the wagon turned and started down a dirt road, the ride became bumpier. By the time they reached Aunt Nester's doorstep, she thought Polly might have cracked a tooth or two, based on her anguished groans.

As soon as Daniel helped her aunt descend from his side of the wagon, Polly moved over and Jane heaved a sigh of relief. She bent down to accept her aunt's kiss. "I'll be home by tomorrow night. Try to get some rest."

Her aunt chuckled. "With four young ones around? Not likely, but a bit of brandy in my coffee will help. 'Keep your chin up and your smile bright.'"

Jane grinned, easily recalling the childhood rhyme. "And everything will be all right," she murmured and watched her aunt disappear into the frame farmhouse.

To reach Sam and Polly's home, Daniel followed her sister-in-law's directions and backtracked a mile to reach the main road, turned north, and continued their journey another half a mile to where the road widened and assumed the official name of Old Mill Road. Just beyond yet another bend, the home where she and Sam had grown up and where he lived now with his wife came into view.

The two-story stone and brick house was visible from the road, but the barn and assorted outbuildings were hidden from passersby. Captured only in her own mind, sweet childhood memories were now soured by Polly's sinfulness and Jane's guilt for not trying to end the affair before Hiram had left.

She had not been back here since that fateful day when she had seen Polly and Hiram together. Viewing it now only reinflated that awful memory until she thought her mind would explode. If only she had not decided to visit Aunt Nester that afternoon. If only she had not taken the shortcut through the woods so Hiram and Polly would have heard her approaching. If only . . .

"You can pull the wagon right up the drive to the back door so I don't have to worry about soiling my skirts," Polly suggested.

Daniel complied without comment and delivered her to the back of the house. Jane kept her gaze centered on the barn and tried to picture all her parents' furniture and household items still stored in the loft. Hiram had not wanted to redecorate the living quarters after their marriage. After Sam had gotten married, he had furnished the house to suit his new bride. Now that Aunt Lily was going to refurbish the cottage, Jane was hopeful she could offer her aunt the furniture, some of which had belonged to Lily's mother, Jane's grandmother.

Fortunately, Polly did not walk around to give Jane a farewell embrace after Daniel helped her from the wagon, and he urged the horses forward as soon as Polly closed the door to the house behind her. Supremely grateful to have plenty of room to sit alongside him without having to be afraid she would fall off the seat, she kept her silence until they were well on their way on the main road again.

The closer they got to Peterson's mill, a few miles up the road, the faster her heart began to beat, yet oddly, she could feel the blood draining from her face. Feeling faint, she dropped her gaze and tried to breathe evenly. As they entered the covered bridge over Mill Creek and crossed from sunshine into shadows, she could not keep from imagining the exact place up the creek where Hiram had been found. Despite her best efforts, she began to tremble.

As soon as the wagon cleared the bridge into sunlight again, Daniel slowed the horses. "I'm sorry. I would have taken another road, but there is none. Are you all right?"

Unable to speak, she nodded.

"Just hold on. We'll put this behind us in just a few minutes."

She was certain he meant well, but she was equally

positive she would never put the terrible circumstances surrounding Hiram's death behind her if she lived to see the turn of the century.

True to his word, however, he guided the wagon quickly past Peterson's mill and up and over the endless hills in the valley, which lay waiting for spring to awaken them from a long winter's nap. Squares of small homesteads with smoking chimneys dotted the valley, and barren fields bathed in bright daylight sat ready for spring planting, creating a patchwork quilt of calming rural tranquility. The air was crisp and cool, but the sun was warm enough at midday that she needed nothing more than her cloak and the lap blanket to keep her warm.

Lulled by the rocking motion of the wagon and the rhythmic creak of wagon wheels, she was tempted to remove her bonnet and feel the sunshine on her hair, but dismissed the thought as totally improper. Not that traveling alone with a man who was not her husband was any more appropriate, but she had little choice in the matter. Aunt Nester obviously did not seem to find fault since she had suggested the trip, and Jane decided it must be her status as a widow now that made traveling alone with Daniel acceptable.

What was entirely unacceptable was the way she felt sitting so close to him. She recognized the not-so-subtle fluttering of physical attraction, but it was her fascination with him as a complete and complex man that frightened her because she had never experienced anything as powerful as this before.

In a flash of wisdom honed by experience, she realized how wrong she had been to let physical attractiveness and unrealistic schoolgirl fantasies blind her to what was important and infinitely more seductive—a man's heart and soul.

She could have saved herself five years of heartache if she had remembered that, and the longer she knew Daniel Colton, the more she suspected he had a heart and a soul that would make every day more precious than the last for the lucky woman who one day claimed his love.

She had no reason not to have these feelings for Daniel, other than common decency. She had barely begun her widowhood, but since she had not been happily married and did not grieve for the loss of a beloved spouse, she could scarcely expect anything to be common or decent, especially where Daniel was concerned.

Suddenly, the prospect of spending time alone with him in Lancaster seemed a very foolish thing to do. She could not think of a valid excuse for turning back to Sunrise until the image of Mercury Pine suddenly appeared in her mind's eye. "Maybe going to Lancaster isn't a good idea after all," she ventured.

He took his gaze off the road for a moment and smiled at her. " 'No second thoughts or wishful thinking,' remember?" he quipped, quoting her own argument earlier when he and Aunt Nester had tried to convince her to try to sell the dibbles and the rest of the expensive leftover goods.

Had the man memorized every word she said? "Aren't you worried about Mercury Pine? What if he's in Lancaster and sees us, or what if we pass him on the road along the way?"

"That's possible, but very unlikely," he advised without looking at her again. "He's more likely on his way to Philadelphia to see his publisher, where he'll admit coming here was a waste of time and start scouring the newspapers and court dockets for a new assignment."

"That doesn't sound like the man you described to me," she argued. "Just because he was run out of Sunrise doesn't mean he'll give up."

"Ordinarily, I'd agree with you, but Pine actually prefers big cities. He lost his eye to a small-town mob seeking vengeance a number of years back. He won't risk that happening again."

She shuddered. "That's . . . that's awful!"

When he looked at her, his features were hard. "How Pine earns his livelihood is much more so. The man's worse than a leech. He takes perverse pleasure in destroying people, innocent or guilty, all for profit, while spewing licentiousness in the name of the public's right to know all the facts. I don't condone what that mob did, but I understand it. I'll just take extra precautions while we're in Lancaster in case I'm wrong. I won't let him anywhere near you."

She gazed deep into his eyes and saw a deep well of protectiveness lined with determination that made her feel both safe and threatened at the same time.

"I can understand you might think we can avoid him, if he's there, but we could turn around and wait a few more days to be more certain he's gone."

He faced the roadway. "Going back to Sunrise isn't an option. And to a certain extent, how long we stay depends on how long we have to wait for an appointment with Hiram's lawyer."

He paused and took a deep breath. "Settling the issue of whether or not your husband drew up a will is important, but it's much more critical for you and me to confer together. Often, and alone. We can't do that in Sunrise without constant interruptions or worry that someone will overhear our conversations, at least not until I get Lily's house in habitable condition. Unfortunately, we can't wait that long, so we'll have to take the time we need in Lancaster to get some matters settled."

Her heart started pounding, and she gripped the edge of her seat again. "I don't understand what's so important—"

"Quite possibly your life," he said softly as he pulled on the reins and brought the wagon to a halt. When he looked at her this time, his feelings were well concealed behind a mask of professional detachment. "Sooner or later, someone is going to stand trial for murdering your husband. Whether you're prepared to face it or not, my primary responsibility now over the course of the next few weeks will be to make sure it isn't you."

Riveted by shock and stunned with outrage that sent

her heartbeat careening out of control, she felt her entire body turn cold and then numb. "You . . . you think I murdered my husband?" she stammered.

"I never said—"

"And . . . and you *lied* to me! I don't have to see Mr. Harris in person at all, do I?" she charged, annoyed with herself for being misled by her growing feelings for him. Based on their debate in the store the first time they met, she should have suspected he had an ulterior motive behind his insistence she travel to Lancaster with him.

"Do I?" she repeated, daring him to lie to her again.

He flinched. "No. You're right. I stretched the truth. I could have handled the will by myself, but we've yet to confer about the circumstances surrounding your husband's death. With the murder investigation already under way, it's imperative we do that immediately."

"Take me home." She stared straight ahead, refusing to meet his gaze or to listen to anything more he had to say.

"I can't do that. Do you have any idea how precarious your situation is right now? You're more than likely the sheriff's primary suspect."

"That's ridiculous," she snapped, breaking her own promise to herself to ignore him. "He's mistaken. If Noah was handling the investigation, he wouldn't consider the notion I killed my husband for more than the blink of an eye. He knows me. He knows—"

"He's not the one you need to worry about. Sheriff Fleming is, but you're right again on one point. He doesn't know you, which definitely works against you, at least for now."

"He's an outsider, but he seems fair and he's—"

"Doing his job, and whether or not you believe it, he'll be looking at the most obvious suspect first—the victim's wife."

Totally exasperated by his arguments as much as his constant interruptions, she could not decide whether to climb down and walk back to Sunrise or to put a gag on him to keep him quiet long enough to let her form a complete sentence. Thundering through her frustration was the real fear that Daniel was right and Sheriff Fleming would be so thorough, he would find out about Hiram and Polly. If he used that against Jane as a motive, the real murderer would go free and unpunished. More importantly, Sam's marriage would be destroyed in the process when more than likely it was someone other than Polly who had killed Hiram.

Caught between acting like a sulking, spoiled child and walking home or ripping her petticoat to fashion a makeshift gag to keep Daniel quiet, she lifted the heel of her foot and nervously jiggled her leg in rhythm with her racing heartbeat. She stared straight ahead and tried to think of a reasonable, rational, adult alternative.

"Talk to me," he urged. "I'm sorry I misled you, but if you're honest, you'll admit you'd never have agreed to come to Lancaster for any other reason than the settling the will."

Chicken feathers! Not only did the man have an uncanny ability to recall conversations verbatim, but he also had the annoying habit of cutting straight through details to the heart of the matter. She caught her bottom lip with her teeth and admitted he was right. She would not have left Sunrise had she known what he had planned to do.

When she did not respond to his plea, he sighed and clicked the reins. She had to use both her feet to keep her balance again as the wagon started moving forward. Up ahead, she saw the intersection of Old Mill Road with the turnpike that connected a number of small towns and villages along the Susquehanna with Lancaster to the northeast and Columbia in the south. Hoping her silence would convince him it was useless to try to change her mind and he would turn around at the crossroads, she was more than disappointed when he reached the turnpike and headed toward Lancaster.

She wanted to erase the sigh that escaped her lips the moment she heard it, and the prayer she had silently said to be sure he had missed her sound of disappointment went unanswered.

"We need to talk," he insisted again. "You can sit there like a statue for the next three hours or you can start talking whenever you're ready. The sooner you talk, of course, the less time we'll have to spend in Lancaster. In any case, we're not going back to Sunrise until you do."

She narrowed her gaze and pursed her lips. Since she wanted to get back to the village as soon as possible, it would be in her own best interests not to waste the time spent on the road to discuss the matter with him and wait till they reached the city. She knew defeat was inevitable, but she refused to surrender to his demands without setting a few ground rules of her own, given their obvious disagreement on justice and how strictly the law should be followed.

She sat up extra straight and took a deep breath. "Rule number one," she began, speaking firmly, "you can't ever lie to me again or deliberately mislead me. Anything you do or plan to do on my behalf must be explained to me and approved by me," she added to prevent him from doing anything she considered unethical.

"Agreed."

Since she detected sincerity, albeit a token of reluctance, in his promise, she moved on to her next concern. Unless he stopped interrupting her, they could ride to the Canadian wilderness and back again before she completed a single sentence. "Number two. You can't keep interrupting me every time I try to answer your questions or counterargue a point. You're being a bit of a bully. Just listen till I finish. Don't jump all over my words."

A deep sigh. A deeper intake of breath. "Guilty as charged. I'm sorry."

When she reached out and touched the reins, he brought the wagon to another halt and she turned to face him directly when she spoke to him. "I know Aunt

Lily is paying your fees, but I won't consider letting you represent my interests during the sheriff's investigation unless you can tell me honestly and without any doubt you believe me when I tell you I am totally innocent and played no role in my husband's murder."

If he did not believe in her innocence, she would have to weather the investigation alone and rely on simple justice to protect her. She prayed with all her heart he would believe in her, and as she looked to the days and weeks ahead, she realized how very much she needed to unburden her heart and share her concerns with him, although she would never reveal the secret of Hiram's affair with Polly.

She had no one else to count on to be objective. Aunt Nester was too quick to take Jane's side. Sam's loyalties and first concerns were for his wife, however undeserving she might be, but he was also as biased as Aunt Nester where Jane was concerned.

Her only worry was whether or not she could set aside her fascination with Daniel as a man and focus only on his role as her lawyer, a task that would require her total concentration and best efforts. She locked her gaze with his and scarcely drew a breath as she waited for him to respond and tell her whether he would be her friend and ally . . . or whether she would be alone.

Chapter 11

Daniel gazed deep into Jane's luminous sable eyes. Mesmerized, he had a rare glimpse into the virtual treasure chest of her heart—one filled with the sparkling facets of a spirit far more precious than any he had ever known.

His heart slammed into the wall of his chest, and he caught his breath, captivated by the sheer, shimmering radiance he beheld. Like precious stones cushioned in a bed of purest gold, goodness and integrity, loyalty and honesty, devotion and compassion glistened softly, but the most brilliant of all was her innocence. Her heart was pure, as translucent as her character, blemished only by the silhouette of loneliness.

Fully entranced, he almost forgot to breathe as love, the one emotion he had waited all his adult life to experience, beckoned sweetly, tempting his heart as well as his soul. Stunned, he knew he had found the one woman on earth whose idealism, faith in humankind, and trust in justice shined bright enough to penetrate beyond the penumbra to the darkest shadows of his cynicism. She illuminated the nobility of the dreams that had inspired him to study the law so many years ago.

When she lowered her gaze and shuttered his view of her heart, his pulse slowed to normal and his irrational heart argued with his rational mind.

He could so easily fall in love with Jane.

He could *not* fall in love with Jane. Not now. Maybe not ever, particularly if she was charged with murder.

He was her lawyer, and a strict code of ethics created a barrier between them even he would not dare to violate. Yet even as he denied the deepest yearnings of his heart and soul, he knew it was too late.

He loved her. Regardless of ethics or reason, he loved her, and his heart rejoiced by skipping a beat and then pounding with the surety of her innocence.

Ever so reluctantly, he placed a shield around his heart and detached his feelings, just as he had had to do for every other case, to be his most effective, but it had never been so hard or so painful.

If he was going to successfully prepare her for the sheriff's additional questions during the course of the investigation, he had to start acting like a competent lawyer instead of a man who loved her and wanted to protect her so much he could not think clearly. As a likely murder suspect, she deserved a lawyer who remained levelheaded, not a lovesick fool who let his emotions interfere with his responsibilities.

His feelings, however, had never included love, and yet only the power of love gave him the strength to deny himself the one emotion he had waited so long to claim.

"I do believe you, and I apologize for acting so badly," he murmured, his gaze never wavering as he waited for her reaction, watching her carefully for any hint he should say more to convince her he was confident of her innocence.

When she raised her gaze, her full lips eased into a gentle smile that tugged at his self-control. "Thank you," she whispered. "I couldn't bear to spend the next few weeks waiting for the sheriff to uncover the truth about what happened to Hiram if you had any doubts about my innocence."

No doubts. Only love I have no right to share with you.

"I do want to make a few suggestions about our stay in Lancaster, but there are also questions I need to ask. That doesn't mean I doubt you," he cautioned, vowing to remain strong in his commitment to help her by summoning up every legal skill he possessed. "I simply need to know as much as possible to be properly prepared to help you when we meet with the sheriff. Just be assured that anything we discuss is strictly confidential. Not even the courts can order us to reveal what we've discussed."

Her eyes clouded with confusion. "I already answered the sheriff's questions."

"There'll be more, and when there are, we'll both need to be prepared." He checked the sky, frowned, and clicked the reins. "Let's ride while we talk. I'd rather not arrive after dark since I still don't know the city that well."

"Neither do I," she admitted. "I found it rather intimidating. So many people and shops and wagons!"

He chuckled. "Philadelphia is even worse. After a time, I think you'd like it. Lily does, although she misses her family, especially now that Philippe's gone."

"Maybe it would be different if she had had children," she offered.

He detected a hint of sadness he thought might reflect her own state of mind now that she, too, was alone as a childless widow. Before his heart interfered, he steered the conversation back to the critical issues they needed to discuss. "It's important for us to find out as much as we can about your husband's stay in Lancaster, although I'm certain the sheriff has already begun investigating. We need to learn several things."

When he paused to take a breath, she surprised him by continuing his thoughts. "He must have stayed at a hotel, at least for one night. We should find out which one."

"Good. What else?" he prompted, anxious to let her control the topics in their discussion as much as possible.

"If we find the hotel, we might locate his travel bag . . . and . . . and the missing ledger books. If he was coming home, he should have had them with him . . . unless they were stolen by the person who . . . who killed him." Her voice broke, but she quickly regained her composure. "Why would anyone steal the ledger books? They're totally worthless to anyone else."

He guided the horses around a large hole in the road-bed before answering. "Not necessarily. We don't know what debts the lawyer was able to collect and which ones he could not. Maybe your husband met up with someone who had been badgered into paying a debt to him and decided to get the money back, although it's hard to imagine someone using a slow-acting poison to do the job."

When she shuddered, he instantly regretted being so blunt and realized he was trying so hard to remain de-tached, he bordered on being insensitive. "I'm sorry. I didn't mean to treat your husband's death so coldly."

She settled back against her seat. "I'm sorry, too. I won't be much help if I don't make myself clear-headed." She toyed with her hands, wrapping and un-wrapping them together for several moments before speaking again. "His pocket watch is missing, too. It's very old, but the case is heavy gold. Someone would steal that and try to sell it. I suppose the sheriff will check that."

"He will. And if he finds it, you'll be able to send it to your brother-in-law." So far, he could envision a fairly decent argument that Hiram had met up with someone in Lancaster who poisoned him and followed him as he made his way home to rob him. Granted, the argument had several gaping loopholes, some of which would prove scandalous and highly embarrassing for Jane if the "someone" turned out to be a lady of the night, but for now, Daniel was satisfied enough to pur-sue the idea further. "Was there anything else missing or is there something else I don't know . . . ?"

She sighed. "He still had his keys to the general store on his person, but nothing else was missing, at least not that I know about. He often bought new things for him-self, though . . ." She paused to take a breath. "There is one other thing I should probably tell you. I'm not sure if it will matter or not . . ."

"Tell me anyway," he urged.

"You met the minister, Reverend Reilly?"

He nodded.

"He was coming home late at night sometime in January, and he thought he saw Hiram at the back of the general store . . ."

Daniel listened carefully as she explained what had happened. The more he heard, the harder his heart pounded. By the time she had finished, concern had evolved into real alarm. If the minister had seen Hiram and told the sheriff, Reverend Reilly was now a reliable and very damaging witness who could place Hiram Foster practically at his own doorstep on a night when he could have been killed.

The only mitigating factor would be the minister's new spectacles, which could weaken his testimony if it were the only evidence against Jane; if combined with other circumstantial evidence, the minister's statement would be very damaging indeed.

"But you never saw Hiram that night. You never heard him go into the store or come upstairs." He framed his questions as statements of support rather than questions, although if he had been examining a witness testifying against his client, his words would have been laced with sarcasm.

Apparently, she did not find his statements argumentative and answered his statements with logical explanations. "He didn't come upstairs. I would have heard him, but he could have gone into the store and left again without making enough noise to wake me. But that doesn't make any sense. Why would he travel all that way to secretly take something that belonged to him anyway and then disappear? I would have noticed if something was missing, which there wasn't."

He raised a brow. "Nothing was missing? You're sure?"

"Positive."

"Then if the minister is right, Hiram must have passed by the store on his way to meet with someone else. Do you know if he kept in contact with anyone while he was gone?"

She shook her head. "The mail wagon comes to the general store once a week. Then I distribute the post. I would have recognized his handwriting if he had written to anyone. There was only that one letter in October he sent to me."

Her answer was too quick and too certain, as if she was keeping the door closed to something he should know. He set her answer aside, reluctant to push her now, not when she was otherwise willing to share what she knew with him. He would ask to see the letter later and hoped she had saved it.

Off in the distance, he sighted a toll gate and posed two more quick questions before they would have to stop their conversation. "If we assume your husband was on his way home, how did he get there? He couldn't have walked from Lancaster. Do you remember hearing anything about a stray horse or an abandoned wagon or coach being found sometime in January?"

She tilted her head to the side. "No. I don't think so, but he could have gotten a ride with someone traveling the turnpike. He often came home that way since we don't have stagecoach service in Sunrise. He didn't like riding much, and if he had rented a horse from a livery in Lancaster, he would have had to return it."

He added another reason to pose robbery as a motive. "Only one last question before we have to stop while we pay the toll," he promised. "As far as you knew, your husband was going to Baltimore and other cities, yet he had a playbill from Indiana which suggests he may have gone there as well. Do you know why, or do you have any idea where else he might have gone? If we can somehow trace his travel route, we might better understand why someone decided to follow him or join him in Lancaster."

She unfolded her hands and gripped the edge of her seat so hard he saw her knuckles whiten. When she sat forward again, her chin tilted up just a smidgen. Given fair warning he had touched on a sensitive subject, he braced for her response.

"Hiram traveled wherever the winds of self-indulgence happened to blow him long before we were married." She spoke quietly, but her tone of voice was oddly bereft of anger or resentment. "He was constantly in debt and forever seeking a quick and easy venture that inevitably failed. When his father became ill, Hiram came back to Sunrise. Everyone in the village was surprised, including me. He helped care for his father until the day he died. By the time Hiram inherited the general store, he was a changed man. At least that's what we all thought. He left for his first business trip a month after we were married. He came back with tales of the Caribbean when he was supposed to have been in New York. Several years ago he went to New Orleans to see his brother; instead, he wound up in Quebec and came home three months later than he had told me to expect him.

"Why did he go to Indiana?" she whispered. "We'll probably never know, just as we'll never be able to trace him easily to any other city or territory he might have visited since last fall. Our friends and neighbors won't give it a second thought because he's done all this before, and that's why I'm telling you now. Hiram was a wanderer at heart. It's public knowledge in Sunrise, so I don't want you to think I'm betraying him by talking about him after he's gone."

Daniel held the shield around his heart steady and resisted the ridiculous notion of bringing Hiram Foster back to life so he could strangle the life out of the shallow, selfish bastard for treating his wife so poorly.

He reined in the horses and slowed them to a walk as they approached the toll gate now only several hundred yards away. "Thank you for telling me. I was just hoping he might have mentioned Indiana in passing at some point, or maybe you might have remembered asking him something about his destinations before he left."

She bowed her head and her voice softened to just above a whisper. "I often tried to ask, but he always became angry and made it very clear I had no right to ask him anything about his trips. He hadn't even intended to say good-bye when he left, but he did. After he ordered me to make sure I opened up the store on time."

When she looked up at him, he was surprised her face was calm and her eyes were devoid of tears. Instead, he saw regret, but no lingering affection or deep sorrow. "Hiram was my husband. I won't ever speak out against him, and I'll defend him if I can. Before he left, he was as happy as he could be in Sunrise, but the last time I saw him, he had only one response when I asked him not to leave early: 'Don't question me. Ever.'"

He shoved the shield away from his heart without a second's hesitation. "Jane, I'm sorry. I'm sure he didn't want to leave you on unhappy terms. If he had known those parting words would be his last, I'm sure he would have acted differently," he offered to somehow ease her painful memory.

She turned away and let out a soft sigh that nearly broke his heart. With every ounce of self-control he possessed, he gripped the reins hard with both hands to keep from pulling her into his arms.

Chapter 12

The Golden Swan had lived up to Aunt Nester's recommendation, but Jane felt as out of place there as a hand-whittled carving plopped into an expensive dollhouse designed for crystal figurines.

Elegant and gracefully decorated, the suite Jane occupied on the third floor had thick burgundy wool carpets underfoot that complemented the drapes woven to duplicate the imported wallpaper striped with silver and gold in a large sitting room with an ivory marble fireplace. A dining area was directly opposite a bedchamber with a lady's vanity and writing desk, a matching set of wardrobes, and a four-poster bed with a canopy draped in lace.

For propriety's sake, Daniel had taken a single room on the second floor, insisting she take the suite so they would have a private place to take their meals and confer. With the sheriff unavailable, they had learned little after nearly a full day in the city, but had not encountered Mercury Pine.

Attempts to find the hotel where Hiram had stayed in January had been a cold, fruitless exercise that had taken most of the morning. All of the hotels had refused to cooperate, sympathetically but firmly invoking the right of clientele to privacy despite Daniel's best efforts to convince them otherwise.

On a brighter note, Hiram's lawyer, Efrem Harris, had agreed to see her this afternoon. She had come to Harris's inner office with only her own unpleasant memories of their first meeting for company while Daniel tried again to arrange for a meeting with Sheriff

Fleming for tomorrow morning. She tried to maintain an outward confidence so when the lawyer did arrive, he would not find the panicked, desperate woman she had been in January.

She sat facing his desk with her back straight and her feet planted flat on the floor. Elbows bent, her arms rested on the sides of the mahogany chair, and her cloak and bonnet lay folded beside her. She hoped her black mourning gown would temper Harris's previous tendency to treat her as an annoying interruption.

She was sorely tempted to leave, but as if on cue, he entered his office and quickly took a seat. "My deepest condolences, Mrs. Foster, and please forgive me for keeping you waiting. How can I help you today?" he asked in the deferential tone of voice she remembered only too well.

Following Daniel's advice, she addressed her purpose here directly. "I've come to see you about my husband's will. I believe you have it on file here."

He frowned, and her expectations plummeted. When he sorted through a sheaf of papers before pulling one aside, she was not sure if he was going to deny her right to see the will or tell her one did not exist. "I never prepared a will for your husband, although I broached the subject several times. I have here a record of every meeting with him where I asked him to draft a will. He always refused, which leaves you in quite an unfortunate position."

Unfortunate? Bleak or dismal was more appropriate. Her cheeks warmed, and she recognized the rush that flowed through her veins as anger. In death, Hiram remained as true to his nature as he had been in life. Selfish and irresponsible, he had cared only for his own needs, and she should have known not to expect him to worry about what would happen to her after he was gone.

Anger, however, was a destructive emotion, and she took several even breaths of air to cool her thoughts. Apparently mistaking her anger for distress, Harris offered her a glass of water, which she promptly declined.

"Refusing to draw up a will is not as uncommon as you might think," he commented. "The law is designed to protect—"

"My attorney has explained the law," she interrupted. "Since my husband did not draft a will, then my business here is almost concluded." She kept her gaze steady and looked him straight in the eye. "My husband gave you our ledger books for the general store in September. To properly file an accounting for his estate, I need to have them returned to me. I'll wait while you secure them."

"I'm afraid you've been badly misinformed. At no time did I ever review or take possession of any of your husband's ledger books, although I did agree to redeem a number of promissory notes, all of which I have described in my statement to Sheriff Fleming."

Shock temporarily suspended her disbelief, and her pulse began to pound with dread. "My husband told me specifically he was leaving the ledger books with you. That's why I had to create a new one to use while he was gone."

His gaze cooled, sending chills down her spine. "What your husband told you is an allegation, not fact. The sheriff has reviewed all of my notes in your husband's file and seems satisfied. Before you accuse me of lying," he whined, "I suggest you speak with him."

Gulping for air, she gripped the arms of the chair like they were lifelines. With her mind swimming with questions, she could ill afford to drown in anger, either at Hiram or his odious lawyer. If he was telling the truth, where were the ledger books? Had Hiram lied to her? Or had he simply given them to another lawyer?

Stunned by total defeat, her body went numb, and she acknowledged the lawyer's parting comments with little more than a cursory nod and a whispered, "Thank you." She donned her bonnet and cloak, let herself out of the office, and stood outside to wait for Daniel to arrive.

Carefully avoiding the crowds of people passing by, she paced back and forth on the brick sidewalk in the shadows of tall buildings that nearly blocked her view of the sun in the late-day sky. Chilled more by the dismal news she had acquired than the brisk wind whipping down the street, she hoped and prayed he had met with greater success.

When she spotted Daniel on the opposite corner, waiting for a lull in street traffic to cross over, her heart leaped and then fell into a heavy dull thud. Unless she was able to control her growing fascination with him, she faced a very frustrating and awkward evening.

Did all his female clients find him so fascinating? Had they, by chance, fallen in love with him? Probably more than she cared to admit, although she was positive most of the women were far more beautiful than she was.

Except for Debra Modean, she doubted if any of the others had faced the possibility of being charged with murder.

However questionable she found his approach to the law, she believed he would never contemplate anything more than a professional relationship between himself and his client.

She chided herself for even entertaining the idea he might find her appealing, having learned to accept her plainness and the idea that no man would ever see her as attractive, let alone beautiful. She reined in her emotions while several large Conestoga wagons passed between herself and Daniel and obscured her view of him. Her mind cried out a litany of reasons why a worldly man like Daniel would never be even mildly interested in a woman tainted by scandal, most especially a woman he considered hopelessly naive and foolishly idealistic.

Inspired by the memory of that one incredible, heart-stopping moment yesterday when he had told her he believed in her innocence, her lonely heart refused to listen to a single reason. It raced even faster, trying to sew the bits and pieces of her broken dreams back together.

She drew in deep breaths of cold air and wished for more time alone so her mind could win the battle raging with her heart. Within moments, however, Daniel rushed across the street and smiled apologetically. "I'm sorry I'm late. Let's get out of this wind," he urged as he took her arm.

His touch sent warm tingles racing up her arm that added the final stitches to the patchwork of her impossible dreams. One touch. Just one touch, and she knew the battle had been waged and won by her heart. But this time when her heart broke, it would shatter for good.

"No will. No ledger books. Did he have anything to say that was positive or helpful?"

Daniel's voice echoed her own frustrations as they sat in front of the fire in her hotel sitting room. A short distance separated their chairs, but she wished she had pushed them further apart while Daniel had stoked the fire back to life.

She was close enough to hear him draw a breath and see the flames mirrored in the black silk cravat he wore at his neck. The glow from the fire softened his strained features and flickered in the dark waves of hair that framed his face, sending dangerous messages to her heart she could not control when she was this close to him.

She gazed, instead, at the fire and waited for her pulse to stop racing before she answered him. "He said he gave a full statement to the sheriff. When we talk to him tomorrow, maybe we'll learn more."

"Fleming's out of town till Friday. They think. And they wouldn't tell me where he'd gone."

"But today's only Wednesday. We can't sit here for two days waiting to see him. I have to get back to open the store," she protested, although she was more worried about the nights she would spend here with Daniel.

"You really shouldn't go back until we've filed the paperwork involved with your husband's estate. With no will, the court has to appoint an executor to devise and administer the estate until it's settled. Do you have someone in mind to recommend in a petition to the court?"

"Can't you do it?" she asked, prepared to hold him to his promise to give her the right to review and approve any legal action he would take for her. Relieved he had not suggested they prepare a false will, a notion so blatantly illegal, she also felt guilty for even thinking he was unethical enough to suggest it. Given Aunt Lily's high regard for him, she wondered if she had not rushed to judgment when assessing his character.

"Maybe it would be better to ask Sam."

She dropped her gaze and studied the hem of her skirts. "Sam wouldn't have the time. His business is barely profitable, and he's already lost days because of what's happened."

"He's your brother."

She tilted her head to the side and looked at him quizzically. "Wouldn't the court see him as more biased than you would be?"

His eyes narrowed, and he raked his hand through his hair. "You're right, of course. I'll draw up the papers tomorrow asking for a temporary appointment as executor. While I'm doing that, you should write to Hiram's brother. Tell him what's happened, explain the lack of a will, and tell him I've offered to handle the settling of the estate. I'll also prepare a statement to that effect you can send to him. All he needs to do is sign it and return the document to me, which I'll forward to the court along with a request to remain permanently as executor."

She twisted her hands together and stared at the fire again. "I was hoping to find out about their father's pocket watch before I wrote," she murmured. In truth, she did not know if she could actually write about the gruesome circumstances surrounding Hiram's death when thinking about it still made her tremble.

"They may never find the watch," he cautioned. "The faster we contact Aaron, the sooner we'll know what he intends to do with his share of the estate. How well did you know him?"

Daniel's questions, formally spoken and stated, helped her to maintain her composure. "Aaron left Sunrise long before his father became ill. He never wanted to be a shopkeeper. He was a lot like Hiram in a way. He couldn't be happy staying in one place for long. When several families moved west, he went with them and quickly found work on one of the riverboats. Eventually, he worked his way up to pilot, and I gather he's found a way to satisfy his urge to travel."

She paused and wondered how two brothers could be so alike, yet end up so differently. Was it fate that led Hiram to an early, unhappy end, or was it simply that his brother had a stronger character and avoided the same poor choices Hiram had made?

Daniel shifted in his seat, distracting her from her thoughts. "It doesn't seem likely, then, to expect he'd want to return to Sunrise to operate the store."

"No," she whispered. Her heart filled with dread and beat weakly. "He'll probably just want the proceeds, which means he'll want to sell the store."

"Or keep it as an investment. In fact, I think that's how you should approach the whole matter." He sat forward and riveted his gaze on her face. "Offer to continue running the store for him. Naturally, you'll have to share the profits, but with the wages he'd pay you plus your dower interest, you could manage fairly well. You wouldn't have to give up your living quarters, either."

Her eyes widened. She thought over his suggestion, which seemed not only practical, but perfectly legitimate, and now understood why Aunt Lily considered Daniel her friend as well as her lawyer. A glimmer of hope chased away the doom that shadowed her hopes for the future. "Do you think he would? He knows me well enough to trust I wouldn't cheat him, I should think."

"Especially if you offer to have your books audited twice a year. Unless he's hard-pressed for funds in a lump sum, he might like the idea of having an extra income dropped into his lap on a regular basis."

"I'll start a letter right now. If I can show you a draft in the morning, you'll be able to suggest any changes I should make and we can post the letter tomorrow afternoon."

When he cocked his head and grinned, her heart skipped a beat. Twice. "What about supper?" he asked.

She rose from her seat before her heart decided to leap out of her body and join his. "I've got too many thoughts running around in my head to be hungry," she lied, fully aware that most of her thoughts at that very moment centered on the man who sat much too close to her. "I think I'd rather start working on the letter now. I'll ring for service if I want something later."

When he did not push the idea of dining together any further, she walked him to the door. "Can we leave tomorrow, or do we have to wait another day to see the sheriff?"

"We should stay until Friday. I left a message for him to expect us at ten o'clock so we can be back in Sunrise before nightfall. I know the delay is frustrating, but since he has Harris's statement, we'd better see what the lawyer had to say."

She sighed. "If the sheriff's not back as scheduled, I think we should leave and try to meet with him another time."

"That's fair. I'll see you tomorrow morning at ten. By then I'll have the proposal ready to file with the courts, and I can review your letter."

"I'll be ready," she promised and closed the door behind him as soon as she could. She went straight to the lady's desk and started composing her letter before she had time to think twice about how easily she had avoided spending the night in Daniel's company. Her heart, however, continued to beat with love for him that was growing stronger every moment, and each beat tightened the stitches that held her dreams together.

Chapter 13

Their first day in Lancaster had been a blur of disappointment. Yesterday, their second, had been filled with optimism as Daniel had filed the petition with the court and posted Jane's letter to Aaron Foster. Grateful to see Friday finally dawn, Daniel could not help but worry what would unfold during the meeting with Sheriff Fleming. He tried to brace himself for the worst scenario, one that would place Jane at the forefront of suspects.

He finished dressing and stood in front of the mirror to comb his hair and saw the reflected image of his bed. He groaned out loud. Judging by the tousled bed linens, the maid would no doubt assume he had not spent the night alone. In fact, he had not been alone. He had not gotten any rest, either, but the woman who had robbed his sleep and left his body aching and unfulfilled slept one full floor below.

Love.

He put down the comb and eased into his frock coat, fully convinced love was certainly the most troublesome emotion he had ever encountered. Sleep-deprived, his nerves were raw and on edge. Since he had yet to get a full night's rest since meeting Jane, he actually considered how long it might take before he simply died from sheer exhaustion. He had even composed a short epitaph for his tombstone in the long hours between midnight and dawn:

HERE LIES A SORRY MAN,
LOVE'S VICTIM FOR SURE.

MAY HE FIND SOME SLEEP
ON A FAR DISTANT SHORE.

Chuckling at his irreverent sense of humor, he reined in his emotions and left to meet Jane in the lobby of the hotel.

By the time they arrived at the sheriff's office and sat down together, Daniel was in full control of himself, alert, and ready to act responsibly as her lawyer.

After getting the preliminary pleasantries out of the way, Fleming took charge of the meeting. "I wish I could say we've apprehended the person responsible for your husband's death, Mrs. Foster. I can't. I can tell you we've developed several substantial leads, all of which point away from someone he knew in Sunrise."

While Daniel kept his surprise hidden, he saw relief wash over her face. Her eyes glistened as she moistened her lips, but she did not prompt Fleming to provide specific details. Daniel, however, knew his responsibilities included asking questions to make sure they were not being misled. "Can you be more specific?"

The hulking man nodded. "So far, we know Foster arrived here in Lancaster late on January tenth. He checked into the Bell and Candle and paid for a room for two nights. The next day he closed his account at Keystone Bank." He paused and checked one of the papers on his desk. "He withdrew 162 dollars from the account, met with his lawyer, Efrem Harris, and received 228 dollars the lawyer had collected from promissory notes, bringing the total amount he carried to 390 dollars."

"In bank notes?" Daniel asked, stunned by the amount as well as the man's blatant foolishness.

"As far as we know," Fleming cautioned. "From that point on, we can only make reasonable conjectures about the rest of his activities." He stopped and looked at Jane, and his dark eyes filled with compassion. "I was able to recover some of the clothing your husband left behind, which the hotel had stored away. Unfortunately, there's no sign of his pocket watch or any of the funds, and his travel bag is missing as well. It appears the coroner was correct when he placed the date of death as far back as January, since your husband never checked out of the hotel the following day. Obviously, we can't inspect the room for clues to try to discover what happened to him, but we can make a few reasonable suppositions."

Daniel watched her closely. Although she appeared calm, he saw the slight upward tilt of her chin and knew she was ready to hear more. "If you could share some of your suppositions with us we'd be grateful," Daniel suggested.

The sheriff never took his gaze from Jane. "One of the chambermaids recalled your husband quite clearly and mentioned seeing him return to his room the night he arrived and the next night just before supper with a red-haired woman she recognized as one of the street's fallen angels."

He stopped to clear his throat. "Among your husband's belongings, we found a lady's hairbrush containing several strands of red hair. At this point, we can only assume the lady in question discovered the funds he had on hand and returned the second time to poison him. Either she knew very little about how long the poison would take to act or did not want him to be found in the hotel. We can't be sure. In any case, she and possibly an accomplice either followed him or accompanied him when he left. I think you can envision the rest."

Daniel did, and apparently Jane did, too. She bowed her head as if to hide the shame of learning her husband had been unfaithful to her. Her chest heaved as she took in deep breaths of air. No sound came from her lips, and yet he had the feeling the sheriff's revelations did not come as a total surprise to her.

Still, he was impressed by her valiant effort to retain a small shred of dignity, while contempt for Foster embittered his relief that Jane was no longer a suspect. "Have you located this woman?"

"Not yet. We're still looking, although these kind of women come and go as frequently as the tides change. If she did perpetrate the crime, she certainly stole enough money to disappear a long way from here. One of my associates is checking along the turnpikes at the inns and taverns along the route to Philadelphia and neighboring counties. With her red hair, she might be more memorable, at least that's our hope."

As a lawyer and officer of the court, Daniel wanted nothing less than to see her caught, tried, and convicted. He was so outraged, he might even consider sending a personal invitation to Mercury Pine to attend the trial so the whole world would see Foster for what he was: a lying, philandering, callous bastard.

As a man who loved Jane too much to ever see her hurt again, Daniel wanted the red-haired mystery woman to disappear forever so Jane could put the shame and scandal behind her and build a new life for herself. Even then, she faced an uncertain future, unless Aaron agreed to let her run the store.

It took all the self-control Daniel possessed to focus on the investigation rather than Jane right now, but he had to be sure she had been ruled out as a suspect. "Will you be coming back to Sunrise?"

"Not that I can foresee, but I'll keep you informed," the sheriff responded.

"Thank you." Hearing Jane respond in a steady voice surprised him, and he was equally amazed at how quickly she had recovered.

"I do have a few questions," she murmured, giving Daniel a side-glance, which he acknowledged with a nod. "Did you find the missing ledger books? His lawyer claims he doesn't have them. Do you know where they are?"

With a shrug of his shoulders, Fleming gave away his answer. "Either he didn't bring them to the hotel, or he had them with him in his travel bag when he left. My guess is he started feeling ill, packed a bit haphazardly, and decided to go home. When he finally died, no longer able to resist a robbery attempt, she and her accomplice quickly covered the body with rocks and stones and left the scene with the travel bag. Once they were far enough away, they no doubt destroyed all the evidence and kept the money."

Daniel pressed his feet hard against the floor and clenched his hands into fists to keep from getting up and consoling her in an embrace that would scandalize them both.

"Go home," the sheriff urged sympathetically. "There's nothing more you can do here. Try to put what happened out of your mind and remember your husband, whatever his faults, was coming home to you."

He sighed when she did not respond to him. "I know none of this is any comfort to you right now, but it won't make your grief any easier if you dwell on how your husband died. Perhaps you should take a brief time away."

Just as Daniel expected, she shook her head. "No, I . . . I need to get home and reopen the store." When she stood up, she clutched the sheriff's hands. "Thank you for being so kind," she whispered, turned, and left the room with a solemn dignity that left the sheriff speechless.

Awe riveted Daniel to his seat before he had the wherewithal to follow her. Reeling with how quickly she had been exonerated from any role in her husband's death, and how right she had been to trust that justice would not overlook her innocence, his heart began to race. Settling her husband's estate would take little time and effort. With the ethical barrier between them crumbling, he would have the right to pursue her, although he wondered how receptive she would be to his suit.

She had made it clear at their very first meeting that she found his pragmatic approach to the law questionable. Following the shocking discovery of her husband's body, she had turned to him for legal guidance and support, yet en route to Lancaster she had made him promise to give her final approval on any legal action he would take for her benefit.

If he had any hope of one day claiming her heart, he would first have to win her trust and respect. And if he stumbled on his way out of the shadows of his cynicism to reclaim his faith in the law and the perpetual triumph of justice, he was blessed to have Jane, a most incredible woman, for inspiration.

Granted, she needed time to mourn her husband's passing, but Daniel would use that time to prove to her, as well as himself, that he was worthy of her love.

Still dazed by the sheriff's findings, Jane did not have either the energy or sympathy to care as the wagon once again approached Peterson's mill. She kept her gaze focused on the covered bridge just ahead and almost wished she could stop the wagon in the middle of the bridge and stay hidden in the shadows until she could think of a better way to share with the villagers the news that had branded her name with more scandal.

She could not lie about what had apparently happened to Hiram, but the absolute truth was so sordid and ugly her skin felt dirty. She could not imagine saying, "My husband was poisoned by a redheaded prostitute," any more than she could add, "He still loved me and tried to come home, but the poison killed him and she robbed him before he could reach me."

She shuddered and tried to compose a less scandalous explanation. "Hiram was murdered and robbed by persons unknown, but the sheriff is still following several clues." No, that sounded too much like she was still a possible suspect, which she was not. She also needed to make it clear no one in Sunrise had played a role in his death.

Apparently misreading her shudders, Daniel urged the horses to go faster as they passed the mill and through the bridge, putting her right back into the sunshine before she could fashion an acceptable explanation to offer the villagers.

When they drove past Sam and Polly's home, she said a silent prayer of thanksgiving that Polly was not involved in Hiram's death and added another fervent prayer that she would remain faithful to Sam in the future. Maybe she would, now that he owned his own business and had the potential for earning the funds to support her expensive tastes.

Jane doubted he would ever move permanently to the city, which Polly preferred, but predicting Sam's behavior where Polly was concerned was something Jane had long since given up. At least she had been able to protect him by keeping his wife's affair with Hiram a secret.

It would serve no purpose to confront her or tell Sam now, especially since the sheriff was searching for someone who had never been to Sunrise and most likely, never would.

Her secret was safe and her freedom from being investigated guaranteed, but if she ever heard rumors that proved to be true about Polly betraying Sam again, Jane would resurrect that secret and use it to send Polly packing to the western frontier.

When they passed the fork in the road that led to Aunt Nester's home, Jane began to panic. She still had not thought of a way to tell anyone what had really happened to Hiram. She gathered up her courage and turned to the only other person who knew about and understood her dilemma. "I don't know what to tell everyone," she began, breaking the silence that had sat between them like a third passenger. "I can't lie, but I don't think I can tell the whole truth, either."

His expression was grim. "I'm not sure I understand why you would try to protect your husband's reputation."

"I'm not," she admitted. A flush of guilt warmed her cheeks. "There's already enough speculation about that. I'm ashamed to admit it, but I can't bear the thought everyone will know and look at me . . . and always wonder what I might have said or done to encourage him to seek another woman's bed."

His eyes widened, and when he looked at her directly, disbelief turned his hazel eyes to dark brown. "You're not at fault here. The reasons your husband strayed have nothing to do with you and everything to do with his weak character. *He* broke his vows to *you*. 'For better or for worse' is supposed to be taken literally, but apparently he had no qualms about exploiting you in the former and betraying you in the latter whenever it suited him."

Surprised by the cold tenor in his voice, she blinked hard and took several gulps of air to calm her thumping heartbeat.

"I'm sorry. I didn't mean to sound so . . . so . . ."

"Cold. And angry," she provided when he seemed unable to find the words. His lack of control was strikingly uncommon and totally out of character, although she suspected he cared deeply about each of his clients.

"I was totally out of line. I apologize. I was just trying to think of how you could explain what happened, too. You seem to be a whole lot better handling frustration than I do."

She doubted it. Not when every one of her thoughts centered right now on the man beside her and how she might explain her growing attraction for him to anyone, including herself. "I hesitate to tell the whole truth," she admitted, "especially if Aaron decides to come back to Sunrise. Scandal has a nasty habit of dying slowly, if ever."

"Indeed, but there's a big difference between being totally honest and reserving the right to keep some things private. Why don't we just say the sheriff has a suspect in Lancaster, and his investigation will be continuing there? It's the truth without any scandalous details. If anyone presses you for more, simply tell them you were too distraught after you'd learned Hiram didn't leave a will to worry about anything other than your future."

She respected the reasoning behind his suggestion and smiled. "I think I can do that," she murmured. His sensitivity touched her and gave her a new insight into the ethics she had once misjudged as questionable. How could she fault a man whose only motive seemed to be to protect his client?

He finally smiled. "That's good, since we're practically home."

When she looked up, she was amazed to see the last bend in the road before they would arrive at the center of the village. Her pulse began to race and anticipation filled her spirit. Sunrise. Home. Family. They were all waiting for her just around the bend.

The moment they neared the curve, Daniel pulled hard on the reins and stopped the wagon as a pair of riders approached. Ben Holtzman and Noah Washburn halted and greeted them with no trace of a smile on either of their faces.

Noah spoke up first after he tipped his hat. "Jane. Mr. Colton. Ben and I were just on our way to Lancaster to see the sheriff. We were hoping you'd still be there, too."

Too stunned to speak and too shaken to think clearly, Jane was grateful Daniel was in better control of his faculties. "Obviously we wouldn't be here if we hadn't concluded our business with the sheriff," he said firmly.

Noah's face flushed bright red, and Ben intervened. "While you were gone, evidence was uncovered that demands an explanation—evidence that can't be ignored. You can talk to us here or in Lancaster, but in any event, you have some explaining to do, Jane. I just hope to God you can."

Chapter 14

"Mrs. Foster isn't going to explain anything right now. If you have something to discuss with her, you'll have to wait until she's had a chance to rest."

Daniel's voice was controlled and even, but his body was rigid. His hands held a firm rein on the horses, and his gaze focused only on the two mounted men directly in front of the wagon. Just as alarmed and thoroughly confused, Jane watched Noah shift in his saddle and avert his gaze.

Ben, however, refused to back down and locked his gaze with Daniel's in a tense standoff of wills. "We need a few simple answers that should be quick enough to supply," he countered. "Otherwise, we're riding straight to Lancaster, and she'll have to answer to Sheriff Fleming."

She put her hand on Daniel's arm and felt his tension. "I can talk with Ben and Noah now."

"Not here you can't," he gritted, refusing to break his stare at the mayor to look at her.

While the two men glared at one another, Noah frowned and shook his head. "I'm sorry, Jane. We've had a time of it today. Do you think we could go back to the store? I promise we won't keep you long. Maybe once you and Ben get a chance to talk this out, he won't be so all-fired upset."

"I'm not upset!" Ben snapped. "I'm just tired of people trying to tell me what to do, when to do it, and how to do it."

When Noah sighed, his chest practically caved in. "He only asked to have Jane talk to you later. It's not their fault Libby's been twisting your ear off trying to make you listen to her."

Ben took off his hat and scratched his head. "I'm sorry, Jane. You too, Mr. Colton. Libby found the blasted note this morning before I did and she had to tell Penelope and between the two of them we haven't had a minute's peace. We'll have even less once we turn around, and everyone sees us all together."

"He's right," Noah said to Jane and Daniel. "Maybe we could ride a ways to find someplace to talk that's a little more private than the store."

When she felt Daniel's muscles flex tighter, she realized she was still holding onto his arm and dropped her hand. "We could go back to Aunt Lily's house. The old Mcintyre place," she explained, just in case Ben and Noah had not heard the news. She leaned closer to Daniel and whispered, "I'm sure this is all a mistake or a misunderstanding. Once we settle the matter, you can take me home."

His gaze wavered with indecision.

"It can't be that serious," she insisted, anxious to learn more about the note Ben mentioned before her imagination ran wild. "They haven't talked with the sheriff, but we have. Once we straighten out whatever concerns them, we can tell them what we've learned."

He exhaled slowly. "Lead the way, gentlemen."

Less than ten minutes later, the impromptu caravan congregated at the end of the dirt lane alongside the stone cottage, where the surrounding overgrowth provided natural cover so anyone passing by could not observe them. While Ben and Noah dismounted and tethered their horses to nearby trees, Daniel helped her down from the wagon.

They gathered at the back of the buckboard where Ben pulled a piece of paper from inside his pocket and handed it to Daniel. "Someone slipped that under my front door during the night."

Daniel held the note so she could read it, too. The handwriting was badly scrawled. She did not recognize it, but the message was clear enough to shake her soul as well as her body:

> The grieving widow has fooled all but one.
> Search. Search. Search for the truth.
> Time is running out.
>   A reluctant witness

She gasped and pulled the note out of Daniel's hand to read it again, but her hand trembled and shook the paper so hard she could not focus on a single word. "Who . . . who would write such a thing? A . . . a witness? This note is obscene and slanderous!" she cried and shoved it back at Ben, who quickly stored it in his pocket.

Daniel took her arm and scowled at her accusers. "This is a wicked hoax. Is this what had you all upset and ready to ride to Lancaster? An anonymous note?"

Ben glared back. "Of course not. By itself, the note is practically worthless. Or would have been if we hadn't found this." From his pocket, he retrieved a small package wrapped in brown paper and tied closed with twine. He laid it in front of the travel bags that had been lashed in the back storage area of the wagon. "This is the reason we're both concerned and anxious to hear an explanation from Jane."

When she tried to reach for the package, Daniel held her back and scowled at the constable. "Found it? Where?"

Noah's face and neck immediately flushed. "We only meant to look around like we normally would when a crime had been committed just to prove . . . We didn't think we'd find anything, but Ben thought we'd better—"

"Where?" Daniel demanded.

She held perfectly still with her gaze riveted on the package and her mind swirling with worry. What had they found that had both men, lifelong friends of hers, so worried that they were willing to ride all the way to Lancaster to show it to the sheriff?

"We searched the general store which we had every right to do," Ben answered.

"And just where did you get the key?"

Ben looked at Daniel and smirked. "The back door is always open. Isn't it, Jane?"

When she saw the look of complete amazement on Daniel's face, she swallowed hard. "This isn't the city. Sunrise is a small village. Sometimes people need to drop something off before I open the store. I thought Aunt Nester had locked it before we left, though."

He let out a long sigh. "So the door was open, and you two just went in and conducted a search on the basis of the note?"

"We were trying to prove the note wrong so we could dismiss it; instead, we found this behind a drawer in Jane's desk.

When Ben reached down to unwrap the package, Daniel held her steady. "You conducted a rather thorough search, if you found it behind a drawer."

Noah grimaced. "The drawer got stuck when I tried to open it, so I had to jimmy it a bit and found this caught underneath the bottom."

With the whole of her concentration focused on the package Ben was unwrapping, the conversation around her seemed like distant echoes. Her heart began to pound, but the moment the contents of the package lay revealed in a shaft of sunlight filtering through the tree branches, her heart literally stopped.

Although it was badly dented, she recognized the item immediately and gasped. "It's . . . it's Hiram's pocket watch!"

With her legs shaking, she managed two awkward steps to reach the watch and place it into the palm of her hand. She fumbled with the clasp and managed to open the case. Even with vision blurred by unshed tears, she could read the two initials engraved on the inside of the cover: BF. "Beckett Foster," she whispered and traced the spiderweb of cracks in the crystal covering the face of the timepiece.

No wonder Ben and Noah were so concerned. She had made an issue of the watch with the sheriff and had even asked Dr. Birchfield to remind the sheriff it was missing. To compound matters, she had also mentioned the missing watch to Daniel several times while they had been in Lancaster.

Now she held the very same watch in her hand without a single, plausible explanation of how it came to be hidden behind a drawer in her desk when she had seen Hiram refer to this very watch as he had left!

Daniel, especially, must judge her either a complete fool or worse—a liar. She closed the case and laid the watch back down, dreading the moment she would have to look into his eyes and see disappointment or contempt glistening in their depths. Her heart thudded in her chest, and she knitted her brows together trying to ease the dull ache in her head that now began to pound mercilessly.

"Are you sure Hiram was wearing the watch when he left?" His voice was so gentle and reassuring she almost forgot to draw a breath. When she looked up, she found him gazing at her with such total trust she nearly cried. "He . . . he checked the time when he was leaving. He didn't want me to be late opening the store. I-I don't understand how—"

"It's fairly obvious," he said, loud enough for the other two men to hear. "Someone must have found the watch. Maybe one of the mill workers who discovered the body found the watch nearby. Maybe Hiram dropped it at some point when he was trying to get home. Or maybe the murderer tossed it away. The point is, whoever ultimately found the watch decided to play a cruel trick and try to implicate you. With the back door to the store unlocked, it wouldn't have been very difficult for someone to slip inside to hide the watch in your desk while you were gone."

"N-no. I guess not, but why would someone do

that?" The pain in the back of her head tightened into a band of pressure that stretched across her forehead.

"I'm not sure," he admitted and looked over at Ben and Noah. "Maybe you should be more concerned about this 'reluctant witness' than you are about Jane. If she did poison her husband, which she most emphatically didn't, why would she have gone to such great lengths to make an issue of the watch when she already had it? It doesn't make sense, and it will make even less when we tell you what Sheriff Fleming has learned in his investigation."

Too overwhelmed to listen closely as Daniel shared the details of the sheriff's investigation and the problems with the estate, she tried to think of anyone in Sunrise who would try to blame her for Hiram's murder. Her thoughts were jammed by her headache, and she gave up trying just as Daniel concluded.

". . . For Jane's sake, and out of consideration for Hiram's relatives, I think you'll agree it's best not to divulge the sordid details to anyone else. I'm certain the sheriff would appreciate your discretion as well."

She dropped her gaze, too embarrassed to look at either Ben or Noah. She could only pray they would keep their own counsel. If their wives knew the full story, she was not sure what she could expect. She could only imagine how many people saw them searching the store and what rumors had already been started.

Ben spoke up first in response to Daniel's explanation. "I guess I just wasn't thinking straight, and I'm sorry. I guess I should have listened to my wife after all."

"Me, too," Noah added. "Things like this just don't happen in Sunrise. I think we all need a little time to let this die down a bit."

"I understand," she murmured, trying to soften the echo of her own words in her pounding head. "Will you be needing the watch? I should send it to Aaron."

"I'll lock it up in my safe for now, along with the note," Noah suggested. "I doubt we'll ever find out who sent it, but after this past week, I'm not sure I know much of anything anymore."

She rubbed her forehead and closed her eyes to block the light in a futile attempt to ease the relentless pressure in her head while the two men mounted up and returned home.

She had endured years of an unhappy marriage and recent months facing uncertainty and worry. She had withstood the initial shock and scandal surrounding Hiram's murder, relieved that simple truth and justice had quickly cleared her name only to find it besmirched again. She had even managed to keep relatively hopeful when faced with the possibility of losing her livelihood as well as her home because of one sustaining part of her life: Sunrise.

No longer a quiet hamlet, the village would now be little more than a mill churning gossip into accusations and grinding new rumors with every passing day until Hiram's murderer was apprehended. Even then, it would be years until the scandal was forgotten.

She tried to prepare herself to face the villagers, but the safe haven she had anticipated returning home to was gone, and she felt utterly bereft and alone.

When she swayed on her feet, Daniel put his arm around her shoulders. "Are you all right?"

"I'm just . . . tired," she whispered, her throat raw from choking back unshed tears. She sank against him and leaned her head against his shoulder when he eased her into his embrace. Her strength had already been weakened by the burdens she had carried alone for nearly six months and sapped by the harrowing week that began with Hiram's death. Now, the cruel accusation against her drained what little strength remained.

She clutched at the lapel of his coat and burrowed her face into the hollow of his neck where she could feel his pulse beating against her forehead. She squeezed her eyes shut and tightened her throat to keep the tears at bay, but she only managed to exacerbate the pressure in her head. She put her other hand to her lips and pressed hard against her chin to muffle her cries and held on to him with her other hand to keep from collapsing.

When strong arms held her close and gentle hands stroked her head, she lost her battle to keep her sorrows and disappointments hidden. The dark clouds of anguish stored in her spirit burst with the fury of a sudden storm, unleashing torrents of tears and leaving her gasping for breath. One by one, the clouds released the last remnants of guilt, shame, and fear, draining the cold, destructive emotions from her spirit to make room for healing and hope.

The storm abated as quickly as it had struck.

Lethargic in both body and spirit, she held him close and listened to the slow steady beat of his heart, stunned by the resilience of her own body, which was quickly returning to normal.

The entirely abnormal position in which she found herself being embraced by him in return melted the stitches holding her patchwork dreams together. Each tattered piece shifted position before sliding into place to create a new dream, one she could actually see and feel and touch, unleashing long-dormant physical desires that left her trembling anew.

She had waited all of her life to be held by a man who had the heart and soul to cherish her as a woman who was precious to him—the only way she could describe how Daniel made her feel. Her heart pounded at her brain to set the blinding truth free, casting permanent shadows on her feeble attempts to deny it with reasons or excuses.

She had fallen in love with him.

Not with the same force of the tidal wave of pure emotion that had swept over her when Hiram had proposed, swamping her common sense and logic and drowning her doubts.

Daniel had walked into her life and had captured her heart. It was as if she had been set adrift in a sea of gentle tides that ebbed and flowed against the shores of her mind as well as her heart and spirit. Although he had first struck her as a man with questionable ethics and a cynical view of the very system he dedicated his life to uphold, she knew he was a man willing to challenge and circumvent any and all obstacles that prevented justice from prevailing.

Although still troubling, his pragmatic approach to finding legal solutions for clients caught in difficult circumstances was not based on contempt for the law. It reflected his commitment to truth and justice, regardless of the cost to his own reputation. He was a man she could respect and admire. A man whose loyalty, sensitivity, and compassion shaped his principles.

And she loved him, as deeply and completely as a woman could love only the man who had been created to be her partner in life.

For several long heartbeats, she let herself pretend he loved her, too.

Reality intervened swiftly, just as it had when she had first realized her husband could never love anyone else because he only loved himself. This time, reality hurt even more. She had no hope Daniel would ever return her love, especially now that she had been cast under suspicion as a murderess. She knew from bitter experience she could never again suffer the pain she had endured by clinging to illusions.

She could never claim his love, but her dreams still belonged to her, and as long as she had her dreams she could survive, one day at a time.

She wiped her tearstained face with her hands before she stepped out of his embrace and tucked away the bittersweet memory of a moment she would never forget. Anxious to relieve the awkwardness that seeped in between them, she let out a deep sigh and kept her gaze averted. "I'm not sure I know what to say except thank you. I don't know what came over me just now."

"No matter how hard you try, you can't be a statue or a machine. You're human. With what you've had to endure, especially over the past week, you should be surprised it didn't happen sooner. I'm glad I was here to help."

His voice sounded strained, but professional, and she had no doubt this was not the first time he had been placed into the role of comforter for one of his clients. "It will likely happen again now that you're home and will be trying to get your life back to normal," he cautioned. "Unfortunately, that won't happen right away, and you'll have a better time of it if you realize only time is going to help make it easier," he advised.

She wanted to think he had chosen his words only for her and her unique situation, but he must have offered the same advice to his clients countless times before. "We should start back now," she suggested, although she was not quite ready to face the villagers, who were surely anticipating her arrival.

He glanced at her and then the cottage. "Would you mind if we stayed long enough to pry open a shutter or two to peek inside? I have no idea how much work will be involved to get it ready for Lily."

She smiled, grateful for the temporary reprieve. "You really were raised in the city. Let me show you something." She led him to the front of the cottage and brushed away a dried hornet's nest before she opened the door.

He stared at her for a moment and shook his head. "Doesn't anyone here use locks?"

Her smile faded. "Not usually, but that will probably change now. In any event, you can go inside without worrying. By now, Aunt Nester has spread the word to most everyone that Aunt Lily purchased the house."

He followed her inside and left the door wide open to provide light since all the windows were shuttered closed. She wrinkled her nose against the stale, musty air as they made a quick tour through the chilly rooms. Small but adequate, the cottage had only four rooms: a large all-purpose room with an enormous hearth along one wall and a corner boasting a rusted hand pump for water and three small sleeping rooms. Except for a coating of dust and an empty crate or two, the cottage was completely bare and sorely in need of sprucing up.

"I'm surprised," he ventured with a final glimpse around the largest room. "I thought it would be a lot worse."

"With a thorough cleaning and a fresh splash of paint, you could have the cottage livable in a week or two."

"Except for furniture," he reminded her.

She grinned. "I think I have all you'll need stored in the loft of the barn at Sam's house. Most of the furniture belonged to my parents. You could use it until Aunt Lily gets back and decides how she wants to decorate, although I think she'd like to keep some of the pieces. They were her mother's."

He narrowed his gaze. "Why aren't you using the furniture? Or Sam? Lily wouldn't want to take any-thing—"

"Hiram never wanted any of my parents' things and Sam furnished the house to suit Polly, so the furniture is only sitting in the loft collecting dust. It can sit here just as well."

"I would like to move out of the room at the tavern," he admitted.

"Then it's settled. While we drive back to the store, I'll suggest a few people you might want to ask to help you get the cottage in order first."

Relieved to have something positive to occupy her thoughts, she left the cottage wishing she, too, had someone to help put her life in order. Unfortunately, Daniel was the only one she wanted.

Settling the estate and refurbishing the cottage should only take a few weeks, and then he would be going back to Philadelphia. Until then, she would have to find a way to distance herself from him, physically and emotionally, if only as practice for spending the rest of her life without him.

Chapter 15

❀ Early one Saturday morning, more than two weeks after returning to Sunrise, Jane hid her disappointment poorly. With a heavy frown, she went through the newest posts delivered by the mail wagon for the third time before sorting them for the recipients to collect during the week.

"You'd better wipe off that frown quick, or it'll be permanent," Aunt Nester warned. "Aaron's probably been away and hasn't gotten your post yet. He'll write soon enough. In the meantime, there's plenty of work to be done today to keep you busy. Speakin' of which, where's Daniel? I thought he'd be here by now with that caravan of wagons."

"It's only seven o'clock, and everyone else is meeting us at Sam's." She glanced around the store and managed to smile. Stocked as fully as it had ever been, there wasn't a space on the shelves or counters to add as much as a hairpin. Decorated tin trinket boxes filled the glass case, replacing the items she had planned to give away. Until the estate was settled, the boxes containing the dibbles and sundry other unsalable items were once again taking up needed space in the storeroom.

Equally amazing, most of the villagers had greeted her return home with far less gossip than she had expected. Apparently, Libby and Penelope had never mentioned either the note or the pocket watch to anyone else, Jane included.

Life was slowly gliding back into its usual routine, and she had even managed to avoid Daniel, who had been supervising the restoration of the cottage. A tad nervous about spending most of today with him, she was glad they would not be alone.

She did feel guilty leaving Aunt Nester alone in the store again. "Are you sure you don't want to come with us? It wouldn't hurt to close up the store for a few hours. You might want to choose some furniture for yourself."

Her aunt scowled. "Can't scarcely move around in my two rooms as it is. Besides, Libby and Penelope are stoppin' by to keep me company. After helpin' Daniel clean the place, we figured we needed a rest. And you need to stay open to make whatever you can. Libby's bringin' dinner and Penelope baked somethin' up. I'll save you some if she didn't burn it too bad." She grinned and plopped a plug of tobacco into her mouth.

Chuckling to herself, Jane grabbed her cloak as soon as she saw Daniel pull up in front of the store. "I'll be back as soon as I can. Once he picks out what he wants, I'll have Sam bring me home." She planted a kiss on the top of her aunt's head. "Don't gossip too much today," she teased and scooted outside before her aunt could spit out the tobacco juice and respond.

With the wagon seat nearly level with the raised sidewalk, she joined Daniel without needing assistance, but she would have gladly accepted help to stop her heart from racing.

Dressed casually in form-fitting dungarees, a work shirt open at the neck, and a thickly padded vest, he greeted her with a smile. Jolts of desire shot straight through her body to her heart which pumped the delicious, but dangerous sensations to the soles of her feet and back again.

"Ready for moving day?" he asked.

If her heart did not stop racing, she was ready to move straight to the end of the seat and jump off. "Ready," she managed and braced herself as the wagon moved forward.

"Any good news today?"

"Nothing in today's post. Maybe next week."

SUNRISE 159

"Don't worry. That's my job, remember?"

Did he have to be so attractive *and* solicitous? She quickly changed the subject before she lost complete control of her emotions. "Who's coming today besides Sam?"

He grinned. "Louis took care of that. George is coming by as soon as the mill closes at noon, and he said he'd try to borrow one of Peterson's wagons. I hope that's all right. If it bothers you, I can send someone—"

"No, that's . . . that's fine."

"How's George doing at the store? He seems like a hard worker."

She smiled. "He is. He thinks he might be able to send for Matilda before the end of the summer. I haven't been up to the loft since Sam got married, but I think there's a lot more furniture stored there than you'll need for Aunt Lily. If there's still some left after you've picked out what you want, do you think he'd be offended if I offered the pieces to him?"

When he glanced at her, the sun glistened in the golden highlights in his eyes. "Wouldn't you rather save them for yourself?"

She shook her head. "I probably won't have any use for them. The furniture in the living quarters over the store isn't mine to replace. If Aaron sells the building, he'll probably offer it furnished."

"And if he doesn't?"

"Then I'll just keep what I have," she responded, more content to have her parent's furniture used and enjoyed by a young couple just beginning their lives together.

When they arrived at Sam's property and pulled up in front of the barn, they were the fourth wagon in line. While waving a greeting to the helpers gathered around a table Polly had set with refreshments, Jane could scarcely contain her surprise.

Dressed in a white gown trimmed with aqua flowerettes, Polly held a matching parasol over her head to protect her from the sun. The silly goose was visibly trembling in the morning chill, too vain to cover up her beautiful gown with a cloak when she had an audience of men around her.

Bypassing the refreshments after telling Sam, her cousin Louis, and several others to enjoy themselves while Daniel picked out the furniture he wanted, they went directly into the barn. Unlike Polly, Jane had no qualms about doing the dirtier work today, and she actually looked forward to seeing her parent's things again. She pointed to the ladder leading to the overhead loft where Sam had already hung several ropes to be used to lower the furniture.

"We can both go up to the loft while you pick out what you'd like to have for the cottage. There's no sense wasting effort and lowering anything else," she suggested. She removed her cloak and bonnet and hung them on a nail in the wall.

Shrugging away the self-consciousness that always surfaced when she was with Polly, she found Daniel studying her with a stern look. "You shouldn't climb up there with those skirts. It's too dangerous."

She grinned at him. "Only if you peek. Be a gentleman and watch the door for me. I can hitch up my skirts and climb the ladder faster than you will. I've had lots of experience chasing after Sam when he used to try to hide from me up there."

"I still think—"

His mouth slammed shut, and he spun around to face the door the moment she reached for the hem of her skirts. Less than a minute later, she was standing in the loft with her skirts properly arranged and her apron straightened. "Your turn," she cried, enjoying his look of wonder when he turned around.

He crossed the barn and started up the ladder. When he paused halfway up and looked down, she saw beads of perspiration covering the creases in his forehead. The knuckles on both hands gripping the sides of the ladder were nearly translucent, and his breathing was quick and rapid. "It's the ladder. I fell off one when I was six or seven," he moaned and closed his eyes. "I'm afraid this is about as far as I can make it on my own." His shoulders shook as he chuckled softly.

"What's so funny?" she asked, concerned he might actually fall off the ladder.

"I'm trying to think of a more humiliating moment in my life, but I'm afraid I can't."

"There's nothing humiliating about being afraid. Everyone has fears about something or another."

"Name yours."

"Lightning." She shuddered. Even saying the word brought back memories of the night her parents had been struck down during a summer storm. "Take a deep breath, keep your eyes closed, and just take one rung at a time," she suggested, trying to shove her memories back into the deep recesses of her mind. "You'll make it to the top in no time."

He chuckled again. "Then I'll have to worry about getting down."

"That's easy to resolve. We'll tie a rope and send you down like a piece of furniture," she teased. "Now take another rung."

He actually managed two more before he stopped again and started to chuckle infectiously, all the while clinging to the ladder as if his life depended on it.

"Now what?" she asked, trying hard not to chuckle herself.

"You really would truss me up and send me back down like that, wouldn't you?"

"In a heartbeat. Now come on. Three more rungs and you can feel the floor of the loft with your hands. Unless you want to wait for the others to watch."

"Not a chance." He took the remaining rungs so fast she thought he might fly through the roof. When he finally stood up, he wiped his brow with the back of one hand. "Well, now you know my deepest, darkest secret."

She gulped, praying her love for him was not written all over her face. "Compared to what you know about me, I'd say you're still way behind," she murmured.

He cleared his throat. "Jane, I—"

"Let's start with the furniture in the front," she suggested to avoid opening a discussion that would be uncomfortable for both of them. She walked several yards ahead and started lifting off the badly yellowed sheets protecting the furniture, unleashing a smaller cloud of dust than she had expected.

"You're going to have to help me out here," he said as he joined her and surveyed an assortment of small tables stacked in front of several crates. She quickly chose three tables, which he set aside just as the others gathered below.

While Daniel secured and lowered the tables to the men waiting below, she checked the crates. One held a collection of linens he would need; the other contained some of her childhood mementos, which she had him shove to the side.

They had been working less than half an hour, but after crawling around to inspect the furniture, her hands were already covered with grime and her apron looked like it had been washed in mud. When she chanced a look below, she saw Polly looking just as dainty fresh and sparkling clean as ever, of course. Resisting the urge to accidentally blow a few dust balls in her sister-in-law's direction, she decided Polly was not worth the effort.

Sweet, devious Polly. What a hypocrite she was, standing there like a pristine princess who would faint at the very thought of climbing a ladder when she apparently did not have a problem crawling into bed with another woman's husband!

On second thought, Jane wished the dust balls were filled with scarlet paint that would splatter all over Polly's pretty little dress and sink clear through to her cheating heart. Deciding ultimately that virtue was a far better choice than vindictiveness, Jane knelt down and leaned back on her haunches to wait for Daniel to finish lowering the crate of linens so he could help her finish moving a chest of drawers.

The sound of galloping horses approaching the barn caused a stir below, and everyone below scurried out to see who had arrived. Moments later, Ben and Noah entered. Solemn. And alone.

When they shut the barn door behind them, she felt a lump of dread congeal in the pit of her stomach. Frozen in place, she remained leaning back on her haunches and watched as each man climbed the ladder, scarcely aware Daniel had moved quickly to stand beside her.

Without a word of explanation, Ben simply took a piece of paper from his pocket and laid it on her lap. She closed her eyes and swallowed hard.

"The minister found this when he went to the church to practice tomorrow's sermon. Someone must have slipped it under the door during the night. He's sure it wasn't there yesterday."

Struggling for air, she did not have the courage to read the note until she felt Daniel lower himself to sit beside her. With a fervent prayer she would remain calm and levelheaded, she opened her eyes and looked at the note.

Same badly scrawled handwriting.

Same hateful, cryptic accusation.

She bowed her head and started to tremble, unsure whether she shook with anger or the very real fear that someone was trying to make very sure only one person would be held responsible for the death of Hiram Foster: his widow.

Chapter 16

✳ Daniel read the note a third time. The message remained just as ominous:

> Let the world judge and condemn the widow who has broken God's covenant and man's laws. The truth will be found in the place where He was born.
>
> A Follower

Anger scalded his disbelief, and he pulled the letter from Jane's lap. "Follower." He hissed, certain the mayor and the constable had also caught the double entendre in the signature. He forced his mind to function logically. Why would someone who claimed to have witnessed the murder allegedly follow Jane around while she hid the evidence instead of reporting the crime to the authorities immediately? Why refuse to come forward now?

Instinct and experience told him this was no "Follower of the Word," either. The murderer, not a witness, was manipulating the evidence, revealing it one piece at a time to implicate Jane. It would be pointless to try to figure out who that murderer was right now or argue against a search of the barn. Until he knew what had been hidden here, he would be unable to undermine its value as he had done with the pocket watch.

Jane, however, claimed his immediate attention first. A ghostly pallor covered her face, and her gaze was vacant, reflecting only total shock. He helped her to her feet and put his arm around her waist meaning to hold on to her until she was steady on her feet. When he felt her trembling against him, he pulled her closer.

She did not pull away and looked up at him with eyes pleading for him to believe in her innocence. His anguish was so profound, his heart ached. Maintaining his role as her lawyer, which reinforced the ethical barrier between them, was more critical now than ever before.

And more difficult.

Being objective and clear-minded had been relatively easy in the past for one very simple reason: He had never fallen in love with the client he had been representing.

"Everything will be all right," he promised her. "It doesn't matter what they find," he whispered. "I believe in you."

She closed her eyes and leaned her head against his shoulder. As she took rapid, short breaths of air, her trembling began to ease. With a soft sigh, she opened her eyes, stepped beside him, and gripped his arm with her hand. When she spoke, she addressed Ben and Noah in a low, but steady voice. "I have no idea what you'll find here or where you'll find it, but I give you my word I haven't been inside this barn since Sam got married."

"Maybe we won't find anything at all," Noah suggested, "but we do have to look around. Might take a while to check through everything stored in the loft. Do you want to stay and watch, or would you rather wait in the house with Polly?"

"I'd rather stay here."

Once again, Daniel thought she answered a little too quickly and a bit too firmly, but he suspected she might simply want to be there if and when the alleged evidence was discovered, if only to dispute it.

"Noah and I will conduct the search. Wish we could let you help, Mr. Colton, but since you're Jane's lawyer, you're not exactly unbiased. We could make this faster, though, if we asked some of the other men to help."

Daniel disagreed. "Sam's her brother and Louis is her

cousin, so they'd have an interest in protecting Jane as well. I don't know about the others, but I'm more concerned about conducting the search with as much confidentiality as possible."

Noah looked at the furniture and frowned. "He's right, Ben. Let's make this as quick as we can without anyone's help. We'll start at the back and work our way through."

Daniel led Jane to the side of the loft and stood with her as the two men began their search. Piece by piece, the furniture moved from the back of the loft to crowd together at the edge, and the men searched each piece thoroughly.

The tables Daniel had not selected were upended, drawers in chests were removed and then replaced, and crates were emptied and haphazardly repacked. The air grew thick with dust and heavy with tension as time and time again, the men came up empty-handed.

Through it all, Jane remained stoic and silent. Her expression remained troubled. The lines across her brow deepened and her lips were pursed, but her chin never dropped. By the time the officials were nearly finished, their coats had long been abandoned and their shirts and trousers were stained with dirt and dust.

Ben slapped his grimy hands against his legs and eyed the dresser Jane had moved earlier. "I'll take the last piece here while you check below. See if the dirt's been dug up recently, check the stall out, and then go back outside and go through the furniture they have in the wagon."

Chest heaving, he wiped his perspiring brow with his shirtsleeves. "And don't say anything to anybody. Looks like this just might have been one nasty, almighty hoax this time. If I get my hands on this note writer, I'm gonna strangle him myself."

After Noah descended the ladder and started to pace back and forth across the ground floor, Ben pulled the dresser around and searched it completely.

"There's nothing down here," Noah cried. "I'm going outside."

"I'm done. Nothing here, either," Ben grumbled. He paused, stared straight ahead, and narrowed his gaze. "What's in that crate?" he asked as he nudged the dresser aside to reach a wooden crate pushed up against the wall.

A flash of recognition crossed her face. "That's filled with my things, but I haven't looked through them in years. I think there's a daybook or two, my old school slate, and some of my parents' letters."

Ben opened the crate, looked inside, and shrugged his shoulders. "That's pretty much what's here," he mumbled. He rummaged through the contents, which Daniel couldn't see. "Looks like a sampler, skeins of embroidery thread, and an old handkerchief."

He lifted out two daybooks, thumbed through them, and set them aside before retrieving the school slate and putting it on the floor. Lastly, he removed a stack of yellowed letters tied together loosely with a faded blue ribbon.

When the ribbon slid off and fell back into the crate, he spread the letters apart and held them like he was holding a hand of cards. His fingers instantly froze in place, and Daniel caught a glimpse of what had been carefully hidden between the old letters.

"Bank notes," Jane whispered, and closed her eyes briefly while she took several small gulps of air. The blood in her face literally drained away, and when he reached down to take her hand, it was even colder than he had expected.

Using the lid of the crate for a makeshift table, Ben carefully pulled the bank notes from between the letters. At the same time, the barn door swung open and the sound of rushing footsteps and raised voices momentarily distracted all three people in the loft, and they stared below.

Noah raced ahead of Sam and blocked his way. "I said you can't come in here."

Sam shoved him aside. "She's my sister, and you can't stop me." He looked up to the loft as Louis and the other men scrambled into the barn. "Jane? What's happening?" he shouted as he crossed the short distance to the ladder and started to ascend.

"Get out," Ben snapped. "All of you! This doesn't concern you."

"Like Hades it doesn't," Sam spat as he charged up the ladder, stared at the pile of bank notes and letters on the floor, and hurried to Jane's side. "Are you all right? What are they doing up here? Why won't they tell me anything?"

Her eyes filled with tears, and she hugged him. "It's all right," she murmured. "Daniel is here with me."

Polly's cry screeched through the barn. "Sam? Don't leave me down here all alone! Sam! Please, I don't understand what's happening."

Jane flinched, and her brother looked torn between the two women in his life. Daniel looked below and saw Polly, her eyes wide with fright and her face stained with tears.

He wondered which woman would get Sam's attention, although Jane made it easy for her brother to choose. "Go be with Polly. I have to stay here with Daniel and Ben a little longer, but I'll explain everything to you later." At least Sam had the good grace to leave reluctantly.

"Noah! Get the rest of those folks outside. I'm almost finished," Ben barked as he hastily counted the notes.

Daniel did not have to be closer to try to read the numbers on the notes. He had already guessed their worth. He grabbed her hand again, which was even colder than before.

When Ben finished, he approached them with a pained look etching his features. "I know you told me Hiram had been carrying a good deal of money, but I forget the precise amount."

There was no sense lying. Ben and Noah could easily

check with the sheriff to verify the figure, and it would not do Jane's cause any good to do anything less than fully cooperate.

Before Daniel could answer, Jane supplied the number with her eyes wide and shining with tears. "Three hundred ninety dollars."

"Exactly," Ben whispered. "Exactly."

Her entire world had exploded right in front of her face, splintering into shards that had scattered at her feet. Jane could not understand it, explain it, or wish it away, but she could not imagine how she would ever put her life back together any more than she could turn back the hands of time or simply evaporate into thin air.

By late afternoon, the village was virtually smoldering with gossip and wild rumors that even the twin village guardians could not extinguish. Jane stared out her bedroom window into the street and half expected to see flames shooting from nearby roofs and black smoke billowing skyward.

She could not see the tavern itself, but judging by the heavy street traffic that had passed by, half the village must be gathered there to munch on every tidbit of today's events while adding spicy details of innuendo and supposition.

Somewhere in this village or on the outlying homesteads, there was a murderer who had taken Hiram's life and was very slowly, but cleverly, trying to make sure Jane would pay the ultimate price for the crime.

Ben and Noah had already left for Lancaster, carrying both anonymous letters, Hiram's pocket watch, and the bank notes. Sam was home consoling his wife, but he was thoroughly outraged at the accusations against his sister and the person who had violated the sanctity of his homestead. Aunt Nester was downstairs in the general store with her knitting needles ready to jab the first person who dared utter a single word against her niece.

Daniel was waiting for her in the parlor. Steady as a rock, he had stayed by her side, never wavering in his support. Ever professional, he had not argued the point when Ben and Noah had insisted on taking the two sets of evidence to Sheriff Fleming.

She dropped her hand and let the drape fall back into place, wishing she could curtain her own worries as easily. Would anyone in Sunrise be willing to give up a year's income just to see Jane accused of murdering her husband, or were the funds hidden in the barn the ones Hiram had been carrying? Anger simmered just below the thin veneer of her self-control, fueled by the irony that Hiram was being canonized as a victim while she was being condemned and branded with vicious accusations.

Along with Sam, since the money had been hidden in his barn. He was her brother, and everyone knew they were devoted to one another. Tears welled and spilled down her cheeks. If anyone learned about the affair, there would be only one person better to blame than Jane: Sam. The aggrieved spouse and the outraged brother, he would have a double motive to commit murder.

Innocent, unsuspecting Sam. A man she had helped raise to adulthood. A man who loved his wife so completely he was blind to her faults. A man who could no sooner commit murder any more than Jane could.

She wiped the tears from her face, more determined than ever to protect him. As long as no one else learned of the affair, Sam would not be subjected to gossip and innuendo for long. He was away so frequently and the barn so rarely used, anyone could have slipped into the barn unnoticed, a point Daniel had argued with Ben and Noah earlier. She hoped the villagers would remember that, too.

With her confidence jarred, but not destroyed, she left her room to go to the parlor to rejoin Daniel. He was not there, but he must have heard her footsteps coming down the hall.

"I'm in the kitchen," he called.

She found him seated at the table, which was set with pieces of paper cut into sizes equal to the size of playing cards. "That doesn't look very appetizing," she teased, attempting to erase the scowl on his face and lift her own spirits at the same time. "I think I'd rather have something hotter and definitely sweeter."

He waved the back of his hand over the papers. "You're right. This is definitely cold and bitter stuff, but extremely palatable if you have a taste for getting away with robbery, conspiracy, and murder. I've plotted out everything we know so far. Take a look and see if you can tell the one crucial ingredient that's missing and undermines the circumstantial evidence that's here."

Both curious and challenged, she stood beside him and quickly scanned the papers. At second glance, she realized they had been clearly arranged in a specific order. "Do you always sort through the facts in your cases like this?"

He shrugged. "I find it helps to keep everything in perspective, especially when I need to lead a jury by the hand so they see what I want them to see instead of the opposing counsel."

Her heart started to pound. "Jury? Do you expect me to be formally accused? There's going to be a trial?"

"No. I'm sorry, I didn't mean to imply that at all. I just used the system now to organize my thoughts. Sheriff Fleming will no doubt want to talk to you about what Ben and Noah have uncovered. We need to be prepared to answer his questions, but more importantly, pose some of our own."

Her heartbeat slowed to a series of heavy thuds, and she gripped the top of the chair in front of her with her hands. As she studied the papers on the table, she realized how meticulous and thorough he had been. Every action she had taken since early January had been recorded, from her initial trip to the city to see the lawyers through today, as well as information the sheriff had provided and the evidence that had surfaced here in Sunrise.

Daniel had even included the minister's alleged sighting, information regarding the unsettled position of Hiram's estate, and her accident in the general store when she had broken the bottle of concentrated tobacco juice.

The individual pieces of circumstantial evidence against her were like small twigs yet to be gathered together as kindling. Stacked together atop logs of available facts, they were volatile. Adding evidence about Hiram's affair would be like striking a match and starting a bonfire that would incinerate her, and probably her brother as well.

She wiped her moistened palms on her skirts and took a deep breath. She would have to be very careful not to say anything that would give Daniel the remotest reason to suspect Hiram had been unfaithful to her with Polly.

While her heart beat out rhythmic pleas for her to be totally honest with Daniel, her mind rebelled. There was only one way she could protect Sam right now. When her conscience started screaming in protest, she muffled it with a compromise—of sorts.

She would discuss everything with him now as truthfully as she could. If and when he posed questions about Hiram's fidelity, she would sidestep until she had no other choice. Then she would have to lie, her conscience be damned.

Chapter 17

✾ Daniel tapped his finger on the table and nodded toward the cards he had made of paper. "You have a logical mind. Tell me what's missing."

Standing beside him, Jane gripped the top of the chair in front of her even harder. "There's no eyewitness to the crime. Is that what you mean?"

"That's a good observation, but an eyewitness isn't as essential as something else." He pointed to the first two rows of cards. "These represent opportunity and means. We can prove you weren't in Lancaster with Hiram, and the sheriff can't prove he ever arrived home, despite what the minister may or may not have seen. That takes care of opportunity. As for means, the poison itself is commonplace. There isn't a woman in the entire area who doesn't keep concentrated tobacco juice in her cupboard to kill garden pests."

She raised a brow. "You're from the city. How would you know that?"

His smile added a sparkle to his otherwise serious expression. "Your Aunt Nester told me about it after your accident in the store. Now, look at the evidence. While it can appear to be overwhelming, remember it's all circumstantial. So . . . what's not here? Think like a gossipmonger, if you will. Whether it's murder or robbery or simple mischief, people always want to know . . ."

"Why," she whispered, scarcely able to find the breath to utter the word.

"Exactly. Why would you or anyone else murder Hiram? Motives usually fall into several common categories. Self-defense, profit, honor, jealousy, and revenge. As far as you're concerned, we can eliminate every one."

When she was unable to manage a smile, he apparently mistook her expression for confusion. "Since Hiram died without a will, your inheritance is questionable. You were far better situated economically when he was alive, so that eliminates profit. Poison as a method wouldn't typically support the idea of self-defense, and honor is more commonly associated with men. That leaves only two motives left: jealousy and revenge. There's no way you could have known about the red-haired woman in Lancaster, which means you didn't and don't have a motive."

Her pulse began to race. Her palms moistened again, and she wiped them self-consciously on her skirts. Jealousy and revenge would be the perfect motives to explain why she would murder Hiram for his affair with Polly.

". . . Which brings us straight back to the motives again, but this time, for someone else." He pointed to the cards representing the anonymous notes, the pocket watch, and the funds. "There are several possibilities we have to consider. First, the sheriff could be right about the red-haired woman and robbery was the motive."

"Why would she kill him and not keep the money? And how would she know where to hide—"

"She wouldn't." He narrowed his gaze. "What if someone from Sunrise stumbled along, interrupted the crime, and suspected you were involved? It was dark. He might have seen a woman bolting away from the scene . . ."

"And finished the robbery?"

"It's possible," he argued. "It's hard to predict what a witness to a crime might do. One of the notes was signed 'a reluctant witness,' remember? Maybe someone saw the crime in process and was too scared to report

it to the authorities and later felt guilty for not speaking
up when the sheriff arrived."

She shuddered. "But I didn't kill Hiram!"

"Of course you didn't, but the witness thinks you
did. Unless . . ." He hesitated and looked up at her.
"Unless the sheriff is wrong and someone else in Sunrise
had a motive to kill your husband and planned to implicate you all along."

"At this point, I don't know what to think." She
rubbed her temples with the tips of her fingers to ease
the pounding in her head.

Concerned, Daniel got up from his seat, took her
arm, and settled her into her chair. "I know how hard
this has been for you," he said gently, "but the questions I have to ask you now will be even more difficult.
I want you to listen to me very carefully and take your
time to think through your answer before you respond.
Can you do that for me?"

She nodded and shifted her gaze to the top of the
table still littered with cards.

"This wasn't the first time he was unfaithful to you,
was it?"

He had asked her the one question she could not
answer. She swallowed hard, struggling against the
truth to keep it from bursting from her lips. She hated
to lie, detested the very notion, but she could not tell
him the truth. As much as he professed to believe in her
innocence, she could not even be sure he would believe
her now after waiting all this time to tell him about the
affair.

She tried to stop trembling and failed.

She tried to stop her heart from racing. It beat faster.

She did not even try to control the anger against
Hiram that was bubbling and churning in every part of
her body. He had mocked Sunrise and all she held dear.
He had callously betrayed his vows to her. Even in
death, he had soiled her name with scandal and now
he took from her all she had left: her character.

She tilted her chin and clenched her teeth together so

hard, her jaw ached. Was it a lie if she did not answer him? Would her refusal to answer make him assume her answer was no?

He exhaled slowly. "I'm not here to judge you or your husband, but I can't help you unless you tell me the truth."

When she did not answer him a second time, he sighed and gathered up his work. His movements were uncharacteristically quick and jerky. He refused to meet her gaze. "I'm going back to Lily's. Louis promised to have the rest of the men deliver the furniture and bring my things over from my room," he said as he stood up and pushed his chair back against the table. "I have work to do. When you're ready to talk to me and tell me the truth, let me know. In the meantime, talk to no one else, except for your aunt."

He walked out of the kitchen and never looked back. When she heard the door close behind him, she wondered if this meeting had been their last.

When Daniel approached the cottage and saw Louis and George unloading the furniture from several wagons, he did a complete about-face, crossed the main road, and walked through the woods to the river. Following along the riverbank, he passed the raft landing and quickly found the outcropping of rocks he had used as a private hideaway the day he arrived in Sunrise.

After he climbed up and onto the ledge, he sat down with his back against a section smoothed by the elements. He inhaled the subtle fragrance of spring, headier than only a few weeks ago. Varying shades of green dusted the trees. Wildflowers, their tight buds promising a future rainbow of colors, challenged the undergrowth for the last rays from a setting sun that dappled the forest-covered earth and danced in the strong currents and swirling waters of the Susquehanna.

He cleared his mind and sat quietly. He felt the warmth of the sun on his face, smelled the mingled country scents, and studied nature struggling to renew herself in the ancient ritual of the seasons.

The foliage along the bank of the river below rustled. Curious, he narrowed his gaze and followed the slow, subtle movement beneath the leaves. He grinned when a long slender face and neck poked through the underbrush and moved from side to side before the animal emerged into full view. He had not seen a box turtle in years, but he recognized the thick chunky body and mosaic shell patterned with shades of dark orange and brown.

He held perfectly still and watched the turtle hunt. Moving slowly, but steadily over small rocks, the animal devoured insects crawling beneath the greens. Occasionally it pulled a fat nightcrawler from the moist soil.

Slow and steady. That was exactly how Daniel had approached his legal career. He had plotted every move, studying law and adapting tactics used by unscrupulous lawyers for a nobler goal: to see justice prevail, even when undermined by the law itself or unprincipled lawyers. Earning a reputation as a champion of justice, albeit one of dubious ethics, he acquired the legal expertise necessary to protect the innocent when falsely accused. His objectivity and compassion were additional components that contributed to his successes as a criminal defender, but emotion had never been a factor.

Now that Jane's legal problems had multiplied, potentially defending her in a murder trial would be difficult. He had fallen in love with her and thus would be hard-pressed to keep his feelings for her from undermining the very skills he had worked years to perfect.

Like the plodding turtle hunting through the underbrush a few feet away, he had always scratched his way through facts and allegations before accepting anything as true or valid. Self-reliant and purposeful, he had never let damaging evidence or mistruths overwhelm him. He analyzed, evaluated, and acted, whether that meant supervising a far-reaching, independent investigation or stretching the boundaries of accepted procedures to achieve his goal: an acquittal for his client.

Debra Modean. Alexander Whitehall. Sherman Cattell. Sarah Pugh. The names of some of his previous clients echoed in his mind. All of them had been innocent. All of them had been charged with serious crimes, and all of them had been judged innocent by a jury because Daniel had performed all of his duties well.

His confidence was not restored by pondering old cases and former victories since he had never had clients question his legal strategies, let alone demand control of their legal defense. Jane had done both. If she were eventually charged with murdering her husband, Daniel had no answer to the dilemma he would face if he had to defend her. Given the philosophical differences that existed between them, he could be forced to break his promise to her and defend her in a way that violated her strict code of integrity and simple faith in justice.

Unless he viewed defending her—and saving her—as one final opportunity to both redeem his cynicism and replace it with the idealism and integrity that would mark him as the lawyer of unusual distinction he wanted to be.

He lifted his gaze and stared at the rushing water. The gently shimmering reflection of the sunlight reminded him of Jane, the jewel shining softly who had captured and dazzled his heart so completely, he had let love consume his thoughts, cloud his judgment, and clog his mind.

Thinking about Jane inspired bitter self-recrimination for allowing the evidence to stack up against her. Mired in a misery of his own creation, his thoughts flowed from hope to despair and back again. When the sun began to dip behind the mountains and the air grew chill, he scanned the riverbank.

No sign of the turtle. He looked more carefully, got a brief glimpse of frantic movement, and clambered down from the ledge. Just as he had suspected, he found the turtle lying upside down and struggling to right itself just below a bed of slippery rocks. Limbs flailed futilely, and the animal craned its neck backward trying to nudge the ground with the side of its face and head in order to rock back and over onto its feet.

"You're feeling just as helpless as I am at the moment, aren't you, fella?" With one deft movement, he flipped the turtle right side up. Blood oozed from a scrape on one side of its head and one eye was swollen shut as a result of the turtle's desperate bid to escape certain death.

Using one hand to hold the injured turtle by the shell, he scooped water from the river with his other hand and trickled the cool liquid over the animal's face to wash away the blood and soothe its injured eye. Satisfied that was all to be done, he sat the turtle under the shade of a clump of wild onions.

Rewarded for his efforts with several long scratches from the turtle's sharp nails, he trailed his hand in the water for a few moments. The turtle had been given a second chance, but he was the only one who could rescue himself from the mistakes he had made here in Sunrise.

Love, as troublesome as it might be, was also an emotion filled with great power, inspiring him to admit his mistakes and doing what he should have done the moment he learned Hiram Foster had been murdered.

He would learn the truth and see the real murderer brought to justice.

To his credit, he had made a feeble attempt today by organizing his thoughts and recording all the details to date on the cards he had displayed on the table for Jane. His efforts had unraveled in a way he had never anticipated.

He closed his eyes and brought her image to mind, reliving the moment she had refused to answer his questions about Hiram's fidelity or lack of it. She had struggled against the truth he had seen shining in the tears that filled her eyes, but she found it impossible to deny it by giving voice to a lie.

He could not imagine surviving a marriage as troubled as her marriage to Hiram apparently had been, or having the courage it would take to ever trust anyone enough to want to marry again. That issue aside, Daniel knew she would only remain silent or tolerate the possibility of lying in order to protect someone she loved.

He knew her well enough to suspect when he introduced the idea that someone else in Sunrise had committed the murder, she had only refused to answer him because she was protecting one person: her brother.

Taking his assumption one step further, Daniel drew a troubling conclusion: Hiram had been having an affair with Sam's wife, Polly, the brightest jewel in all of Sunrise.

What he saw was not a love triangle, but a love quadrangle filled with lust, betrayal, honor, and vengeance that someone like Mercury Pine would love to exploit.

Had Sam killed Hiram? Had Polly? Had they done it together? Or had Hiram indulged in other affairs, opening up a list of other possible suspects?

His heart began to pound with the certainty there was no "reluctant witness." Somewhere in this village skulked a murderer who was going to escape punishment by placing the blame on Jane unless Daniel acted quickly.

He turned away from the river, his grim expression softening only when he saw the turtle once again hunting for food. Instead of returning to Lily's cottage, he made his way to the road that led back to the village and a future he refused to relinquish without a fight.

He did not bother to waste any energy bemoaning yet another sleepless night.

He had not spent years perfecting his legal skills only

to forget them now, and he had not waited all of his life to find Jane, only to lose her forever.

Humming along to the melody that echoed in his mind and heart, he could only pray that his soft jewel would be as strong as a diamond while he was gone.

Chapter 18

Frustration and disappointment, longtime companions, normally supplied energy. Adding anger had created a synergy of powerful proportions, but Jane had used it well.

By the time she heard Aunt Nester mumbling her way up the staircase at the end of the business day, Hiram's bedchamber had been completely scrubbed and their quarters stripped of anything he had worn or collected in his travels.

Flushed from her efforts, Jane left the piles of his belongings temporarily stashed on the chair and settee in the parlor only long enough to open the door before tackling the mess again.

Her aunt entered the parlor, glanced about the room, and rocked back on her heels. She sniffed at the perfumed scent in the air and scowled at Jane. "Thought you were supposed to be restin'. And what's all this? Guess I won't be gettin' any rest relaxin' on the settee."

"Or anywhere else in here," Jane groaned as she hauled a deep wooden box closer to the lump of garments she needed to fold. "I set out some cold supper for you in the kitchen. If you need to rest a bit first, you can use the chair I moved into your room."

She arched her back and stretched sore muscles. "I need to get this done so George can cart it away first thing in the morning."

"Cart it away to where?"

"Anywhere. As long as it's gone. After what's happened, no one here would wear any of this." She picked up a black cashmere coat and folded it neatly before

placing it into the box. "He can take it all to Columbia.
It's closer than Lancaster. Whatever he can't sell, he can
give away. I don't ever want to see any of it again."

Her aunt snorted, walked over to the box, and rifled
through the pockets in the coat. When she pulled a coin
out, she shook her head. "I'll check and fold. You do
the packin'. No sense givin' money away."

She shrugged her shoulders. "I thought I'd give
George a share of the proceeds and turn over the rest
to Reverend Reilly."

"Charity best start right here since you haven't heard
back from Aaron yet."

While her aunt tackled pairs of winter undergarments, Jane folded and packed two pairs of leather
gloves and a collection of mufflers, content to let her
aunt's comment go unanswered. Charity had nothing
to do with her decision to strip her home of Hiram's
personal belongings and everything to do with easing
her troubled state of mind after Daniel had left.

She was ready and more than willing to banish everything connected to her husband, including any and all
memories of the life they had shared together. If she
had any other option to earn her livelihood, she would
gladly take it, lock the general store and toss away the
key so hard and fast it would land hundreds of miles
away in Aaron's lap, her inheritance, if any, be damned.

Unfortunately, she did not have that luxury. But she
could control her surroundings and eliminate all remnants of Hiram's existence, starting with her husband's
clothing, still scented with his cologne.

"What did Daniel say when you told him you were
gettin' rid of these?"

Jane's heart flip-flopped. "I didn't tell him. He's my
lawyer, not my guardian." Her cheeks warmed, and she
bent down to lay the mufflers atop the coat. She hoped
he was still willing to be her lawyer, although her heart
pounded with longing for him to fill a much different
role in her life.

"Thought this might be part of the estate, that's all.

What if Aaron decides he wants any of the clothes or expects the proceeds? You got enough trouble as it is. Wouldn't want you to land yourself in any more."

Jane let out a long sigh. Aunt Nester was absolutely right, although she had no idea how she had underestimated and understated Jane's position.

Accounting for Hiram's clothing or their proceeds fell at the bottom of a very long and complicated list she had mentally compiled since Daniel left several hours ago. Truth be told, she was far more concerned about Daniel, the accusations against her, and trying to argue against them without involving her brother than the technicalities of the law regarding the proper handling of Hiram's estate.

With her conscience pricked, Jane was nevertheless bound and determined to clear out Hiram's possessions by the morning and settled on a compromise, of sorts. She dismissed the thought she was doing something Daniel would find not only acceptable, but practical as well.

"I'll still have to pay George, but I'll set the rest aside until I hear from Aaron. He probably wouldn't fit into the clothes anyway." She attacked a lump of socks while her aunt started on a pile of trousers.

"I almost forgot that. Wonder if he's lost any weight." She chuckled. "Sure was a man with a wide girth. Had a big heart, too, just like his mother. For your sake, I hope he hasn't lost any of that," her aunt murmured. In one of the pockets of a pair of striped trousers, she found another coin and a handkerchief, which she added to the coin she had found in the coat.

Once again, Jane let her aunt's remarks go unanswered. They worked together, filled the first box, and started on another when her aunt pulled her hand out of a pocket of one of Hiram's frock coats. Dangling from her fingers was a tawdry red and purple lace garter.

Jane dropped her gaze for a moment, waiting to hear an acerbic comment. None came. From beneath her lashes, she saw her aunt slip the garter into her apron pocket without saying a word. The contempt on her face was so harsh, she would have cracked the mirror on the wall behind her had she glanced in that direction.

"Think I'll have my supper now," she announced as she wiped her hands on her skirts. "Be a dear and bring my platter here so I can keep you company."

Jane guessed her aunt's real intentions and loved her all the more for being so protective. "You'll be more comfortable in the kitchen," she suggested, hoping to search through the rest of the garments and complete the task her aunt had intended to do while Jane was in the kitchen.

"Not unless you join me."

Jane played twice as stubborn. "I've already eaten."

"Eat again."

"I'm too full." She dug her heels in deeper. Revealing Hiram's liaison with the red-haired woman to her aunt, which Jane had finally discussed after being pestered to death, had been hard. Finding evidence indicating he had been with other women while traveling went beyond embarrassing.

Her aunt shrugged her shoulders. "Then I'm not gonna eat. I'll wait till we're done. You'll be hungry by then."

Momentarily stonewalled, but not resigned to defeat, Jane opted for the only argument that had never failed her: the truth. "Aunt Nester, we both know Hiram—"

"Lord forgive me for speakin' ill of the dead, but that husband of yours was a scoundrel and a pitiful fool." Her aunt's eyes misted with tears. "Let me do this for you. It was my fault for not locking the back door to the store last week, and this time it was my stupid idea to hunt through his pockets. I never thought I'd find anything that would hurt you."

Her aunt swiped at tears, and her expression hardened. "He never wandered at home, or I'd have been forced to poison the man myself, if your brother didn't strangle him first."

Jane held her bottom lip with her teeth and swallowed the lump in her throat. She could not speak. She could not control her racing heartbeat. She could scarcely breathe, but she did find the wherewithal to nod and walk out of the room.

When she reached the kitchen, she said a grateful prayer Aunt Nester did not know about Polly. Her aunt's reaction to finding evidence of Hiram's additional infidelities and her assumption that Sam would have avenged Jane's honor only reinforced her determination to remain silent about the affair.

She set a kettle of water to boil and arranged two cups and saucers, a teapot, condiments, and napkins on a tray with her aunt's supper platter. By the time the tea was brewing, she was fairly certain her aunt had had enough time to complete the loathsome task.

When she reached the parlor, Aunt Nester was gone. Judging by the sundry, but less scandalous items her aunt had discovered and the garments lying askew with their pockets turned inside out, Jane assumed her aunt had finished. There was no sign of the garter or anything else she might have found.

Jane was still holding the tray when Aunt Nester came out of Hiram's old bedchamber, paused in the doorway, and frowned. "Afraid I lost my appetite. I'm just gonna lay down a spell. If you leave the clothes, I'll pack them up for you after I put my things away. It'll be nice to be able to use the chest of drawers and the wardrobe instead of living out of that old travel bag."

Straightening up, Jane tightened her fingers around the edge of the tray. "I'll finish up here. Would you like me to put the tray in your room in case you change your mind?"

"Just put it all back. My stomach is wamplin' somethin' fierce. If I get hungry later, I'll fix somethin'. Don't stay up too late."

"No, I won't," she promised. With her heart as heavy as the tray in her hands, she went back to the kitchen, sat the tray on the table, and went back to finish packing.

Far less fastidious than she had been earlier, she made quick work of folding and packing up the last of his garments. She put the trinkets he had collected into a small box. When she tried to move the boxes littering the parlor out to the landing, she realized they were now too heavy to move.

Content with knowing George would be able to carry the larger boxes away in the morning, she put the smaller one on the landing. She would have George put it in the storeroom and ask Aunt Nester to add the cache of goods she had found in Hiram's pockets. She hoped to dispose of the small box eventually in the trash pit behind her aunt's home where someone would not be able to find it.

With hours to fill before taking to her bed, Jane went downstairs in search of her ledger book. With two days of entries Aunt Nester had made to correct and Sam's books to reconcile, she had little doubt she could occupy her mind rather than waste time worrying about what she would say to Daniel if and when they met again to discuss the growing evidence against her.

The telegrams had finally been sent, but the knot still twisting in Daniel's stomach left no room for an appetite. Although he had not eaten since breakfast, he bypassed the tavern on the outskirts of Columbia, half the distance from Sunrise compared to Lancaster. The information and directions he had gotten from Louis had been accurate, although he was still glad he had the compass Jane had given him in case he took a wrong turn in the dark. He headed back to Lily's home, satisfied he had done all he could do.

For now.

Feeling every bit like a beleaguered general ordering seasoned replacements midway through a battle poorly waged with new recruits, he only hoped he had not waited too long. The analogy was a bit off-kilter since he had been acting alone so far, but he did have men he trusted and respected who would respond to his urgent calls for help.

He had employed Robert Ludlam for nearly a decade now, and there was not a finer investigator in the country. Half coonhound, he could almost follow a person's scent through water, and considering Foster's love for cologne, Daniel imagined Ludlam would be able to trace the deceased man's travels with his nose stuffed closed. Half man of the cloth, Ludlam could also get a hardened pickpocket to return his booty and apologize to his victims.

Another bad analogy. Daniel laughed out loud and nearly spooked his mount. He patted the horse's neck to calm him. Ludlam was already a convicted pickpocket when Daniel had represented him at his second trial, won an acquittal, and hired him all in the same day. Now gleaning information instead of wallets or jewelry, Ludlam was Daniel's self-appointed advisor and confidant. He was also the only man who could yank Daniel's conscience, if necessary, or set him straight if he veered off the track.

For legal assistance, Daniel had contacted his associate, Benjamin Hastings. His grasp of criminal law more than compensated for his lack of experience. At twenty-six, he was as intelligent and zealous as a . . . "Forget the analogy," he murmured out loud and chuckled softly this time, certain the prematurely gray, long-haired bachelor would not appreciate being compared to a sheepdog, although this analogy rang true.

The man could herd up obsolete statutes and court opinions, bark orders, yet keep witnesses happily in the flock and sense trouble in the jury box better than any lawyer Daniel had encountered in his career. He had hired him with one ulterior motive: He did not want Hastings working for opposing counsel.

Neither man would be arriving in Sunrise anytime soon, and Daniel had solved the lack of telegraph service there by paying the telegraph operator in Columbia a large sum to insure the man would make the four-hour round-trip journey to bring any telegrams the same day they arrived.

In the meantime, Ludlam would travel directly from Philadelphia to Baltimore while Hastings should arrive in Lancaster by Monday to engage a local lawyer as the final member of their team. While some might protest Daniel was acting prematurely since no formal charges had been filed against Jane, no one would argue the possibility was real.

He looked forward to spending the night in Lily's cottage rather than in Columbia as he had originally anticipated when he had left Sunrise just before sundown. While he hoped Jane would want to see him tomorrow, he was now prepared to wait for at least a few days. He had taken time today to do a lot of soul-searching, and he prayed she had done the same.

The turnpike was dark and deserted. The air was brisk and cool in this hour just shy of midnight, similar to the last time he had ridden back to Sunrise, only to find out later that Mercury Pine had been following him. This time, Daniel was more alert for signs and sounds of other travelers on the off chance he had been followed again.

With Pine long banished and no indication anyone else was about at this late hour, Daniel was confident he was riding alone. He was sorely relieved Pine was nowhere near Sunrise with the way the evidence was pointing toward Jane, and Pine's mockery of the ditty echoing once again in Daniel's mind was still vivid.

He did not sing the words aloud; instead, he hummed the melody to help ease the lonely ride and the ache in his heart. He slipped his hand into his coat pocket and wrapped his fingers around his compass. She would always be his jewel shining softly, and he let the compass slide back into the folds of his pocket, knowing his heart would lead the way back home to her.

Chapter 19

After a fitful sleep, Jane had convinced George to haul away every single box, after which she had scrubbed the floors and stored the smaller box filled with useless trinkets on the top shelf in the storeroom along with the items waiting to be given away.

Accompanied by Sam and Polly, Jane had even attended church service and survived only slightly scathed. Neither Ben nor Noah, or either of their wives, had attended. Some members of the congregation had greeted her with restrained smiles, others refused to meet her gaze. Worry about Aunt Nester, who pleaded no relief from her stomach disorder earlier, had kept Jane from dwelling on the very mixed reactions her presence in church had inspired from the congregation.

Sam and Polly's invitation to spend the day at their home taxed the little patience and energy she had left.

She politely, but adamantly refused. Ignoring her brother and his wife, she went straight to her desk and removed her cloak and bonnet. "The store is open this afternoon, and I won't ask Aunt Nester to get out of her sickbed so I can go visiting," she repeated.

"Close the store for today," Sam argued. "You don't need customers here gossiping or asking you questions. You saw what happened in church. I don't know why they bother to attend if they intend to spend the rest of their hours condemning you."

"I can't hide upstairs forever, and I'm not about to let anyone intimidate me, either. Sooner or later, we'll learn who's responsible for killing Hiram and trying to see I take the blame. In the meantime, I have a business to run. Speaking of which," she added to redirect the conversation, "I think you've put your own business on hold long enough on my account, don't you?"

He scowled at her and put his arm around Polly to draw her nearer to him. "We've both decided I should stay close to home. I don't want to leave Polly overnight, not with the scoundrel who skulked into my barn on the loose. I'll keep to the deliveries I can make in a single day for now."

Polly nodded, dabbing the corners of her eyes with a frilly handkerchief. "I don't want to be alone at night until . . . until it's safe again. Sam wanted me to go home and visit with my parents for a spell, but I'd only worry about him." She looked up at her husband with a tremulous smile. "I'd miss you too much if I left."

When he hugged her even closer, Jane dropped her gaze. The affection shining in Sam's eyes for Polly only added another layer of guilt to Jane's soul, and she turned her back to don the apron she had draped across the back of her chair. "Polly, why don't you go upstairs and see if Aunt Nester is feeling well enough to visit with you for the afternoon? I need Sam for a few minutes anyway to review his books."

"Go on," Sam urged. "If she's still feeling poorly, see if she'll take a cup of coffee."

"But no brandy," Jane cautioned, fully aware her aunt could bluster Polly into doing just about anything. "Make the coffee before you even ask her. If she argues too much, come and get me."

After Polly gave Sam a peck on the cheek, she went upstairs. For the next fifteen minutes, Jane and her brother sat head-to-head at the desk. "That's about it," she announced as she shut his account book. "It'll get a lot more complicated as your business grows."

He put his hand on her shoulder and squeezed gently. "Thanks, darlin'. I really appreciate your helping me."

She grinned and nudged him with her elbow. "That's what sisters are for." When she looked into his eyes, her smile faded. "I'm sorry you've been caught up in my troubles. I wish I wish I could keep people from—"

"Stop right there," he insisted. "I'm your brother. I don't know who killed Hiram or why, but I do know one thing for certain: You had nothing to do with his death." His eyes glistened, and he caressed her hands with his. "After Mother and Father died, you were there for me. Always. I want you to know I'm here for you now."

She turned her hands and laced her fingers with his. "This is different, Sam."

"No it's not. We'll get through this together." He smiled gently. "Sound familiar?"

She choked back tears and nodded. "Together," she whispered. This time, guilt showed no mercy and yanked hard at the secret she had stored deep in her soul. Hiding the truth from him was no better than living a lie—one that was festering and creating a gulf in the open, loving relationship they had always shared.

Only the proof she had found in her ledger book documenting Sam's week-long trip deep into York County at the time Hiram was in Lancaster gave her any solace, proving Sam could not have been involved in the murder if the affair ever came to light.

"Sam? Oh, Sam!" Polly rushed from the back of the store, looking like she had waged a battle in the kitchen and lost. Dark brown blotches stained her pale yellow skirts and gobs of something sticky oozed along the bottom of the lace hem, drizzling a trail behind her as she walked. The heart-shaped locket she wore was snagged on her bodice, forcing her to slump her shoulders to keep from breaking the thin, intricate chain around her neck.

"Help me! My necklace is going to snap and break," she cried. "I made the coffee first, just like you said. Then I knocked on her door. She wouldn't answer so I knocked again. That's when I tipped the tray and the coffee spilled, then I dropped the tray and the honey pot fell and broke and splattered . . . Oh, look at my gown," she wailed, finally dissolving into tears that ended her rambling.

Sam immediately rushed to his wife and looked over her shoulder as he fumbled with the locket. "I'll take care of Polly. Why don't you go upstairs and check on Aunt Nester?"

Only too happy to oblige, Jane hurried past them toward the back of the store and rushed through the foyer to the staircase. Careful to sidestep the trail of honey, she made it halfway to the landing when she heard the door below open. She looked back over her shoulder and gasped when she saw a woman emerge from behind the opened door and the shadow of a man behind her.

Jane swirled about faster than she had intended when her foot glided across a gob of honey. "Aunt Lily! What—" She grabbed at the banister and caught herself, but lost her hold and her footing in the next breath. More honey!

She pitched forward and squeezed her eyes shut as if not seeing her impending fall would prevent it. With petticoats and skirts tangled around her legs, she braced her arms in front of her and slammed hard against a solid force that kept her from hitting the floor.

Her eyes flew open, but with the air sucked out of her lungs, she could only stare at the chest of the man who had apparently lunged forward to save her. Familiar arms wrapped around her so tightly, she could scarcely move or draw a breath.

Her heart was pounding, almost as hard as his as they swayed precariously, and he held her against him as he fought to regain his balance. "Easy," Daniel cautioned when she tried to squirm free. "We've got one step separating us from disaster for sure."

He lifted her down to the floor and set her on her feet while he stayed one step above her and kept his hands on her shoulders until Aunt Lily rushed over and embraced her. "Jane? Are you all right? I never meant to frighten you into falling down the stairs. Poor darling. Daniel told me what's happened."

"I'm fine. On all counts," Jane managed between breaths. "It was the honey. I thought you were in France, and I was just so surprised to see you I forgot to look where I was going."

"Aunt Lily!" Sam's voice boomed in the foyer. "I thought you were in France!"

Her aunt grinned. "Daniel, I think I detect an echo. Why don't we all go upstairs so I can save time and talk to everyone together? Jane looks like she could use a few minutes to gather her wits."

That was such an understatement, Jane nearly collapsed. She would have if Daniel had not grabbed her shoulders to keep her upright while she battled her near fall and the far greater danger of being locked in his embrace.

Sam frowned. "What's the matter with you?"

"Your sister tripped down the steps," Daniel said. "Fortunately, she didn't fall far enough to get hurt."

When her brother eyed the steps, his frown deepened with guilt. "You slipped on the honey, didn't you?"

"It was my own fault," Jane insisted as she eased from Daniel's grasp. "I was so surprised to see Aunt Lily I was careless. We shouldn't use the steps until I've washed them down." She turned, saw the cleaning bucket and rags George had used earlier, and quickly retrieved them. "It'll only take a few minutes."

She paused as if struck by a thought she had left somewhere on the steps before she fell. "Aunt Nester! I was supposed to be checking on her."

"Nester?" Aunt Lily smiled. "She's perfectly fine. We visited at my house while you were all at church. She went to see Libby, but I'm sure she won't be long."

Jane narrowed her gaze. "I thought she was ill and resting upstairs."

"She's feeling much better."

Thoroughly puzzled, she shrugged her shoulders. Aunt Nester certainly did not need Jane's permission to leave or do anything else, but an odd feeling came over Jane. She quickly dismissed it as far less important than cleaning up the mess Polly had made.

"Why don't you take Aunt Lily into the store to visit with Polly? I'll have this done in no time."

Daniel and Sam reached for the bucket at the same time. Daniel was faster and grabbed it out of her hand. "I'll clean. You supervise while the rest of these folks have a reunion. I'll send for all of you when we're done."

Aunt Lily chuckled and linked arms with her nephew and guided him back into the store. "Don't even try to argue with him, Sam. Take me to your wife. I'm anxious to see her again."

Daniel removed his vest, went to hand it to Jane, and grinned. "Maybe I'd better put this in the storeroom for now."

"It's only my slippers that are sticky," she argued and wiped her hands on her skirts to make sure before she took his vest and glanced up the steps. "I'd really feel better if you'd let me do this." Actually, she would much prefer to see Polly on her hands and knees cleaning up the mess she had made, but chose not to invite a second disaster.

His grin deepened, and he kept the bucket out of her reach. "I insist. Top or bottom?"

Warm tingles shot from the top of her head and the bottom of her toes, colliding together in her heart. "Top," she murmured, wondering why her mind had suddenly turned to mush and her pulse was racing. "But be careful using the steps. It's hard to see the honey on the wood."

He sidestepped his way up the stairs and knelt down on the landing. After rolling up his sleeves, he started wiping the floor. "Satisfy my curiosity. How did you manage to traipse this honey all over without knowing it?"

She laughed softly, although the real question she asked herself was how he had slipped into her heart so easily without her realizing it sooner. When she told him what Polly had done and how she had reappeared in total disarray, he chuckled and quickly apologized.

"I'm sorry. I didn't mean to laugh. Polly just strikes me as a woman who'd be better off displayed on a shelf like a china doll. Pretty to look at, but not much else," he commented as he finished the landing and knelt back to survey his work. When he looked down at Jane, he frowned. "That wasn't very kind of me, was it?"

Although surprised by his candor and insight, she held back a chuckle. "No, but I probably shouldn't have told the tale so humorously, either. She's young yet, and Sam adores her. She'll come around. One of these days."

Daniel lowered the bucket to the third step and washed a section of the banister. "I gather she isn't from Sunrise. Where'd he meet her?"

Relieved he did not revert back to the questions he had posed yesterday, she smiled. "Columbia. Her father owns several warehouses there where Sam takes some of our shipments. Apparently, she's accustomed to an easier life, but Sam's young and hardworking. He'll build his business in no time so he can provide more for her."

"Spoken like a devoted sister. You're still very close to your brother, aren't you?"

Guilt tugged at her conscience again. "We'll always be close," she insisted, perhaps more to convince herself than Daniel. "It's a shame you never had a brother or a sister."

"Actually, I did," he murmured. "My younger brother, John, was only two when he died. I was only four or five so I don't really remember him. Since my parents never had any more children, I grew up pretty much surrounded by adults."

She dropped her gaze and found it hard to imagine growing up without Sam, or not having him with her after their parents died.

Fortunately, Daniel changed the topic back to the

present as he wiped his way further down the steps. "I'm surprised they didn't settle near her family."

Her hands tightened around his vest. "Sam wouldn't leave Sunrise. He inherited my parents' home, and there's been a Glennings living there for over a hundred years. Polly wasn't very thrilled, but she visits her family whenever Sam's going to be away for more than a few days."

"Tradition is hard to break, I suppose."

She nodded. "Sam might one day have a house in the city like Aunt Lily, but he'd never completely turn his back on Sunrise. His roots are here, and someday his children will grow up here."

Although Sam and Polly had never discussed the very personal matter of children with Jane, she was sure he wanted a large family. The children he would someday have with Polly would only be hurt if the affair with Hiram ever became public knowledge, yet another reason for Jane to keep her own counsel.

"Finished!" He had no sooner folded the cleaning rag over the lip of the bucket before he retrieved it again. "Off with the slippers, or you'll track more sticky stuff on my handiwork. I might as while wipe the floor where you're standing, too."

She wriggled her toes. Removing her slippers would not be enough, but she could hardly remove her stockings in front of him! She felt a blush crawling up her neck, threatening to reach her cheeks unless she did something. Quick. She tugged the rag out of his hand and handed his vest back to him. "I'll do the floor. While you get the others, I'll slip upstairs to change my . . . my slippers."

His lips twisted into a knowing grin. "Try not to do that. Slip, I mean. The stairs are still wet."

Ready to crawl up on her hands and knees before her cheeks burst into flames, she heaved a huge sigh of relief when he turned away and went back into the store. She tiptoed into the storeroom and shut the door before removing her stockings and slippers. They would not fit into her pockets, but she was too embarrassed to carry them with her. She shoved them behind a box on the bottom shelf and made quick work of wiping the floor before scampering upstairs in her bare feet.

Yet another sticky trail zigzagged across the parlor rug and an unholy mess greeted Jane in the hallway where Polly had left the overturned tray and its spilled contents. She was half tempted to turn around and lock the door till Polly arrived and tidied up the disaster she had left behind.

That event was as likely to happen as finding Jane's attraction for Daniel easy to control. She clenched her jaw and went to the kitchen to pump out another pail of water, deliberately avoiding a glance into the mirror.

With her hair coming undone and her feet bare, she felt every inch a common maid summoned again to clean up for a spoiled princess. "At least there's one man Polly hasn't managed to dazzle," she grumbled. The memory of those few minutes downstairs when he had made her feel as precious as royalty herself sweetened her mood immediately.

She had only filled half the bucket with water when she heard loud shouts muffled by the distinctive thunder of horses galloping close enough to the general store to make the dishes displayed in a corner cupboard rattle.

Before she could draw another breath, the sound of shattering glass and shrill screams pierced the air. Alarm sent the bucket flying, her feet racing downstairs, and her heart pumping so fast she expected it to burst.

Chapter 20

Horror magnified Jane's fear when she burst into the general store and slammed straight into devastation so unexpected she could scarcely believe her eyes.

Shattered glass from the two display windows and the glass inset in the front door, along with half a dozen large rocks, littered the front of the store. The lamp on her desk had been upended, its globe smashed beyond repair. Whoever had thrown the rocks had even hit some shelves and knocked stock to the floor.

Polly wept uncontrollably in Sam's arms near a side counter, both apparently shaken but unhurt. Her heart pounding, she raced straight to Aunt Lily and Aunt Nester. Pale and trembling, they were seated together near the warming stove, and Daniel had crouched down with his hands braced on either side of them. His shoulders and vest glistened with crystal shards, testimony to the protection he must have given to both women.

"Are you hurt? What happened? Who did this?" Jane gushed. Standing next to Daniel, she frantically searched for any visible signs either of her aunts being hurt by flying glass or of other debris and saw nothing but an odd combination of fear and relief etched on their faces.

Aunt Lily managed only a wan smile, but Aunt Nester's eyes flashed with anger. "We're fine, thanks to Daniel. Ornery fools! If I get my hands on the scoundrels who threw those rocks—"

"Everyone here all right?" Cousin Louis rushed into the store, setting off the bell and startling Jane and her aunts as well. Sweat poured down his reddened face. "I tore after those two when they left the tavern, but I couldn't find them. When I finally did, I couldn't catch up to them or get here to warn you. Blast it all! They should have gone to services with their wives. Came in half soused and got all riled up over nothing but scurrilous gossip!"

When Daniel stood up and flexed his shoulders, shards of glass dropped to the floor, but Jane was more concerned with the abrasion just above his right eye with blood trickling from several small cuts.

"It's not bad. Caught a rock," he said and accepted her handkerchief to press against his wound before addressing her cousin. "Who were they?"

"Jack and Willy Coombs. Hiram's cousins," he spat. "Held court, convicted Jane, and then mounted up with some friends to ride for justice, so they claimed."

Jane shuddered with outrage. "Justice? This is vicious vigilantism! Someone could have been badly hurt. And I can't afford to pay for new windows and fix the door. Just look at my store!" Simmering just below her anger, fear sent alarm trickling up and down her spine.

Reaction to the anonymous notes and the discovery of the pocket watch and missing funds ran far deeper than the disapproving glances she had received earlier in church. Jack and Willy had tried to intimidate her before with talk of engaging a lawyer. Now she was completely shocked they had turned to violence that now truly threatened her family as well as her business.

Louis's face flushed deeper red, and he dropped his gaze. "I'm sorry. I tried to get here to warn you, but they had horses and got here ahead of me. When I saw them throw the rocks . . ."

She apologized quickly. "I didn't mean to make it sound like it was your fault." She pressed her fingertips to her temple and sighed. "I'm just upset."

"Upset?" Sam strode forward, his arm gripped protectively around his pale but silent wife. "You should be outraged! Since Louis saw it happen, you can file charges against Jack and Willy, to name two, and make them pay for the damages. Isn't that right, Daniel?"

When he nodded, he winced. He removed the handkerchief and gingerly touched the bruising over his eye, and she was glad to see the bleeding had stopped. "How likely is it they'd have the funds to make restitution?"

Aunt Nester snorted. "Neither one scratches enough from the land to feed their families. 'Course they always seem to have enough for hard liquor."

Relief that no one had been hurt cooled her anger, and Jane shook her head. "I don't want to file charges. If they were addled, they didn't really know what they were doing. I'm sure some of Hiram's other relatives are upset, but they aren't resorting to violence. I don't want to antagonize them by involving the law. Besides, Noah's not even here."

"You don't have to file charges against them today," Sam argued. "If you let them get away with this, they'll come back and do even more damage. And who's to stop them? You? Aunt Nester?"

His expression tightened. "You two shouldn't be here alone. It's too dangerous, and it won't get any safer until they find out who killed Hiram. You have to close the store and move in with us. Aunt Nester can go home with Thomas, at least until everything settles down."

"I can't do that," she protested. "People need supplies. They need to barter their goods. What they don't need is for me to let a pair of drunken fools frighten me out of business. I've fought too hard and too long . . ."

Emotion choked the rest of her argument and unshed tears of anger and frustration blurred her vision. When would the legacy of shame and suspicion Hiram had left behind end? How long would she be able to survive here in Sunrise if the villagers turned against her? They had known her for years, trusted her, respected her for always being fair and honest. Why were they so quick to judge her guilty now? Had Hiram stolen the last precious thing she had left—her very existence in Sunrise?

She looked to her family for support, only to meet with disappointment.

"Sam's right. You have to close the store," Aunt Nester urged.

Aunt Lily nodded sadly.

Daniel's expression remained grim, but he remained silent and did not argue to support her.

"Go upstairs and pack a few things. You're moving in with us," Sam repeated, sterner than the first time. "I'll take Aunt Nester home when you're ready to leave."

"Move in with me, Nester," Aunt Lily suggested. "I still have a spare room, even with Daniel visiting."

Aunt Nester tilted up her chin. "Thank you, anyway. I have two rooms at home. I'm goin' up now to pack my things. Just got 'em put into the drawers, too. Pity," she grumbled as she got to her feet.

"Then I'll help you pack, and we'll take Polly with us, too," Lily said.

Jane gasped. "You're . . . you're both agreeing with Sam?"

"He makes sense. You don't." Aunt Nester huffed. "Sometimes a woman just gets too emotional to think straight." She glanced at Jane's feet and smirked. "Kinda like runnin' barefoot over glass. Sit down and make sure you didn't slice open the bottoms of your feet before you walk back upstairs to pack for yourself," she suggested before she and her sister left, escorting Polly along with them. Louis mumbled his own excuse for leaving and scrambled out of the store.

Too stunned to speak or understand why she had been abandoned by her aunts as well as her cousin, Jane looked down at her feet and groaned. She had rushed down to the store so quickly she had completely forgotten to put on a new pair of slippers. She sat down, ran her fingers over her bare feet, and smiled weakly when she saw several large slivers of glass only inches away from where she had been standing. "No damage done," she offered to the two men staring at her.

"Which is more than we can say for your store." Sam crossed his arms over his chest and shook his head. "You were lucky this time. We all were. I don't want there to be a next time. Just once, try to listen to reason."

Her mind reeled, but she could not make room for reason while horror and anger battled for dominance, and disappointment filled the little space that remained.

Sitting down made her feel like a child being reprimanded, so she quickly remedied that as best she could. Carefully avoiding the glass on the floor, she stood up, although his greater height and bulk still gave him the advantage. "I'll agree with you that Aunt Nester should go home. I don't want her hurt or upset like this again."

He scowled. "But. That's what's coming next, isn't it? You think you're staying here? Alone? Think again."

"I have thought about it."

"For all of two minutes!"

No. For almost a lifetime.

She caught herself before she uttered the words out loud. Anger was a volatile, hard-to-control emotion, but it had its finer points, too. She could let anger destroy her, or use it to her advantage. The choice was hers to make, but she really had no choice at all.

She turned her anger inward and let it sweep away fears that had trapped her far too long. She had earned the right to make her own decisions and refused to let anyone, especially her own brother, rescind that right ever again.

She gazed, instead, at Daniel, but the deep concern etching his sober features gave her little hope he would support her now against her brother. She counted on him to be faithful to his duties as her lawyer to bring him to her way of thinking. "You're the executor temporarily responsible for Hiram's estate. Do you think the courts will perceive this single act of vandalism as sufficient to close the store when you submit an accounting? Aren't you supposed to represent the interests of the creditors as well as all the heirs?"

His eyes lit with surprise before they shuttered any further emotion. His grim expression disappeared behind professional detachment, and she could almost see him mentally shifting roles, from friend and protector to professional advisor.

Sensing she had touched the right nerve, she pressed her case. "Submitting expenses to make necessary repairs and perhaps instituting precautions would also demonstrate your commitment to be fair and equitable to all the heirs."

The corners of his lips twitched, but he set them in a firm line, and she wondered if he had been going to smile or frown. "I assume you have some suggestions to offer," he said.

She took a deep breath, grateful he had not rejected her idea outright. "You'll need to repair everything whether the store stays open or not. Replacing the broken window glass with wood and installing a new door, one with glass panes high along the top this time, would also make it safer to operate the store, at least temporarily," she added to allow for some sort of compromise.

Her brother snorted. "Not if they take a shotgun to the storefront or set it on fire. No, it's still too risky. The store stays closed, and you're leaving with me now."

"I doubt violence will escalate to that level, Sam. And Jane has a point," Daniel argued. "She's also a sensible woman who has a deep commitment to her friends and neighbors. She has a right to reopen."

She caught her breath, and her heart swelled with more gratitude, along with her respect and admiration that only deepened her love for him.

"She can't give in to violence," Daniel continued. "Once she does, she becomes a victim, which only invites more harassment. The store should reopen, but not without a few changes. Along with the necessary repairs, I'd like new locks on the doors, just in case someone has a duplicate key for the old ones. During the day, I'd think Jane would be safe enough, especially if you were able to be here. If anything like this happens again, though, I'd agree with you and close the store until the sheriff's investigation is completed."

She exhaled slowly and accepted his compromise as reasonable and fair to all concerned. She prayed Sam would listen to Daniel, whose words about her echoed back and challenged her to take a deeper look at her life for the last five years.

She did not like what she saw in her mind's eye. First, a long-suffering, but dutiful wife, then a poor widow—victimized by a husband thoughtless enough to die without a will and a cruel tormentor who had unleashed outrageous and scandalous accusations that she was a murderer.

What had happened to the woman who had fought, day after day, to make a home for herself and Sam after their parents died? Had she been forever destroyed, or did the courage and fortitude she once possessed still exist, dormant for far too long?

She swallowed hard.

Inspired by Daniel's faith in her, she admitted to her mistakes, set them aside, and reclaimed control of her fate.

Once again confident of vindication when, not if, the real criminals were apprehended and her innocence was proven to those who doubted her, she also realized she could not do it alone. She needed Daniel's experience and guidance, and he needed to know the truth.

She had been wrong not to trust him. The splinter of guilt festering in her soul for keeping Polly's affair from Sam remained, and she would lance it with one concession: She would have to tell Daniel so he could defend her and her brother should the need arise. Lying to Daniel was not fair—to any of them—but she would have to make very sure he understood she expected his total and unconditional confidence.

She took a deep breath and gazed directly into her brother's dark eyes. "I love you for trying to protect me, but after I get some fresh water to clean up Daniel's cuts, I'm going to find a pair of heavy boots and some gloves so I can clean up the store. If you and Louis could fix the storefront this afternoon, I could reopen tomorrow, and I'd welcome your help during the day. If you really care about me, you'll see I'm doing what's right for everyone. Please don't argue with me, Sam. You never win anyway," she added with a smile, hoping to influence him as easily she had always done in the past.

With a reluctant smile, he dropped his arms to his side and shook his head. "You win. The store reopens, but if there are any more problems, the store closes. Agreed?"

Her sigh of relief released the huge bubble of pressure in her chest. "Agreed. Thank you, Sam."

He cocked his head and grinned at her. "I'll be sure to remind you this was all your idea," he warned. "I don't suppose you'd like one final opportunity to reconsider or talk this over with Daniel again?"

She grinned back at him and noted Daniel's surprised expression out of the corner of her eye. "Not a chance."

"I'll remind you of that, too, but right now I'm going upstairs to get Polly. We'll be back in an hour." He turned and walked toward the back of the store.

An alarm bell in her mind sounded off so loudly she thought Sam and Daniel might both have heard it. "Let Polly stay home and rest," she called after him. "She's been badly frightened, and I don't want her to get hurt cleaning up the glass."

He looked back over his shoulder. "I'll help you do that while Polly's upstairs unpacking."

She caught her breath, too shocked by the idea that exploded in her mind to keep from stammering out a single word. "Un-unpacking?"

He chuckled and turned around to face her. "You'll be open tomorrow, but you only won half the argument." When she frowned, he shrugged his shoulders. "You didn't really think I'd let you stay here alone at night, did you? By suppertime, we'll be all moved in."

When she scowled at him, he laughed. "There's no need to say 'thank you' again. All you have to do while we're gone is decide which room you want us to take." He turned around and disappeared into the foyer before she could think of a retort.

Flabbergasted, she squeezed her eyes shut and flexed her hands, determined to dig a hole for a basement and move her things there before he got back.

After struggling like a fish who had swallowed the hook along with the bait, Jane had little choice but to relent graciously when Sam returned with his wife. Apparently not satisfied with vandalizing the store, the vigilante posse of cowards had ridden to Sam's and broken every single window in the house.

She had never seen Sam so furious. Even Polly had surprised her. Instead of taking to her bed or pleading to escape to the safety of her parents' home, she had also been energized by adversity. She worked as hard and as efficiently as everyone else to clean up the store, a change Jane found utterly remarkable.

By eight o'clock that night, Sam and Polly had settled into Jane's room, half again the size of Hiram's former room where Jane had stored her own things. With help from some of the villagers who had been as shocked and outraged as Jane and her family, the store was ready to open in the morning and Sam's home had been boarded up.

With a new respect for herself and the power of anger properly channeled to reunify her family, Jane was ready to tackle the last item on her unwritten agenda. She was halfway out the parlor door when Sam spied her leaving.

"Hold it right there."

She let out a sigh and turned around, but kept her hand on the door latch.

He caught up to her with a quizzical expression on

his face. "Where do you think you're going at this hour?"

"To a meeting with Daniel, and if I don't hurry, I'll be late."

"Why isn't he coming here?"

"Because we need to talk privately. He's my lawyer, remember?"

"He doesn't know you're coming, does he?"

She flinched and dropped her gaze, unable to give voice to a lie.

"I knew it. Daniel wouldn't ask you to travel around in the dark to come to Aunt Lily's for a meeting. He'd come here, where you'd have all the privacy you'd need downstairs."

Refusing to let her brother deflate her newfound confidence or restrict her freedom, she met his gaze and stood her ground. "I'm not a child. I'm a thirty-two-year-old widow, Sam. I've buried my husband, who left me tottering on the threshold of economic disaster because he didn't take the time to draft a will. I'm trying to withstand public suspicion and gossip, not to mention anonymous notes, evidence planted against me and malicious vandalism, because a few people can't or won't be satisfied waiting for the real criminal to be caught."

She paused to take a short breath. "I'm also trying to do my best to cooperate with my lawyer to make sure I'm not charged with a crime I didn't commit. Given all that, do you honestly expect me to be afraid of walking less than a mile in the dark?"

He opened his mouth to reply, apparently thought better of it, and took a deep breath instead. "I'm sorry. I just don't want anything to happen to you," he murmured.

"Neither do I. That's why I have to see Daniel tonight. We should have met earlier today, but with everything that happened, I have to meet with him now. If it'll make you feel any better, I'm sure he wouldn't mind walking me home, and I'll wake you to let you know I'm back."

"I wish I could take you there, but I don't want to leave Polly here alone."

She smiled and reached up on tiptoe to peck his cheek. "Your place is here. I won't be that long."

"I'll wait up. If you're not back in an hour—"

"Entertain your wife by reading a book with a happy ending together, but if you dare come after me, Samuel Alexander Glennings . . ."

"All right. All right. You win, but try not to be too late. We have a store to open in the morning. And make sure you lock the door behind you. Did you remember your new key?"

Grinning, she held up the key to the new lock Daniel had recommended and slipped out the door before Sam could pose another argument. Once she was outside, she inhaled the distinctive scent of spring in the warm, still night air. While she made her way around the store to the main road, she heard the distant rumble of thunder and froze still.

Another rumble. Her heart started to pound, but she forced herself to concentrate, counting the seconds until the next heavy roll of thunder threatened a storm coming. Judging a distance of several miles away, she started forward again, but quickened her steps. If she hurried, she could make it to Aunt Lily's house long before the storm arrived.

Nearly running now, she followed the curve in the roadbed, but she could not race ahead of the still-awful memories of the sudden spring storm that had claimed her parents' lives on a night just like this one.

A bolt of lightning crackled and split the darkened sky with blinding light that illuminated her way and rekindled the vision of her parents' charred bodies she had stored away so long ago.

She ran faster, panting for breath. She held her hand against the stitch in her side and lifted her skirts with the other. With the next ferocious bolt of lightning, she saw the lane leading to the cottage just ahead.

Spurred on by a burst of energy and propelled by pure, unadulterated fear, she tore up the lane. Heavy rain and hailstones the size of marbles pelted her, stinging her face and drenching her wind-tangled cloak. She lowered her head to let her bonnet bear the force of the storm and held her cloak closed as she plowed forward.

Through vision blurred by the downpour, she could see the front door now. Light poured out the curtainless front window only a few hundred feet away, and she could see Daniel seated in front of a fire.

"No-o-o-o!" she cried as her feet slid out from under her and she sprawled forward, landing on her knees in the mud. With the air knocked out of her lungs, she gasped to take a breath as the storm intensified, celebrating the opportunity to claim yet another member of her family.

Heavier rain. More hail. Thunder. The ground shook beneath her legs. Lightning exploded directly overhead now. A loud pop and the smell of burning wood was just behind her. Ahead: safety.

If she had the courage to reach for it.

She gulped for air, paralyzed by terrifying fears, old and new, but kept her gaze riveted on Daniel. The words she had used to help him battle his fear of ladders yesterday sprang to her lips.

"Take a deep breath, close your eyes, and take one rung at a time." She rose to her feet before doubt could intervene. Substituting careful steps through slippery mud for rungs on a ladder, she kept her gaze locked on Daniel's face and form and moved forward.

When she reached the front door, she leaned against it and pounded hard, completely oblivious to the dark figure who had been following her and stood hidden in a copse of trees, observing her even now.

Chapter 21

Lost in thought, Daniel was only vaguely aware of the storm battering the cottage. The sound of heavy banging eventually roused him, and he looked up to see rain sheeting against the front window. Immediately suspecting a loose shutter as the source of the persistent noise, he was halfway to the window when he realized someone was banging on the door.

Fear that Lily had gotten caught in the storm as she returned from supper with Nester and her family inspired a muttered oath as he unbolted the door and swung it open.

Jane immediately stumbled through the doorway so quickly he had no time to move out of her way. When they collided, he grabbed her around the waist and braced his legs to keep them both from falling. One-handed, he fought to close the door against the powerful winds that blew cold rain inside.

Panting heavily, she was shaking so hard he expected to find half her bones shattered. He pulled her close, his heart beating as frantically as hers pounded against his chest. "You're safe now," he crooned, stroking her quaking back to calm the demons of fear that had propelled her into his arms.

"Why on earth did you venture out into this storm?" he asked, attempting to distract her and keep her from dwelling on her frightening experience.

Her hands gripped his shoulders so hard the tips of her nails dug into his flesh. "Y-you said I sh-should tell you when . . . when we c-could talk," she stammered.

He could not tell if she was still trembling from fear

or the cold, drenched bonnet and mud-covered cloak she wore. Regret for his challenge to her yesterday collided with dangerous sensations coursing through his body. The added pressure of her breasts crushed against his chest inspired a low moan he caught before it reached his lips. With all of his sensations already magnified, he closed his eyes and savored the feel of her in his arms and the musky scent of spring rain that engulfed them both.

Physical longing joined forces with emotional need so strong he could only draw one deep, ragged breath at a time. He had spent hours in front of the fire reliving the entire day, over and over again in his mind, torn between his conflicting roles as her lawyer and the man who loved her with all his heart.

He had no inner struggle now.

Not when he had the rare opportunity to hold her in his arms.

Believing for only a moment he could be both her lawyer and her beloved, he comforted her with loving touches and soft words, and his spirit unleashed a torrent of emotions. Love was the greatest and most powerful, erasing every single one of his reservations and suspending, for one incredibly blessed moment, all of his newly made vows to distance himself until he had fulfilled his professional duties to her.

He loved her dearly, this amazing woman whose courage today had revealed yet another facet of the goodness in her heart, which had captured his own.

In that very hallowed moment, he listened to his heart rejoice and knew she loved him, too.

Awed by the sheer magnitude of this overwhelming truth, his spirit nearly exploded with joy. He closed his eyes and felt her heart beating against his chest. If he had the power, he would fly her far away from here on wings of pure and perfect love to protect her forever.

It was a dream and a fantasy, but he embraced it knowing full well she could never leave Sunrise until he cleared her name and proved her innocence.

Only her uncommon courage and her faith in him gave him the strength to accept his role as her legal defender until he had the right to claim more.

Heart to heart, soul to soul, they stood together, bathed in soft fireglow. No tender words were spoken now. No vows were made. Yet for several wondrous, long heartbeats, they were joined as one in spirit, their hearts united forever by love.

The glory of physical union was a siren call, luring each of them to rocky shoals neither was yet prepared to cross, but the promise of fulfillment was powerful and relentless.

One incredible heartbeat after another, Jane clung to him. Locked in his arms, she felt as though she had plunged deep into the calm eye of the storm that raged outside, threatening everything else in the universe. Except for them.

Her mind reeled with the wondrous discovery that flooded her heart and spirit. He loved her. He loved her! She could feel it in the gentle touch of his hands as they stroked her back, in the power of his crushing embrace. She had heard it in the soft timbre of his voice only moments ago when he had murmured words to comfort her fears.

She had no fear now, only tremendous joy. Before reality intervened, she basked in his love, returning it in equal measure, savoring the joy and storing this moment in her heart until one day, she prayed, they would be able to openly declare their love for one another.

If that day never came, if they were never to know the full wonder of sharing each day together as husband and wife, she would always have this moment to sustain her dreams, reminding her that she had found true love, once upon a stormy night when nothing else mattered except for the two of them.

The storm outside abated. An eerie silence, broken only by the sound of their labored breathing, filled the room, supplanting the magical moment that had forever banished her fear of storms.

From this day forward, she would never again hear the crackle of lightning or the rumble of thunder without reliving the only moment in her life when she had so completely loved a man and been loved just as deeply in return.

Reluctant to have this moment end, she did not resist when he set her back from him. She toyed with the soggy ribbon tied beneath her chin as doubt filtered into her mind and heart. Had she imagined what had just occurred between them?

She glanced up at him, but found only concern gazing back at her. "You're going to catch cold. You're drenched," he chastised gently. "I'll be right back. I need to get you a quilt."

When Daniel disappeared into another room, she quickly removed her cloak and bonnet and placed them in front of the fire to dry. Fortunately, her gown was relatively dry, except along the hem. Her slippers, however, were a soggy, muddy mess. She eased them off and laid them along the edge of the hearth.

He returned moments later with a heavy quilt that had belonged to her mother, lined the seat of her grandmother's rocking chair, and pulled it closer to the fire. "Sit here and get warm while I get you something to drink."

She scooted into the rocker and tucked her stockinged feet beneath her before wrapping herself in the quilt. When he came back and handed her a small snifter of brandy, she wrinkled her nose.

"Just take a few sips," he urged. "I'll be right back."

He left the room again. When he returned this time, he had changed into different clothes, and she realized she must have soaked him when she had barged into him earlier. She cradled the untouched glass of brandy in her hands and dropped her gaze. "I'm sorry. I didn't mean to carry the storm in with me. Has Aunt Lily already gone to bed?"

"She's still at her sister's. I assume she's been delayed by the storm," he said as he angled a chair next to her so when he sat down, he was to her right and close to the fire, too.

Anxious about being alone with him, she snuggled in her bulky cocoon and let the fire warm her face. "I didn't realize how quickly the storm would hit, or I would have waited till tomorrow," she offered, wondering how to broach a topic bound to be awkward for both of them.

"I'm glad you reconsidered, especially after what happened at the store today."

His words were softly spoken and nonjudgmental. His expression was concerned, yet completely professional. "I should tell you first what I've set in motion on your behalf."

She listened carefully as he outlined the team of men he had organized, particularly impressed at how quickly and efficiently he had acted even though she had not been cooperative with him yesterday. Her decision to speak to him honestly tonight was reinforced by his commitment to help her and her trust in him was heartened by how he had kept his promise to keep her informed of his efforts on her behalf. Yet she still found it difficult to begin.

Her life had been virtually snatched away from her, and every aspect would be recorded or investigated, creating page after page in a book without any clue how this chapter of her life would end. He made it even harder when he smiled, and she relied on simple honesty as a starting point. "I'm not sure I know how or where to begin."

"Coming here took a lot of courage, even discounting the storm. Would it help if I posed a few questions?"

She nodded and took a sip of brandy, letting the fiery liquid send warmth coursing through her chilled body.

"In Lancaster when you were told about the woman who had been seen with your husband, was that the first time you learned he had been unfaithful to you?"

Her pulse began to race, and her eyes misted with

tears. She wrapped her hands around the glass of brandy as her mind focused on the painful memories she had kept hidden from the world. Hiram had been an adulterer, but he had betrayed her in spirit from the day he had proposed, breaking his promises to love and cherish her long before he had broken his vow to be faithful to her.

Yearning to bring the years of loneliness and disappointment to an end, she could feel the truth buried deep in her soul struggling to be set free. She closed her eyes long enough to take a single deep breath for courage, but she could feel Daniel's gaze caressing her with his spirit. With only the sound of the crackling fire to disturb the silence in the room, she took even breaths of air.

Admitting to the truth hurt more than she had expected, but her pain was for her brother, not herself. She could no more change the truth about what Hiram had done or the nature of their marriage any more than she could relive or erase the past five years of her life.

If she had any chance for a better future, it lay in facing the past, without pretension and without assessing blame, and moving forward, hopefully made stronger and wiser by her experiences. She could only pray Sam would be able to do the same if he ever learned the truth about his wife.

"No. It wasn't the first time," she whispered in a voice hoarse with emotions she could hardly control.

"Do you suspect he was unfaithful to you when he traveled prior to his last trip?"

She moistened her lips. "Perhaps." When the vision of the red and puple garter flashed through her mind, she amended her answer. "I had never really thought it might be true until yesterday."

She quickly detailed how she and Aunt Nester had gone through Hiram's clothing and her aunt's attempt to spare Jane by going through his pockets alone. He listened, but gave no indication of his feelings about what she was saying until she had finished.

"That must have been terribly hard for you to discover."

She sat her glass down and slid her feet to the floor before she started to rock. "It's one thing to have suspicions. It's quite another to find mementos . . . Aunt Nester has them now."

He did not comment and moved directly to another question. "I know Hiram traveled extensively, but I wonder if you could think back and make a list of his trips with dates and locations."

"A list?" His question surprised her, but she trusted he had good reason to ask for such a list. "I could try. It would be easier if I had the old set of ledger books. I still don't understand what happened to them."

He shrugged his shoulders. "We may never know," he admitted. "Could you make the list?"

"It might take a little time, and I can't guarantee it will be completely accurate." Her mind was already rearranging bits and pieces into order when she remembered the box she had put in the storeroom. "I do have a small box of trinkets he collected on his travels. They would help me recall the places he visited, but the dates . . ."

When she glanced at him, he smiled encouragingly. "I wouldn't ask you to do this if it wasn't important."

She looked away and tugged the sagging quilt back up over her shoulders. Finding the rhythmic, rocking motion soothing, she continued. "Is there anything else?" she asked, anxious to get the whole truth out and be done with it.

"Did your husband have an affair here in Sunrise with Polly?"

Her heart almost leaped out of her chest. She rocked forward and braced her feet on the floor before she locked her gaze with his. "How did you—When did you—Why—" She was too shocked to frame a full question. Fully frustrated, she gave up and pulled the quilt tighter around her body until she could think straighter. "How did you know?"

"When you didn't answer my last question about Hiram's infidelity yesterday, it wasn't hard to imagine why you couldn't. Sam is the only person you would try to protect. From there, I simply made the logical deduction that you had somehow discovered your husband was having an affair with Sam's wife." He paused and softened his voice. "Your brother doesn't know, does he?"

Her eyes widened, her fingers gripped the edge of the quilt, and her heart raced even faster. "No. He mustn't ever know! The affair is obviously over, there's nothing to be gained by telling him now. You told me anything we discussed would be confidential. You can't tell him. You can't tell anyone. No one else knows, but me!"

His gaze hardened. "Your Aunt Nester suspects as much."

"That's impossible," she snapped. "She would have come to me before now. She would have told Sam—"

"She came to me."

"You?" Chills ran through her body. "She came to you? I don't believe you."

He took something out of his pocket and held it up for her to see, but kept it beyond her reach. She stared at the distinctive tortoiseshell hair ornament and recognized it immediately as Polly's.

"She brought this to me this morning while you were all at church, along with the other items she found in the pockets of his clothing. She didn't want you to know, or Sam for that matter, but she thought it might be important. She was right."

He slid the hair ornament back into his pocket. "She's worried, and she has every right to be. The hair ornament only invites conjecture and doesn't constitute proof of the affair beyond the fact that your husband liked to hoard mementos from his conquests. If you knew about the affair, that's a good enough motive as far as the sheriff will be concerned. How long had the affair been going on? When did you know? How?"

He paused and the expression in his eyes softened

with compassion. "These are hard questions you may
have to answer for the sheriff one day, but I wouldn't
be doing my job if I didn't pose them to you now."

She tilted her chin and held on to her dignity with
all the strength she possessed. "A week before Hiram
left, I found him with Polly. I don't know if it was the
last time they were . . . together. It certainly wasn't the
first."

Oddly enough, her words were softly spoken, even
to her own ears. Describing the awful scene that had
played over and over in her mind was akin to discussing
a repetitive nightmare once daylight had broken.

"You're positive they were . . . physically intimate?
They weren't just talking privately?"

She could not honey-coat the scene she had witnessed
if she tried, but cutting through the sordid details made
it palatable. "They were making love in the . . . the dining room of my brother's home," she whispered.

She closed her eyes and bowed her head. The few
words she had overheard echoed back from that fateful
day. She blocked them out with words of her own.
"Sam was away just for overnight. Hiram told me he
would be in Lancaster overnight. It had been unbeara-
bly warm all day, so after I closed the store I decided
to take advantage of the cooler evening air. Mrs. Singletary had brought several pies to the store. Peach, as
I recall."

She paused, mired in small details that were pro-
longing her explanation. She cleared her throat before
resuming. "I wrapped up two pies and delivered one to
Aunt Nester and her family. After a short visit, I used
the shortcut through the woods to get to Sam's house.
I-I felt sorry for Polly. She was alone so much. That's
when I found them. Together."

"They didn't hear you coming or notice your presence?"

She shook her head, wishing with all her heart they
had. "The back door was open. When she didn't answer
my knock, I slipped into the kitchen to put the pie

someplace safe. That's when I heard their voices, and I knew Polly was far too busy with my husband to be lonely for her own. I was hurt and angry. The door to the dining room was open just a crack, just enough to see them together like that. I had to leave. I was afraid I was going to be physically ill, right then and there. I ran into the woods, tossed away the pie, lost my supper, and ran home."

Trembling, she rocked faster and caught her lower lip with her teeth.

He gave her a few minutes to collect herself before he continued. "Did you confront either of them later?"

"No. I was too ashamed. And too hurt. Polly is my brother's wife! I knew I had to do something—at least talk to Hiram—but I couldn't find the right words until the day before he was scheduled to leave on his trip. He promised we would have time together that night, but then he altered his plans and left that night, claiming he had no time for me. I was upset, but knew nothing would happen while he was gone, so I was just waiting for him to come back to confront him."

"What about Polly? Or your brother?"

"I couldn't," she argued. "She would only deny it, and Hiram wasn't here to take his share of the blame. I thought if I could force Hiram to end the affair when he came home, Sam would never have to know. I still don't want him to know."

"Are you sure you have that right? He's not a child anymore. He's a married man whose wife has betrayed him."

His question went straight to the splinter of guilt festering in her soul, nudged it, and sent shards of pain shooting through her body. She stilled the rocker and challenged him with a warning look. "I can't tell him. Not now. Now when they haven't found Hiram's murderer, and neither can you."

His gaze never wavered. "What if your silence is protecting the murderer? What if Hiram came back in January to see Polly instead of you? What if she's trying to put the blame on you?"

"Polly?" She rolled her eyes. She dismissed his accusations as ludicrous, although she herself had considered Polly a suspect. For all of ten seconds. "Polly wouldn't have any reason to do that. You've met her. She's a flighty, vain woman without a lick of common sense or backbone. Can you honestly say you can envision her poisoning Hiram, following him until he dropped dead, and then burying his body under a mound of rocks? In the middle of the night?"

She was rattling off her words so fast she nearly forgot to take a breath. "If he did stop to see her, he would have collapsed between Sam's home and the general store, not in the other direction near the mill. And what about the anonymous notes? Do you think she scurried around the village at night and risked being seen? Not a chance," she grumbled. "Hiram was killed on his way here by someone he had met in Lancaster. He never got as far as Sam's house. Like you suggested yesterday, the note writer is probably someone who witnessed the crime and mistakenly thinks I was the woman running away. Polly is an adulteress, nothing more," she argued.

Despite the soft fireglow bathing his features, Daniel remained grim. "Beware the jewel shining brightly," he murmured and gazed directly into the fire.

She furrowed her brow and shook her head, unable to decipher his cryptic words. She was certain he would eventually reach the same conclusion about Polly as she had. In the meantime, she reminded him to keep their conversation confidential. "And I won't have you or your investigator poking into the affair or Sam or even Polly, for that matter," she added. Ready to dismiss him again if he broke her confidence, she relied on him to keep his promise to adhere to her demands.

She stood up and folded the quilt before laying it across the seat of the rocker. "I'll have the list for you tomorrow."

"I'll stop by to pick it up," he offered, his eyes deeply troubled.

She had just put her slippers and cloak back on when the door opened and Thomas escorted Aunt Lily inside. She quickly accepted his offer to take her home, more at peace with herself than when she had arrived.

She wished she could say the same for her lawyer.

Chapter 22

By the middle of May, Jane had reached the breaking point. Overworked and under stress that had increased by leaps and bounds, she crawled out of bed every day more harried and worried than the day before.

"Not today," she vowed, excited by her decision to claim a temporary reprieve. She slipped downstairs to the storeroom to check on the handmade sign she had painted before retiring. "Dry and ready to hang," she pronounced and carried the sign with her as she walked through the foyer into the store.

Still unaccustomed to the gloom, she hoped she would be able to replace the wood covering the windows with glass sometime soon. She put the sign on top of her desk, but did not bother to light the lamp. Anxious to finish before a single customer arrived, she secured a hammer and a handful of tacks, confident she was not the only one who needed a respite.

Everyone around her was tense, walking on a tightrope of uncertainty. They were waiting for the sheriff to return and to plunge them into a deeper chaos than already existed now with the arrival of trade season.

Sunrise was again an occupied town. Small river craft carrying lumber and other resources clogged the Susquehanna, and the raft landing just below the village center bustled with activity. Rafters, a local term for men who steered the products downriver to Columbia or further south, milled about the streets and crowded the store to purchase additional supplies by day and turned rowdy in the tavern at night.

The tiny village was a hotbed of gossip, old and new that divided the local residents and fascinated visitors. The jail overflowed with the riffraff Noah arrested and held overnight until Ben levied the usual fines and sent the troublemakers on their way.

Jane's problems were nowhere near resolved. Daniel had heard nothing from the investigator, although he had gone to Lancaster to meet Abe Smitherman, the local lawyer his associate had engaged. The sheriff had not appeared to question her about the pocket watch or the funds found in Sam's barn. Aaron had yet to respond to her first letter or the second Daniel had sent after the store had been vandalized.

She fared no better with her family. Aunt Nester visited regularly, but neither one broached the subject of Polly's hair ornament. Aunt Lily had gone back to Philadelphia, but expected to return by the end of the month. Sam had grown restless being cooped up in the store most of the day, and Jane could scarcely think about Polly without fuming.

The woman had literally taken over Jane's home! She had cleaned every room from ceiling to floor and rearranged the furniture. Cupboards, trunks, and storage spaces had been reorganized until Jane could not find a single thing without asking Polly where she had put it.

Claiming the first floor as her exclusive domain, she had put her foot down when Polly attempted to extend her efforts to the storeroom, half tempted to hand the young woman the tortoiseshell hair ornament she was certain Polly was trying so desperately to find, hidden in the guise of spring cleaning.

"Today will be different," she promised herself and carried her sign and her tools outside.

She tacked up her sign and stood back to assess her handiwork: CLOSED TODAY DUE TO ILLNESS.

"We are sick, and we need a day free from the crowds, the gossip, and the endless work," she mumbled to justify the message on the sign. Without hesitating a moment longer, she closed the door and went straight back upstairs.

By the time Sam and Polly appeared for breakfast, Jane had everything ready, but held her surprise until they had finished their meal. That's when she handed Sam a basket filled with enough food to last for the day and marching orders to stay away till dark. "Take a ride to visit Polly's parents or friends, find a secluded spot to be alone, or just ride around in circles," she teased when he halfheartedly tried to argue with her.

"And what will you do all day?" he asked while Polly went to fetch one of her parasols.

"After I stop to see Aunt Nester so she doesn't worry, I'm going riding."

His eyes widened with disbelief. "Riding?"

She grinned.

"You haven't been riding for years."

"I'm sure I haven't forgotten how. I just need to get away for a few hours, then I'm going to take a cool scented bath, read a little, and munch on sweets for supper. Sounds decadent, doesn't it?"

His eyes began to twinkle. "Not unless you have company."

"Sam!" She smacked his arm playfully. "That's indecent. I'll be alone, of course."

He cocked one brow. "You shouldn't be riding off by yourself. Ask Daniel to go with you."

Another grin. She could not help it. Just thinking about spending time alone with him today made her happy. "I already did. He's going to the livery to get mounts for us, and I'm meeting him at Aunt Lily's house at eight o'clock. I didn't want anyone to see me riding off when we're all supposed to be too sick to open the store. They'll find out soon enough tomorrow. In the meantime, I have to change into a riding skirt."

She pecked his cheek with a quick kiss and went to her room. By the time she finished changing and returned to the kitchen, Sam and Polly were gone. She checked the clock in the parlor and had ten minutes to get to Aunt Lily's and still be on time. She was halfway down the staircase when she heard a loud rapping on the back door.

"Some people have gumption," she muttered, wishing she had made two signs instead of just one to convince her customers the store was closed for the day. She stepped into the foyer and had half a mind to escape through the front door, but quickly had second thoughts. What if Daniel had misunderstood and come here instead of waiting for her at Aunt Lily's?

Hoping that was the case, she slid the bolt free and swung the door open wide. Hope evaporated beyond wishful thinking into absolute fantasy, and she stared straight into the faces of her worst nightmare.

Five men, not one, stood shoulder to shoulder in front of her door, each more frighteningly somber than the other. Hiram's brother, Aaron, stood in the background, his anger distorting his features.

Her heart pounded. Her legs grew weak, and she held on to the edge of the door for support. Terror unlike any she had ever known snaked up her spine and around her heart, but it was the grim expression on Daniel's face that scared her the most.

Frantically fighting to keep tears at bay, she scanned the other men's faces as Daniel stepped beside her. Noah and Ben kept their gazes to the ground, as did a balding man she did not recognize who was standing next to Daniel.

Sheriff Fleming, a full head taller than the others, looked directly at her, his dark eyes resolute and without an ounce of compassion. "Jane Glennings Foster, I have been authorized to place you under arrest for the murder of your former husband, Hiram Benedict Foster."

"I didn't kill Hiram. Why are you doing this to me. I'm innocent!" she cried.

"I'm sorry," Daniel murmured. "I should have been warned, but the telegraph lines from Lancaster to Columbia are down." Guilt flashed through his eyes

"Let's go inside. The sheriff agreed to give us time to talk alone." He looked away from her and nodded. "Half an hour."

The sheriff signaled the others to leave. "We'll have everything worked out by then."

Daniel closed the door and slid the bolt home. He ushered her up the stairs and sat her down on the settee before he took a seat in the chair facing her. "We don't have much time now. We will later, but for now, the sheriff agreed we could have a few minutes so I can explain why you've been formally charged and arrested."

Attentive, yet coolly professional, he sat on the edge of his seat. "I'm sorry, Jane, but I have some very disturbing news."

"You have 'disturbing' news? Disturbing?" The bubble of hysteria in her mind burst and escaped her lips as a sarcastic laugh. "After being charged with a murder I didn't commit, I hardly think there's anything worse you could tell me. No," she corrected herself. "I'm certain there's nothing worse."

He flinched, but did not back down. "Hiram divorced you, Jane. Last October."

"He—he *what*?" she blurted out, too shocked to keep disbelief from turning her voice into a shrewish warble.

"Hiram went to Indianapolis and secured a divorce last October. I haven't seen the documents yet, but Abe Smitherman has. He's the lawyer from Lancaster I've engaged on your behalf, and he came with the sheriff to assure me it's a legal divorce."

"Divorced? I'm *divorced*?" Had she fallen into some sort of snake pit filled with incredible lies? "That's impossible. Surely I would have had to be notified. He couldn't just go off and obtain a divorce, just like that."

"Yes he can, and apparently, that's exactly what he did. Unfortunately, that's not all he managed to do."

Still jolted from two shocks, she scarcely had time to take a breath before he stunned her again.

"He also sold the business. Or tried to. He accepte a bid for the general store, but the sale was never nalized because Hiram never provided the new ledge books. The sheriff recovered the missing ledger bool from the lawyer handling the transaction in Boston an he has his own theory why Hiram never returned t complete the sale."

"That's absurd," she argued and categorized he high-pitched voice as natural under the circumstance rather than bordering on hysterical. She tried to focu her jumbled thoughts on one she could sustain fo longer than a heartbeat. "This has to be a mistake. He never been to Boston. We didn't have any supplier there. Why Boston, of all places?"

Daniel dropped his gaze for a moment. When h looked at her again, he had shuttered the pain smo dering in the depths of his eyes. "His fiancée lives i Boston. They were to be married this summer."

She stared at Daniel for several long moments. Ur able to change or successfully challenge the truth sh found churning in his eyes, she held perfectly still whi her mind still reeled with the objections she had trie to lodge against what he had told her.

Anger, terrifying and all-consuming, overwhelme her. "He divorced me and set me aside to marry anothe woman? He sold or tried to sell the store? What kin of demented monster would do that to his wife? Wha was supposed to happen to me? How was I to live? C face my family, my friends?"

She hissed, her body rigid with rage hot enough t melt her bones. "May his soul rot for eternity!"

"That's precisely where the state is arguing you trie to send him when you poisoned him," Daniel mu mured. "The sheriff believes Hiram came home and tol you about the divorce and the sale of the store. In re turn, you poisoned him to prevent anyone else fro learning what he had done. We have a little less tha two months before your trial on July ninth to prov otherwise."

There was no proof of her innocence. She knew it, and so did he. And so did the person who had cleverly murdered Hiram and used the damning evidence against her. She laid her head back and closed her eyes. When tears welled, she willed them away.

Scarcely two hours ago, she had thought today would be wondrously carefree.

She had been wrong.

Instead of harboring that same illusion now, she met reality head on, certain she had now experienced the worst life could offer any woman. She had been an orphan, a spinster, an unhappily married woman, a widow, and then a divorcée, all in the space of half a lifetime.

And now, just when she had found the man of her dreams and she dared to believe he returned her love, she was charged with a crime so heinous her very life was at stake.

Would fairness and justice ever prevail against the darker forces that had taken over her life, or would she be condemned by a jury, forever immortalized as a murderess and denied the fulfillment of her dreams?

Self-loathing topped Daniel's list, just ahead of stupidity, incompetence, and recklessness, but he could not afford to waste any of his time chastising himself now. He had a lifetime ahead of him to do that.

He had his own plans for Mercury Pine, who had left Sunrise, tracked Foster's trail to Indiana and Boston, located Aaron Foster, and returned to Lancaster handing Sheriff Fleming a motive for murder on a silver platter. The circumstantial evidence was powerful enough to convict Jane twice.

She was first and foremost in his mind now, and he held his ground in his battle with the sheriff and the local officials as they gathered in her parlor while she packed a few of her belongings. "No. I don't think I can make it any clearer than that, gentlemen. I will not allow my client to spend half a minute in that pitiful excuse you call a jail."

Noah scratched his chin. "Got no choice from what I can see."

The sheriff supported the local constable. "The renovations to the county jail begin in less than two weeks and will probably take the whole summer to complete. Until they are, all new prisoners have to be held in the local jails until they're escorted to Lancaster a week or two before their trials. Case closed."

"The case is not closed," Daniel argued. "How long do you think she'd last in there with the rabble he arrests every night?"

"If you're that worried, then send her to Columbia. There's a decent jail there," Fleming suggested.

"And twice as many riffraff." Daniel snorted. "It's also another two hours from Lancaster, which is where she should be. I need to meet with her on a regular basis and coordinate the efforts of the rest of my staff there."

Ben finally entered the foray. "It's obvious we need to reach a compromise. This time of year we need some sort of jail for the troublemakers Noah arrests. Most of them are harmless enough once they sober up, but I wouldn't want Jane or any other woman in there with them."

"Exactly," Daniel agreed.

Fleming frowned. "What's your compromise?"

"No one will be using the new schoolhouse between now and July. If you two gentlemen agree, we can have it converted into a temporary jail and ready for Jane by late today."

"I have no objections," Daniel offered, although he had a whole host of arguments against this mockery of justice that the sheriff had already refused to consider.

Fleming shrugged his shoulders. "None here either." When he stood up, his towering figure dominated the room. "I'd like to search the premises now since I already had a look at the barn where you found the missing funds as well as the mill area on my way here."

"Abe, stay with the sheriff and document anything he takes. I'll stay with Jane in her room. There's no need for her to watch this."

Praying he would have the time to wage and win the most important legal battle of his life, by whatever means necessary, he walked the short distance to her room and slipped inside, hoping Jane would find her principles much more pliant now that her life was at stake.

Everything Jane had ever held sacred had been ransacked or destroyed, and nothing could ever erase the horrendous sense of violation that deadened her senses and numbed her disbelief and anger.

Oblivious to the chirping crickets and the distant hum of revelry in the tavern, she sat hunched at the head of her cot in her makeshift jailhouse. With her arms wrapped around her bent legs, she rested her cheek on her knees and stared into the darkness.

Her home, all of her personal belongings down to the laundry, had been studied, searched, and some even confiscated. Probing hands and eyes had scoured every shelf and crate in the general store and the storeroom. She should have taken Daniel's advice, but she had refused to cower in her room instead of observing the sheriff's search.

She had lost everything. Divorced instead of widowed, she had no claim to any of Hiram's estate. She had no home and no livelihood. An eventual acquittal would never be enough to eradicate the damage done by the murder allegations against her. Stripped of her reputation, with her character blackened, the respectable place she had once held in society was gone forever.

After her conviction, scandal and heartbreak would be the only legacy she left behind, and she closed her eyes to hold back the tears that welled when she thought about her family.

Bless them all. Faithful to her even now, her family had rallied to support her. Aunt Nester had bullied

Noah into letting her transform the stark utilitarian one-room schoolhouse into a cozy room. Louis promised to bring meals from the tavern, and Sam . . .

She choked on her unshed tears and let them cascade down her cheeks. Sam had been so outraged by the charges against her, by what Hiram had done to her, and by Aaron's announcement he was returning to Sunrise to operate the general store, Sam had tossed the keys to Aaron and taken Polly home.

She sniffled and used one of her plain handkerchiefs to wipe her face. Poor Daniel. He was still the executor of Hiram's estate, but had given his associate a directive to file a petition with the court in the morning to be removed.

"Daniel." Her whisper was half cry and half plea. Of all the losses she had suffered today, or would sustain in the future, losing her dream of one day finding happiness with him was her deepest and most painful.

She loved him beyond all reason, and she knew in her heart of hearts that he loved her, too, but there would never be anyplace for an alleged murderess in his life. Even if by some miracle he convinced the jury she was innocent, the charge itself was too scandalous for a man in his position to overlook or overcome.

Love alone could not withstand the whispers of gossip and scandal or the ongoing suspicion that would shroud her name for as long as she lived if she were to be acquitted.

Love was precious, and she had waited too long to find love only to see it tainted or destroyed. She also loved him too much to expect him to risk his name, his reputation, and his career by one day linking his future to hers.

Grief, heavier and more profound than she had ever thought possible, filled her heart and soul. She had no sense of guilt or hypocrisy to distract her this time. Her grief was real, her despair total, and her heartbreak complete as she bid one final farewell to her dreams and slipped into the deep dark void of sleep to embrace the nightmares waiting for her.

Chapter 23

"Jane Foster is going to be convicted and hanged for a crime she didn't commit."

Daniel's ominous prediction broke the silence in the Lancaster hotel room he had reserved for Jane's defense team. Returning from his first visit with her in the county jail, he issued the call to arms, but everyone here knew only too well time was running out. Her trial was scheduled to begin in exactly fourteen days, and he had little hope of saving her life.

The tension in the room was thick and palpable. The case against her was formidable. Her confidence in him remained high, and he hid the fear gripping his heart beneath a calm, but grim expression.

With little more than a few hours' sleep each night, he was surviving on sheer determination, driven by frustration and the very real possibility his prediction today would come true.

"Our one and only job remains the same: to make sure that doesn't happen," he added, his voice firm and his posture rigid. Seated at the head of a rectangular table stacked with legal books, court documents, and research, he glanced around the table and met the somber gazes of the men he had gathered together. To his right, Abe Smitherman, their local attorney, sat next to Ben Hastings, Daniel's Philadelphia associate. Robert Ludlam, pickpocket-turned-investigator, was alone on the opposite side.

Each man had been working independently, with Daniel coordinating and orchestrating their efforts on Jane's behalf. Today was the first time they would pool their individual findings and examine the case against their client, and he hoped they would be able to find a glimmer of hope in an otherwise damning collection of evidence against her.

Anxious to begin, he nodded to the local attorney. "Let's start with the prosecution. Abe, summarize for everyone what the prosecution's argument will be."

Perspiration beaded the top of the bald man's head, and he paused only long enough to mop it. "This is what Attorney General Ford intends to prove. Foster left Sunrise, stayed in Baltimore briefly, and proceeded directly to Indianapolis where he waited six weeks to petition for a divorce, which was granted on October twenty-seventh."

Pausing to fiddle through his papers, he took a long pull on a glass of water before continuing. "From there he traveled to Boston and contracted with a lawyer to sell the general store, providing ledger books to document its worth. He also proposed to one Ada Shaw, a widow he had met and apparently courted on previous visits. She accepted, and they set a wedding date for the end of July. He signed an agreement to sell the store in the first week of January and arrived back in Lancaster on the tenth. That day he closed his bank account, met with his lawyer and collected on some old promissory notes. Then he traveled to Sunrise to retrieve the ledger books Jane had been using which he needed to finalize the sale of the business."

He took in a deep breath of air and finished his glass of water. "Up to this point, the evidence they have is rock solid. They found the divorce decree with the lawyer Foster had in Boston. Along with bank and hotel records and testimony from his landlady in Boston, both of his lawyers, the minister in Sunrise, and one Moira O'Leary Quinn, the red-haired prostitute, there's little we can dispute."

Daniel furrowed his brow. "What about the widow, Ada Shaw? Has she agreed to testify?"

"No. Apparently she's too distraught. Why?"

"Just curious. Don't you find it odd she never once tried to contact Foster? He'd been gone for months. She knew where to find him, yet she never wrote a single letter."

"Neither did his lawyer," Hastings added. "I wonder why."

"I can tell you," Ludlam offered. His deep-set, black eyes snapped with disgust. "The vermin told them he was going to be traveling to western New York to check on his investments there, which don't exist, I might add. Looks to me like he didn't want to be contacted, which follows the pattern he had used with his wife."

Hastings frowned and shook his head. "That might have mollified his intended wife, but not his lawyer, or the buyer for that matter. They must have been anxious to complete the sale."

Daniel's frown was deeper than Hastings's had been. "From what Abe told me earlier, Ford isn't going to pursue the matter. If we do, he'll only argue Jane simply destroyed the correspondence since she handled the posts delivered by the mail wagon. Which is exactly what he'll do if we decide to introduce Foster's letter from October as evidence and argue there were never any more. The whole issue is best left unaddressed in court."

He looked around the table and saw the others agreed. "Abe is right, however. To this point, there's little reason to try to dispute anything. We're better off concentrating on what they will try to prove happened next."

Picking up his cue, Smitherman continued. "They allege Foster returned home, confronted his by-then former wife, packed up the ledger book he needed to finalize the sale of the business, and bathed before he left. Desperately angry and finding herself divorced, homeless, and her life virtually destroyed, she emptied out some of his cologne, and replaced it with concentrated tobacco juice. When it didn't take immediate effect, she was forced to follow him when he left. After he finally collapsed, she took his travel bag, covered his body with rocks, and simply went home and pretended he'd never come back. She hid or destroyed what evidence she could and hired herself a lawyer, namely Daniel, to get the court's permission to operate the store just to keep up the pretense she had been abandoned."

He sighed and looked around the table. "Cold and shrewd pretty much sums up their portrayal of Mrs. Foster, although her reputation among the villagers was quite the opposite. Even fooled the sheriff. I understand he's not too happy about that. He thought she was innocent."

"Until the anonymous notes surfaced and Pine showed up," Daniel snapped, thoroughly disgusted with himself for inadvertently attracting Pine to Sunrise in the first place.

Equally disappointed with himself, he reined in his emotions. He quickly regained the detachment that had forced him to distance himself from Jane as well as her family—detachment he needed more than ever to function analytically. "How do they intend to explain the anonymous notes?"

"A witness too frightened to come forward? Someone who doesn't want to invoke the villagers' wrath by accusing one of their own? Who knows? It doesn't matter to them," Smitherman charged.

"But it's critical for us to know," Daniel countered. "Jane is innocent, which means whoever wrote the notes is either a witness or the actual murderer. That's where we need to concentrate."

He pressed his fingers to his temples and rubbed his brow to ease the pressure pounding in his head. "The evidence they have is all circumstantial. Review it again. There's got to be something we're overlooking."

Hastings pushed back his long-styled hair behind his ears and spoke up after rifling through the papers in front of him and pulling one aside. "I've got the evidence list here. There are the notes, of course, the pocket watch, the three hundred ninety dollars, Jane's gown and petticoats, stockings, slippers, and handkerchief, all stained with tobacco juice, the coroner's report, and the new ledger book from the general store. What they don't have, fortunately, is the bottle of poisoned cologne or an eyewitness," he added, although the frustration that laced his voice dimmed his enthusiasm.

"Or the mementos Foster kept from his conquests," Daniel murmured, sending a silent prayer to Providence or luck, whichever was responsible for inspiring Jane's aunt to bring them to him before the sheriff searched Jane's living quarters.

Finding nothing helpful in the evidence, he looked to Ludlam, who had arrived in Lancaster only hours ago, for help and directed his next question to him, hoping to hear some positive input for a change. "Have you been able to locate anyone in the nearby vicinity, other than Polly, who had enjoyed the late Mr. Foster's attentions?"

Ludlam leaned against the back of his chair and steepled his pudgy hands atop his ample stomach. "As far as I could find out, Polly Glennings was Foster's only paramour locally. My guess is he restricted his appetite in Sunrise to a family member, which give him leverage if and when he decided to end the affair, which he always did. I've got a long list of women he bedded and abandoned in other cities, none of whom knew he lived in Sunrise."

Daniel shook his head and sighed. The prospect of winning an acquittal looked bleak. He did not share Jane's faith in either his skills or simple justice to clear her. Unlike Jane, he had seen too many innocent people wrongly convicted. Like it or not, he could still only see one possible defense for Jane: to point an accusing finger at her sister-in-law, just long enough to establish doubt in the jurors' minds by suggesting someone else wanted to see him dead.

Given Polly's unusual beauty, it would be easy for them to accept the idea Foster found his sister-in-law irresistible, especially when they saw how very plain Jane appeared when compared to Polly.

The jurors, however, would only accept what they could observe or were told by witnesses, and the wisdom of his father's ditty had never seemed more apropos. The jurymen would not be able to see into Jane's heart unless he showed them the way, but finding a way to discover the truth lying in Polly's heart was bound to be difficult.

Gut instinct, however, prodded him to violate his promise to Jane not to introduce the affair in court and to pursue the proof he needed to persuade her, and later the jury, that it was entirely possible Polly had committed the crime of murder. If he could document the affair without Jane's testimony, that might be enough to save her.

Troubled he had no other choice, he furrowed his brow. Something Ludlam had said tugged at his instincts, and he replayed Ludlam's words in his mind as well as today's entire discussion. His ability to recall conversations verbatim once more served him well. He separated several words or phrases from their original context and linked them together in another.

He immediately had a different perspective of things, and the scenario taking shape in his mind placed Polly in the accused box instead of Jane. If he and his team worked hard enough to develop the proof they needed, they might even get the charges against Jane dropped before the trial began.

His heart pumped faster to keep up with the thoughts and ideas that raced through his mind, and he spoke aloud for the benefit of the others, who might be able to contribute additional insight. "Ludlam suggested Foster deliberately chose Polly for a bed partner to make it easier to end their affair. I wonder . . ."

He looked directly at Ludlam. "Shuffle through that mound of papers you've collected and find the list Jane made with dates of Foster's trips."

"Got it." He handed it to Daniel, his expression defensive. "I've been here, there, and everywhere on that list. What do you think I missed?"

"Not you. Us," Daniel corrected as he scanned the list. He circled the trips for the past year and a half and gave the list to Hastings. "Foster usually stayed overnight in Lancaster at the start of every trip to make stage connections. I don't care how, just find out where Foster stayed and whether or not he was alone. Ludlam, copy the dates and get to Columbia this afternoon. Find out if our little adulteress really did visit her parents as often as she's purported, and while you're at it, see if there's anything else you can learn about her. Abe, get access to the ledger books that cover the same time period."

Smitherman's eyes filled with puzzlement. "What am I looking for?"

"Deliveries Sam made. Find out where he was, calculate how long he might have been away, that sort of thing."

"Enlighten me. I'm confused," he admitted.

"If I'm right, Foster and Polly might have met in Lancaster while Sam was also away. If we can prove that, it's circumstantial evidence of the affair—evidence we can use since Jane isn't willing to testify about it."

"If you can get her to agree. So far she's refused to consider introducing the affair in court under any circumstances," Hastings argued.

"She might not have a choice. Not if I'm right and Polly did more than have an affair with Foster, who forgot one very simple law of nature: For every action, there's a reaction. Gentlemen, I think the prosecution is right about one key point. Foster was not going home when he died. He was leaving home and returning to Lancaster. The question is, whose home did he visit last? His own, or Polly's?"

He narrowed his gaze and scanned the faces of the men around him as he spoke. "Reverend Reilly thought he saw Foster near the general store. What if he did? What if Foster did go to the store and retrieved the new ledger book he needed and then stopped to see Polly for one last tryst? What if she somehow found out he was leaving to marry another woman? Any threat she might have made to stop him would have been met by an equal threat from Foster to tell Sam about the affair. Murdering Foster would have eliminated that threat. She could have returned the ledger book to the store since the door is never locked. She could also have written the notes and planted the evidence against Jane."

The more he thought about his theory, the more it seemed plausible, with the exception of picturing Polly scurrying around at night by herself.

"It might work," Hastings admitted. "It's sure better than anything else we've got."

Smitherman looked doubtful, but Ludlam had a gleam in his eye. Daniel could feel the excitement and the certainty building and coursing through his body. "We need proof, gentlemen. And we need it fast. You know what you each have to do. Ludlam, I'll ride out with you. We'll all meet here together in one week. Any questions?"

There were none spoken, but Ludlam had a quizzical expression on his face. "Are you coming with me to Columbia?"

Daniel shook his head. "I'm going back to Sunrise. It's on the way. Maybe you can help me figure out how I'm going to search through Polly's home. It's the only place the sheriff overlooked."

Chapter 24

Solitary isolation had its merits. So did the baggy gown, the bland, unpalatable food, and the stark cell in the Lancaster County jail Jane had called home for nearly two weeks.

She had been deprived of all stimulation, except the daily plethora of construction noises that echoed incessantly from dawn to dusk. Only her dream that she and Daniel would one day be together shined through her dire circumstances and enkindled her goal to prove her innocence and win her freedom without shaming her brother in the process.

On the eve of her trial, a clock somewhere nearby struck the hour. Two o'clock. Daniel was an hour late. She paced about her cell, wondering how she had landed in this awful place. She scarcely remembered her late-night journey to Lancaster, but the memory of her last visit with her family in Sunrise was indelibly etched on her soul.

Polly had been too distraught to come to say farewell, a singular blessing for which Jane would be eternally grateful, but one by one, the others had come to say their last good-byes since she could have no visits from them in the county jail. Aunt Lily and Aunt Nester came, their faces lined with grief, their eyes swollen from crying, their last hugs desperate. Louis, ever-dutiful, had brought her a small basket of sweets to take along, too moved to care about the tears washing his face.

The hardest good-bye had been with Sam. Dear, dear Sam. Her heart wept for him, even now. He had tried to be stoic, but in their last moments together, he had crushed her in his arms and hugged her, his chest heaving with deep sobs, his grief as profound as when their parents had died.

Once far removed from Sunrise and her family, the bitter reality of her situation had descended swiftly, evident in her desolate surroundings. A rickety table and a single chair sat just inside the door to her cell. A cot with a thin mattress rested along the outer wall below a high, barred window that met the ceiling and provided meager light and even less air. Only a thin curtain of self-control separated anger and doubt from her faith that justice would eventually prevail and acquit her of the false charges against her.

She did not dwell on how or why this had happened to her; instead, she counted on Daniel's expert legal skills and her own reputation as a moral, upstanding woman to undermine the circumstantial evidence against her and to convince the jury of her innocence.

Perspiring from the stale summer heat in her cell, she walked to the basin on the table, dipped a rough cloth into the tepid water, and washed her face and arms.

She had no sooner replaced the cloth than she heard the sound of footsteps approaching her cell. When the key turned the lock on her door, her heart began to pound, and she prayed Daniel brought good news.

She turned to face the door. The moment she saw the grim expression he wore, she knew her prayers had gone unanswered. She sat down on her cot and waited for him, her gaze averted from the perpetual sneer the keeper wore whenever he escorted Daniel inside.

Just as he had done every day since her arrival here, Daniel placed the chair in front of her and sat down with his back to the keeper, who stood just outside the door, guarding them both. The lines furrowing Daniel's brow and creasing the corners of his eyes were deeper than she remembered from yesterday.

Frustration worried his gaze. "How are you faring?" he asked, again keeping his voice barely above a whisper to prevent the keeper from overhearing their conversation.

"Better than you are," she admonished gently. "You look like you haven't slept for months. How are you going to defend me in court tomorrow if you're exhausted?"

His expression hardened. "Better put, how can I defend you when you won't listen to me or take my advice?"

"Because I have more faith in justice than you do," she countered.

He leaned toward her, his expression troubled. "There isn't any time left to argue anymore, not with the trial opening tomorrow. If you don't testify about Hiram's affair in court to plant the seeds of doubt in the jurors' minds that you weren't the only woman who—".

"No. We've been through this before." She held on to the edge of the mattress to keep from reaching out and touching him. "I won't have Sam shamed in court, and I won't hand the prosecutor another motive. He has enough already—"

"Enough to guarantee you're convicted if you don't. I know it's risky and it's difficult for you to do, but we don't have any other choice now."

Her heart began to pound, and it was hard not to shout the words to try to make him understand her position. "We have the truth on our side. You've admitted the evidence is all circumstantial, and there are no eyewitnesses. You're a skilled lawyer, Daniel. I know you can whittle away at the evidence, and when you present the witnesses to testify to my character, the jurors will have to believe in my innocence."

His eyes widened. "After all that's happened, you simply can't still be that naive. Not with your life at stake! And you're overestimating my skill—"

"No I'm not," she argued, empowered by the fear he was too worried about her to be thinking clearly. "How could you take my testimony about the affair and point to Polly as a possible murderess, making accusations that would destroy my brother's marriage and completely shred her reputation, without proof? I know you're a better man than that."

He flinched as though she had lanced his conscience with a knife instead of her words, and she gripped his hands. "We've been through this countless times. Nothing has changed. You have to have faith in the legal system. In justice and truth to triumph over iniquity. You can't let fear erode your faith in yourself, either." She swallowed hard, loving him enough to spare him from the ordeal of defending her. "You have two other lawyers who can present my defense. Maybe you should let them."

His eyes flashed with pain so deep her heart constricted. "Is that your way of dismissing me? Again?"

"You were right when you predicted I would," she reminded him with a sad smile.

"And I'm just as right about this, too," he murmured, caressing the back of her hand with his thumb. "Jane, I—"

A sharp rap on the open door interrupted him. "Time's up. On your way, Mr. Colton, or I'll have to report you to the warden. Wouldn't want your sweet little murderess here to be without legal advice, now that her trial's ready to start in the morning, would you?"

When Daniel's eyes flashed angrily, she tugged on his hands. "If you lose your temper, they won't let you come back for a few days. I need you, Daniel. I can't go through the trial without you."

He squeezed her hand before letting go as he stood up. "Didn't you just dismiss me?"

She smiled up at him. "I suppose I did, but if you don't come back, I won't get to convince you that I'm right. You can win this trial for me, Daniel, and for you. I believe in you." Her eyes welled with tears. "Please try to get some rest. Tomorrow is an important day," she murmured. She prayed he would somehow find a way tonight to finally let go of his jaded view of justice and his skepticism so that righteousness would shine through his words in court and illuminate her innocence.

When she sat in the prisoner's dock tomorrow, she would be strong, using dignity and courage when the evidence against her was presented. Silent, her demeanor alone would illuminate the principles that would guide Daniel as her defender.

And as the one true love of her life.

Thunder roared, an ominous precursor to the lightning that gashed the night sky. Blustery winds blew sheets of cold rain that drenched the balcony outside the hotel suite where Daniel stood, welcoming the natural storm as only fitting.

His very soul was a tempest of raging emotions.

Damn the fates for being brazen enough to give him a woman who inspired him to believe again in the nobility of the legal system and the faithfulness of justice, and tempt his heart with true love—only to ridicule him, in the end, for being a fool!

The trial that began tomorrow was bound to end in a verdict that would be a travesty, mocking the very principles and ideals that marked Jane as a woman of unusual faith and character.

Unless he broke his promise to her and gave the jury an alternative suspect: Hiram's mistress, Polly Glennings.

Now facing the dilemma he had fought so hard to avoid, his thoughts mirrored the violent, unexpected storm pounding his body and the city around him. Anger crackled through his spirit. His hand clenched into a fist, smashing the trial notes he had made and studied for hours on end after his last visit to Jane, but bitter reality gave him no reprieve.

The woman he loved with all his heart was locked in a jail cell. There was nothing he could do to prevent her from being convicted and taken from him forever unless he reverted to form and stretched the boundaries of ethical behavior, destroying Polly's name with nothing more than innuendo.

Ludlam had disappeared since leaving for Columbia, and Jane refused to testify about the affair. Revealing Polly as Hiram Foster's mistress and then extending that claim into a theory about how Polly might have murdered Foster, an allegation unsubstantiated by any evidence, would violate his ethical duty to his client. It would also extinguish any hope of his own redemption as a lawyer who used tactics above reproach.

Disgust lifted his arm and opened his fist to offer the trial notes back to Fate. The wind quickly accepted, blowing them away. Rain drenched the notes, which fluttered madly to the ground below, illuminated by the light pouring from hotel rooms.

He watched with hearty satisfaction as they dissolved before his very eyes, but his dilemma remained.

He lowered his arm and closed his eyes. Shudders wracked his body, and the cold that emanated from deep within his soul conspired with the chilling ache in his heart to join forces with the natural elements assaulting him. The rain cascaded down his face and the wind whipped at his clothing.

On a night such as this, he had held Jane in his arms. He wished he could hold her now. For courage. For inspiration. For just a moment, if only to know what to do.

Her parting words echoed in his mind, and he knew he could resolve his dilemma by simply stepping down and letting one of the other lawyers defend her in court. Although Hastings and Smitherman were competent attorneys who could present Jane's limited defense, Daniel would never forgive himself for abandoning her. Not now. Not when she faced the ultimate punishment for murder.

No. He could not avoid his dilemma and still hope for his own redemption and her acquittal, yet however he decided, he still faced one inevitable result: He would lose Jane forever.

If he broke his word to her and won her freedom, she would never forgive him and he would lose her. If he kept his promise, he feared she would be convicted and condemned to death. The world would lose one of its finest creations, and his very soul would be destroyed.

Thunderclaps became the sound of workmen building the gallows. Cracks of lightning became bursts of applause from the crowds as they watched the hangman slip a noose around her neck.

"No!" he shouted, glaring up at the heavens. Heavy rain stung his eyes and gale-force winds sent him stumbling back a step.

"No," he repeated. He braced his feet and defied the power of heaven and earth to take her from him and challenged Justice to reassert herself.

"Damn the evidence. Damn *you*!" He cursed Fate, his voice muffled by the storm as it intensified. He reached into his pocket, retrieved the compass Jane had given him, and held it against his heart. Love for Jane kept his heart beating, reminding him there was nothing he could ever do or achieve that would have any meaning without Jane by his side.

He took a deep breath of the humid air and brought her image to mind. Her dark eyes glistened. Her lips curled into a smile, but it was her heart that reached out and touched the very essence of his dreams and his love for her.

And it was love, strong and enduring, that resolved his dilemma, washing it away as powerfully and completely as if it had never existed and replacing it with faith—in Jane as well as in himself.

He bowed his head and pressed the compass harder against his chest, committed forever to the precious jewel who had captured his heart. With only hours left before court would convene and the jurors would be seated, he had no time to waste. He would go back inside and make new trial notes, prepared to defend her with honor and the highest ethical principles as his guide, and fight for the verdict Jane deserved: not guilty.

Chapter 25

By the third day of her trial, Jane's naivete had evaporated into cynicism and her stoicism had disintegrated into agitation. Her belief in justice now smoldered just shy of contempt. The ironic juxtaposition of her principles with Daniel's gave her a new understanding, if not respect, for him.

The moment she studied the evidence to be introduced today, she leaped to her feet and leaned over the railing on the prisoner's dock. "No. That's not—"

"Silence, Mrs. Foster! And I'll have quiet in this courtroom as well!" Judge Gordon Welsh banged his gavel repeatedly to restore order and glowered Jane back to her seat. "I warned you three times yesterday not to test the patience of this court by interrupting testimony. Obviously, you have no regard for this court or your counsel, who has failed to persuade you to take my threats seriously."

He banged his gavel again. "Bailiff, remove the defendant at once. See that she's kept locked in her cell and denied visitors for the remainder of the day."

"With all due respect, Your Honor—"

"Sit down, Mr. Colton. Your client is neither deaf nor feebleminded. She understood my directives, yet deliberately and repeatedly ignored them again today."

"But, Your Honor—"

"Another word, Mr. Colton, and I'll hold you in contempt, order you removed as well, and send for Mr. Smitherman to continue in your stead."

Stunned, Jane plopped back into her seat and watched Daniel sit down dejectedly. Disappointment and frustration flashed through his eyes when he glanced at her, and shame filled her heart. As the surly bailiff approached her, he blocked her view of Daniel, and she gripped the edge of her seat.

Panic sent her heart racing and another objection from her lips. "Please, Your Honor, I have to speak to my attorney," she pleaded.

"You had ample time to do that last night."

"But it's important—"

"Silence," he shouted and glared at the bailiff. "Remove Mrs. Foster at once. If she says another word, gag her."

The bailiff grabbed her and applied pressure that numbed her arm and sent pain shooting through her body. "Shut your mouth and come quietly. Forget the gag," he hissed. "I'll drag you outta here by your hair."

The hard glitter in his eyes sent chills down her spine, and she had no doubt he would carry out his threat. She glanced at the jurors who sat in tiered benches to her right and saw nothing but condemnation in their eyes.

She could not cry out again and dared not take the risk for fear the judge would extend her punishment.

Choosing to leave with whatever dignity she could muster would not change their minds, any more than Daniel's impressive cross-examinations these past three days. Still another defiant display would only antagonize them and harden their minds against her before Daniel had an opportunity to present her defense.

She yanked her arm away and stood up by herself before descending the single step that led from her seat on the platform to the courtroom floor. The bailiff immediately took her arm again and held her so tightly she could almost feel the bruise forming on her flesh—a black-and-blue reminder she would have of her behavior today.

With her head lowered, she left the courtroom. She kept her gaze on the planked floor, half expecting to find the tattered remnants of the justice she had hoped

to find in court laying about, trampled by distorted testimony and slanted evidence.

She had not helped her own case yesterday by repeatedly calling out to dispute the testimony against
her, but the graphic description of her time with Hiram
offered by the red-haired prostitute had been horrifying.
Later, when Efrem Harris had portrayed Jane as a
greedy, desperate woman whose only interest was
claiming funds to which she was not entitled, she could
not remain silent.

Frightened by the judge's warnings, she had been
able to keep her composure until late afternoon when
Aaron Foster had taken the stand. He attacked the skills
she prided most, making outlandish claims that she had
been inept and grossly incompetent as a business-
woman, citing of all things the crate of useless items
like the garden dibbles. At that point, she protested
loudly, even over the sound of the judge's banging
gavel.

But she just could not let what she had seen today
in the evidence go unchallenged!

When the bailiff opened the east door and escorted
her outdoors, she squinted against the bright afternoon
sunshine and took a deep breath of moist, humid air
before he locked her into a covered wagon that would
take her back to her cell. As the wheels creaked forward, she braced her hands on either side of the dark
enclosure to keep her balance.

Tomorrow in court, she would have to keep her frustration in check and her emotions under control if she
had any hope of speaking to Daniel again.

Before it was too late.

Before her fate was sealed.

And before Hiram's murderer had a chance to claim
a second victim, and possibly a third: Sam.

Disheartened by Jane's outburst and stunned by the
judge's order to have her removed, Daniel sat alone behind the table reserved for the defense attorneys. Mean-

while, the other members of his team worked feverishly
back at the hotel to prepare for opening Jane's defense
tomorrow.

He hid a scowl, loosened his cravat, and scanned the
courtroom. He could only liken the atmosphere to a
bawdy theater filled with a zealous audience ready to
explode into applause when the prosecution rested its
case this afternoon.

The three judges sat behind a bench on a raised platform along the north wall, their expressions now as
black as the robes they wore. Spectators filled every
available seat on the benches dominating the southern
half of the room.

Somewhere in that throng, members of Jane's family
sat together, praying for a miracle, but expecting the
worst, especially now that Jane had antagonized the
judges again and the jury as well. He had not seen her
family arrive, but he knew they were there, just as he
knew Mercury Pine was recording yet another one of
Jane's outbursts that were bound to find their way into
the murder pamphlet Pine was writing.

Daniel suspected the rabid journalist would release
the first of his pamphlets tomorrow, if he repeated what
he had done to Debra Modean. An accounting of Jane's
trial to date would no doubt be delivered to a printer
before the echo of the judge's gavel ending today's session faded.

When he focused on the center of the room, his fears
for Jane, who had quickly unraveled once testimony
had begun, multiplied. Standing in front of a railing
along the perimeter of a semicircular platform, two tipstaves with staffs stood on either side of a small gate
and guarded the jurors on the right side. Directly opposite, the tiered benches in the same area, reserved for
witnesses waiting to testify, were now empty.

Between them on a separate railed platform facing
the judges, the prisoner's dock was occupied by only
the ghost of the woman who had been exiled from
court. Shattered by the cold realities of the court pro-

ceedings, Jane had been difficult, if not impossible, to control, as shown by her outburst only moments ago.

He had spent hours with her last night, preparing her for today's testimony, yet he could sympathize with her horror of seeing her nicotine-stained garments displayed for the court. He envisioned them scandalously illustrated in Pine's pamphlet, shook his head, and tightened his cravat again.

He was more frustrated now than anyone would suspect, most especially his client. He still had not heard from Ludlam. Hell, he did not even have a client in the courtroom! And he would not be able to speak to her again until tomorrow. Considering all the good he had done her, he might as well have turned her defense over to Smitherman or Hastings.

The very thought of seeing Jane convicted and executed made him tremble, and he shuffled through the papers on his table as though they held the key to the miracle it would take to save her.

The courtroom finally grew silent again. Sheriff Fleming, the final witness, was still on the stand, waiting to complete his testimony. Attorney General Ford approached the witness stand, ready to resume. Daniel set his papers aside, prepared to listen carefully and take notes.

"Before we were interrupted," Ford began, "you were going to describe the garments you submitted and the court has already accepted as evidence."

He took the clothing from the table and handed it to the sheriff, who held each piece up, one at a time, as he spoke. "I found the gown and petticoats . . . the slippers . . . and the stockings in Mrs. Foster's wardrobe. As you can see, they're badly stained with concentrated tobacco juice, the poison used to murder the victim."

Ford took the items from Fleming and displayed them, once again, on a table reserved for evidence. This time, he carefully draped them so the jurors could see the amber stains and enjoy a titillating view of Jane's undergarments as well.

Daniel scribbled a quick note to use during his cross-examination.

"These are the stains?" Ford asked as he waved his hand across the display.

"Correct."

"And you're positive the stains were made by the same poison used to kill Hiram Foster?"

The sheriff shifted in his seat. "As much as anyone can be. If you lift the petticoat, you'll note a circular stain midway up."

Ford lifted the garment and pointed to a round stain. "Here?"

"Yes. We put a small amount of concentrated tobacco juice on the petticoat to compare the color to the other stains. As you can see, they're almost exact. The stains on the hem, of course, are a bit lighter, but the garment has been laundered."

Daniel crossed off his note.

Anticipating his opportunity to undermine the sheriff's testimony by introducing Jane's accident in the store and have it later corroborated by Libby Holtzman and Penelope Washburn, he was unprepared for Ford's next point.

"You have one remaining piece of evidence you collected. Please describe where you found the item as you hold it up for the court."

Fleming held up a badly stained lady's handkerchief. "I found this in the crate where the local constable discovered the funds stolen from Foster the night he was killed. Unfortunately, it was overlooked at the time.

Daniel leaped to his feet. "Objection!"

"Denied, Mr. Colton."

"Permission to approach the bench, Your Honor," he countered, his heart pounding even harder.

"I object," Ford said quickly.

A heavy sigh. "Mr. Ford. Mr. Colton. You may approach, but let's keep this short. I've little patience left for verbal shenanigans."

Daniel did not have to take any documents with him

to the bench. He had memorized every one, including the discovery document listing the evidence he would argue against now. Standing shoulder to shoulder with his opponent, he addressed the three judges in a whispered voice to prevent the jury from overhearing. "Your Honors, the prosecution clearly listed the handkerchief along with the other garments as being found in the defendant's home, not the crate in the barn loft."

"An oversight we regret," Ford argued. "We only discovered our mistake during the dinner recess when we reviewed the evidence with the sheriff. It was too late to notify—"

"And it's too late to use the evidence now since you didn't," Daniel countered as vehemently as he dared. "That's a violation—".

"It was a mistake, nothing more. In the interest of justice—"

"Exactly. In the interest of justice, I ask the court to acknowledge a violation of discovery law and refuse to let the handkerchief remain as evidence."

The chief justice did not bother to confer with his two colleagues. "Denied, Mr. Colton. Take it up on appeal, and you'll get the same answer since neither you nor your associates found the mistake, either. If you take one more minute of this court's time objecting, I'll hold you in contempt. Return to your places, gentlemen, and let's end this day with a prayer that tomorrow both the defendant and her attorney will be better tempered."

Daniel was already in contempt, of the very system he had served for over a decade, but he returned to his seat as ordered. Jane had been agitated to have her garments displayed for the world to see. She would be completely unnerved if she were here now.

She would also have a right to be angry with him. He should have caught the mistake earlier. More specifically, Smitherman should have noted the discrepancy, since he had accompanied the sheriff when he had gone to the barn loft en route to Sunrise to arrest Jane

and failed to record the handkerchief as confiscated evidence. Smitherman had also recorded the garments
taken from Jane's home, but Daniel embraced his own
share of guilt. He had been too concerned about Jane
to concentrate on what the sheriff had taken, a mistake
that haunted him now as he clearly recalled Ben saying
there was a handkerchief in the crate.

The sound of the judge's gavel forced him to set his
anger aside. For the next hour, he listened to the rest
of the sheriff's testimony and conducted his cross-
examination.

"The prosecution rests," Ford announced.

The chief justice's voice rang out one last time. "Mr.
Colton, be prepared to present your arguments when
we reconvene tomorrow morning at nine. This court is
now adjourned." He banged a gavel and the three
judges left through the north entrance before the extra
tipstaves hired to control the crowds opened the doors
on the southern and western sides of the building to let
out the boisterous spectators who shouted verbal epithets at Daniel as they left.

He spied Pine slithering out the door and scowled
openly this time. When someone nudged him hard from
behind, he clenched his fists and turned, ready to slug
the imbecile who dared violate the inner sanctum of the
court reserved for attorneys and their staff.

With one quick glance at the man standing only
inches away, his heart began to pound, and he dropped
his fists. "Ludlam!"

"Bearing gifts. I left them for the others to open and
study while I came here to get you."

"They'd better be sweet," Daniel grunted, doubtful
anything could salvage today, let alone the trial. He
grabbed his papers and stuffed them into his case.
"Let's get out of here," he grumbled and led his investigator to the closest exit instead of crossing the room
to use the door reserved for attorneys and their staff.
As they descended the steps to the brick sidewalk, the
spectators recognized Daniel and turned into an ugly,

unruly crowd that pelted him with angry words and showered them both with pamphlets.

"Go to your whore! You should hang with her!" one shouted.

A woman tossed a bottle that narrowly missed Daniel's head and struck his shoulder instead. " 'Champion of the Sheets'? You should be disbarred!"

Daniel grabbed Ludlam, shoved him back away from the crowd, and snatched a pamphlet from the ground. "Inside," he shouted. "We'll have to leave another way."

Breathing heavily, he pushed a way clear for both of them. They escaped back into the building unscathed, and he spoke briefly with one of the tipstaves, who promised to secure the other exit for them. He dropped his gaze and glanced at the cover of the pamphlet he had recovered.

Ludlam snatched it away before Daniel could focus on more than the cover illustration, but too late to stop rage from exploding into an expletive. "Bastard!"

"That he is," Ludlam agreed. "But you won't do your lady any good if you read this instead of what I brought you."

"She's not—"

"Your lady? You might have fooled Smitherman and Hastings, but I'm the expert on people, remember?"

"I'll kill him," Daniel hissed.

"And I'll help you. After the trial. And after we get your lady, er . . . client cleared. Your choice," he challenged. "Read this pamphlet now. Let him goad you into a fury, and you'll lose this case. Focus on the evidence I have, which will be enough if you're clearheaded and use it right, and you can take her home with you where she belongs."

Daniel flinched. "I'm in total control, just like I've been all day."

"Sure you are." He handed Daniel his wallet and smiled. "Filched this when I first got here, so that argument is lost. You ready to win a more important one?"

Daniel shook his head, put the wallet in his pocket, and grinned, positive Jane's faith in the system was about to be rewarded. "You win. I'll read the pamphlet later. Let's go take a look at that information you've collected. We have fifteen hours till court reconvenes, and we can't afford to waste a single minute."

Chapter 26

✢ "It's not enough. Maybe if we had more time . . ."

At midnight, Daniel raked his hand through his hair and did not make an effort to keep his disappointment from embittering his words as he sat across the table from his investigator.

Ludlam had compiled background information on Polly Glennings that went as far back as her years in boarding school. The legal team had correlated Foster's trips, Sam's hauling assignments, and Polly's alleged visits to her parents. Coupled with the tortoiseshell hair ornament found in Foster's coat, the evidence proving Polly as an adulteress was circumstantial. Extending that accusation to murder would be nearly impossible—and arguably unethical.

Too exhausted to wage the battle controlling his emotions any longer or to keep up pretenses Ludlam had already discounted, Daniel leaned back in his chair and stared at the papers that littered the table.

Misery filled his heart. Guilt left no room in his soul for anything else. From his pocket, he took out his compass and held it in his fist, wishing her gift would now show him the way to win an acquittal.

"I can't save her," he whispered. His voice cracked, and his chest tightened. "It's too late. The jurors won't accept any of this circumstantial evidence without some kind of solid proof Polly committed the murder."

Grim-faced, Ludlam narrowed his gaze and stared at him from his seat on the other side of the table. "That's not a given fact. Don't underestimate them. Or yourself, for that matter. You've won acquittals before with less, or have you already forgotten Debra Modean?"

Daniel's laugh was harsh. "Hardly. Neither has Pine, although he's gotten closer to crossing the line between legitimate allegations and libel with his latest pamphlet. 'The Champion of the Sheets and the Devious Divorcée.' " He spat the title of the pamphlet and clenched the compass harder.

"I warned you not to read it."

"Most of Lancaster already has."

"But you of all people should have been one of the few who didn't. You claim you can't abandon her and let Hastings and Smitherman defend her. If you still mean that, then start acting like her lawyer instead of the grieving man about to lose her. You can't be both."

Stunned, Daniel glowered back at him. "You're awfully quick to point an accusing finger. I needed this evidence weeks ago, not now when it's practically worthless."

"And you would have had it if you hadn't been so quick to give in to your client's demands. You didn't do that with Debra Modean, did you?"

"Of course not! I—"

" 'Of course not,' " Ludlam mimicked and leaned across the table. "Do it now. Take what you have to Jane and tell her she's not going to take the witness stand, but you're going to use the affair to defend her with what you have. Tell her it's her only chance."

"I can't do that. It's too late an hour, and the judge ruled no visitors tonight, remember?"

Ludlam glared at him. "Then go into court tomorrow and take Polly apart, layer by pretty layer, and show her to be a cunning murderess willing to see her sister-in-law die for a crime she didn't commit."

Chest heaving, he shoved the papers on the table toward Daniel. "And put that damned compass away so you can work. You know what direction you have to take and how to get there, or you're not the lawyer— or the man—I thought you were."

The words lashed at him were so cold, Daniel was

momentarily frozen in place. Nearly paralyzed by the harsh truth, he almost forgot to breathe. When he did, he took in slow, even breaths of air and waited for his heartbeat to return to a steady rhythm.

Thank Providence, Ludlam had held true to his nature, remaining as objective as a mirror that only reflected what had been placed in front of it. The image of himself Ludlam gave was brutally honest, yet a fair indictment. One of the spectator's taunts, *You should be disbarred*, rang damnably true.

Ludlam was right. Daniel could not be her lawyer and the man who loved her beyond all measure at the same time. Committed to defending her, his choice was limited to only one, but when the court day ended tomorrow, his role as her lawyer would be the only one left to him.

He could not risk warning Sam in advance for fear Polly might learn of Daniel's plans, and Jane would never forgive him for using the circumstantial evidence he had to reveal the affair between Polly and Foster in open court, devastating Sam and destroying Polly by implying she was a murderess.

And unless Daniel was brilliantly successful, he would find himself right back where he had been when he had first met Jane—in the shadows of ethical behavior where the means he used to win an acquittal mattered far less than achieving his goal.

The double-edged sword he was about to unsheathe sliced through his heart, but he felt no pain. His heart had gone numb the moment he had made the only choice he could to save the woman he loved.

He put his compass back into his pocket and glared at Ludlam. "Well, what are you waiting for?" he snapped. "Wake up Hastings and Smitherman. Tell them I expect them here in an hour, or I'll fire both of them. You, too, if you don't wipe that grin off your face before you get back!"

Ludlam pounded his fist on the table and rose so quickly he upended his chair. "I'll have them here in half an hour. In the meantime, do me a favor."

"What?" Daniel barked as he rifled through the papers.

"Use the next half hour to change. You look like you've been to hell and back."

"That I have," he murmured, but knew the hell he had been through during this case was nothing compared to the one that waited for him in the future without Jane by his side.

Jane crumbled the disgusting pamphlet surreptitiously slipped under her door and threw the outrageous accusations to the other side of her cell. She thought her angry gaze would be enough to incinerate the pamphlet, but when that failed, she tried to stomp it with her feet until it disintegrated.

Not that it would matter. The keepers had tacked dozens of pamphlets to her cell walls and had taken the time to open the pamphlets so each page was displayed for her to see. Even on tiptoe she could not reach high enough to tear them down, and she shook with frustration as well as anger.

"Scurrilous knaves," she spat, giving up her effort. Like a mother bird who had returned to the nest only to find her babies eaten by predators, she fluttered about her cell. If she could sprout wings and fly out the window, she would peck out Mercury Pine's remaining eye and curse him to the lifetime of darkness he deserved.

Her heart pumped so fast she could almost feel the blood coursing through her veins. Her feet smacked at the floor, creating a furious echo bound to bring the keepers to investigate. "Let them come." She issued the challenge in a loud voice. What could they do to her that the jury was not already prepared to do? Short of ending her life now, instead of sometime within the next few weeks, she had nothing to lose.

But Sam did.

"I'm such a fool," she cried. "A simpering, stupid

idiot! I should have known. I should have listened to Daniel." She drew in heaving gulps of air and vividly recalled seeing the evidence to be presented today that had jolted her out of her doldrums, sparked life back into every one of her emotions, and sent unmitigated terror straight to her heart.

Focusing on her brother helped to dissipate her anger over the pamphlets and redirect her energies toward something she could change or control. She had to talk to Daniel before anything happened to her. Or to Sam, although he was probably safe for now. What about tomorrow or next month or next year? There would be no way she could protect him unless she told Daniel what she had seen today in court.

Pacing about the cell was pointless and making noise to bring the keepers was self-defeating. Neither action would bring Daniel here, not with the judge's order restraining him from visiting. She glanced up at the pamphlets on the wall and, hissed. If she could control herself in court tomorrow, he would be able to visit her, and on the off chance he had not seen the pamphlets, she had to get them down before he did.

She lugged the rickety table and chair over to the wall and hiked up her skirts. With a prayer the table would not collapse under her, she stepped from the seat of the chair to the tabletop. Holding her breath, she reached up, yanked one pamphlet free, and let it fall to the floor.

Within half an hour, she had every single pamphlet down from the wall. She was also flushed and short of breath. After gathering the pamphlets together in the folds of her skirts, she collapsed onto her cot. She cradled the pamphlets with their hateful illustrations in her arms and wept.

What had been the most beautiful moment of her life had been grotesquely distorted into a sordid rendezvous, sketched for all the world to see on the cover of the pamphlet. She did not have to look at the largest illustration again to bring the image to mind.

Centered on the narrow cover, the front of Aunt Lily's cottage had been drawn beneath a sky filled with dark clouds and streaks of lightning. Pine had exaggerated the height and width of the front doorway to accommodate the figures of Daniel and Jane embracing in front of the fire.

She shuddered, horrified Pine had been following her the night she had gone to see Daniel and had been caught in the storm. She was outraged he had violated her privacy as well as Daniel's, portraying their impromptu embrace meant to comfort as only one moment in a continuing sinful liaison between the Champion of the Sheets, as Daniel had been dubbed in the title, and the Devious Divorcée—Jane.

Her tears flowed freely now. Even though she had not read every word of the eight-page pamphlet, she had seen enough to glean the major points. In addition to a complete documentation of the prosecution's case against her, Pine added an editorial postscript snidely hinting Daniel had seduced Jane, like he had done with a previous female client, namely Debra Modean.

She did not, however, waste a single tear over the illustration of the lovely Modean or the caricature Pine had sketched of Jane's likeness on the back of the pamphlet. She knew this was a deliberate attempt to ridicule her plainness, a personal attack she overlooked because she was more distressed Daniel had been targeted by the pamphlet.

With her tears now spent, she dried her face with the hem of her gown and stuffed the pamphlets under the thin mattress on her cot. When Daniel did arrive tomorrow, she did not want him to see them or waste time discussing what was an outrageous, blatant attack on both of them.

While she resumed pacing back and forth across her cell, she rehearsed what she would say to Daniel, arranging and rearranging her words so she could make her point succinctly and Daniel could go to Sam and warn him immediately.

She wished she could tell Sam herself and admit to withholding the truth about Polly's affair as well, but the judge's order notwithstanding, she was not permitted to visit with her family.

Thanks to Jane's stubborn refusal to let Daniel pursue the possible implications of Polly's affair with Hiram, there was nothing else to tie Polly to Hiram's death. It might be too late to convince the jurors of Jane's innocence. She might be condemned to losing Daniel forever, but she had to save Sam.

The longer she paced, the more she realized she could not afford to wait until tomorrow night to tell Daniel and tried to figure out a way to tell him in court—even if that meant she would be banned from the rest of her trial.

A terrifying thought flashed through her mind, and she began to tremble. What if Daniel had become so upset with her today in court he decided to let his associates finish her defense? Violent tremors shook her body and she fell to her knees as the distant sound of thunder and a coming storm broke through the silent night.

She would not blame Daniel if he turned away from her now, not after she had let him down with her performance in court today. How could she face her eventual conviction without Daniel? And if by some miracle she was found not guilty, how could she face the fact she would be so tainted by the scandal surrounding the trial, she would be condemned to a lifetime without him?

Sobs tore from her lips until her throat was raw, but eventually, Sam was the one who claimed her tears.

Only Sam.

And the certainty that the adulteress who carried his name was a murderess as well.

Chapter 27

As near to being frantic without completely losing her mind, Jane had taken her place in the prisoner's dock and held on to the railing with one hand for support. With the court once again in session and the spectators more unruly than yesterday, the judges were not in a mood to tolerate so much as a sigh from her lips.

Desperately relieved to see Daniel at the table reserved for her team of defense lawyers, she had tried repeatedly to catch his gaze, but failed. Moist with perspiration, the handkerchief where she had hidden the remnant of the note she had hoped to slip to him was in her other hand. The keepers had confiscated the long message she had written to Daniel on the back of one of the pamphlets with the snub of a pencil he had inadvertently left behind in her cell.

She had managed to hold on to a very small piece with only a few words, but hoped they would be enough to trigger Daniel's memory and alert him to the mislabeled evidence.

Her family sat in the tiered benches behind her that were reserved for witnesses waiting to testify. She fought the urge to try to make eye contact with Sam for fear the very sight of Polly sitting by his side would infuriate her to the point of total explosion. Instead, she kept her gaze on the state seal hanging on the wall above the judges' heads and prayed for justice to prevail in the interim and touch the jurors' minds as well as their hearts when her family testified.

With a tenuous hold on her dignity, she sat as straight as she could and still keep keep her hands on the railing. Her love for Daniel had never been stronger or her admiration greater. He had done his best to undermine the circumstantial evidence against her and knew he would launch the only defense he could today, given the severe restrictions she had imposed.

The number of witnesses who had agreed to testify to her character was small, but she prayed the proceedings would last at least another day so she could talk to Daniel later tonight and make sure he had understood her message.

When Aunt Lily took the witness stand first, followed by Aunt Nester, Jane thought her heart would break. Both women had changed considerably these last few months. The wrinkles on their faces were deeper and their bodies more frail, but it was the streaks of gray in their hair that testified greatest to the worry they had endured.

Their words describing her moral character were gifts of purest gold that brought tears to her eyes. Apparently, even the attorney general was moved. He had waived his right to cross-examine each of them.

She was not surprised Daniel did not question Aunt Nester about the hair ornament she had found in one of the pockets in Hiram's garments, but she was honest enough with herself to admit she was relieved. Almost as much as when Libby Holtzman reiterated Penelope Washburn's testimony that the garments in evidence were the ones Jane had worn when she had accidentally knocked the bottle of concentrated tobacco juice off the shelf in the general store.

Not to be outdone, the attorney general had cross-examined them skillfully. He extracted an admission from each of the women that they could not say with certainty the garments were not already stained before. He categorized the accident as staged for the benefit of the wives of the local officials who would later be investigating Foster's murder.

Her cousin Louis quickly followed. He, too, bore the effects of his concern for her, and he never wavered once during cross-examination, classifying the charges against her as outrageous.

"Honorable judges, the defense now calls Samuel Glennings to the stand."

Daniel's words sent chills charging up and down her spine. Polly would have to be next. She was the only witness left.

Her heart began to pound. The room started to spin. She closed her eyes and gripped the railing even harder. After Sam's testimony, Daniel would briefly question Polly and rest their case. Then attorneys for both sides would argue in summation.

Jane was not sure if she would be allowed to see Daniel then. Would they make her wait until after the jury's deliberations and verdict? How long would that take? She needed to tell Daniel now!

With her head bowed, she heard Sam's footsteps and listened as he swore to tell the truth. On the verge of panic, she had no recourse now. After taking a deep breath for courage and saying a fervent prayer that Daniel would respond instinctively, she let go of the railing and feigned a swoon. She slid off her seat to the floor of the platform and hit her head hard in the process.

Judging by the collective gasp, the sound of rushing footsteps, and the harsh rapping sound of the judge's gavel she heard, she had been successful in fooling everyone. She kept her eyes closed, but allowed the tiniest sliver of light to intrude so she had an extremely limited view of the activity around her.

The moment she saw Daniel, who was the first to come to her aid, she moaned and hastily slipped her damp handkerchief into his hand. "Read the note," she mumbled, hoping to sound incoherent to the others who crowded around him.

"Get back!" he shouted as he cradled her in his arms without attempting to move her out of the prisoner's dock. "Is there a doctor present? She needs a physician!"

"Order! I'll have order in this courtroom!" One of the justices banged his gavel, attempting to restore order. "Mr. Simmons, clear the spectators. Mr. Rawlet, send for Dr. Chase. Court is adjourned for a one-hour recess." He banged the gavel again. And again.

She pressed her face against Daniel's waistcoat and inhaled his scent while savoring the feel of his arms around her.

"Jane," he murmured. "Oh, my Jane."

She snuggled closer and prayed he would not only understand her note, but also use what she told him to protect Sam. If Daniel failed to convince the jurors of her innocence, the very thought she would leave this world and enter the next without so much as one sweet kiss from him to remember while she waited for him to join her in eternity was too much to bear.

This time, when her surroundings faded, the black mist that enveloped her was all too real.

After the physician assured the judges Jane had sufficiently recovered from her very ordinary swoon, Daniel argued for an additional hour for her to rest. He won, but lost no time celebrating his victory.

He went directly to the second floor to a room ordinarily reserved for the city council and rejoined his staff. He still had Jane's handkerchief in his hand, but her tattered note was safely secured in the room. When he saw the state's evidence against her sitting on a table, he smiled. For fear of tipping his hand, he had asked for all the evidence to be taken upstairs during the recess. Ludlam had already separated the item Daniel really wanted to see.

Without acknowledging his staff with more than a nod, Daniel studied the item, carefully examining it before reading Jane's note again. He closed his eyes and concentrated as his mind sorted through endless scenes and conversations he had held or observed from the first night he had met Jane through today.

Images flashed. Phrases and full sentences echoed.

And then again. Seconds stretched to minutes that quickly consumed almost all of the hour he had been given.

The silence in the room was heavy with curiosity and anticipation, but he ignored it, concentrating harder, categorizing and classifying his memories until he was able to link several scenes and conversations together with Jane's note.

I never knew you had such fine things.

Polly's words echoed loudest in his mind now. "And I should have remembered," he whispered. He picked up the proof he needed. Although dismayed it had been sitting there all along as part of the state's case against Jane, he was proud of her for calling this evidence to his attention. Her faith in the system not only had been well-founded, but also rewarded with the very proof he needed to prove her innocence.

Jane had done her part. Now it was up to him to see justice was done, and he prayed her faith in him would be rewarded as well.

His heart pounding, he wrapped her note with her handkerchief and placed it back into his pocket. When he turned to face his staff, he took a deep breath to ease the pounding in his head. "Gentlemen, let's go back into court and win this case. If I'm right about what Jane was trying to tell me, she's spent her last night in jail."

"And if you're wrong?" Smitherman asked quietly, voicing the concern Daniel saw written in Hastings's expression.

"Then even God will show no mercy on my soul," he responded and quickly led them back to the court-room.

Chapter 28

✻ The hush that had fallen over the courtroom when proceedings resumed added an echo to Sam's poignant testimony. As his cross-examination ended, Jane dabbed at her eyes with her fingertips, praying Daniel would now be able to make good use of the handkerchief-bound note she had given him.

"She raised me," Sam repeated, responding to Daniel's last opportunity to erase the prosecutor's mocking questions. "I know her better than anyone else in the world. She could not, did not murder her husband."

Sitting tall, with his shoulders squared and his head held high, he was her valiant defender. His troubled gaze, however, was riveted on the jury, as if silently pleading with them to trust her brother, if they refused to believe anyone else who had preceded him to testify to her character.

"Mr. Glennings, yesterday the prosecution suggested your sister deliberately staged her accident in the general store to cover up her crime. How would you categorize Mr. Ford's allegations?"

"Ludicrous," Sam spat. "My sister is the most honest person I've ever met. Lying or conspiring to hide the truth is contrary to the very essence of her character."

Jane cringed in her seat. Each of his words rained salt on the secret festering in her soul. Shards of pain shot straight to her heart and shame shadowed her spirit. She had failed to live up to Sam's expectations, as well as her own. It was a mistake that might cost her her life, but adding to the pain of ending her days on earth without Daniel's love, the prospect of losing her brother's respect and his affection once she told him the whole truth left her nearly numb.

However just, an acquittal would condemn her to a life of loneliness too profound to consider.

"Yet you'll admit these are her garments?" Daniel asked, pointing to the table draped with the evidence.

A flush of crimson stained Sam's cheeks. "I assume they're hers."

"But you're not sure?"

"No," Sam admitted. "My wife, Polly, would know. She kept house for the three of us when we lived above the general store after the vandalism."

Jane's pulse began to race with wild hope that Daniel had understood her sorry remnant of a note, and she edged forward in her seat.

Mr. Ford's voice rang out. "Objection, Your Honor. The defense made no argument against the introduction of this evidence when it was presented. To question the ownership now tests the court's patience."

"I withdraw the question and have nothing further for this witness. The defense now calls Mrs. Polly Glennings."

Sam left the stand and walked directly past Jane to return to his seat. His sad smile of support made her tremble. She dropped her gaze and prayed harder than she had ever done before as Polly was sworn in and took her place on the witness stand.

When she looked up, her sister-in-law sat primly, her dark blue eyes wide with fear that added a haunting look to her features. Dressed in a black silk gown that accentuated the pale ringlets that flowed from beneath her bonnet to curl about her shoulders, Polly looked as beautiful as she did vulnerable.

Daniel kept his back to Jane as he began. "Mrs. Glennings, how long have you known the accused?"

"Since my marriage to her brother, a little more than two years ago," she murmured.

"Then you're not from Sunrise."

Her eyes widened. "Heavens, no. I was raised in Columbia. I-I only moved to Sunrise after I married Sam."

"You never met her before then?"

"No."

"Not at boarding school, perhaps?"

She tilted her chin up. "No. Why would you assume that? As far as I know, she never went away to school. She was too busy at home, raising Sam after their parents died and later, working in the store to support them. She never had the opportunity to go away like I did."

"To attend schools like Miss Braynard's Academy in Philadelphia or The Female Academy in Scranton?"

She smiled. "Exactly, although I finished my education at Miss Willsey's Academy in Lancaster," she said proudly. "Jane had to seek employment, although I doubt she ever wanted to go away. She's very content living in a small village."

"It must have been hard to leave your family when you moved to Sunrise."

Ford stood up before Polly could answer. "Your honor, I fail to see the relevance of these questions. The whole point to having Mrs. Glennings here is to testify to Mrs. Foster's character, not give us this woman's life history."

"It's exactly her life history I need to document to demonstrate the close relationship Mrs. Glennings and Mrs. Foster enjoyed," Daniel countered.

"The objection is overruled. You may continue to question the witness," Judge Welsh ordered before looking toward Polly. "Do you need to have that last question repeated?"

"No, Your Honor. I missed my family very much."

Daniel nodded sympathetically. "Did you visit often?"

She dabbed tears away with a handkerchief trimmed with black lace. "Not as often as I would have liked. Sam traveled a great deal, but occasionally when he was gone for more than a few days, I did get to go home to see my family."

"You didn't stay and help Jane to run the store?"

An unsteady smile did not disguise the horror that sparkled in her eyes. "Certainly not. Sam wouldn't allow me to tend store."

"So you went home instead."

"I already said that," she pouted, revealing a flash of temper for the first time.

"Did you ever take Mrs. Foster with you?"

Polly rolled her eyes. "She had to tend the store."

"But you did consider Jane as part of your family, didn't you?" he asked, deftly forestalling the objection Ford had apparently been ready to make as he retook his seat.

"Of course. And her husband 'as well."

"Indeed." Daniel paused and turned to address the judges. "I respectfully request permission to treat the witness and her testimony now as hostile to the defense."

"Objection!" Ford leaped out of his chair.

Polly wore a mask of confusion that mirrored Jane's bewilderment. Unfamiliar with legal maneuvers, she strained forward to try to hear the verbal sparring taking place between the lawyers.

"This is Mr. Colton's own witness. If she's hostile to the defense, then he shouldn't have called her to the stand," Ford protested.

"I have evidence the court and the jury is entitled to consider."

Hostile to the defense? Jane's mind latched on to the prosecutor's words, and her heart trembled. Had Daniel understood her note, or was he only going to question Polly about the affair with Hiram? She gripped the railing so hard her fingers were numb and held her breath while she waited for the judge's ruling.

"I'm going to overrule the objection. Proceed, Mr. Colton, but if the evidence is not forthcoming soon, I'll reverse my decision."

"Understood. Thank you, Your Honor." Daniel turned away from the judge, he gazed directly at Jane, his expression frozen in a professional mask he wore for the first time in the trial. She acknowledged him with a nod, knowing full well the testimony Polly was about to give would spell doom for herself and for Sam, even if Daniel proved Polly was nothing more than an adulteress.

She captured his gaze and held it as long as she could without invoking the court's wrath. Her heart was literally lodged in her throat when he turned away to face Polly.

"Mrs. Glennings, please tell the court why you were expelled from boarding school in Philadelphia and Scranton."

Disbelief and anger crackled in her eyes. "That's a lie. I wasn't asked to leave. I was homesick, which is why my father arranged for me to finish school closer to home."

Daniel squared his shoulders. "Isn't it true you were expelled from Miss Braynard's Academy for repeatedly violating curfew and slipping out at night to meet beaus? Do the names Paul Ashton or Michael Zane sound familiar?"

When she gasped, her lips twitched, and her eyes widened to the size of saucers. "Certainly not!"

"Do you also deny you were asked to leave The Female Academy in Scranton after they discovered you were the one who slipped something into George Ballinger's punch at a soiree when he spurned you and turned his attentions to Sarah Wells?"

Daniel's allegations came so fast and furiously, Jane was completely overwhelmed and shocked by what he claimed. Polly had completely dissolved into tears and played the role of victim so well, Daniel looked like a bully.

"They were schoolgirl pranks," she insisted between spells of tears. "I was very young and foolish. I'm not proud of what I did, but at the time, I thought the rules were too strict and unreasonable."

"Rules," Daniel said coldly. "You still consider some rules unreasonable, don't you?"

Polly dried her tears and sat up straighter. "I'm not a schoolgirl any more. I'm a grown woman, and I've tried to be a good wife and a friend to Jane, even though we had little in common."

Daniel walked over to the evidence table where Jane's garments were still displayed. Jane held her breath, unable to think or feel anything other than the pounding of her heart as it slammed against her chest.

"Do you recognize these garments as belonging to Jane Foster?"

Polly nodded.

"You have to voice an answer for the jury to hear. Is this her gown and petticoat?"

"Y-yes."

"Her slippers and stockings? And her handkerchief as well?"

"Yes."

He picked up the handkerchief, carried it back with him, and handed it to her. When she refused to take it, he unfolded the pale green lace-trimmed handkerchief and held it up in front of her.

Unearthly silence reigned in the courtroom. The judges leaned toward the witness. The jurors were each visibly on the edges of their seats, but Jane's gaze locked on the handkerchief she had noticed yesterday.

"You said earlier you and Mrs. Foster had little in common, but there is something you did share, surprisingly. A love for fanciful handkerchiefs like this."

Polly barely nodded, her eyes flashing with fear.

"Do you remember the day you ironed her handkerchiefs? You were surprised, weren't you? Jane doesn't give the impression she'd own anything like this. I believe you said you thought she was too 'prim and practical-minded' to own such finery."

A trancelike nod.

"Do you remember what she said in response?

Polly shook her head, but Daniel did not stop her to make her give voice to her answers now.

"Then let me refresh your memory since I was there. She said she saved them to use on special occasions. She didn't use them every day. Would you agree that meant when she was working in the store on the day of her accident?"

Polly blinked her eyes and emerged from her trance. "M-maybe."

"And she would have carried a handkerchief like this?" He pulled the handkerchief Jane had slipped to him with her note and held it up next to the one in evidence.

"I suppose."

"Then why is this fancy handkerchief stained with poison? The one she used to sop up what spilled onto her foot would have been a plain one like this, wouldn't it?"

Polly's lips turned white and started twitching.

"This isn't Jane's handkerchief at all, is it? It's your handkerchief, Mrs. Glennings. You put the poison in Hiram Foster's cologne and mopped up some you had spilled. You hid it or left it behind in the crate stored in the loft of your husband's barn when you stored away the funds he'd been carrying."

"No! That's a lie. A wicked lie!"

"Are you saying you've always been faithful to your husband?"

Polly blanched. "Of course! How dare you ask me—"

"I do indeed. The Black Crow. The Golden Swan. Do you remember staying at those hotels with Hiram Foster?"

"No! Never! Sam, don't listen to him. He's lying!" She huffed, and her eyes glittered with hatred.

Daniel pointed to the papers on the defense table as though he held a sword in his hand. "I have it all, Mrs. Glennings, including dates when your husband's trips away from home coincided with Mr. Foster's. I have sworn affidavits from hotel employees. You were much more than a sister-in-law to Hiram Foster. You were his lover," he charged and held up the tortoiseshell hair ornament for all to see. "He kept this as a memento, didn't he?"

Polly's face mottled with red splotches as she leaned back away from him. "Get away from me! Wh-what a horrid, cruel accusation!" she sputtered. "You're lying. That's . . . that's not mine."

"Yes, it is, and I have witnesses ready to testify to that fact."

She glared at him, but remained silent.

"He betrayed you, didn't he? Just as surely as the wife he divorced. When he stopped on his way back to Lancaster, he told you he was leaving to marry another woman instead of you, didn't he?"

"That's not true," she moaned. "Sam, it's not true. I love you. I'm your wife—"

"No!" Sam said, his voice grim and steely. "You can't be my wife. You can't be the woman I thought I married. You're nothing but a lying, conniving—"

"Stop! You can't deny me or turn away from me," Polly cried, her face distorted with rage.

Judge Welsh nearly leaped out of his seat. "Silence! Mr. Glennings, sit down and control yourself, or I'll be forced to have you removed from this courtroom! Mrs. Glennings, I advise you to confine your remarks and respond only to the questions posed to you by Mr. Colton." The judge's words bellowed over the harsh echo of the gavel he banged as he spoke, his reprimand hardened by his dark expression.

Jane shrank down in her seat, shocked by Sam's outburst, but too intimidated by the judge's scowl to turn around to look at her brother. She kept her gaze locked, instead, on Polly, who remained silent, but her eyes were wild and unfocused.

"Continue, Mr. Colton," the judge advised.

Still facing his witness, Daniel took a step closer to her. "And when he told you he was leaving, Mrs. Glennings, you were angry, weren't you? That's when you threatened to tell his wife where he had gone, but he brushed you away. He swore he'd tell your husband you'd been unfaithful if you carried out your threat, destroying your marriage without a second thought, didn't he? Was it after you made love that he threatened you? Is that what infuriated you enough to poison the cologne he used before he left, just like you once slipped concentrated tobacco juice into George Ballinger's punch when you were younger?"

"I didn't do that! I didn't!"

Daniel struck hard again. "And did you then follow him, slipping through the night like you had done so many times in boarding school, until he finally expired? Why did you try to use the pocket watch and the funds he was carrying to put the blame on Mrs. Foster? Were you afraid the sheriff would find out you were the real murderer?"

"Liar!" she cried. "I didn't do that. I-I couldn't do that. You're despicable! And you're . . . you're desperate! You want to clear Jane so badly you're willing to put the blame on me!"

"No," he argued, waving the stained handkerchief in her face. "You put the blame on yourself."

Polly shook from head to toe, exploding into a rage and leaping at him with her fingers curled as though she was ready to rake her nails across his face. "Bastard! I should kill you, too!" she screamed, unleashing total chaos in the courtroom.

Jane buried her face in her hands, sobbing with relief burdened by guilt and dreading the look in Sam's eyes when he found out she had known about the affair all along.

The three judges barked orders. A gavel banged incessantly. Spectators screamed a litany of epithets that drowned the judges' orders as tipstaves swung their staves in wide arcs to protect the jury as well as the hysterical witness Daniel had just goaded into confessing to murder.

He pinned her arms to her sides and held her until the court crier intervened and hauled her aside. Stunned by his victory, he rushed to find Jane. He found her crushed within her brother's strong embrace.

"It's all over now," Sam crooned to his sister, who had buried her face against his shoulder. "We have each other. We'll be all right. I promise."

In the midst of utter chaos, Daniel stood beside Jane and her brother, shielding them with his body from the onrushing spectators. When order had been restored, he turned and addressed the judges. "Your Honors, I respectfully request—"

"Granted!" Judge Welsh proclaimed. "Jurors, you are dismissed. Jane Glennings Foster, you are freed and declared innocent by this court of any and all charges against you. Polly Glennings, you are remanded to the custody of Sheriff Fleming and charged with the murder of Hiram Foster. Bailiff, escort the prisoner to the county jail. This court is adjourned."

When Jane's family emerged to surround Jane and her brother, Daniel bowed his head and averted his gaze. He watched as the tipstaves cleared the courtroom and Jane's brother protectively led her away. When he heard a number of heavy footsteps approaching him from behind, he looked up and waved his associates away. He was disinclined to accept their congratulations when his heart was filling with joy he had saved Jane's life and a deeper grief . . . for the woman he had loved and lost.

Daniel faced the deserted judges' bench, alone with his thoughts. He had won an amazing victory, yet now wondered where to go or what to do.

He had a legal practice he could resume, but he had no desire to enter a courtroom anytime soon, if ever again.

He had saved Jane's life, only to lose her as part of his own. She might be able to put today's shocking events behind her one day, but he would always be a reminder of the pain he had inflicted on her family, however necessary that had been to save her life.

He took the compass from his pocket, a bittersweet memento of the precious jewel who had captured his heart. " 'So you won't ever lose your way,' " he whispered, repeating the words she had used when she had given him this gift.

But without Jane, he was condemned to life as a bird of passage, wandering everywhere and anywhere, yet never finding a home.

Not without Jane.

"Sir?"

Startled, he looked up and found a tipstaff nervously standing in front of him. "We'd like to lock up now. Court's been adjourned for over two hours."

He closed his fist around the compass. "I'm sorry. I lost track of time. I didn't mean to keep you waiting."

When he turned to walk toward the closest door, the tipstaff called after him. "Sorry, sir. You can't use the north door. That's reserved for the judges."

Daniel changed direction. As he approached the east door, he held the compass up and watched the needle shift direction and point due east. "At least it's accurate on direction," he murmured as the tipstaff rushed ahead and opened the door for him.

He stepped through the doorway and froze. Even as he heard the door behind him close and the lock click into place, his hand was still extended, the compass still pointing east.

To home.

To Jane.

"Jane?"

He blinked his disbelieving eyes as she rushed up the steps to meet him. When she reached the top step and stood only a few feet away from him, he looked down at the compass. His heart pounded in his chest the moment he saw that the needle pointed straight to her heart.

With her cheeks flushed, her lungs burning, and a

stitch in her side from her desperate race back to the courthouse, Jane gasped for breath. Blessed relief that she had found Daniel outweighed her curiosity as he slipped the compass she had given him into his pocket. Suddenly feeling self-conscious, she wished she had had time to freshen her appearance and change out of her prison gown before seeing him, but need far outweighed what little vanity she had left after months in prison.

"They . . . they told me you were still here. I . . . ran . . . I ran all the way here to see you before you left," she blurted out before she had even caught her breath or her heartbeat had found some semblance of a normal rhythm. While stumbling over her explanation for her disheveled appearance, she straightened her skirts and struggled to regain her composure. But the moment she caressed his beloved features with her gaze, her heart refused to cooperate and beat even faster. Her legs grew weak, and every pore of her skin tingled with physical attraction stronger than she had ever felt before.

From the deep recesses of her heart, the dream that one day a man would find her physically attractive tugged at her heart, daring her to believe Daniel found her anything other than a rather plain woman to behold, a dream too incredible to ever come true.

"How's Sam?" he asked, his face etched with compassion and sincere regret for the pain the trial had caused her brother.

Her eyes welled with fresh tears, and she attempted a smile. "He's back at the hotel with Aunt Nester and Aunt Lily. I . . . I told him the truth," she said.

Daniel frowned. "You didn't have to tell him you knew about the affair. Even if he somehow found out, you could have blamed me for not letting you tell him—"

"No. He's my brother, and he was Polly's husband. He deserved to know the truth," she whispered before dropping her gaze. Guilt shadowed her elation at being vindicated. At long last, the secret that had festered in her soul had been lanced, and she knew the love she shared with her brother was strong enough to survive the grave mistake she had made by keeping the affair a secret from him.

She drew in a deep breath and took a single step forward, determined to lay claim to her love for Daniel even though the scandal surrounding her trial would make it almost impossible for him to accept her love. When she looked up at him and saw his love for her still simmering in the depths of his hazel eyes, her heart skipped a beat. Disbelief turned into sheer wonder at the power of love to conquer any and all obstacles, if only given the chance. "I don't know how to begin to thank you," she murmured, hoping to find the words to erase the guilt in Daniel's eyes and give their love one last opportunity to be fulfilled.

He shook his head. "I should be the one offering gratitude. You made me see what I'd become and inspired me to believe in justice in a way I'd long forgotten. You encouraged me to be the lawyer I'd always hoped to be, but in the end, it was your own courage and faith in truth and justice that led to your acquittal, not my skills as a lawyer."

His words cut straight to her heart and unleashed every hope and dream she had ever dared to embrace. Like the first colorful flower of spring, her feelings for Daniel had braved scandal and guilt to fully blossom, filling her spirit with the fragrant essence of true love. "You were brilliant today, just as I knew you would be. I never lost faith in you," she said.

She swallowed hard, anxious to let him know she shared a guilt that matched his own. "If I'd listened to you in the first place, the sheriff would have investigated Polly right away. I probably wouldn't even have been arrested."

"But you were. I shouldn't have let that happen, but I did—"

"That was my fault, not yours."

He squared his shoulders. "My incompetence didn't

end there," he argued. "I missed the handkerchief in the evidence list. Thank God you noticed—"

"We would have discovered the handkerchief together, if I hadn't been so stubborn and spent more time arguing with you than studying the evidence. Then I lost my faith in justice when I needed it the most: in court. After how badly I behaved yesterday, I was afraid you would decide to let one of the other attorneys finish the trial, but you didn't. You came back to defend me."

His eyes widened and pain clouded his eyes. "I would never turn away from you. Never. And if I'd been the lawyer you deserved, you might never have been forced to stand trial, but I was . . . distracted by the most fascinating, obstinate, and courageous woman I've ever met."

She caught her breath, too afraid to believe what her heart was trying to tell her. "D-distracted?"

"Completely," he whispered.

His hazel eyes simmered with emotion so raw she had to bow her head and avert her gaze to keep her heart from leaping out of her chest.

When he tipped up her chin and gazed into her eyes, she caught her breath and held it for several very long heartbeats. When he caressed her cheek, her legs grew weak and her heart began to pound.

"I love you," he whispered. "I want you. And I ache for you, Jane. Every moment of every day. I can't imagine life without you. Marry me, and let me spend the rest of my life proving how very much I adore you."

Awed by the intense physical longing in his gaze, she began to tremble with the hope that their love would survive this nightmare experience of a trial. "I love you, too."

"My precious, precious jewel," he murmured and pulled her into his arms, showering her face with kisses that scattered every thought in her head and left only room for sheer joy and physical pleasure. He captured her lips, devoured them, and left her hungering for more, even after he paused to let them catch their breath.

Cradling her face with both hands, he chuckled and kissed the tip of her nose. "I think we'd better find a preacher. Fast."

Nearly giddy, she nodded. "Reverend Reilly isn't returning to Sunrise till tomorrow. He should be back at the hotel."

He grinned, scooped her into her arms, and started down the steps before she realized what he was doing.

"I can walk," she argued, although she had little desire to move as much as an inch away from him.

"I'm not putting you down until we've said our vows. Even then, I'm not letting you out of my arms until I take you to my room. *Our* room," he insisted. When he reached the bottom of the steps, he paused and kissed her again. "Do you have any idea how very beautiful you are?"

Her heart nearly stopped beating, then beat faster than ever before, racing to that secret place in her soul to capture, at long last, the most impossible of all her dreams.

"You are beautiful," he repeated.

And when she looked into his eyes, she knew it was true.

Epilogue

One week shy of their first anniversary, Jane and Daniel finally returned to Sunrise.

Anxious to see the home he had had built for them on the main street of town while they enjoyed an extended wedding trip through Europe, Jane sat next to her husband in a wagon loaded with trunks of new clothes and mementos of their travels.

She carried her greatest treasure, Daniel's love and devotion, in her heart. Warmed by the late summer sun, she held his arm as they passed Peterson's mill and neared the covered bridge. Memories resurfaced, still painful, but eased by the happiness and contentment she had found in her marriage. She inched closer to the man who had taken each and every one of her dreams and turned them into a precious reality. She could scarcely believe how quickly she had been able to set the past aside and find the joy that had long eluded her.

She prayed Daniel was right when he told her the villagers had been able to do the same. She had no grievance with those who had turned against her, but she knew from experience that forgiveness was only accepted when it came from within. Her hope that she and Daniel would be able to take their place in the village alongside friends and neighbors, as well as family, was real, especially now that . . .

When Daniel stopped the wagon in the middle of the covered bridge, her thoughts immediately centered on him. "Is something wrong?"

He put his arm around her and smiled. He captured her lips in a kiss that left her breathless and longing for the privacy of the hotel room in Lancaster. Though they had left only a few hours ago after a night of passion that should have kept her satisfied for months, she blushed when he broke their kiss and gazed at her.

Breathing heavily, he grinned. "I wanted to do that the last time we traveled together under this bridge, but under the circumstances—"

"Under the current circumstances," she teased, "I suggest you take me home. Quickly," she urged as she laced her hands around his neck and kissed him until she nearly fainted, forced to stop and take a breath of air.

"We'll have precious little time alone when we arrive," he argued, and she batted his hand away when he attempted to unpin the brooch at the top of her gown.

"It's only Sam and Aunt Nester. They were kind enough to help get the house ready for us, but I don't think they'll stay very long if I tell them I'm overtired," she purred, finding her role as wife and vixen a most powerful and pleasant experience.

He caressed the side of her breast with his hand. "I'm not sure you'll be able to convince them how tired you are. Maybe I should just tell them the truth. That you can't wait to bed your husband again—"

"No. I'll take care of it," she promised as her cheeks grew warmer still. Once again satisfied with telling less than the truth, she also knew if she and Daniel did not take to bed and sleep, instead of spending every night exploring the physical delights of the marriage bed, she might one day have permanent love circles under her eyes.

He chuckled as if he could read her thoughts and flicked the reins to set the wagon back into motion.

Squinting until her eyes readjusted to the bright afternoon sunshine, she tightened her hold on his arm when Sam's house came into view. Sam had traveled to Indiana immediately after the trial and secured a divorce. Only weeks later, Polly had been evaluated by several physicians and pronounced insane. Thanks to the efforts of Sheriff Fleming, Polly's attorneys had reached an agreement with the attorney general, Mr. Ford. With her mind completely disintegrated, she would spend the rest of her days in an asylum for the mentally deranged, sparing them all the ordeal of enduring the scandal of a second murder trial.

Sam lived in their family homestead again, although he had completely redone the interior and removed every bit of furniture he had bought for Polly. Jane bowed her head and sighed, grateful Aunt Nester had moved in with her brother to keep house for him as well as to help him as he came to terms with all that had happened.

She had to grip the edge of her seat when Daniel urged the horses to go faster as they passed the home where she had been born and had raised Sam to adulthood. And where she had discovered the futility of trying to save a marriage that had been doomed to fail from the very moment it began. Her heart still trembled at the thought of what she had seen that fateful day, but strengthened by Daniel's love, she had let peace, instead of anguish, fill her heart until it overflowed, leaving no room for the past to taint a single moment in the present.

When the wagon finally rounded the bend in the roadway and entered the village proper, Daniel slowed the horses to a halt. She looked at the roadway straight ahead and her heart literally pounded against the wall of her chest.

Daniel let the reins go slack and gripped her hand. "Everything is going to be all right," he reassured her.

Her throat choked with emotion, she could only nod as tears sprang to her eyes and cascaded silently down her cheeks.

Ribbons. Dozens of dazzling white ribbons decorated the trees that lined the bluff overlooking the river. Flags proudly flew from each storefront alongside handmade signs, their welcoming messages blurred by her tears.

When the church bell began to toll, villagers poured out of stores and homes to line the street, their faces smiling, their voices raised in welcoming cheers that touched her very spirit.

He locked the brake, descended from the wagon, and lifted her from her seat to stand by his side. "Welcome home," he murmured and escorted her down the middle of the street past the general store and the church to their new home where Reverend Reilly, Mayor Holtzman, Constable Washburn—accompanied by Libby and Penelope—Sam, and Aunt Nester had gathered on the front porch. She waved to her cousin Louis who was tending several open-pit barbecues alongside his tavern while his wife and several of her friends stood ready to serve the food already piled high on rows of planked tables.

"You knew, didn't you?" she managed. "We promised we would never have any secrets from one another," she gushed, her words softened by the guilt she carried for keeping a very special secret from him—one she had hoped to share with him on their first night home in Sunrise.

He paused, his face solemn, but his eyes were twinkling. "Some secrets are worth keeping. Your friends and neighbors told Aunt Nester they wanted to surprise you. They wanted to make sure you knew how much they regretted everything that happened and how glad they were you decided to come home."

"Home," she murmured, treasuring more than ever the tiny little village that would sustain her and those she loved in the years ahead.

He led her along the cobblestones that led to their home, but she tugged on his arm and made him stop when they reached the sign that hung from a carved post and faced the street. "Daniel Colton, Attorney-at-Law." She read the sign aloud and looked up at her husband. "Are you sure you want to practice law here?"

"Absolutely."

She searched his gaze and saw truth shining back at her along with love based on mutual respect and a physical attraction that grew deeper every day they spent together as husband and wife.

And deeper still, she hoped, when they were alone later tonight and she told him of the new life she carried in her womb. The first of many children, she hoped, who would grow up here in Sunrise, where they would face all of life's challenges supported by life's most wondrous gift of all: love.

Survey

TELL US WHAT YOU THINK AND YOU COULD WIN

A YEAR OF ROMANCE!
(That's 12 books!)

Fill out the survey below, send it back to us, and you'll be eligible
to win a year's worth of romance novels. That's one book a month
for a year—from St. Martin's Paperbacks.

Name _____

Street Address _____

City, State, Zip Code _____

Email address _____

1. How many romance books have you bought in the last year?
    (Check one.)
    __0-3
    __4-7
    __8-12
    __13-20
    __20 or more

2. Where do you MOST often buy books? *(limit to two choices)*
    __Independent bookstore
    __Chain stores *(Please specify)*
        __Barnes and Noble
        __B. Dalton
        __Books-a-Million
        __Borders
        __Crown
        __Lauriat's
        __Media Play
        __Waldenbooks
    __Supermarket
    __Department store *(Please specify)*
        __Caldor
        __Target
        __Kmart
        __Walmart
    __Pharmacy/Drug store
    __Warehouse Club
    __Airport

3. Which of the following promotions would MOST influence your
decision to purchase a ROMANCE paperback? *(Check one.)*
        __Discount coupon

     __Free preview of the first chapter
     __Second book at half price
     __Contribution to charity
     __Sweepstakes or contest

4. Which promotions would LEAST influence your decision to purchase a ROMANCE book? (Check one.)
     __Discount coupon
     __Free preview of the first chapter
     __Second book at half price
     __Contribution to charity
     __Sweepstakes or contest

5. When a new ROMANCE paperback is released, what is MOST influential in your finding out about the book and in helping you to decide to buy the book? (Check one.)
     __TV advertisement
     __Radio advertisement
     __Print advertising in newspaper or magazine
     __Book review in newspaper or magazine
     __Author interview in newspaper or magazine
     __Author interview on radio
     __Author appearance on TV
     __Personal appearance by author at bookstore
     __In-store publicity (poster, flyer, floor display, etc.)
     __Online promotion (author feature, banner advertising, giveaway)
     __Word of Mouth
     __Other (please specify)_____

6. Have you ever purchased a book online?
     __Yes
     __No

7. Have you visited our website?
     __Yes
     __No

8. Would you visit our website in the future to find out about new releases or author interviews?
     __Yes
     __No

9. What publication do you read most?
     __Newspapers *(check one)*
       __*USA Today*
       __*New York Times*
       __Your local newspaper
     __Magazines *(check one)*

    __People
    __Entertainment Weekly
    __Women's magazine *(Please specify:_____)*
    __Romantic Times
    __Romance newsletters

10. What type of TV program do you watch most? *(Check one.)*
    __Morning News Programs (ie. "Today Show")
      (Please specify:_____)
    __Afternoon Talk Shows (ie. "Oprah")
      (Please specify: _____)
    __All news (such as CNN)
    __Soap operas   *(Please specify: _____)*
    __Lifetime cable station
    __E! cable station
    __Evening magazine programs (ie. "Entertainment Tonight")
      (Please specify: _____)
    __Your local news

11. What radio stations do you listen to most? *(Check one.)*
    __Talk Radio
    __Easy Listening/Classical
    __Top 40
    __Country
    __Rock
    __Lite rock/Adult contemporary
    __CBS radio network
    __National Public Radio
    __WESTWOOD ONE radio network

12. What time of day do you listen to the radio MOST?
    __6am-10am
    __10am-noon
    __Noon-4pm
    __4pm-7pm
    __7pm-10pm
    __10pm-midnight
    __Midnight-6am

13. Would you like to receive email announcing new releases and special promotions?
    __Yes
    __No

14. Would you like to receive postcards announcing new releases and special promotions?
    __Yes
    __No

15. Who is your favorite romance author? _____

WIN A YEAR OF ROMANCE FROM SMP
(That's 12 Books!)
No Purchase Necessary

OFFICIAL RULES

1. To Enter: Complete the Official Entry Form and Survey and mail it to: Win a Year of Romance from SMP Sweepstakes, c/o St. Martin's Paperbacks, 175 Fifth Avenue, Suite 1615, New York, NY 10010-7848, Attention JP. For a copy of the Official Entry Form and Survey, send a self-addressed, stamped envelope to: Entry Form/Survey, c/o St. Martin's Paperbacks at the address stated above. Entries with the completed surveys must be received by February 1, 2000 (February 22, 2000 for entry forms requested by mail). Limit one entry per person. No mechanically reproduced or illegible entries accepted. Not responsible for lost, misdirected, mutilated or late entries.

2. Random Drawing. Winner will be determined in a random drawing to be held on or about March 1, 2000 from all eligible entries received. Odds of winning depend on the number of eligible entries received. Potential winner will be notified by mail on or about March 22, 2000 and will be asked to execute and return an Affidavit of Eligibility/Release/Prize Acceptance Form within fourteen (14) days of attempted notification. Non-compliance within this time may result in disqualification and the selection of an alternate winner. Return of any prize/prize notification as undeliverable will result in disqualification and an alternate winner will be selected.

3. Prize and approximate Retail Value: Winner will receive a copy of a different romance novel each month from April 2000 through March 2001. Approximate retail value $84.00 (U.S. dollars).

4. Eligibility. Open to U.S. and Canadian residents (excluding residents of the province of Quebec) who are 18 at the time of entry. Employees of St. Martin's and its parent, affiliates and subsidiaries, its and their directors, officers and agents, and their immediate families or those living in the same household, are ineligible to enter. Potential Canadian winners will be required to correctly answer a time-limited arithmetic skill question by mail. Void in Puerto Rico and wherever else prohibited by law.

5. General Conditions: Winner is responsible for all federal, state and local taxes. No substitution or cash redemption of prize permitted by winner. Prize is not transferable. Acceptance of prize constitutes permission to use the winner's name, photograph and likeness for purposes of advertising and promotion without additional compensation or permission, unless prohibited by law.

6. All entries become the property of sponsor, and will not be returned. By participating in this sweepstakes, entrants agree to be bound by these official rules and the decision of the judges, which are final in all respects.

7. For the name of the winner, available after March 22, 2000, send by May 1, 2000 a stamped, self-addressed envelope to Winner's List, Win a Year of Romance from SMP Sweepstakes, St. Martin's Paperbacks, 175 Fifth Avenue, Suite 1615, New York, NY 10010-7848, Attention JP.